To John N. Frary, Patron

THIS SIDE
OF JUDGMENT

THE MEN ON THE HILL stood close together between a bright orange hovercraft and a stand of dead-looking larch, branches bare even of snow. They spoke little, and all of them faced the road, shoulders hunched as if against a brisk wind, although the air was still.

A distant whine broke the silence. One man went to the edge of the hilltop. He was in uniform: nylon jacket, striped pants, a bone-colored Western hat. The jacket was open in spite of the cold, revealing a pistol belt. On the shoulder a patch read SHERIFF'S DE-PARTMENT with IRONWOOD*MONTANA below. He shaded his eyes and looked out over a white expanse broken only by the dark gray of a newly plowed road. "That'll be Johnny," he said quietly.

A cruiser pulled up behind the two cars already parked. An officer emerged, dressed like the sheriff. Putting on his hat, he walked to the packed snow lining the road. He hesitated a moment, as if looking for an easier path, then made his way along the trail of footprints leading to the hill.

Halfway up, he stopped to face a splash of dark red, clotted and sunk deep. He studied it without expression before going on.

"Well, Johnny," the sheriff said as the deputy reached the top.

"You're not going to like this, but"—he nodded over his shoulder. "Take a look."

Without a word the deputy walked past the hovercraft. There, under the trees, lay a body. Female, unclothed, height and weight average, hair black . . .

He squatted for a closer look. The other two, a rancher in a sheepskin jacket and an overcoated man wearing an armband marked VIGILANCE-501-COMMITTEE gathered behind him as if waiting for answers.

The corpse had a boneless, doll-like appearance. Both arms were broken all along their length, one pulled completely out of the socket. The hand on the other was bent back flat against the wrist. The ribs had been crushed on the near side, jagged edges poking knifelike through skin. The breasts had been mutilated.

But the face . . . the face was just gone, an oval of raw meat speckled here and there with shining bone. A hole gaped in the lower part, and there were broken stumps of what must have been teeth.

He raised his head. The sheriff was pulling at his mustache. "We got a real winner out there somewhere, Johnny."

"That we do."

A soft throbbing echoed from the hills. On the eastern horizon a small dot grew into a lifter, its curved, deltoid hull white as the snow below it. The deputy got up, brushing off his pants.

Edging closer, the vigilante said, "What do you think, Nast?"

The deputy turned away. "I think that's a dead girl."

Banking toward them, the lifter lost height, red cross visible on its tailfin. As it passed overhead, the trees swayed and a wave of warm air crossed the hilltop. Halting at a level spot at the foot of the hill, the lifter dropped to the snow, setting down daintily.

A small figure in a camelhair coat emerged, followed by two men carrying a folded stretcher. Fumbling on a pair of sunglasses, the coroner climbed the hill. "What you got for me?"

The sheriff gestured toward the trees. "Right back there."

Walking past him, the coroner whistled. "Where did *you* come from?" he muttered as he set down his black boxes. Kneeling next to the corpse, he cracked open the largest unit. The system hummed as it powered up. "You gentlemen will want to give me some room."

They moved back. The emergency team stood off by themselves, mumbling to each other. To one side the sheriff spoke to the vig, who gave Nast a brief glare.

"Remains have been moved," the coroner said without raising his head. He attached a probe to the body and stuck another into the snow.

"That was Wes," the sheriff called out.

"I didn't think it was right, her lying out there like that," the rancher said, his voice tight.

"It's okay, Wes," the sheriff said. "We've been through it."

"I thought it was a dead steer," the rancher went on in a voice so quiet, it was barely audible. "I couldn't turn the hover. It was like I was pushed here."

"Thirty seconds," the coroner called out. He got up and turned to the vig. "Ben, step aside there. You're in hologram range."

The sheriff walked up to Nast. "You want to see to this?" he asked.

The deputy nodded. "Okay. What's Lassiter doing here anyway?"

"I was having coffee with him when the call came in. It'd be nice if you weren't so hard on him."

Nast smiled mirthlessly. "Hell with the vigs," he said.

A beep sounded, and the coroner went back to his boxes. "What you thinking, Stan?" the sheriff called out.

"I'm thinking I'll head back to the lab and see if I can get a time of death. No question about cause, I don't believe."

The sheriff grimaced. "Right. Johnny's handling it. I'll have him call you."

"About two, I guess," the coroner said. Behind him the emergency team was shifting the corpse to the stretcher. One of them straightened and made a gagging sound.

Going to the hovercraft, the sheriff spoke to the rancher. The vig paused to say a word and with a sulky glance at Nast headed downhill. "Thanks for coming, Ben," the sheriff called.

The coroner reached the lifter, the stretcher just behind him. Turbines keened as the hatch closed. The sun vanished, obscured by clouds.

"Told Wes you'd call for a statement," the sheriff said, returning to Nast. "He's worried about his girls. Can't say I blame him." He shook his head. "He ain't been right since the war."

"Who has?"

The sheriff glanced up at him, eyes narrowed. "You sure you want to take this on, John? This is one bastard we might not catch."

"The corpse would have been visible from the road." Nast spoke simply, without emphasis, as if they had discussed this before. "Wonder why it was dumped there?"

"You're looking for reasons," the sheriff said. "Whoever did this doesn't have . . ." His words were lost as the lifter took off and roared overhead. Then the fans of the hovercraft began turning behind them. Shrugging, the sheriff bobbed his head toward the road.

Halfway downhill Nast came to a halt at the single splatter of red. His eyes were thoughtful, as if he were trying to imagine one spot on earth that hadn't been soaked in blood.

The sheriff looked at the red uneasily and went on. After a moment Nast followed, shivering and raising the collar of his jacket. It would snow before dark, and spring was still a long way off.

CHAPTER 1

*. . . Ross Bohlen is another problem. It's
high time something was done about this individual. I was in fact
considering dismissal following the Lower East Side incident, but
decided this would be a harsh step to take while the man was hos-
pitalized. I am well aware of Bohlen's record of success, but we
have to ask ourselves if such a man is properly representative of
the Agency. We've discussed this in the past, and I believe the
phrase used was "natural-born killer." As the Agency enters its
third phase, the sophistication of personnel will become a crucial
factor. In lieu of the fact . . .*

The subject of the memo crumpled it and tossed it into the
corner. Going to the window, he gazed out at a typical Washington
February, forty degrees and not a patch of snow in sight. Bohlen
was from the north woods and thought he knew what winters were
like. This wasn't a winter.

From the window he could see the Capitol dome, the Washington Monument, and the very tip of the Reagan Memorial. The
sidewalks below were packed, most of the men wearing the fur
hats in style this year, big Mongolian things that made them look

like detachments of the Golden Horde come to slaughter the bureaucrats. Bohlen smiled. He knew where they could start.

The memo had been marked RESTRICTED TO STAFF, with the copies numbered. He'd fished it out of the secure files after his request for field duty had come back. Denied, like the previous three, with no explanation this time, not even the excuse that he was recuperating. Just a scrawled no followed by a pair of initials: HC.

The same letters ended the memo. HC: Harland Cummins, former head of the University of Arkansas compsci department, former assistant director of COSSF, appointed the director of same after Marcus Amory's death, and undoing the old man's work ever since.

Bohlen snorted. Born killer—Cummins had some nerve taking that line after what happened at Key West.

The printer hummed behind him. He went over and tore off the sheet. Another memo, another HC. Bohlen flicked it away. Jesus, Cummins wasn't even in town and he was sending memos. Out in Hawaii, giving some kind of speech to a Pacific Alliance meeting.

Kicking the chair back, Bohlen sat down. He supposed he ought to do some work, earn his keep until Cummins ordered his butt dragged out onto the pavement. He stared at the screen with loathing. Records—good place for a psychopath.

He'd been sitting here processing old data since he came in off sick leave a month ago. Requisitions, timesheets, expense forms— the most worthless files you ever saw. Good to have you back, Ross. You look great. Straighten out those old W-2s, why don't you?

And that was it. Not word one about what had happened up in NYC. No debriefing, no interview, no investigation either. They didn't know who the shooter had been, but he wasn't a chiphead, and that was all that . . .

"Ross?" Lu called out. He looked up. The building was an old

Maxim's hotel commandeered during the war, and this office was two singles with a door between them. "Yeah?"

"Awful quiet in there."

"You woke me up."

"Uh-huh. Well, I've got something for you."

Bohlen snarled silently. More goddamn records. "What?"

There was a tap of heels, and Lu appeared in the doorway. She was dressed like a French schoolgirl gone bad—a black dress that could have been looser than it was, white tights, and clunky strap shoes, the Marianne Look or some damn thing. It rather suited her, although Lu resembled a Midwestern college student more than anything else, a sorority type who played a lot of volleyball.

"It's an anomaly," she said. "Out west someplace. Maria sent it up from Analysis. Thought you'd be interested."

Bohlen frowned. Maria was one he'd miss when he was shipped off to the pound: Amory had snatched her from Naval Intelligence at the beginning, and Ross had been her favorite bad boy ever since. She was no idiot, which was more than could be said for the rest of the analytical section. "What's so special about this one?"

Lu bit her lip. "There's a murder. Really nasty."

"Yeah? Put it onscreen, will you?"

As she vanished from the doorway, he called out, "Where's it from, anyway?"

"Montana. Irontown, or something."

The monitor beeped. Lines of print appeared: dates, locations, time of day, type of intrusion, and the programs used. Seeing the dates, he wondered if Maria had lost it: stale data, two-three years old, all from California. "Lu," he hollered, "what's this West Coast crap? I thought you said . . ."

"Scroll, Ross," she called back.

He went to the last entry. Ironwood, Montana. Never heard of it. Someone had needed mad money; the intruder had tapped a bank, the Ironwood First State, probably a farmer's outfit with no modern countermeasures. The time code told him that whoever it was had been in the system for nearly thirty seconds, plenty of time for mischief. Sloppy, though, as if he hadn't cared whether he was detected or not.

The programs involved were listed in the upper right corner. Birdman, Dog Story, Caligula, all standard intrusion software, all evolutionary and able to adapt to countermeasures, all illegal as hell. He scrolled back through the California entries, San Mateo, Marin, San Francisco, Palo Alto, and saw that they were duplicated on each. Oh, a couple of others here and there, but imps usually loaded half a dozen or more, and this had to be a chiphead spike or Maria wouldn't have sent it to him.

He switched to the murder report. The Crimewatch logo came up, along with a warning that BurCyb would get you if you were accessing illegally. He turned away, tapping the desktop, a staccato rhythm with three fingers. The screen lit up. He looked back and winced in spite of himself.

It was a photo of the crime scene: a nightmare image, all blood and bone, far beyond brutality, nearly an abstraction illustrating the worst that the world could hold. It took him several seconds to realize that the victim was female. He frowned. Someone had not liked this woman, or perhaps any woman.

He punched for ID and another picture came up, from a driver's license issued in California. It was impossible to reconcile with the one he'd just seen: a pretty face, cheekbones a bit too prominent and the lips a little thin, but some people would have said she was a beauty. There was a hint of Eastern ancestry around the eyes and in the clearness of the skin. The hair was black, worn in the old New England style popular a couple years ago, parted in the middle with rolls on either side of the head.

Sandra Nagawa-Butler, Oakland, California. Turned twenty-one last December. Height 5'8", weight 110, eyes brown. No record apart from a few speeding tickets. Blood sample from a donor drive showed no trace of illegal substance or STD. Life history, according to the bureaucracy: local schools, two years at UC,

Santa Cruz, associate degree in fine arts. Enrolled currently at an art institute in San Francisco, studying modern dance. No record of displaced person status, which fit. Not many had fled the Bay Area; the Medranistas had gotten no farther north than Tehachapi.

So what the hell had she been doing in Montana? He ran a search for relatives, a boyfriend, maybe a tour by a dance group— did they do that? He came up with nothing, which was no surprise. Identification had been made only this morning, from DNA records, and what Crimewatch had so far was minimal.

He went back to the pathologist's data accompanying the photos. No exact time of death, just an estimate based on body temperature. Switching to the intrusion entry, he checked the time. It was right in the range. Somebody had killed that girl and then made an after-hours withdrawal. Or vice versa. Or simultaneously.

Bohlen didn't like that. Chipheads weren't stupid; crazy they might be, but stupid, never.

Granted that it was a chiphead at all. There were still such things as casual murders, even in this enlightened age of vigilance committees, retroactive warrants, and national security police. But a murder coincident in area and time with a nonhacker cybernetic intrusion was a bad sign. Particularly a murder like this one.

"Lu," he called out. "What's Analysis doing with this?"

"Nothing. The California sequence was downgraded to inactive last year, so—"

"Who ordered that?" Bohlen said, knowing the answer.

"The director."

"HC," he muttered as he bent over the keyboard. "HC, HC . . ."

"What?"

"Nothing." He read the California entries. Eight murders, beginning right after the war and ending last year. The victims were of both sexes, all ages, races, economic strata. The youngest was a San Jose girl of twelve, the oldest a businessman of sixty-one found on a highway north of Sacramento. The only connection was MO: they'd all been beaten to an unimaginable degree, just like the dancer. The sequence had been flagged due to an unexplained series of anomalies in the same area. He split the screen so that both lists appeared. Only one real match, in Palo Alto: the murder had occurred a day after an intrusion. Not much, but Amory might have sent a team out on it.

The list seemed familiar. It took a moment for him to realize why: this was the sequence Frank Ricelli had been investigating when he was killed. Run down by a car outside Frisco . . .

Bohlen leaned back, about to ask Lu why the Hillbilly had deflagged the file, but then thought better of it. She wouldn't know; Cummins never indulged in explanations. That was beneath him.

Instead he tried to get hold of Maria, diddling the call so it wouldn't be recorded. He wasn't supposed to contact Analysis over an open line. In fact, he wasn't supposed to call them at all—COSSF's flow chart contained nothing called Records.

But it turned out she wasn't around. The guy who answered—Bohlen didn't know his name, though he knew who Bohlen was—told him that one of her kids had gotten sick at school and she'd left for the day.

As he cut off, Lu appeared. She backed against the doorway, eyes lowered. "You're going to be mad," she said.

He raised his eyebrows.

"That Montana thing," she went one. "I was checking to see if anything new came in, and . . . well, they arrested somebody."

She bit her lip as he stared at her, and he forced himself to relax. Am I getting that bad, he thought. Lu was one person he didn't want to rage on; she was in the same position he was. Cummins detested her too, for some unfathomable reason, and had dumped her here as the last step before kicking her out into the street. She didn't talk about it, but he knew it depressed her.

He gave her a smile. "It's okay."

"Sorry, Ross."

As she turned away, he called to her. "Throw me the report just for the fun of it, huh?"

The monitor beeped and went through the logo-and-warning cycle again. He leaned closer when the report came up. The entry had been made that morning. It would have been nice if it had been cleared before he'd gotten into an uproar, but Crimewatch took most of the day to process incoming data for softbombs, viruses, and other surprises.

The report was in copese, a dialect that Bohlen rather enjoyed, more to listen to than anything else, though reading it also had its pleasures. He would have expected something coming out of Montana to be a bit more laconic, along the lines of "I done seen him and I catched him," but he knew that was asking too much.

. . . several reports received of an inebriated white male perpetrating a disturbance . . . (A drunk raising hell, in other words.) *. . . Deputy Frostmoon took the call and upon arrival at the scene observed suspect inflicting grievous harm on a canine belonging to . . .* (Kicking a dog. How awful. And what kind of name was Frostmoon, anyway?) *. . . Frostmoon endeavored to put suspect into custody, who resisted . . .* (Bohlen smiled. Done catched him.) *. . . in the ensuing altercation, Frostmoon was forced precipitously to the pavement . . .* (Ralph got knocked on his ass.) *. . . Deputy Nast appeared on the scene and moved to assist Frostmoon in subduing suspect . . .* (Nast . . . he was the one investigating the murder. Okay.) *. . . suspect attempted to abscond, with Deputies Frostmoon and Nast in close pursuit. Suspect evaded several initigtives to seize him during the chase but was finally apprehended and put under restraint . . .* (They beat the living hell out of him.) *. . . while Frostmoon escorted suspect to the patrol vehicle, Nast collected several articles shed by suspect. At this point in time several members of the Polk County 501 appeared at the scene . . .* (501? What the hell was that? A vigilante outfit?) *. . . demanded suspect be placed in their custody due to a report that he*

11

had destroyed and/or damaged a solar collector at the do-
micile of one member present, also occasioning some alarm
in the member's household. A disagreement transpired
. . . (Right; a bunch of vigs trying to horn in on a legit
arrest. Must happen every other day out there.) . . . Dep-
uty Nast calmed the situation, enforcing an understanding
upon the 501 contingent that the Polk County Sheriff's
Department possessed overriding jurisdiction . . .

Eloquent stuff; modern-day poetry. He couldn't see why somebody hadn't written a blank-verse epic in cop talk. But how did it
tie in with the murder? Wait, here it was:

. . . suspect's possessions included, among other items, a
bayonet and an electromagnetic sap . . .

A slapper. He thought of what had been left of the woman's
face. A slapper would have done the job: a foot of steel spring
snapped out by superconducting coils at two hundred feet per second. But there had to be more to it than that.

The perp had been carrying a ratty piece of military ID: DEX-
TER, JAMES—PRIVATE FIRST CLASS. Bohlen went through his record, a whole string of PI and D&D busts going back to just after
the war, with a couple of visits to dryout clinics that obviously
hadn't taken. Nothing more violent than a few brawls, but . . .
He read the last entry and smiled. Two months ago he'd had one
too many in Stockton.

That was it. Dexter roars into town, terrorizes the neighborhood, is caught with a nasty piece of hardware, and was in Northern California a while back. So he killed the girl. Q.E.D.

And that was exactly what Nast's report said: *. . . illegal*
weapon . . . Northern California vicinity . . . uncontrolled vio-
lent behavior . . .

Done seen him, done catched him.

He switched over to comm mode and called Montana. Only

one number; must be a small department. The screen put up a clearing signal, so he overrode. Against regs, but everybody did it. If you waited to be cleared for an outside line, you'd never get anything done.

A woman answered, moon-faced, her hair in a braid wrapped around her head. "Polk County . . ." she began brightly. Bohlen cut her off. "Patrolman Nast, please."

"That's Deputy Nast," the woman said.

"Right. Thanks."

She smiled solicitously. "Now, who's calling?"

"Ma'am, do you see that symbol on the bottom of your screen?" She nodded amiably. "That means federal security. Now, is he around?"

The woman's eyes widened. "From *Washington*?"

"That's right, Washington."

"Oh . . . I'll get him."

The screen displayed a picture of the departmental shield. A lot of mountains, sun bursting through clouds, in the foreground a guy on a horse. The horse looked like the smart one.

There was a flicker, and he found himself contemplating a blank wall. A shadow moved across it, and he heard a high-pitched voice winding up his introduction: ". . . from *Washington*." Then Nast appeared.

Bohlen didn't know what he'd been expecting; whiskers, big hat, a wad of chaw in one cheek. Nast fit another mold: brown uniform shirt, strap of a Sam Browne across one shoulder, sandy hair cut to within an inch of his skull, skin wrinkled in harsh folds around the eyes. The epitome of the small-town cop. The only thing that marred the image was a bandage above his right eyebrow.

Nast gazed into the screen, not at Bohlen but through him. The thousand-yard stare, they called it.

Bohlen felt his hackles rise. He'd come across the type before; the army was full of them. A lifer—seen it all and liked none of it. He hadn't been able to stand them then, and nothing had changed since.

"Nast," the cop said quietly.

Bohlen leaned forward. Stay calm. Remember, you're asking for cooperation. Keep things light and easy.

He pointed at the bandage. "Looks like you had a rough one. That wouldn't have been Dexter, would it?"

"Who are you?" Not even a smile.

"Name's Bohlen. I understand you're holding this Dexter for the, uh . . . Butler murder. That's the name, right?"

The cop said nothing. Okay, Bohlen thought, you want to play hardass, we'll play. "I'm interested in your train of thought there."

Nast's eyes narrowed slightly. "You read the report?"

Bohlen nodded.

"That's it."

Still nodding, Bohlen picked up a sheet. It was another memo, but Nast didn't have to know that. "Okay. So Dexter comes around, goes on a spree, teases Fido the Pup, and runs you and your pal Frostmoon a race across the prairie. All this a day after he mauls a woman so bad, it took a DNA tag to identify her."

"Looks that way."

"Yeah," Bohlen said loudly. "And it looks like he planted the Manhattan bomb and was a go-between for Medrano and Castro, too. What are you trying to sell me?"

Nast's face reddened. "What's your problem, mister?"

"I've got a few. Bloodstains. That was a pretty soggy job. Any on Dexter? The slapper? And opportunity. How'd he run into her? In California? Carried her over his shoulder since December, I suppose. *I* was in Frisco last summer. Why don't you book *me*?" Crumpling the memo, he shook it at the screen. "You think you got a case?" He flicked it over the monitor. "There's your case. Now you got something you want to tell me about this?"

Nast moved his head. No more than an inch, but it was as if he'd almost lurched through the screen. "What the hell do you mean?"

"Long time between homicides out there, huh? You wouldn't

be keeping the caseload clean? Pinning it on the first schmuck to come along? Who gives a shit about Dexter? Piece of trash thrown up by the war. That how you do things in Ironburg?"

Bohlen paused.

Eyes wide, Nast was leaning forward. "If you were standing before me," he said, his voice almost inaudible. "I would put your ass on deck."

Bohlen was opening his mouth to reply when the screen went dark. He raised his hands as if to drag Nast out of the monitor bodily, then dropped them.

He'd handled that just fine; one of his better moments at external liaison. He cast an eye at the door. No wonder Lu was so spooked. Things were starting to get to him: the shooting, all that time in the hospital, three months of deskwork, and on top of it all, HC.

He went to the window. Five blocks south was DuPont Circle, where the bomb had been planted. In a van parked by a bookstore, sitting there for two days while the town quaked in hysterics waiting for Medrano's next move after his attempt to pancake Manhattan. When it was towed, the crew at the impound lot hadn't known what to make of it. The Navy bomb team had, though. "About thirty kilotons," the chief said after they cut through the roof. "Never could have gone off. Lousy design."

If it had, the edge of the fireball would have been right about where Bohlen was standing, give or take a yard.

His breath fogged the glass. He drew a target, then wiped it clear with his sleeve. What to do about Ironville? That cop's story was a crock. His burnout could have killed the girl, unlikely as it might seem, but burnouts didn't leave implant spikes behind. Only chipheads did that, and if it was a chiphead, then this was COSSF business.

That's what the Computer Subversion Strike Force was for, whatever Cummins was saying these days. Set up in the second year of the war to take on a problem that BurCyb and the FBI

Computer Crime Unit had never encountered and didn't know how to handle: the Cybernetically Enhanced Individuals. The chip-heads, the imps—a self-styled elite who had taken the next step in cybernetic evolution, and come to the conclusion that this made them superhuman, and eligible to grasp the reins of destiny. And that the worst days of a war to the knife between their country and a Latin megalomaniac was the time to do it.

There had been no more than a handful of them—estimates ranged from 180 to 300—but they'd managed to turn the country inside out all the same. Placed in positions close to the comps that ran things, in Defense, the CIA, Human Services, Treasury, the FBI, they used the trapdoors they had smuggled through data encryption to delete a byte here, diddle a program there, all according to orders given by people who knew nothing of the world outside a university campus. Information was power, and whoever controlled information controlled everything—and everything was what the imps had been shooting for.

COSSF was a dedicated agency, its only mission to track down CEIs and apprehend them. In practice, apprehension meant killing. Apprehension was where Bohlen came in. That was his job, and he was very good at it.

Once Marcus Amory got mad at him for some forgotten reason—antagonizing outside law, maybe. "You're a knucklehead, Ross," he'd said. "But you have one thing going for you: situational awareness. Fancy word for intuition. The old fighter jocks had it. Total gut grasp of what's happening at any given moment: they always knew when there was an enemy plane nearby. With you it's intellectual. You know when something is off, when a piece just doesn't fit. And that is why we put up with your antics. But," he went on, just as Bohlen was beginning to feel cocky. "It's a good thing you have it, because without it you'd have the mentality of a stone."

He felt it now. Right behind him: some mad, twisted remnant of the great cybernetic crusade that had pushed the interface a little too far, tapped one time too many, and then bang, over the border

16

into blood country. If the old man was still around, Bohlen would be flying west right now. But not under the Cummins regime. Since the Hillbilly had taken over—and Bohlen longed to know how he'd pulled that trick!—it was third phase this, reification that, heuristic management the other, anything but what the COSSF had been created to do. Mushmouth had even gone in front of Congress last fall to say that the chiphead problem was essentially solved.

Bohlen knew better.

But he needed more data. Glancing at the clock, he went back to the desk. Nearly one o'clock out on the Coast; he might catch Floyd before he went clomping out to lunch . . .

The comp buzzed as he touched the keyboard. He stared at the monitor, afraid that his call had let something into the system, but that wasn't it. He felt his face grow hot as the words came up:

DAILY WORK QUOTA FOR RECORDS COMPILATION IS FIVE HUNDRED AND TWENTY (520) ENTRIES. YOU HAVE AT THIS TIME COMPLETED ONLY ONE-FIFTH (1/5TH) OF THAT TOTAL. UNTIL QUOTA IS FILLED THIS STATION WILL DISREGARD ALL ATTEMPTS AT USE OTHER THAN . . .

He clenched a fist and lifted it to the screen. So there was a quota now, was there? He'd give 'em quotas. He leaned toward the monitor, which was now explaining that a report was being placed in his file. "Off," he said softly. The screen went dark.

He stood clutching the edge of the desk. "Shit," he muttered. There was a sound from the other room: Lu, probably wondering what was going on. He paced a couple of minutes to cool himself down, then went to the door. "Let's knock off and go out for a drink."

Lu squinted back at him. "What about Madeline?"

"I'll call her too."

She smiled. "You do that first."

"Okay," he said, turning back to the room. The crumpled memo still lay in the corner. He gave it a kick as he went past.

CHAPTER 2

THE SKY WAS SLATE-GRAY and low, with a hint of snow in the air. What had already fallen lay more than a foot deep, and Telford made his way through it along the tracks of the few cars that had passed. The only supermarket left in town was a half-mile from Sarah's place, and he'd had to walk it.

Ahead the towers of Essex glowed, the flashing signs—Prudential, Sony, Transorbit, Eurex—making the day seem darker than it was. Beyond them was the spire of the Empire State, unlit these five years.

The grocery bag was getting away from him. Canned stuff, unbalanced and ready to topple. He clutched it against his chest and juggled it until the cans settled. The bag was made of the new ecoplastic, slippery in spite of the buff finish. He thought of the jokes about the bags degrading in people's hands. If it was ever going to happen, it would be right now, to him.

He resumed walking, went past a small white house abandoned and falling to ruin. It had once been a doctor's office—standard practice in the 20th, remaking homes into offices—and the sign remained, dangling on a piece of wire. SANJI PATEL, LI-

LICENSED OPTOMETRIST. Telford wondered where Sanji was now.

Across the street stood Newman Hall, a small Catholic college gone bust and converted into cheap apartments. Almost empty now, although it had been packed with evacuees from Manhattan not long ago. Climbing the knoll at the corner, he paused to look around. Nothing out of the ordinary, no sign that anything had changed in the half hour he'd been gone. He had no reason to believe that the Cossacks knew who or where he was, but that didn't excuse sloppiness. You had one mistake coming, if you were lucky. Telford had already made his.

He waded on. The checkpoint straddling the border of South Orange and Essex blinked at him. Unmanned, comp-driven, programmed to report anyone who crossed without a city ID. Essex Inc. wasn't fond of people wandering in unannounced from the suburban slums.

At the door he punched the entry code, balancing the bag on one knee. A buzzer sounded as it swung open.

Inside he stopped to listen, then went on up. An old dorm, hallways bare and cold though the apartments were actually pretty nice. When he opened the door, an image arose: the sick horror that had greeted him in New Orleans. He shut his eyes and went in. There was no sign of Sarah; she was probably still asleep.

He set down the bag and rubbed his hands. They were aching with cold, and they'd be chapped tomorrow. Better pick up a new pair of gloves; winter wasn't over yet by a long shot. His last pair had vanished, left behind in that hotel room in Louisiana, most likely.

He put the food away and cleaned up the foul mess in the kitchen. Old food, half-empty cans, a patch of stickiness, what he guessed was spilled liquor, covering a quarter of the floor.

Finishing up, he opened the cabinet under the sink and winced when he saw the urn where he'd put it last night. He looked over his shoulder, half-expecting to see Sarah gazing back at him, but the room was empty. Reaching in, he pushed the urn all the way to the back, arranging the cans to hide it. He didn't want her to know about that. Not now, probably not ever. He'd sneak it out later, bury it somewhere, a spot fit for poor Briggs's ashes to rest.

Telford wasn't all that hungry, but he decided to eat anyway. A can of chili, a couple of rolls. He put it away quickly, without really tasting anything.

Sarah came out as he was washing the bowl, so quietly, he didn't hear her until she reached the kitchen.

He turned to see her standing in the doorway, wearing the nightgown he'd put on her last night, with a blue robe over it. She looked better today, but that didn't mean much. Her face was ashen, her eyes bloodshot, her hair a knotted nest dangling to her shoulders.

And yet the beauty was still there—a hint of it, anyway. If she'd only cool down, cut out the booze, take care of herself, it would come back. Not the way it had been, perhaps, not fresh and new as when he'd first met her, but something worthy. If she'd only get a handle on things . . .

But there was no getting a handle on what was wrong with Sarah.

She gave him a ghost of a smile. "Good morning."

"How you feeling?"

Crossing her arms, she leaned against the doorjamb. "My head hurts."

He started toward the bathroom. "I'll get you . . ."

She grabbed his arm, just a touch before dropping her hand. "No, it's all right. I just took something."

He looked down at her face, then backed off, remembering that she didn't like anyone that close. She plucked at the front of her gown, her face stiff.

"I'll get you some dinner," he said, turning back to the kitchen.

"I'm not very hungry."

"Come on, Sarah. You've got to eat. I'll make some soup. How's that?"

Her only answer was a shrug. She watched as he opened a can. Then she went into the living room.

While the soup cooked, he made a jug of orange juice. Sarah had always liked OJ. He carried bowl and glass out, and she smiled at him, sorry to be such trouble, not wanting to admit that nothing he did for her could ever be called that.

As she ate, he went through a copy of the *Times* he'd picked up, reading aloud anything odd or silly enough to amuse her. There was plenty of that.

She finished and lay back on the couch. "They still call it the *New York Times*," she said.

"Yeah, well—*Hackensack Times* doesn't have quite the same cachet."

She laughed. A quiet laugh, but real just the same. "Why didn't they just move to Brooklyn?"

"Got me." Telford pointed to her glass. "More juice?"

"I'll get it . . ."

"No, you sit right there." He left the glass and brought her the pitcher.

"How long can you stay this time?" she asked as he poured.

"Long as I like, babe."

"Nobody calling for help out there?"

He felt a twinge, thinking of the ashes only twenty feet away. "Nope. Pretty quiet all around."

"You need somebody to help you, Jase. It's too hard for just you alone."

"There isn't anybody else."

Sarah went on, her voice small. "I'd like to help."

He held back his answer, not wanting to hurt her, afraid he'd say something that would tell her just how empty that hope was. Finally he spoke. "You do help me, Sarah."

The glass turned slowly in her hand. "If I could pull things together here . . ." Her eyes met his, and she smiled, a bleak smile, full of sadness. She knew.

"You'll do it," he said, winking at her. "You ain't whipped yet, kiddo."

She put her glass down and yawned, raising her hand to her lips.

"Still a little beat?"

"I feel like I haven't slept at all."

"You need more rest. Go on and crash out. Tell you what," he added as she got up. "When you're back on your feet, we'll go downtown. See a show, have a good meal. How's that sound?"

"That'd be nice."

"Yeah. We could both use a good time."

"That's for sure," she said, and padded to the bedroom. At the door she stopped. "And Jason . . . Thanks for taking care of me last night." She dropped her head. "And all the other nights."

The door closed before he could answer. He gazed at it a moment before turning away.

He went to the window and pulled back the drapes. It was full dusk, though you wouldn't know it to look at Essex painting the entire eastern sky with light. Hell of a sight, if you didn't remember Manhattan before the Times Square Fizzle.

Strange how that had worked out. People were still living in the sections of Queens that had been dusted, but you couldn't give Manhattan real estate away, even though the bomb had spewed hot stuff only over Midtown. The rest of the island was clean, but empty, except for the decontamination crews and a few thousand squatters, as if Medrano's plan had succeeded and the device had cut loose with all thirty kilotons. It was the latest New York myth, and maybe the last.

The Big Apple now was Essex. Old Newark, sold to a US-Eurasian consortium after being burned down during the PC riots in the nineties. Big uproar over that, selling a whole American city to foreigners, even though only half the money was overseas and there hadn't been much of a city left. Good thing Essex had been around when the war started, otherwise a million Manhattanites would have wound up camping out in the Jersey swamps.

He thought of what he'd said to Sarah, and a small wave of pleasure rose within him. Yes—get her out of this hole, a night on the town . . . No, erase that; a whole day. She'd want to get her hair done, some new clothes . . . God knows how long she'd been cooped up in here.

He was about to let the drapes fall when his eyes caught something just outside the window, an object reflecting the light of the room.

The good feeling vanished, replaced by hollowness. Raising the window, he reached out. Flower boxes were attached to the ledge, a sorry attempt at a homey touch, and the bottle was wedged between the bricks and the corner of the box.

He pulled it inside. Vodka, a cheap house brand, perfectly chilled, seal intact. He clutched it tightly, as if he were holding her soul to him, remembering the other bottles, the ones he'd dumped last night. Six empties and one half full. All the same rotgut trash, raw alcohol good only for getting blasted as quickly and thoroughly as possible.

Christ, but there were times he could just give up.

He emptied the bottle in the sink, running the water in case Sarah was still awake, then threw it down the garbage chute. He almost wished he'd saved some for himself, but it was just as well. It would only have gagged him.

She'd never told him what it was that tortured her so. Either it was too personal, too strange, or too obscenely frightening to put into words. He understood that, understood it well. He had his own bad nights.

He'd thought for a while, even hoped, that it wasn't PS at all, just alcoholism, something that would have happened anyway. But he knew her too well for that. No, it was PS, all right. He rubbed the spot behind his right ear where the EC microcomp lay flush against his skull. Pelton's Syndrome, the sickness that came out of the interface.

It was a long way from Big Sur to here. He recalled how she'd looked back then, that first night they spent together . . . Actually, he didn't remember much at all; he'd been too disoriented from his first attempt at tapping the day before. But he'd done all right, evidently. He found out later that Nathan had suggested it to her. Not an order, Nathan Kahn never gave orders, but sex had its place in his system as everything else did, and that night it had been therapy for the new kid, Jason Telford.

She'd been standing in front of the mirror when he awoke, a trim little behind sloping up to a waist which from that angle seemed impossibly small. Sarah was an older woman, all of twenty-two, and he'd been awed by her. But there was a touch of simple male pride in it too . . .

She laughed, and he raised his eyes to meet hers in the glass, realizing only then that he was fingering his skull where the imp had been emplaced two weeks before. He dropped his hand guiltily. "Go on," she said, turning to him. "Say it."

"What?"

"About the bioplastic. Everybody does."

He flushed, all vanity gone, and she threw herself onto the bed. "Oh, you look so sweet. Now say it." She started tickling him and kept it up until he admitted he was worried about the bioplastic sending tendrils into his brain.

"You stupid," she said, now kneading his shoulders. "It can't do that. It's synergistic, only growing where the trace elements have been laid down. So." She pounded his back with each word. "Don't. Worry. About. It."

He mumbled agreement, and she told him what else not to worry about: the confusion he'd felt after the interface, the lousy job he'd made of his first try, the rumors about some imps running into trouble. Capped with the line he'd begun to think of as the estate mantra: Nathan had it all worked out.

"He likes you, you know," she said, wrapping her arms around him.

"Really?" That perked him up: he was afraid he'd made a fool of himself last night, after the trial run. Nathan had been speaking about something that Telford couldn't quite grasp: the ground state, an idea he'd picked up from some old Englishman—Huxtable? Hurley? he couldn't remember—that the brain was a reducing valve which cut down sensory information to no more than a trickle, that the implants were a regulator, and that soon they'd be able to see the world as it truly was . . .

"Yeah, really," Sarah said, running her hands over his chest. She'd told him last night she liked hairy men. "We talked about you yesterday. He sees something in you." She leaned close to his ear. "I don't know what," she whispered as her hands went lower. "But I know what I see."

There was still some orange juice left. Telford picked up the pitcher and drank the rest. A few months ago they'd tried to make love once again. He'd stopped when he realized she was crying.

Back at the estate she'd talked about what fun it would be to share orgasms through the implants. Now she couldn't bear to touch another human being.

Maybe she hadn't known the bottle was out there. Maybe she hid it while she was drunk and forgot about it. Yes, that's what happened.

But she was better off than most of them, because most of them were dead, victims of Pelton's or the Cossacks. He saw again what had greeted him at the flat in New Orleans: Briggs hanging from the shower nozzle in the dark bathroom, the belt around his neck stretched to twice its length, the face rotted away.

He touched the chip. Nathan's tool, the lever with which he would move the world. The key to heaven that had opened the gates of hell.

As they would open for him, too, in time. Somewhere down the line, Pelton's waited. That horrific week last summer—the voices, the dreams, the mad shimmering at the edge of his vision. Someday the valve would open wide, and when it did, Telford would be washed away.

He was nearly asleep, in that soft, half-dreaming state between wakefulness and oblivion. He told the light to shut off and was surprised it didn't, until he recalled that nothing was computerized here except the phone. It wouldn't hurt to leave the light on. He closed his eyes and let himself drift.

He'd almost dropped off completely when the phone rang. He tensed, then rolled from the couch and stumbled over to it. His eyes widened as he caught sight of the readout, Ironwood, and the number of the lodge. He snatched the receiver.

"Yeah."

"Oh, I'm so glad you're there."

He recognized Naomi's voice. "What's wrong?"

The line was silent for so long that he thought they'd been cut off. Finally she spoke, her voice ragged. "Page was here."

Telford lowered the receiver and stared at it. Page? For a second the name didn't register. Page . . . no, that was impossible. Page was dead, food for worms long ago. "What?"

"He was here. Hanging around all day."

Wait a second, Naomi didn't know Page, she'd never laid eyes on him. "How do you know it was him?"

"He told me." Her voice rose in pitch. "Jason, I'm scared."

That was Page, all right. When he entered a room, fear strolled in right behind him. "Are Cora and Gene okay?"

"Gene was talking to him. I didn't hear what they said. I stayed upstairs. He kept looking at me . . ."

Goddamit, get to the point. "Naomi, are they all right?"

"Yes," she said, enunciating the word precisely. "Jason, you'd better get out here."

He looked at the clock. After ten. There was a redeye at midnight, but it would let him off in Denver and he'd have to wait for the morning shuttle to Butte anyway. "Listen, Naomi, I'll fly out tomorrow first thing. If he comes back, don't let him in. Tell him I'm on my way, he'll have to talk to me."

"I don't know how he found out where we were. None of us ever . . ."

26

"Just calm down. Keep the doors locked, and I'll be there."

He heard her sigh. "Okay." She paused a moment before going on, her voice milder. "I know what I sound like, but he just . . ."

"He got to you. I know. He's good at that." He damn well was, if he'd panicked Naomi like this. She was absolutely solid, otherwise he'd never have put her at the station. Page had been bad enough the last time Telford saw him, over a year ago. With Pelton's he'd be utterly demonic by now.

"Everything else okay?"

"Yes, fine."

"All right. Get some sleep. I'll see you tomorrow."

He waited, but Naomi said nothing more, and he hung up. Hand on the phone, he stared at the blank walls. No pictures, no decorations. It was like a mausoleum, this place . . .

There was a sound behind him. He turned, uncertain he'd heard anything, but it came again. Sarah, calling from the bedroom.

She was under the covers, face toward him, blinking at the light from the living room. Pulling the door half-shut, he made his way to the chair by the bed.

"I heard you talking," she said. "Did you get a call?"

"Yeah."

"Anything wrong?"

Should he tell her? No, not tonight. Let it ride—the morning would be soon enough. Let her get at least one good night's rest. "No, nothing."

Her eyes were open. He could see no details, just the bare structure of her face, a graceful play of gray and shadow. She raised a hand and brushed it across her forehead. "I had a dream."

"A good one?"

He sensed rather than saw her smile. "We were at the estate, all of us. You, me, Nathan, everybody. It was after everything happened, and it turned out it was all a mistake."

"That sounds nice, Sarah."

"Oh, it was. Nathan was just the way he used to be, and everyone was talking, and you . . . Jase, you were so cute then. So quiet, staring at everyone as if you were afraid to talk."

"You telling me I'm not cute anymore, lady?"

Her hand reached out to touch his face. "No, Jason," she said. "I'm not telling you that."

"You're smiling," she went on. "It's so good when you smile."

He sat without moving. He would smile for her forever, if that was what it took.

"Oh, Jason, those were the good times."

He took her hand. "That they were," he said. "The best."

The moment stayed awhile, Sarah gazing up at him in the dimness while he held her hand. Finally she shifted her head on the pillow. "Good night, Jason," she said softly.

"Sleep well, babe."

In a moment she was asleep. He laid her hand on the covers, got up, and went quietly to the living room.

Essex glittered, if anything brighter than before. That was one town that never slept. A few aircraft were visible, collision lights blinking. Cops, businessmen, partygoers, who knew? Resting his head against the cold pane, Telford closed his eyes.

Page. That was what he was known as. Whether another name went with it or if there was any connection to the one he'd been born with was unknown. Just that one syllable, flat and mocking, challenging the world to learn anything more, the group he'd been with, who had implanted and trained him, or what generation he was. A blank concrete wall.

There was a word for whenever someone vanished or died: he'd been paged.

Telford had run into him only twice. First at the estate. He could still see it with perfect clarity: Ronnie lying there holding his leg, eyes bulging at the red pool that crawled across the tiles, Page standing over him, smoke curling from the pistol barrel. He'd looked like something out of a history book, head shaved to stubble, old-style leather coat reaching to his thighs—a police thug from a European dictatorship of the thirties. Telford often wondered whether the look was deliberate or something Page had stumbled on by chance. Or whether this was a case of similar mentalities converging to the same image decades apart.

He'd just appeared. No alarms went off, no one on guard duty saw him. He was simply there, smiling as if it was the damnedest joke in the world, waiting until he'd gathered enough of an audience, then speaking his piece in a mild voice: leave the Stoner group alone. Don't try to track, don't cache any data, don't even think about it. Drop any interest in Betty Stoner lest she become interested in you.

They'd all been too shocked to do anything, all except Telford.

He'd moved quickly: two steps, a kick, and the pistol had gone flying. Dropping back, he'd waited for whatever move would come, but Page just stared at him as if memorizing his face. Then he turned his back and walked out.

No one outside had seen him leave, either.

The second time was at the hub airport in KC. Telford had long forgotten why he'd been on the road that week, or the reason he'd taken that particular route, dangerously close to the old front line and overrun with military and security types. Some desperate errand, most likely. A mission in aid of someone now dead and buried.

He'd been hurrying to catch a connecting flight when there Page was, the same as he'd been in California, down to the coat. A little thinner, maybe, the eyes a little wilder, but that was all.

Page said nothing to Telford, just nodded as if to let him know that he was still around, still taking an interest in things. Telford kept walking and got no more than twenty feet when a sound from behind told him to move.

A chair, torn from the floor, hit where he'd been. He swung around to see Page, hands bloodied, and those eyes, like two holes in the doorway to hell, boring straight through him.

Airport security appeared, along with a few MPs, and Page started running. Telford simply walked off, slowly, as if the whole affair had nothing to do with him.

He had been sure that Page was long gone. Devoured by PS, dusted by the Cossacks, hooked up with the Mob to carry out a few perfect hits before being erased himself.

Now he was back, and not just anywhere, but on Telford's own ground. It was a direct challenge, no less. Telford didn't ask himself why; he knew why.

The thought came that he could call in COSSF. Drop a line to Bohlen, the bare facts, no need to identify himself. It wouldn't take much to get that butcher moving.

But he couldn't go to the Cossacks, not after Key West. They'd had their chance. The thought of giving anyone to them, even Page, made his stomach turn.

He'd have to handle it himself; and if the worst happened— well, at least it'd be better than PS.

He tried to remember the color of Page's eyes. Gray, blue, some light shade like that.

Turning from the window, he shut off the light and went to the couch. Tomorrow would be a long day.

As it was, he lay awake until nearly dawn. He got up, shaved and washed, then went to the bedroom door.

He couldn't open it. Couldn't face her, not after what he'd promised last night. He stood there a few minutes, in the muzziness of too little sleep, half-hoping she'd come out, but the door remained closed. Finally he went to the kitchen, wrote her a note, and put it by the phone. It occurred to him she might be low on money; he'd use a comp at the airport to transfer some funds. A straight transaction, no interface and no problem.

He punched for a cab and left the apartment. Outside, he paused. The sky was still clouded, and there was a fresh layer of snow, bright and unmarked in the cold light of morning. He walked through it to the avenue.

CHAPTER 3

LOAFERS ON THE DESKTOP, phone at his shoulder, Bohlen sat talking to a Bug, telling him in as obnoxious a manner as possible that no, he didn't have any time to spare for him. He'd been doing this a lot lately, it seemed.

The Bug carried on about interagency cooperation, bureaucratic responsibility, the standard rap. Bohlen let him run down, then said, "No."

That set the Bug off, and he started talking Formal Complaint. Bohlen keyed in an instruction not to clear calls from the number currently on the line. He waited for it to be processed. Then he hung up.

He sat back, proud of himself. Interagency cooperation my ass. He'd had nothing but trouble from those bastards. That time up in Essex when they hadn't let him or Delahanty into their office to check on something romping around in their system. They'd had to come back later with an entire armed team, and by then it was too late: whatever it had been was gone.

The Bugs were a jerkdog outfit set up at the start of the war to chase Medrano's saboteurs. By the time they got organized, the Frontero Liberación Aztlan had been pushed back, the FBI had broken up the subversive networks, and the Internal Security Bureau—InSecBu in Washingtonese, and it hadn't taken long to derive a good tag from that—had been left without a mission.

The Bugs didn't let that stop them, devoting their time to kicking in college kids' doors, confiscating manuscripts from writers, and getting in the way of people with real work to do. There was talk of shutting them down, but they had a lot of protection. Bohlen supposed the whole song-and-dance would go on until the wrong person got killed.

He turned back to the monitor. He'd been through the Montana report five times this morning and was going for a sixth. Not that he expected to tease out anything new; he was just killing time until Delahanty slouched into his office out on the Coast and he could run the whole thing by him.

He'd been up half the night thinking about it. First at dinner with Maddy and Lu, then sitting up in bed. When Maddy stole all the pillows, he got dressed and went over to Duff's Alehouse for a couple of beers, hoping they'd calm him down. It didn't work, and when he returned, Maddy was awake and he had to explain it all to her. She didn't say much—the Madwoman was a toughie—but in the morning she held him tighter than usual.

The monitor beeped. Letting his feet drop, Bohlen said, "Switch." The report faded, and a bald man with an oval head and permanently surprised blue eyes appeared. Eddie Frisell, Mushmouth's right-hand man. Left in charge, Bohlen presumed, on the principle that he was the last person to pull anything behind Cummins's back.

"Ross?" he said, as if he wasn't quite sure who it was he was speaking to.

Bohlen smiled. "Hey Eddie. How things shaking?"

"Ross, did you turn down an ISB request just now?"

"Yeah. What about it?"

Eddie's eyebrows bunched together. "Why'd you do that?"

"Since when are we holding hands with those losers?"

"It was an interbureau request," Frisell said, shaking his head slightly. "The director approved it . . ."

Uh-huh, Bohlen thought. Jethro had arranged it before he left, and Eddie had forgotten to send it down. "Well, Land o' Goshen," he said, forcing his eyebrows up as far as they'd go. "He should of damn well told me. I wouldn't make these mistakes then."

An ocean of concern flooded Eddie's face. "I'll have him call you back . . ."

"No, don't bother, I'll call him. I know where he's at."

Eying him doubtfully, Eddie nodded. "All right."

Bohlen was already reaching for delete, but the temptation to tweak Eddie was just too strong. "Maybe I should check with Harland, make sure it's okay."

Eddie almost leaped at him. "No, no, don't do that, it's fine, really. I'll send you a memo . . ."

"Nah, not necessary." Bohlen paused while Eddie regarded him warily. "Harland's out in Honolulu, no? What's he up to, anyway? Running up and down the beach, is he?"

"No. The director's speaking at the Pacific Rim Security Conference."

"He's not speaking all the time. I'll bet he's mixing a bit of a vacation in with it. How long's he gone for, anyway?"

"The beginning of next week."

"Uh-huh. Well, things are running smooth upstairs, I hope. Need a hand with anything, give me a buzz." He touched the keyboard, and Eddie jerked closer.

"Now you're going to call ISB . . ."

"Sure thing," Bohlen said, and cut him off.

"What's Eddie up to?" Lu called out.

"Oh, being an idiot," Bohlen said. He smiled at her sound of disgust. Eddie had spent a lot of time badgering her for a date when she'd worked in Analysis.

A ping sounded as a line appeared onscreen: FLOYD DELA-HANTY PRESENT AT SAN FRANCISCO STATION. Bohlen checked the time. Only two hours late. Now that was unheard of: back when they'd been partners, Del had never ceased going on about how things would change when he got an office. "I'm gonna sit on my butt," he'd said, "and everybody else can hustle. If they want me someplace, they can carry me in a sedan chair."

Bohlen put the data on hold as he made the call. An empty chair appeared, and he was waiting patiently when the band of white at the bottom of the screen shifted and he realized that it was a broad, business-shirted back.

He leaned forward. "Hey, Del!"

"Holonamini," a muffled voice said, and a second later Delahanty loomed into sight, his face red. He fixed Bohlen with hooded blue eyes. "What the hell do you want?"

"What was that all about?"

"Tying my goddamn shoe. You mind?"

"You don't have somebody to do that for you?"

Delahanty lowered his head. "You go to hell."

Making a production of it, Bohlen inspected the clock. "Little early for you, isn't it? I mean, you haven't even been in for three weeks, from what I hear. You got a holo of yourself that swears at people when they open the door. I heard you put a hammock out back . . ."

"Okay, smartass," Del said, reaching for the keyboard.

"No, wait." Bohlen held up his hand. Del was good. He could lock up Ross's unit from where he was sitting, no problem at all. "Del, come on. This is serious."

Ignoring him, Delahanty went on keying.

"Del, I swear."

Delahanty grinned up at him and hit the cancel button. "All right, what is it?"

"Got something for you to see."

"Okay." He reached out of screen range for a second. "My code with E appended."

Bohlen shot him the data. "Came in yesterday. It's hot, nobody else is onto it."

Delahanty looked at the screen and moaned. "Ross, you call this hot? This weird shit has been around forever . . ."

"Last entry, Del."

Mumbling to himself, Delahanty read through it. "Montana," he said once, glaring at Bohlen as if he was scheming to make him look bad. Finally his eyes went wide and he raised his head. "Ross, What are you, nuts? They caught a guy!"

"Yeah, a guy. First burnout rolled through town. They ordered him from the perp catalogue . . ."

Del wasn't listening. ". . . and those worthless spikes. Some damfool hackers. No tie-ins on the murders at all." He waved a meaty hand. "It's been checked, man. It's a big ball of nothing."

"Del . . ."

Shaking his head, Delahanty leaned forward until his face filled the screen. "Ross, those spikes were empty. The intrusions went nowhere. Nothing happened at site or anyplace else. No anomalous actions in any program. The killings could be anybody. They nabbed a guy out here last week with three heads in his freezer, and he didn't have a circuit in his skull." He fell back, arms spread wide. "So why waste the taxpayer's money?"

"Could be piggybacking. Doesn't have to be ripping a system—maybe he's caching something."

"Could be. And it could be it's a short in a kindergarten show-and-tell unit."

Bohlen shifted in his seat. "You ever find one? Or these phantom hackers either?"

Delahanty said nothing, but his expression of annoyance eased slightly.

"Last entry is from Montana."

"Yeah? So what?"

"So if it's a local glitch, how did it get there? Take a bus?" Bohlen plopped forward on his elbows. "A bank, Del. It's a credit snatch. I think it'll show up real soon. And Dexter—what's he look like?"

"Like a loser." Rubbing the top of his head, Delahanty inspected the data once more. After a moment he rolled his eyes to Bohlen. "Buffalo god talking to you?"

Bohlen grimaced. The buffalo god was Del's version of situational awareness, a personal deity where Ross was concerned. Every time Bohlen guessed right, the buffalo god was responsible.

"You think this is hardcopy," Delahanty said, settling back.

"It's got the feel."

Delahanty mulled it over. "So what do you want from me?"

"Ricelli was working on those spikes, right?"

"Aw, Ross. That stuff's buried so deep, I don't even know the filename . . ."

"So put Heller on it."

"Heller ain't here," Del said disgustedly. "Cummins assigned him as liaison to some FBI sting operation. I'm holding the fort with two kids doing postgrad work."

"Put them on it."

Del threw a hand up. "All right. I'll find it for you. When I get around to it."

"You look real busy."

"Ross . . ."

"Take you fifteen minutes."

"Will you stop." Delahanty shook his head at the alternate screen. "I don't know. You could be right. But there ain't been a thing since Key West, and you know what happened there. I been thinking maybe Harland's right and we burned 'em all."

"Bull."

"Yeah, well there ain't no army of 'em out there either. You can forget that. And what are you gonna do about it anyway? Cummins has got you chained there . . ."

"Ross!"

It was Lu. Bohlen looked over the top of the monitor. "Yeah?"

"Ironwood. It's onscreen. You'd better take a look."

He told Delahanty, "Call you back." Del put on a stern expression and began to speak, but Bohlen cut him off.

The screen held a Crimewatch bulletin, addendum symbol

flashing. He ran his eyes across the date and heading to the short paragraph below:

> *Butte Citizens' Committee reports that* DEXTER, JAMES *apprehended for public drunkenness/lewd behavior and ejected from city on Sunday 2/12 at or about 0730 . . .*

Last Sunday: the night of the murder, the night the bank was tapped. He ran through the rest quickly. Dexter had been released yesterday to the local Latin War Vets. Natural enough; they looked out for their own. The vets had filed suit against the sheriff's department, Frostmoon, and Nast for false arrest and brutality. Yesterday . . .

He saw that the entry had been made a little after four. It had nearly been five when he talked to Nast.

He slammed the desktop. That son of a bitch had been jerking him. Nast had known then and there that Dexter was clean. The goddamn hick—frustrating to have your suspect evaporate and the vets rage at you, so let's take a piece out of the next fed who calls. Work off a little steam. Never lay eyes on him again anyway.

He started to call Montana but stopped. No—let it go for now; he'd be paying the deputy a visit soon enough.

Bohlen chuckled sourly. He was getting ahead of himself, acting as if he were still on field duty and not a clerk. What he had to do was boot it upstairs so that Eddie could dither over it until Cummins got back. He knew that, but he ticked off the alternatives just for form's sake. The Denver office was out. The supervisor there was a dumb kid Cummins had put in to answer the phones and make sure nobody stole any stationery. For all his guff, Del would wade right in, but Bohlen couldn't have that—not until there was evidence in hand. Old Floyd had done pretty well nailing the Coast slot, and it would be a fool move to throw that away on a wildcat operation like this one. He owed Del a lot; everything, really. If Del hadn't dusted that guy in Loisaida before he got off a second shot, Bohlen wouldn't be around now to argue with him.

Of course, he could buzz Harland in Honolulu, and give him enough time to think how to fumble it as badly as he had Key West.

If such a thing was possible. Key West—an "unfortunate incident," according to Mushmouth himself. What it had been was a massacre. Six imps blown away while trying to give themselves up, two of them women. How it happened Bohlen didn't know; he'd been in the hospital at the time, growing a new liver, and when he got out, nobody was talking. He'd heard they'd taken sniper fire from the villa, but he didn't think much of that story.

It shouldn't have turned out that way. It couldn't be justified, not as matters stood. If Marcus had been there and thought there was any chance the imps were sincere, he'd have walked right into that building. Alone, sniper or no, as ancient and frail as he was those last months.

Marcus Aurelius Amory. Bohlen once asked him about the name, and the old man had told him that it was in honor of the last great Stoic emperor. That had puzzled Bohlen; he'd always thought that the Roman emperors had partied and had a grand time.

Amory had been in charge of comp security for the old CIA at the tail end of the Cold War. He retired just as the 20th ran out, only to be called back at the outbreak of the Latin War. At first his only contribution had been to concur with the decision to shut down the national datanet and run critical systems in isolation. Amory was left idle afterward, until that idiot Kahn unleashed his pack of demented utopians. From then on he had plenty to do.

They met the night of Bohlen's first op, the raid on the Department of Transportation offices that bagged three imps and turned up the existence of what would later be known as the Stoner Gang.

Bohlen had been assigned to the outfit for only two days and was not happy. Pulled off the line in Nuevo León—due to the compsci minor he'd taken in college, he found out later—and shipped first to Laredo then to Tulsa then on to Washington, he was dumped in a hotel near the Mall, dragged out the next night, handed an M-24, and told to keep an eye on the rear exit of the DoT building while a team went in.

He'd been given no explanation beyond the fact that it was a cybertage matter, which puzzled him: that stuff was supposed to be over and done with. The war had opened with a wholesale effort to cripple the US datanet, which succeeded completely—Medrano would have just been another Hussein or Qaddafi if it hadn't been for that. "Silicon Harbor" was carried out by illegals sent across the border and a few malcontents who worshiped Medrano because he was Montezuma's reincarnation or something. As the Medis attacked, the datanet—a cool hundred billion's worth of fiber optics—had gone down under an avalanche of viroids and trojans, not to mention more novel tricks. The hardbombs, for instance: vans loaded with superconducting coils charged to some unimaginable voltage and parked downtown or across from the local airbase. When the circuit was broken, several square miles were flooded with EM fields of a few million gauss, wiping out all magnetic media in the area.

The night of the raid had been wet, with a cold, steady drizzle, and he was still wearing desert-camo fatigues without even a jacket. He was leaning against a big ornamental planter as the twilight deepened, trying to figure out what to make of it all. One thing he knew: the rumors he'd heard about trained killers with computers in their heads were nonsense. They couldn't fool him with that line.

He'd just about decided that even hunting Medis was better than this, when things broke: sirens blaring, lights flashing several floors up, gunshots and screams. He hunkered nervously against the concrete, handling the rifle carefully—the 24's circuits were known to short out when the weapon got wet. He didn't have long to wait. As chaos reigned overhead, the rear doors opened, and a panicked, howling mob burst out, what seemed like the entire shift doing their damnedest to run as far and fast as they could while making as much noise as possible.

He knew immediately what was happening; after all, Medrano had done the same thing during the invasion. These were decoys, nothing more. Ignoring the uproar, he aimed the rifle at the glass doors. A second later a bearded man emerged, wearing a business suit with an embroidered vest and appearing completely normal except for his clenched teeth and the machine pistol in one hand. Bohlen tracked him, waiting for the mob to thin out. The imp lent a hand by clouting a man in front of him with the pistol, catching sight of Bohlen as he did. He lifted the gun while Bohlen checked to see that no one was in the line of fire, but he raised it over his head before aiming, a stupid move out of Hollywood. The barrel was still dropping as Bohlen pulled the trigger.

The imp staggered but kept on coming. Bohlen fired again, astonished that the man didn't go down, and again, as the pistol began flinging rounds over his head. Bohlen was already saying his goodbyes to the world when he pulled the trigger a final time and the imp—he didn't know the word yet but it would soon fill his days—collapsed twenty feet in front of him.

It took the rest of the team fifteen minutes to get to him—understandably, since the operation had been a botch, ten people killed, including three of their own. He passed the time wiping the rain off his face, shaking his head at the questions from people who drifted back, and staring at the body. Four shots, and the man kept coming. The 24 was a dual-slug weapon; that meant eight rounds, point-blank, and the son of a bitch kept coming . . .

Bohlen remained quiet on the way to the offices, focusing only on the fact that he was going to get out of this as soon as humanly possible. That night, if it could be arranged.

The offices were a shabby basement filled with secondhand hardware. There the team leader—a guy in a trenchcoat with ex-CIA written all over him—pointed in Bohlen's direction as he spoke to a thin old man in glasses, who then came over and asked him to step into his office.

Sitting down, the old man filled an ancient pipe before looking up at Bohlen in that way he had—over the top of his glasses, as if contemplating the most serious thing in the world. Then he smiled and said, "Tell me about it, son."

Bohlen told him everything: the confusion, the terror, the way one woman had slipped coming out the door, the tricky electronics of the 24, the gross image of death on a rainy spring evening. He went on for what seemed an hour, not stopping when Amory poured him a shot of rye, a drink he'd never tasted before. "So, I don't know," he said finally, holding out the glass for a refill and noticing that his hand had ceased shaking.

Amory let him know: this wasn't simply a matter of war-related sabotage, it was something new and strange, something that might make the war seem like a tussle in a local bar. He told Bohlen all that was known about the imps up to that moment, which wasn't enough, but there would never be enough: the learning curve was damned steep where the chipheads were concerned.

". . . it may be that they're right, that this is the biggest step since the wheel. Or it may be the opening wedge of the worst tyranny this tired world has ever seen. Our job is to find out which."

"But who's behind it?" Bohlen was leaning forward, fascinated, the drink forgotten in his hand.

"Chartoff, Sachetti, Stoner, Kahn . . ." Amory frowned at the pipe bowl, as if suddenly aware of a flaw. "Could be any of them, or somebody I've never heard of."

"But if you tracked them down . . ."

"All out west, Ross, and you know what conditions are there." He reached behind him and picked up a book, a thick scholarly volume with nothing but print on the cover. "As for how we grasped the nature of the situation . . ."

Bohlen accepted the book: *Homo Praestamus,* by Nathan Kahn. He'd heard of it: a big campus bestseller about ten years ago. On the back cover a photo showed a cheerful face, bony and prognathic, what hair that remained barely combed. "I thought it would be another twenty years, if at all in my lifetime," Amory was saying. He smiled, quick and sympathetic. "I was mistaken."

He pointed with the pipestem. "Read it and tell me what you

think," he said. "Not tonight; you need your sleep. Take tomorrow off as well. But Thursday be here early."

So Ross Bohlen met Marcus Amory, and he never looked back. Marcus was something new to him, something he hadn't come across before: a truly civilized man. *Decency* was the word that accompanied any thought of Marcus. An odd word for a man who had spent his life in the dirtiest of professions, but the right word all the same. Marcus never lied, either to himself or the men under him, felt every blow they took, and never stopped seeking alternatives, for a way to bring the enemy into the light, as he had brought defectors out of the Marxist empires decades before.

In this, it was Marcus against the world: the government was filled with people capable of learning only one thing at a time, and what they'd learned from the war was that the way to deal with a threat was to smash it flat and keep smashing until nothing remained but a bloody pulp. Marcus explained the reason to Ross once: wars fought by democracies always ended that way. The Reconstruction, the Red Summer, a pol named McCarthy (Gene or Jim something), an episode called Watergate that Marcus himself had been vaguely involved in. War was unnatural, undemocratic, and un-American, so there had to be a scapegoat whenever one came along. It didn't matter who; the more peripheral the better. "Beware the People, Ross," Marcus said. "Most savage of the beasts of the earth for vengeance. Bogeymen are needed, and the implants are available."

Bohlen hadn't given him much help. Nobody had. He recalled the last time he saw Marcus, thin and ill, eyes fixed on the photo of one more bullet-ridden corpse. "Never forget that they're human," he said, "and thus pathetic. Don't demonize them."

That had been a bad operation, damn near a disaster. Two men down, the imp dead, as always. Bohlen was tired, numb, and disgusted. He was sure his face revealed it. He didn't have much to say to Marcus. Looking back, he felt sure that the old man expected that. The thought was one of the few things that made him feel ashamed.

Now Marcus Amory was gone, cut down by a stroke while still in his seventies. The smashers had taken over. COSSF could end up just like the Bugs, or the FBI Latin Bureau, or the House Undemocratic Activities Committee, if things went on the way they were going. And there was nothing that Bohlen could do about it. That goddamn hillbilly . . .

The monitor beeped: Del calling back. He hit the keyboard.

Delahanty peered out at him. "What the hell's going on?"

While he explained, Bohlen sent him the Dexter notification. Delahanty glowered at it, then turned back to him. "I tried to dig up that Ricelli stuff," he said. "It's not there."

"What?"

"Nothing. Not in records, not in his personal file. Even the paper's gone."

Bohlen stared at him in silence. Scowling, Delahanty said, "Now don't you tell me I didn't look—"

"I'm not saying anything of the kind," Bohlen said slowly.

"What are you thinking?"

"Damned if I know."

"So what's the next move?"

Bohlen smiled but said nothing.

"You better watch your step, Ross," Del said, shaking his head. "Cummins is out to stomp you soon as you give him a chance. He's been after you ever since you called him a hillbilly at that meeting . . ."

"He's in Hawaii."

"Ain't far enough," Delahanty grumbled. "Well, I suppose you can get a job with Hector. He needs people. Maybe he'll let you clean ashtrays or something."

"Nice to have a fallback."

"Yeah. Well, good luck. You're gonna need it." Del gave him a smirk. "Montana. You know, Custer got his butt whipped right around there."

"Least I'll be in good company."

Del's image faded, and Bohlen realized that he was sitting

hunched on the edge of his chair, as if preparing to climb into the screen. He sat back, fighting an urge to look over his shoulder.

There was an entire squadron of Zeros back there, and the buffalo god was roaring in his cave. Bohlen hadn't lied to Del; he had no idea what to think. But one thing he knew: there was no question of merely filing it and sending it upstairs. This wasn't simply a solitary chiphead running wild across the cold West. As to what it might be . . .

He glanced at the clock. Just after twelve. If they got a flight in an hour, they could be in Montana by, let's see, take off two hours for Mountain Time . . . three o'clock. Set things up tonight and get cracking first thing tomorrow. Of course, Lu might not want to come along. In that case he'd go in alone. He'd need a full team from Del anyway once he got a line on something.

And Cummins? The devil could have him. He'd be sitting around eating burnt pig with his fingers for the rest of the week as it was. After that, Bohlen would see. There was a reg that covered this kind of situation, modeled after the concept of hot pursuit: an operative was to take any actions deemed necessary without notifying his superiors if he believed that any delay would result in loss of contact with a suspected CEI. Of course, it wasn't meant to apply to somebody sitting at headquarters, but . . .

The worst that could happen was he'd be canned, and that was coming anyway. Better to go out on your feet than with your butt planted behind a desk.

He opened the bottom drawer. Inside was a shoulder holster and a pistol. Lifting them out, he inspected the gun. A Colt Python, thirty years old, the kind they didn't make anymore. An antique in these days of comp bore alignments and laser sights. Del used to tease him about it, but Bohlen told him he considered it humanistic compared to the iron everybody else carried. Besides, there was a lot less that could go wrong with a revolver.

He got up and strapped it on, pausing to feel the scar tissue above his belt. Still a little tender, or was that only his imagination? Funny, you'd think a slug in the gut would have more of an impact, that he'd reflect on his mortality a little before raging back into the field. But he'd changed since that first time in the rain. Not that he'd become fearless, far from it. He knew fear, all right, but was always able to control it, and able, when the danger was done, to put it away where it couldn't get at him. It was something he'd learned, perhaps from Marcus, perhaps from experience: that fear didn't exist in things or events, only inside men. There was nothing out there but the world at large.

He walked to the door. Bracing himself with both arms, he looked out at Lu. She went on with what she was doing for a moment before turning. She frowned when she saw the gun.

"Time to put the warboots on, Louise."

She dropped her hands in her lap. "Ross, what are you talking about?"

"What do you say we head out to Montana?"

He called Madeline while Lu made the arrangements. Maddie said little until he mentioned that Lu was coming along. "You look out for her, Ross," she said fiercely. "I mean it."

"I hope you find whoever did it," she said a moment later. "But I don't know. He's probably gone by now. Who'd hang around after doing a thing like that?"

CHAPTER 4

SLAMMING THE BOOK SHUT, Page went rigid. His gray eyes narrowed as he inspected the room: appliances, cabinets, the telecomp screen.

He tilted his head and listened, his mouth working slightly as his expression flattened out.

He sat a moment, two, then rose abruptly and walked out of the kitchen. Keeping close to the walls, he stepped across the living room. At the front window he squatted down and peered past the curtain. He did this at each window, making his way clockwise back to the kitchen.

He couldn't quite say what he'd heard, or if there had been any sound at all. It had been more a feeling, as of something watching him, a presence at the very edge of perception making careful note of where he was and what he was doing. He'd felt it before, and sometimes there had been a watcher and sometimes not. It was all the same to Page. The one time he ignored his intuition would be the last, of that he was sure.

He thought of Bobby; Bobby playing with him, maybe, a little turn of the tables. But Bobby would have made too much noise, and besides, he knew better than to annoy Page.

His gaze fell on the telecomp. A possibility—it was the easiest thing in the world to rig a comp for surveillance; he'd done it a hundred times himself. But not likely. They wouldn't be so stupid as to think he'd be fooled by that.

He stepped over to it all the same and laid his wrist on the casing. His eyes closed, and he stood quietly for a few seconds. His lips drew back from his teeth; a sound escaped, half moan and half growl. He threw his head back and raised his hand, cradling it as if it hurt.

Nothing in there; no sign of an intrusion or any operational program at all, just DRAMs chuckling away emptily.

He shook his head to clear it of the disorientation that tapping always entailed. The feeling was still there, a slight tug at his mind. Going to the table, he swept up the gloves, pulling them on and clenching his fists. He smiled as the alloy stiffened. He went to the door and slipped outside.

The clouds had parted, and he squinted through the snow-white glare. Backing against the side of the house, he looked about him. His eyes halted at a shed twenty feet away, and a spasm crossed his face before he went on.

It was all clear, straight out to the woodline thirty yards back. The trees were thick, but there was no brush, so he could see a long way in. If they were out there, they were good.

He made his way around the house, pausing at each corner. He found nothing; no cars on the road, no figures in the distance. The only tracks he saw were his own.

Out front he stomped his feet to knock the snow off his boots. He looked the place over. It had its bad points: set on a small hill with only a line of low bushes separating it from the road. In the open and hardly defensible, but everything else was right. It was all vacation homes up here, no town within five miles. The house was off the main routes, and the owner had bought it only a few months back. He'd checked that.

And the area of operations was less than twenty miles away. He lifted his eyes to the low mountain rising to the east. He'd be able to see Ironwood from the peak.

He went back in, pulled off the gloves and laid them carefully on the table.

He was hungry but didn't feel like cooking anything. Opening a cabinet, he sorted through the cans. The Bollingers had stocked the place well, he had to say that. He picked up a can of salmon and pressed the top until it peeled open, then grabbed a fork and wandered through the house, eating out of the can.

The sense of being watched was gone, but he thought about it as he ate. It meant something; everything did, no matter how trivial. All things interconnected, each bound up with everything else, moving, changing, melding together over nothingness, the abyss that lay under all. He knew that, had always known it.

The problem was to see how it fit, what place it occupied in the pattern developing around the events he'd set in motion. He was being told something; he had to work out what.

Walking into the living room, he sat down at the coffee table. He'd cleared that end, pushing the magazines and books to one side. All that remained were a pen, a legal pad, and a neat stack of written-on sheets.

He wrote quickly, holding the can in his other hand. A short list, everything that he knew was coming down today. Bobby pulling in, probably Telford as well, the fact that the local vigs had been out in force this morning. He paused, then wrote "strike force ops" and put a question mark after it.

He thought of making a note of the guy who had waved to him yesterday when he shoveled the driveway, but you had to draw the line somewhere. Occasionally he tried to work in everything, the news, what the weather was like, the dreams he'd had the night before, but after a certain point it no longer made sense. He didn't have the ability yet to integrate it all.

For a moment he wondered if he should put a question mark after Telford's name also, but decided against it. Telford had said he was coming today, and he always kept the promises he made to his flock. Maybe he should put another tap on the lodge comp, but

. . . No, too risky. Bad enough he'd done it last night. If Telford had checked, he might have pinned it.

He took a mouthful of salmon. A chunk fell off the fork and dribbled down his chin. He pushed it into his mouth without looking down. Finger still on his lips, he froze, then started chuckling. He put the can down, took the pen, and crossed out the question mark following strike force.

That was it, staring right at him, exactly what his subconscious had been trying to say. They'd be showing up today too. Synchronicity, all of them arriving at once.

Only it wasn't coincidence. He'd made it happen that way.

Raising the pen to his mouth, he began gnawing on the tip. He couldn't be sure about the Cossacks, but . . . No, it fit the pattern perfectly. Why would it be lining up like this otherwise? He'd sure as hell left enough of a trail for them. What else did he have to do, send them a fax?

He wondered who they'd assign to this one. Most of the original operatives had either quit or been phased out after that old fuck Amory bit the dust, and he'd heard that one of their hotshots had been messed up in New York a while back. It made no difference. They could send them all, just as long as Cummins showed up.

He'd think about it some more later. Dating the sheet, he tore it off and added it to the stack on the table.

Someday he wouldn't have doubts like this. Once he crossed the threshold, burst the paradigm, and entered into true consciousness. It was coming; he could feel it, late at night, close enough to touch . . .

He got up and went to the kitchen, boots light on the hardwood. The clock on the screen read twelve-thirty. If Bobby left on time, he'd be here in an hour, but he was always late. Page frowned. He wouldn't have much use for Bobby Golden once this was finished. Stealing cars and picking up women, that was all Bobby was good for.

He sat down and grabbed the book he'd been reading. The dust jacket was intact and nearly as clean as when he'd bought it years ago—he hated anyone who mistreated a book. He studied the picture on the cover, a dimly lit profile of a cold-eyed man wearing a mustache. A thick volume, nearly a thousand pages. The title was *Stalin's Diaries*.

Opening it at random, he smiled as his eyes fell on a well-read passage.

. . . stared at me with those pig eyes. His face was ashen. I tapped Yagoda's report once again. "That's right, Nikola. It's all in here."

He said nothing, and I went on. "And not thousands, either. Not tens of thousands, no. Millions. The kulaks will be an extinct breed when we have finished."

He began whining to me that they were not kulaks at all but simple peasants, the salt of the earth and so forth. His voice grew louder as he approached my desk and braced his arms upon it. He ended by pounding his fist, crying, "You must do something!"

I confess that I was somewhat startled. I would never have thought he had it in him. Nonetheless I stared at him wordlessly until he came to himself and backed away.

I allowed my reply to wait until I had lit a cigarette. He spent the time staring at the carpet, his fat face twitching. His head rose as I cleared my throat. "Nikita Sergeevich," I said. "You have been my strong right hand. You have been a credit to the Soviet and to the Party . . ." I went on in that vein while he sweated, awaiting my final words. I paused before speaking them, enjoying the sight of him cringing like a Jew before a Cossack. "Nevertheless," I told him. "If you ever speak to me in those tones again, I will bury you."

He said only, "Yes, comrade," when I asked if he understood. I made him repeat the words before dismissing him. He backed out, nearly colliding with the door in his rush . . .

Lifting his head, Page smiled blankly, his face frozen. He lowered his eyes and leafed on, until he reached a page with only the words THE PURGES 1936–39 and an epigram beneath them. His lips moved as he read: "To make one's plans, to select one's victims, to wreak an implacable vengeance, and then to go to bed. There is nothing like it in the world."

He closed the book slowly, hand on the cover, and considered the others stacked on the table. *Mein Kampf,* the *Table Talk,* Goebbels's and Speer's diaries, the biography of Pol Pot. He had read them all, many times, but Stalin was the best. Not just plans being made, not the words of a pretender, not the interpretation of some idiot academic, but the pure product: the thoughts of a man of immense power while that power was being wielded to the fullest extent.

The diaries had been discovered in the Kremlin back in the nineties and published a short time later. Page had the first North American edition. There was some debate as to whether or not they were forgeries, but he didn't listen to that. They were the real thing; he'd sensed it the first time he read them. There was an aura of truth about them that could not possibly have been faked.

He'd read it through six times and some parts beyond counting. He knew where they were; there was no need to mark them. He knew them by heart.

Lately he had been concentrating on the final section, the pages covering 1948 to 1952. Those entries were strange; a nearly incoherent mix of real incidents, elliptical phrases, and snatches of what might be nightmare, dream, or vision. The book's introduction—by some Kremlinologist at Yale—said that the last section was marked by Stalin's growing paranoia and alcoholism, but Page disagreed. Those pages were where the truth lay. They were the testament, the final legacy, the signpost for those who would follow. Page hadn't worked it out yet, but he was convinced it was there, a truth too terrible to be put into clear language.

He reached again for the book but stopped and drew his hand back. He didn't feel like reading now. He was too keyed up, filled with anticipation for what was coming. Another two days, or three, and he'd face that truth himself.

He got up and paced the room. He wanted to go there now, to drive to Ironwood, track down Cummins, see his expression when he realized who it was that confronted him. To finish it, today.

It would happen soon enough. Let it unfold in its own way. Control, that was the key. Control and patience. That was how he'd made it this far, why he was still here when all the rest were dead meat. Be like Iosif Vissarionovich. Slow; slow and sure. To make one's plans . . .

He picked up the gloves and went out. The sun had vanished, and it had grown chilly. Pulling them on, he walked to the shed and reached into his pocket for the key, an old-fashioned metal type. He unlocked the door and swung it wide.

There they were, Gary and Tess Bollinger, frozen where he'd thrown them. Gary had tried to defend his wife and as a result had been messed up a bit, but Tess was nearly perfect except for the odd angle of her head. She lay atop her husband, eyes wide, mouth open. A trace of her final expression remained.

Her hair, long and auburn, was draped over a fertilizer sack. It appeared stiff, and Page idly wondered whether hair could freeze.

He inclined his head to meet her eyes. "Hi, honey."

A car whined on the road. Drawing himself up, Page listened. The sound dropped in tone as it came nearer, and he heard the crackle of tires on ice. A squeak of hinges, footsteps, then a voice calling, "Page?"

He was closing the door when he realized that he'd twisted the latch nearly double. Grimacing, he forced it straight and slipped the lock on. He was about to snap it shut when he thought better of it. Leave it—Bobby might want to take a look.

Out front, Bobby hollered once more. Page said nothing as he made his way around the house.

CHAPTER 5

TELFORD HAD THE CAB drop him off two blocks from the garage. He walked past twice before opening the door, and was relieved to find the Honda intact. Last summer some kids had broken in and vandalized it, forcing him to rent a set of wheels while it was fixed. That was something he hated to do; it left a trail in the circuits much too close to home.

He cleared away the snow and pulled out. As he drove through Billings, he was surprised at all the construction—a lot more than last time he'd been through. It had to be DP money. People were settling in, even though they were supposed to move back to the LA strip once the war damage was cleared.

A shadow fell across the road. Overhead a construction blimp passed with what seemed an entire story of an office building dangling from its belly.

The car beeped. He saw that he was drifting out of lane and turned his eyes back to the road. He'd rather not be pulled over or shut down by radar if he could possibly avoid it. Oh, his paperwork would hold up, he had no doubt about that. He'd run it himself, using one of the six identities he had cached in the government comps. The oblique programs made that possible: loaded in the beginning, still running hot and heavy, as they would be until every single unit in the country was shut down and cleared simultaneously, which would never happen.

Strange how that part of Nathan's dream was still alive—or maybe not so strange. If the crusade had involved only software and machines, he wouldn't have failed. Flesh and blood were what had let Nathan down.

Nathan Kahn had been called a lot of things—polymath, prophet, the reigning genius of the post-hardware era, and also renegade, maniac, and traitor. In Telford's opinion he'd been a little of all of them, but above all, the most important fact, he'd been one of the finest human beings he had ever met.

Nathan had been a man of the 20th, with all that that implied. In school during the sixties he'd been involved with the drug culture of the time: Leary, the other guy with the dolphins, and the one who became some kind of monk. His guiding principle had taken form then: a belief in transcendence, in an unimaginable freedom utterly divorced from the everyday human condition.

Telford smiled, recalling the yoga exercises that had been part of the training at the estate. That had been weird, so old-fashioned, as if they'd been required to wear spats and carry walking sticks.

Nathan brought his convictions with him when he took up compsci in the hardware era of the eighties and nineties. He'd been the spokesman for those opposed to Gilder's thesis that computers were the ultimate justification of capitalism, and by the end of the century he was acknowledged the greatest philosopher of cybernetics since Turing and Wiener.

Machines and software hadn't meant that much to Nathan. They were tools only, secondary to the overriding goal. His theory was that the purpose of computers wasn't to stabilize the economy or solve scientific problems or play virtual reality games. All that was trivia compared to their true role as the key to the next stage in human evolution. He looked forward to the mind/machine interface that would meld the microcosm with the world of men, preserving what was essential in human nature while purging all that was gross, bestial, and degraded. It would make all things possible: it would tear off the veil of maya, seal shut the gates of hell, and then raise the New Jerusalem on earth's green and pleasant land.

The concept was far from new; the ideas had been floating around for decades. But it was Nathan who synthesized them, perfected them, and, in the end, made them seem inevitable.

But because he had no interest in hardware, he almost missed his shot at turning theory into fact. Nathan couldn't be blamed much, as the opportunity came from an unlikely source: a third-rate think-tank vaguely attached to the University of Arizona. It was essentially used as a dump for the wilder adherents of Mauve Era physics. Jack Kogan ran the place, and he was a perfect example of what went on at the Bin, as the rest of the scientific world called it. A product of the Tao/Shiva/Buddha school of quantum physics, Kogan called himself a postrationalist, and that about summed it up. He believed in everything that crawled through the window: holistic healing, biofeedback, acupuncture (he'd patented an electronic version that the FDA made him take off the market), Velikovsky, the Dean Drive. His major obsession was ESP, which, he was firmly convinced, could be explained by quantum theory.

Kogan had spent years on his projects, years in the wilderness, his papers returned without comment, no attention paid to him outside of the supermarket press. He got his funding from Midwestern pork kings, Oriental mystical sects, New Age networks. To those people he was a prince, a real scientist who took them seriously, even if none of his ideas ever panned out.

Except one: charge clusters, what he called ECs. No one knew how he'd hit on the idea; he wasn't speaking to his colleagues at the time. The financing came from some sausage baron, who had heard of Kogan from a channeler he knew. There weren't any papers published until well after the devices hit the market. After that Jack Kogan—*Doctor* Kogan—didn't have to wonder about funding ever again.

It was called a stopped-clock discovery, Kogan hitting the right hour for the first time in his personal twenty-four-hour sweep.

Charge clusters, like the Dean Drive and ESP, weren't supposed to exist. Electrons compressed to a point where they became a solid, hundreds of billions of them packed into a sphere a few Angstroms across. It couldn't happen that way, not with particles of the same charge. But Kogan, working with the other outcasts in crank heaven, had figured out a way to do it: the Casimir effect, the electrons themselves shielding each other from the virtual energy that should push them apart, condensing into packets of pure charge. As it turned out, he'd been wrong about that—but the real explanation was far too complex for Telford to grasp.

It had worked all the same, and the result was pure-charge devices, microcomponents operating more efficiently and powerfully than old-style chips by an order of magnitude. They swept the industry, making the pork king a component emperor and Jack Kogan a figure to be reckoned with for the first time in his life.

Nathan knew Kogan well—they'd worked together as grad students. When the first components came off the line, Kogan called Nathan, thinking he'd be interested. He wasn't. Another kind of chip, a little better than what was already around, was nothing to get excited about.

Nathan didn't change his mind until a year later, when he heard from Allison Keyes, an ex-student who was involved in a project at Wright-Patterson investigating ways of controlling the next generation of tactical fighters, planes that maneuvered at speeds too fast for a pilot to handle. One approach had been to connect a Kogan EC microcomp to the frontal lobes, with bioplastic circuits developed for prostheses.

That idea was abandoned early, when it turned out that the implants could be blown by standard countermeasures, with unhealthy consequences for the pilot. Instead they went with a system using muscle cues read through flight suits. But Allison had been pulling a Von Braun: using the military, which she despised, to develop a technology which otherwise wouldn't have seen a dime. When the project shut down, she headed west with a supply of surplus microcomps and the software to run them.

Telford often wondered how it had been when Nathan first saw those chips of doped silicon, small enough to balance on a finger. Had he envisioned his new world rising out of them; had he smiled or been solemn; had he felt a surge of triumph at the great lever being placed in his hands? Telford would have liked to have seen it.

From that point Nathan moved quickly. He resigned his university position, liquidated everything he owned, and essentially vanished. Within a few weeks he found and bought the estate, a villa at Big Sur that had been owned by a singer on the skids after too much booze and dope. Nathan remodeled, purchased med equipment, training gear, a 6th-gen ultracomp, and Japanese surgical robots for the implants. There was other money: Nathan's version of the pork king, a multimillionaire who had read one of his books and been converted. Telford didn't know his name. It had never been mentioned, and in any case he was killed by Stoner.

Then Nathan brought in his people: students, mostly, a few fellow scientists, individuals he believed he could trust. Zip Dubois, the kid who specialized in oblique programs. Elizabeth Stoner, a socioecologist from Nathan's university. Ronnie Infield, his research assistant. Sarah Nieman, grad student.

The crusade kicked off. Nathan was the first, his own white mouse. The operation went well, and he was up and around in three days. It took him a month to master the technique, and while he was doing that, Zip traveled the country loading programs into whatever hardware he could get at—government, private, corporate. The software he'd written was oblique, using the structure of the host programs themselves and nearly impossible to detect. They could be accessed only through the codes carried in the implants—codes that changed over time as the programs did, adapting to the software they encountered.

Kogan wasn't involved. He'd moved his entire operation north to B.C. as an independent institute. Nathan's project didn't impress him much—he had his own, an attempt to prove that charge clusters could exhibit quantum effects on a macrocosmic scale, explaining telepathy, holism, and so on. Nathan liked the idea and had plans to look into it—to use the implants to explore the quantum state, as he put it. He thought that "macro interaction," in Kogan's words, would prove to be part of the paradigm breakthrough, a method of opening up the reducing valve.

The war began, Medrano's Indio master race pushing a hundred miles into US territory the first day, three times that within a week, slaughtering and burning as they went. Nathan ignored the whole affair. It was unimportant, a small glitch compared to the task he had undertaken: to implant and train individuals and send them out across the country, placed in positions where they could manipulate events in favor of Nathan's plan: government departments, beltway foundations, a few major corporations. First dozens, then hundreds, eventually thousands. A geometric progression, like algae in a pond: the first units would reproduce and spread, gaining the resources to implant and train others. In a short time the country would be saturated, and then would come the world.

The situation had begun to deteriorate by the time Telford arrived. The fiberoptic net, the key to Nathan's plans, had been shut down by Medi sabotage. Stoner had vanished, taking her personal clique with her. Some of the imps—that was what they now called themselves—had dropped out of contact, and rumor had it they were dead. There was word of another group, using the same techniques, along with interesting variations such as assassination and terror. A few of the early subjects were having problems—the first symptoms of what turned out to be PS. The new dawn was revealing a pretty bleak landscape.

But it didn't seem that way to Jason Telford. To him it was a thing akin to paradise, exactly what he'd been looking for: a cause he could lose himself in without a thought, everything a smartass kid could want—rebellion, disreputableness, and conspiracy, all wrapped in the bright sheen of high motives and ideals.

It was probably his background that explained the attraction. Jason's mother—he'd never known his father—had been a doper during the last part of the late 20th drug plague, the days of the synthetics. Laura had kicked the habit by joining Domus Dei, one of the RC splinter groups, when Jason was about seven. That had saved her, but it had been a bitter thing for her son. The endless religious classes, the fasting, the beatings whenever he committed some sin against the harsh regimen they'd somehow extracted from the Gospels. He fled as soon as he could—a government scholarship to a voucher school when he was sixteen. The founder of the Domers, a rogue priest named Weber, excommunicated him, which would have meant absolutely nothing but for the fact that it cut him off from his mother. They kept in touch anyway, Laura calling him on supply trips to the upstate New York town nearest the Domer colony, but then one week she didn't call, and the week after that, and the week after that.

He had to find out from the government that she was dead.

A stroke. Two, actually, one after the other, a legacy of the drugs she'd taken years before. There had been a week between the two attacks, enough time for him to get back, to be there with her, to help her let go. But nobody dared tell him.

He called Weber, knowing he'd get no decent answer. "You chose the path of the world," the old fanatic told him. "You are no longer under God's roof, and the blessed owe you nothing."

Jason cursed him uselessly, and the priest—if he could still be called that, as Rome had ousted him years before—listened until he was finished, then said, "You'll pay for that at Judgment, boy."

Jason quit school and took to the road, headed west. In California he heard vague stories about the estate—nothing concrete, just that Nathan Kahn was up to something at Big Sur. He'd read two of Nathan's books, *Homo Praestamus* and *The Transcendent Mind*, standard campus reading in much the same way that Camus, Rand, or Foucault had been in earlier decades. He had to admit that they'd made no real impression on him at the time.

But in person it was different. By then Nathan Kahn was becoming Biblical, had grown a beard and was speaking more in parables than with the rigorous logic he'd used before. Looking back, Telford saw that this was the earliest sign of Pelton's working on the old man, but at the time he'd been moved in a way unique to his experience: it was as if the estate were a saner, more worthy version of the Domers' obsessions, and Nathan himself a true prophet.

They hit it off well, and Telford became the only one to go through the program without being cleared by someone Nathan knew. He had no idea what it was that attracted Nathan to him. He asked him once. "Enthusiasm," Nathan said. "That and loyalty. I value loyalty above all things."

That pleased Telford so much, he didn't ask how Nathan saw loyalty in the punk kid he was. But it didn't matter—Nathan possessed insight, an insight as deep as anyone ever achieved. Not deep enough, of course.

There were times now when Telford nearly hated Nathan, as he made his way through the wreckage of all that the old man had conceived. But the hatred didn't last long, and it only came when he was exhausted, or dealing with a particularly sad case, like Briggs. Nathan had been a good man attempting a great thing, and the worst that could be said about him was that he had failed.

He recalled the last time they truly spoke, just before the raid. Nathan had been falling apart for months, ever since that blond girl—Telford could never remember her name—shot herself. He spent his days wandering the estate, talking mildly about his plans as if nothing had gone wrong, as if the whole scheme were progressing exactly the way he'd foreseen. His main topic the last few days was the breakthrough, what he called the ascendant threshold. He'd picked that up from Kogan's papers—they were printing his stuff now. Kogan claimed that his charge clusters could act as a bridge between the microcosm and the great world, and Nathan liked that idea. Contact between the realm of quanta and the human mind; the total identification of Man and the universe. He said he felt it coming, that it would occur any time now, and that things would be fine.

Telford never knew how much Nathan understood of what had happened over the previous months: the terror campaign by

Stoner's people, the rape of Desert Oaks by the Cybernistas, the actions of a government alerted to a threat and hardened by war. But perhaps he'd grasped it all, and the talk of a breakthrough was simply self-delusion, the last scrap of comfort for a dying man. But he understood at the end, came back to himself long enough to see clearly and confront, as if this were necessary, the depth of his failure.

At dawn that day, Telford went in to help him get up, as he'd been doing all that summer. He found Nathan sitting at the edge of the bed, one arm in his bathrobe, gazing out at the ocean just visible over the pines that ringed the estate: a Moses awakened to the fact that his promised land was in truth Sheol. Telford knew immediately what the next moments would bring, and forced himself to walk into the room.

The old man remained unaware of him until he reached the bed. He turned, a glint of fear in his eyes that vanished when he saw who it was. He gave Telford a look of despair beyond anything a man should have to endure, and then spoke: "You'll take care of them, won't you, son? All the ones I did this thing to?"

Telford nodded, not trusting himself to speak, looking away as Nathan began weeping, pressing his face into Telford's hands and begging forgiveness from them all.

After a while Telford got him dressed and led him downstairs. By the time Nathan reached the dining room, he was a cheerful old man again, telling jokes and asking after people who had fled or been buried weeks before.

Two days later the raid came. Just before sunrise, helicopters and lifters fell out of the sky, loaded with men trained for death.

They barely escaped—Telford, Nathan, Sarah, a handful of others, leaving behind six dead. The truck Telford had hidden took them over an old logging road invisible from the air to the highway, then north to Oregon. Nathan died that night, and they buried him, father of the aborted new age, in an unmarked grave in the piney woods.

No, he couldn't hate Nathan.

He often wondered whether Nathan might not be proven right someday, as Kogan had. Not about the new consciousness—that was simply mysticism—but the rest of it, the hard-edged ideas on how to run a cybernetic society. If they could beat Pelton's, it just might come to pass, and Nathan would be vindicated.

But that was far down the line. Decades, if not longer. Telford wouldn't live to see it.

The exit for Ironwood was just ahead. Easing off on the throttle, he drove up the ramp. He gazed across the landscape, dead white except for the dark green of the trees on the mountains. Another twenty minutes, if the roads were good.

About a mile on, he saw a roadblock ahead. Slowing down, he felt a chill. It was manned by vigs. Worse than cops, that bunch. They never played by the rules.

A feeling of relief washed over him when he saw that the block was set up past the turnoff to high country. Keeping his speed constant, he made the turn and drove uphill. The vigilantes watched silently as he went out of sight.

Naomi was waiting when he reached the lodge. He had trouble getting up the driveway; it hadn't been plowed since the last snowfall, and he kept skidding before he found the right gear program.

As he pulled up, a curtain fluttered. He looked around the small clearing ringed by ancient pines. The only vehicles in sight were the station trucks, a pickup and an offroader, both with Ecology Department seals painted on the sides.

The door of the lodge opened as he got out, and Naomi came onto the porch. She smiled, but the smile vanished when he reached the steps.

"Hiya, love," he said, taking her arm and walking her into the house. She dropped her head and said nothing.

Naomi Buckner was the last of the breed, the final implant made at the estate. There hadn't been time to put her through training, which was all to the good. She'd never tapped, had no desire to, so Pelton's couldn't touch her.

She was a big woman, at nearly six feet, taller than he, but on the skinny side by current standards. Her features were a touch masculine, strong chin and aquiline nose. She'd run the lodge and the station that went with it for nearly two years with never one complaint. They'd slept together a few times, more for companionship than anything else. Aside from Sarah, she was probably the closest person he had in the world, and he couldn't have gone on without her.

"Everything okay?" he said, shutting the door. She nodded wordlessly.

He glanced around the place. It was a private lodge used for vacations and hunting, and had been taken over by the Feds after the war. They'd turned it into an environmental station for measuring rainfall, temperature variations, pollution levels, and the like. Most of the equipment, aside from the comp that ran everything, was outside, in a pair of metal sheds.

The lodge itself was meant for the staff, and it was by no means a cheap government prefab. Whoever built it had had deep pockets and spent his money well. The building was essentially a log cabin, but bore as much resemblance to old Abe Lincoln's as a Starlifter did to the Wright Brothers' plane. The interior was nicely paneled and insulated. The enormous living room was separated from the kitchen by a low divider. There was a bedroom on the first floor, which Naomi used, and two more upstairs.

Against the wall to his left, on a table by itself, sat the station comp. It was standard government issue, a PC-derived work system that ran the station equipment as well as the lodge functions. Telford had made a few minor hardware mods and loaded the comp up with Zip's defensive software.

He had heard about the stations just after the war and immediately decided to put it to use. It was perfect: a network of outposts in remote areas to collect environmental data, paid for by the government itself, with no supervision, and inspections only once a year. He'd constructed a legend for Naomi in the Fed databanks with as much care as he'd ever done anything. A degree in environmental statistics from the U of Texas at Austin—demolished during the war, along with all records—and certification from organizations that had been softbombed. An average personal history, one that wouldn't stand out in any important way.

So Naomi became Moriah Carter, doctor of environmental science, with a husband named Greg, a war vet who was still getting over engagement anxiety, and a mildly retarded sister whom she'd taken care of since their mother died.

He'd had some notion of doing the same for the other survivors, but gave it up; the station project was just too small, and there was only one Naomi.

He walked to the wood stove at the far end of the room, relishing the blast of heat as he raised his hands to it. They stung from the cold; he needed to pick up a pair of gloves.

"Cora and Gene okay?"

He heard a sigh. "I guess," she said. "Cora's upstairs with her birds. She's upset. Gene . . ." She added a sneer to the name. "I haven't been able to get a word out of him. Did I tell you he's sleeping in the cabin now?"

"No." The cabin was an old shack atop the hill next to the clearing, apparently what the original owner had used before he built this place. "Since when?"

"Since that . . . son of a bitch was here."

"Uh-huh. Any . . . episodes?"

"No, he's been fine except for that."

Telford nodded. Gene had trouble staying away from comps. It was like that with some imps, as if they yearned for the oblivion that interfacing brought. It had been that way for Briggs. He'd told Telford it was a high, an addiction he couldn't kick. Telford didn't understand that; for him tapping had always been an agony.

He turned to face her. "Tell me exactly what happened."

Naomi regarded him quizzically. "Aren't you going to take your coat off?"

He looked down at himself and laughed, then unbuttoned the coat and shucked it off.

Smiling, she dropped her eyes to the rug, kicking the edge with the toe of her shoe. "Are you hungry?"

"No, I ate what they called breakfast on the plane. Could use some coffee, though."

He watched as she went to the kitchen. Damn shame, a woman her age caught in a situation like this: caring for two badly damaged people alone in the great woods. He couldn't blame her if it got to her after a while.

She came back with two cups and a full pot, and sat next to him on the couch. She told him about Page. Just after twelve yesterday, he'd sailed in as she opened the door. He strolled around the place, inspecting it without a word. She said nothing herself; something about him silenced her.

Finally he turned to her and smiled—she closed her eyes as she told Telford this—and said, "Name's Page. You've heard of me."

She asked him what he wanted while he admired the computer, peered into her bedroom, and walked into the kitchen. Ignoring her, he opened the fridge and helped himself to a hunk of cheese, then leaned on the counter with his gaze fixed on her.

She was at the point of panic when Gene came downstairs and caught sight of him.

"His eyes just lit up," Naomi said. "He didn't say a word to me. He just went to . . . Page and shook his hand like he was his long-lost brother or something."

Telford frowned. As far as he knew, they'd never met. But a lot of things he didn't know about had happened between the raid and the setting up of the network.

Naomi went on. The equipment outside wasn't due for servicing, but she did it anyway—at that point nothing could have kept her in the house. She spent three hours at it, replacing parts, calibrating and recalibrating everything, hoping that Page would leave while she was outside. It was growing dark by the time she steeled herself to go back in. They were still talking, and Page stared at

66

her as she went past him to the stairs. On the second floor she found Cora sitting on the bed, arms wrapped around her knees, refusing to speak. Naomi was convinced that Cora had seen Page. She stayed with her, listening, afraid she'd hear footsteps on the stairs. Finally she could stand it no longer and went down to find them in the kitchen, talking over an open wine bottle. "Are you moving in or what?" she said, her voice almost a shriek.

Page set his glass down and came out of the kitchen. His pace was slow, and he stopped only a foot away. Although she was taller than he, it seemed that he was examining her from a great height.

"I was just leaving, ma'am," he said, and walked out without another word.

". . . Gene gave me a dirty look and went upstairs. I called you after I calmed down a little." She stopped speaking for a second. "I finished the rest of the wine myself."

"Don't blame you." He asked her a few more questions; a description of Page, how he'd been dressed. It was he all right, although Telford had never really doubted that.

"He show any signs of dementia—facial expressions, the way he talked, anything like that?"

"No, he was totally calm."

Telford got up and went to the window. He'd always assumed that Page was from one of the groups who went in for tapping in a big way, who virtually made a ritual out of it. That being the case, Page should be wasted by now, but who knew? He might not be interfacing at all, or wasn't as susceptible as most. Pelton's didn't affect everybody at the same rate; it was even possible that some people were immune.

Telford shook his head, thinking of a man like Page having free access to the comps of the world, as shielded as they were.

There was movement outside. He glanced up at the hill beyond the trucks and saw Gene looking back at him. Gene was wearing a lumberjack shirt and jeans, and Telford could see that he hadn't shaved. He was about to raise his hand when Gene's face hardened and he turned away, vanishing into the trees.

Telford stared after him. For a moment, as Gene had swung around, he could have sworn he saw something jutting from under his jacket, something a lot like a gun.

"What is it?" Naomi asked behind him. She was massaging her throat.

"Nothing," he said.

"Jase," Naomi said in a small voice.

He couldn't be sure, but it seemed that her eyes had grown brighter in the dim afternoon light.

She took a deep breath before speaking. "Is it going to happen again? What happened on the Coast? Is he going to bring that here?" Her voice broke, and she closed her eyes. "Because if it is, I can't stay. I couldn't take it, Jason, I just couldn't . . ."

He was going to go to her, to put his arms around her, but was sure somehow that wasn't what she needed. "No," he said. "It won't happen here. I promise you that."

She rubbed her face. "What are you going to do?"

Find out what he wants, what he's here for, whatever the hell it is he thinks he's doing. Telford turned back to the window. It was getting on to dusk, bright snow highlighting the shadows of the trees. Footprints stood out next to his car. Gene made those, he thought. He wondered what he was doing up there, whether he was alone, whether it would be worthwhile to go talk to him.

He watched the shadows lengthen, aware of Naomi's eyes on his back. There was probably only one thing to do, and he wasn't the man to do it. "I'll think of something," he said quietly.

CHAPTER 6

"It's a purple elephant on a field of tuna fish," Bohlen hollered. "It makes no sense and I don't want to hear it."

He and Lu were cruising down the interstate at ninety plus, the car's comp blaring out a federal signal at whatever radar was lurking. He steered smoothly into the broad turns, keeping his eyes slitted against the afternoon sun.

He'd asked her about the Ricelli investigation, on the off chance she knew something. She didn't.

"That's what the report said, Ross. It was an accident. Somebody hit him and kept going, that's all."

"That's not what Hec Salgado thinks."

"I don't know Hec Salgado."

"He quit, Lu. He and Ric were partners, and when the results came in, he had it out with the Hillbilly and resigned. Why'd he do that?"

"I don't know. Ask him."

"I did. He told me the investigation was phony. No evidence of a hit and run. Ricelli's neck was broken."

"Why are you so interested anyway? That happened in California."

Bohlen made a face and said nothing.

"Or is this one of those situational awareness things you always go on about, hm?"

"Never mind."

"I wish I had a psychic talent, Ross."

"It's not a psychic—aw, forget it, Lu."

A dark, ragged line floating above the western horizon decided to become a range of mountains. Bohlen wondered what they were called. The Rockies, the Tetons, the Continental Divide? Whatever, Ironwood lay just this side of them. It wouldn't be long now.

Spotting a truck stop a mile ahead, he pulled into the slow lane. "Coffee," he told Lu as she glanced over at him.

Inside the diner a few truckers sat at the tables. The only customer standing at the counter was an Indian wearing what you'd expect to see on a big-league lawyer: oxfords, a three-piecer, an overcoat. His hair fell in two braids well past his shoulders. As he walked out, Bohlen followed him with his eyes, wondering what on earth the man did. He didn't hear the waitress asking what he wanted until she spoke for the second time.

The waitress was a truly outstanding example of unspoiled frontier womanhood. He ordered two coffees to go and leaned nearer on the counter. But when she turned, he caught sight of a holster belt strapped low on her hip and a revolver butt sticking out of it. He sighed. He had a strong personal policy against flirting with women who carried arms.

Pulling his earlobe, Bohlen turned from the counter. Indian lawyers, armed cowgirls—he was way out west, all right.

He went to the news rack and glanced over it, stopping when he reached the *National Keyhole*. He picked up a copy. Annie Oakley was just setting down the coffee when he returned to the counter.

Back in the car he handed Lu her cup and tossed the paper in her lap. Her lip curled as she unfolded it and read the headline: LOVE-STARVED CHIPHEADS RAPED ME OFTEN.

"Ross, that isn't funny," she said, crumpling the tabloid and making as if to toss it out the window.

"Hold on a second, that's a lead," Bohlen yelled.

She gave him a disgusted look and threw the paper in the back seat.

The mountains were a lot closer by the time Bohlen finished his coffee. Lu had been oohing and aahing over them the last few miles and had just made another remark about how awesome they were. "Okay, they have mountains here," he replied. "What else?"

At that moment they made a sharp turn and were confronted with a few hundred shaggy beasts standing in a snowy field. Lu pointed at them. "That answer your question?"

Bohlen contemplated them. Some kind of buffalo-cow hybrid, or maybe regular cattle tailored for cold weather. "Come on, Lu, let's get on the keyboard."

Laughing, Lu pressed a button on the dash, and a comp slid out, screen lit. There was a beep, and she began tapping the pads. "Montana," she said. "Mostly agricultural. Grain, fuel crops, agri-tech labs . . . and guess what. Cattle."

"No kidding," Bohlen said. "Any industry?"

"A lot of power reactors, oddly enough."

"Tell me about that."

"It says here they lowered the licensing requirements to attract business before the war. With the big population influx they're selling power all over the mountain states now."

"Population."

"Half a million evacuees from the LA area. Doesn't seem like much, but it nearly doubled the state population. They were losing people all through the eighties and nineties."

"How many to Ironwood?"

"Let's see—more than tripled the population over two years. They had three camps outside town. Most of them came in the first winter." She shivered. "That must have been awful."

Bohlen nodded. It must have been. "They all stayed?"

"Most of them. They couldn't go home, with the water system

out. The camps were turned into permanent settlements. Lots of building going on now."

And somebody slipped in during the big march after LA was flattened, Bohlen thought. Utter chaos, millions of refugees, hundreds of thousands dead—their boy might even have picked up an ID from a corpse and be living another man's life. "Let's hear about local law," he said.

"State or Ironwood?"

"Big picture first."

"Okay. Law enforcement statewide is considered strained—hasn't kept pace with population growth. The state police are efficient, though. There's an agreement with the Canadian commonwealths—the state force and the FCMP can operate in both jurisdictions, just like the FBI."

And unlike the COSSF. Saskatchewan and BC had cut a deal with Washington banning all internal security outfits as the price for political association. But that was their business, after all, and the Mounties did a good job on their side of the line.

". . . slack is taken up by local vigilance committees. The statewide organization is called the 501."

"Where'd they get a label like that?"

"Hmmm." Lu scrolled. "It's named after groups back in the nineteenth century. I didn't know they had vigilantes in the frontier days."

"Yeah, they did," Bohlen said. He despised vigs and was glad he wouldn't have to deal with them. "Give me Ironwood."

"All right. Sheriff's department is the main outfit. There's a police department in Redding—that's the evacuation camps—but it's only a couple years old and pretty feeble. Sheriff's got a good-to-excellent Crimewatch rating, though."

"Any vigs in town?"

"They're all over," said Lu.

Not bad, all things considered. He wouldn't have to go dragging his tail between two or three departments, as was usually the case. Just contact the sheriff and work through him. What was his name again? Hough, Leon Hough. Good, solid, backwoods name. Bohlen liked that. A country boy, unsophisticated, easy to handle.

"Anything else?" Lu said.

"No," Bohlen answered after a minute. "Save all that and dump it in my workcase. I'll want to run through it tonight."

As Lu pressed the keys, Bohlen spotted an upcoming sign. "Ironwood exit, two miles," he read. "Almost there."

"Finally," Lu said as the comp slid out of sight.

A short distance off the highway they ran into a roadblock, two cars pulled in front of an overpass. Bohlen eyed it with loathing as he slowed down. "Here's your 501," he muttered to Lu.

The vigs manning it were a scruffy bunch. Two stood in the road, self-importantly waving the car down even as it stopped, while a third, who'd been waiting in a truck, got out. They were wearing badges and red armbands. The first two had on jeans and hunting jackets, while the third wore a snowmobile suit. All three had guns hanging from shoulder straps.

Bohlen rolled down the window when the nearest one came over. He was bearded, with long hair tucked behind a set of large, batlike ears. His shotgun was strapped diagonally across his chest, as if he was trying to look like a Medranista. "License," he said gruffly, holding out a gloved hand.

Thumbing his ID, Bohlen held it up. "Federal security, on official business," he said, looking at the other guy, who had come over to rest his foot on the bumper.

He should have kept his eye on Bat Ears, who reached in and snatched the card. Bohlen looked up to see him squinting suspiciously at it, and was about to object when the vig turned and walked toward the truck.

"Hey," Bohlen yelled. "Where you going with that?"

Ignoring him, the vig kept on walking. The one in front lit a cigarette and smirked at Bohlen through the smoke.

"Son of a bitch," Bohlen said.

"Ross, smooth out," Lu said. "They're trying to get us mad."

"Smooth out nothing," Bohlen snapped. At the truck, Bearded Jackass was in deep consultation with Snowsuit. The card had gone transparent, and he was bending it to see if that would do anything. Jesus, Bohlen thought, if he fucks up the circuitry . . .

"Ross," Lu hissed at him. "They have guns."

"So do we," Bohlen said. "Cover me."

"You get back . . ." the guy in front said as Bohlen got out.

"Later, shithead," Bohlen told him and headed for the truck. Behind him he heard the passenger door open. There was a click, and Lu said, "Hold it!" On her toes, old Louise.

The two vigs by the truck weren't able to make a move before he reached them. The snowmobiler backed off a step and said, "Return to your vehicle."

Paying him no mind, Bohlen went up to Bat Ears and grabbed for the card. "Gimme that."

The vig lifted it out of his reach. "Return to your vehicle," Snowsuit repeated, as if he had been training for this moment for years. Bohlen looked over to tell him to shut the fuck up and saw him slipping the rifle off his shoulder, so he took a wide step and kicked him in the kneecap, hard. With a moan the man went down, and Bohlen grabbed the hood of the suit and slammed him against the truck's side panel. The gun fell to the road, and Snowsuit slid after it, surprise on his face.

Bat Ears was lifting his gun and had it throat level, but Bohlen grabbed the butt and jerked it toward him. The vig spun around as Bohlen gave the shotgun a twist to make the strap a noose then pulled him close.

He looked past the vig's shoulder. Lu was bent over the car roof, pistol in hand. The guy in front was standing, his gun up but aimed nowhere in particular. "Get that barrel down," Bohlen yelled.

Nodding as if he agreed absolutely, the vig lowered the gun. Lu told him to drop it, but he didn't seem to hear. Deciding to let her take care of that, Bohlen shifted his attention to the one at hand.

The vig was stiff, shoulders hunched and eyes wide. Tightening his grip on the strap, Bohlen said, "Where's the card, asshole?"

"I dropped it," the vig whispered.

Searching the snow around his feet, Bohlen spotted it and pulled the vig down to get at it. It flicked on when he pressed it. He shoved it under the vig's nose. "What does that say?"

The vig read off his name and rank in a halting voice.

"Right," Bohlen said. "Now tell your buddy."

"They're federal agents, Pete," the vig called out. Pete, gun butt resting on the snow, nodded again, as if he'd known it all along.

Bohlen turned to see that Snowsuit had gotten up and was bent over, rubbing his knee. He straightened with a sullen look.

Pushing the vig ahead of him, Bohlen stepped forward. "Are you silly bastards registered members of the local safety committee?"

The bearded vig said nothing, but there were grunts from the others. Bohlen looked fiercely about him. "You're lying!" he bellowed. "No legit outfit could be this fucked up!" He shook the bearded vig, who cringed and tried to pull away. "What's this? What's this with the shotgun? You think you're with the FLA or something?"

Ross yanked the strap over the vig's head and booted him away. He lifted the gun and gave it a quick inspection. "A Remington!" he said. "Oooo-eeee! Ten-gauge, too." Raising the barrel, he let off a round. Bat Ears ducked, feet splaying on the snowy pavement. "Awright! Lotta noise—I like that."

"Ross," Lu called out.

Cracking open the magazine, Bohlen popped out a round and threw it at Bat Ears's head. "Give you a hard-on too, does it? You goddamn . . ."

"Lady," Snowsuit bawled. "Is he crazy or—"

Scattering the rest of the shells at his feet, Bohlen swung the shotgun as if to smash it against the side of the van. "No, no," Snowsuit cried. "My insurance ain't . . ."

Ross smiled at him. "Relax," he said, and with a heave tossed the shotgun over the truck and into the snowbank on the other side.

He swung around to see Bat Ears standing as if paralyzed and Pete slipping his rifle behind him lest Bohlen express an interest in examining it. Bohlen was raising a hand to make a come-hither gesture to both of them when Lu called out.

He looked and saw her pointing at the roadblock. A squat man in a gray coat was peering over the parked cars. A few yards down the road his own car sat with the front door open and the motor running. "What's going on here?" the man called out.

The vigs began pointing at Bohlen. "This guy here—Fed security he says—something wrong with him—come round took my shotgun—"

"Quiet," Bohlen said. The vigs shut up, and he approached the man in gray, who first hunkered down behind the cars, then hesitantly came out, slipping something into his pocket.

Hands on hips, Bohlen halted. "Who are you?" he asked.

"I'm Lassiter, deputy director . . ."

"Then you're in charge here?"

"Well yes, I suppose . . ."

"Uh-huh," Bohlen said. He leaned forward and tapped Lassiter on the chest. "Well, deputy director, I'm from Washington, and I'm here to help you. Your posse could use some training." He pointed at the vig in front of the car. "Young Kit Carson there doesn't know enough to plant his ass at the roadblock, while Bat Masterson . . ."

Lassiter blinked in confusion as Bohlen went on. Bohlen continued his lecture until Lassiter turned his head toward Snowsuit. Then he grabbed Lassiter's arm, twisted him half around, and pulled the pistol out of his pocket.

Lassiter lunged for the gun, but Bohlen batted him away. The pistol was a piece of Taiwanese shit with enough electronics for an Earth-to-orbit clipper. He tossed it after the shotgun. "This is all very serious," he said. "Because if you go on letting your firearms do your thinking for you, you're all gonna get hurt."

Lassiter gaped at him a moment, then looked at the vigs.

"Got that straight?" Bohlen asked. "Good. Anything else, just look me up, I'll be around."

With a final glare he went to the car. Lu had already gotten in and was sitting grimly with her arms folded across her chest.

Closing the door, Bohlen looked straight ahead for a few seconds, then turned to the open window. The vigs stared back at him. He leaned out and in a mild voice said, "Will one of you dumbshits kindly remove that roadblock?"

Lu didn't relax until they were a mile down the road. Glancing over at her, Bohlen saw that she was shaking her head. He reached over and patted her hand, laughing when she pulled it away.

Sitting back, Nast went over the report. Nothing special: a DWI that the 501 had corralled on the state highway. An out-of-towner, a biotech salesman who'd had a few too many at lunch with some clients. Nast gave him the works: a sober-up pill, impound on the car, and a day at the hospital for alcoholism tests with a telltale locked to his wrist. The humiliation would teach him even if the fine didn't, and the fine would be a whopper— Judge Pellew didn't much care for drunk drivers.

There was a beep, and a line of print crossed the comp screen. He gave it only half his attention: something about a disturbance at a block south of town. Nast turned back to the typewriter.

The phone rang, the fourth line, the number he'd given Diane. He raised his head to Ralph Frostmoon, who was sitting across the room. "Ralph . . ." he said, his voice sounding shrill even to himself.

Frostmoon looked up and nodded wearily as he reached for the receiver. "Polk County Sheriff's Department . . . Oh hi, Diane . . . No, I haven't seen him. He's out on patrol . . ."

Nast bent over the typewriter, trying to concentrate on the

form, but Frostmoon's voice, tightening as Diane questioned him, made it impossible. He was half inclined to pick up now, but it was too late; no sense making Ralph a liar on top of everything else.

"Okay, Diane," Frostmoon was saying. "I'll let him know." He hung up and rose from the desk. "Call back," he muttered.

"Sorry about that, Ralph."

Frostmoon raised an arm wordlessly as he walked out the door.

Nast gazed after him, embarrassment turning to anger: she had no business putting Ralph through the wringer like that. Nast ought to call her back right now and ask her what the hell she thought she was doing, interrogating another member of the force about her husband, and a guy she barely knew at that.

But he'd better not; it would just cause another blowup, and he was tired of those, tired unto death . . .

He realigned the sheet and started typing again, taking his time, checking every few lines. If he made a single mistake, left anything out, he'd have to begin again from scratch. The hard sheets were chapter and verse, what everything that followed was checked against. After he finished, he'd enter it verbatim, file it in a locked drawer, then compare it with what was in the system every few days until the court date. That was regulation procedure in every department he'd ever heard of, the only way to make sure that nobody was making the bytes do tricks in the electronic files.

A lot of effort for a simple drunk-driving case. Things were easier in the old days.

He slipped the form into the scanner, and looked at it after it was filed. It seemed okay; no errors that he could see. Clearing the screen, he hesitated, then tapped another command.

The screen brightened, and there she was. The dancer, the girl on the hillside.

He leaned back in the seat, taking in the planes of her face, the clear, pale skin, the eyes. It was the eyes that got to him: staring frankly at the camera, calm and serene. MV photos usually looked pretty stupid, but not this one.

She'd been studying dance in Frisco. Ballet—no, modern dance, that's what it was. Hough had explained the difference.

Nast squinted at the image, recalling what he'd seen on the hill: the battered flesh, the bone, the frozen red splatters in the snow.

During the war he was caught in a mortar barrage, an automatic left by the Medis to cover their retreat. He rode it out in a shellhole with a lieutenant who sat a little higher than Nast liked. They were bracketed, shells hitting on either side, and when Nast grabbed his shoulder to get him to pull his head in, the lieutenant collapsed on top of him, turning to show a face torn apart by shrapnel.

It was the same, exactly the same.

They hadn't found a damn thing on the hill, or anywhere else either. The trail led back to the road, and the plows had wiped out all tracks. No oil or transmission fluid on the road, and no blood traces. It took them a day to get a positive ID out of Crimewatch.

He scrolled down, rereading the file. Nothing stood out, nothing called for closer attention. There was little remarkable about the whole business beyond the fact that a young woman had been butchered and tossed into the snow like a dead animal.

What still made no sense to Nast was where the corpse had been found: in plain sight, on a hilltop in the middle of a working ranch right next to a county road. If the perp had wanted to conceal the crime, there were a thousand places to do it within ten miles of where Nast was sitting. A few yards into the woods, in the deep snow under the pines, and a body wouldn't be discovered until spring, if then. The wolves or brown bears would make short work of it if they got there first.

It was as if the body was meant to be found.

The phone rang again, and he picked it up automatically, realizing that it was the fourth line only when he had the receiver in hand. He swallowed as he put it to his ear.

"Nast."

Five full seconds went by before Diane spoke. "You son of a bitch."

He didn't answer, just waited for the rest.

"I checked with the dispatcher," she went on, her voice nearly unrecognizable in its bitterness. "You weren't out at all. You were sitting there the whole time. You told that big fucking Sioux to lie to me. Your own wife."

Wait a second, he thought. Connie wouldn't have told her anything, not over the phone. He started to say just that, but it was too late. He'd been silent too long, and silence was admission of guilt in Diane's book. "Did it go over good? Did you get a good laugh from those animals over there?"

"Goddamit," he shouted. "Haven't I told you not to give me this shit at the station? Can't it wait?"

But she wasn't listening. She was off now, raging at full bore. He held the receiver away, wanting to pitch it across the room. The standard recitation, the usual list of grievances: treating the house like a motel, neglecting her, neglecting the kids. He listened in silence, suppressing the urge to ask what he'd done this time. If he did that, she'd dredge up everything that had happened over the past six months.

As she ran down, he put the phone back to his ear. For the next few seconds they breathed at each other like a couple of kids. God, the childishness of it! How he detested this.

She spoke again, her voice mild, as if the last few minutes had been snipped from memory. "Are you coming home for dinner?"

Closing his eyes, he cursed under his breath. If there was one thing he couldn't take, it was the way she changed her tune in mid-shriek. A tactic, an olive branch, what? It was beyond him. There were times he thought she was flat-out nuts. Mood swings, they called it. He ought to have her committed—at least then he'd get some peace. "I don't know," he said, trying to keep his voice level and making a miserable job of it. "Something's come up."

"I wish you'd tell me before I start cooking."

Before I start cooking. Ten grand worth of hardwired kitchen in that house, and listen to her. It took her about thirty seconds to turn out a seven-course meal. "Look," he said. "I'll get there when I get there."

Dead silence on the line, then: "Fine. I'll let it rot."

"You do that," he said just as she hung up. He clenched the receiver and slammed it down himself. He should give her something worth crying about. Go over to Morley's or the Roadhouse, tie one on, and come home at two or three in the morning, kick the door in, and . . .

He caught himself. No, that was disgraceful. A man didn't do that. Don't even think about it.

His eyes fell on the photo, the dancer from the Coast. Especially not with that in front of you.

Diane didn't know. Oh, she'd heard about the murder, everybody had, but she had no idea that he was investigating it. He'd kept it from her, a small triumph sweetened every time she talked about the lousy job they were doing and why didn't they have trained detectives like in the big towns. When he closed this case, he'd tell her and watch the look on her face then . . .

A dull ache settled in his chest. It would never be closed. He'd never put it together. An image rose in his mind: red blood against dazzling white, stiff limbs, a face that was a face no longer.

Clearing the screen, he picked up the report and headed for Hough's office to get his signature. A few feet from the door he heard an unfamiliar voice, and stopped to listen.

". . . nothing but a pack of fucking incompetents, if you ask me."

"Regardless," the sheriff answered, irritation evident in his voice. "They're an unofficial auxiliary, and I want them treated with respect."

Nast was getting the gist of it. The disturbance at the 501 block; this guy must have been behind it. But what was he doing here talking to Hough?

"Respect, huh? Okay," the voice said. "Next time I run across a roadblock, I'll salute the assholes."

Whoever he was, he'd gotten off on the wrong foot with Hough. The Bear was old school; he didn't like foul language for any reason, said it was unnecessary and uncalled for. The deputies always took bets on how long it'd be before the rookies got chewed out for using what Hough called "oaths."

"See here, mister. You're in a different setting than what you might be used to. The committees perform a serious function in areas such as this."

"Serious function, my ass. They collapsed the minute I barked at 'em. They're spaghetti. You get any real trouble coming down the backroads, Chief, you'd best have a few holes dug on Boot Hill."

"I can see we're getting nowhere with this." Hough's tone was chillier than Nast had ever heard it.

"Right. So . . ." The voice grew cheerful, obviously trying to lighten things up. "I see you play the fiddle."

Nast grinned. The visitor had stuck his foot in it now—Hough had been playing for thirty-five years; he was first violin in the university string quartet and had been a guest player in symphonies from Denver to Vancouver. If there was anything he was prouder of, Nast didn't know about it.

Several seconds passed before Hough answered. "I play the violin," he said.

"Oh," the voice said, barely audible. "Bet you're pretty good."

Behind him Nast could hear someone coming out into the hall. Keeping his face straight, he went to the door.

Hough looked up when he appeared. "Ah, the man I want to see."

As Nast went to the desk, he glanced at the man in the chair. He knew that face—it was the Bug from Washington, the one who gave him a hard time yesterday. Nolan something.

The Fed nodded to him, a cartoon Irish face breaking into a broad smile. "How you doing?"

Nast bobbed his head as he dropped the form on the desk. The guy looked a lot smaller in person than he did onscreen. Nast wondered if he had a trick program to bulk him up. Some of them did that.

"This is Ross Bohlen, from Washington," Hough said slowly. "He heard about the Butler murder and wants to give us a hand." Hough cocked his head. "He thinks an implant gang had something to do with it."

"Chipheads?" Nast said, crossing his arms.

"Yeah, well I didn't have a chance to get into it," Bohlen said, talking fast the way they did out east. "See, we got an intrusion alarm from your town here. It had certain characteristics, kind of like a data fingerprint . . ."

Hough raised his hand. "We know what they are," he said. "Now, Deputy Nast is handling the investigation, so you take it up with him." He gave Nast a get-this-idiot-out-of-my-office look. "Johnny?"

Nast smiled down at the Fed. "I don't think we need to waste the sheriff's time any longer."

Smirking sourly, Bohlen got up. "Right," he said. "Afternoon, Sheriff."

Grunting an answer, Hough picked up the form. As Nast ushered the Fed out, Hough raised his eyes and made a short chopping gesture. Nast nodded back at him.

In the hallway Bohlen opened his mouth, but Nast cut him off. "Chipheads, eh?" he said. "I ran into one of them during the war, down in Mama East. Lot of people say there weren't any with Medrano. What do you think, Bohlen?"

The Fed gave him a smile touched with more than a little scorn. "Who knows?"

"Still keeping it secret," Nast said as he led him to the clerical office. "You serve, Bohlen?"

"415th. Task Force Delgado."

"Guardsman, eh?" As they walked into the room, Mary Ann looked up, and a smile appeared on her round face. "You're the fella from Washington," she said.

"That's me."

"Annie, print me out all the forms for cooperation with outside agencies. Four copies of each, please."

Mary Ann frowned. "I don't think we've ever used those, Johnny. I'll have to track them down."

"Take your time," Nast said. He turned to Bohlen. "Have you got your paperwork?"

"Uhh," Bohlen said. "I'm with COSSF. We don't go in for much paper—"

"You don't?" Nast rubbed his chin. "That's a problem, isn't it?" He paused, Bohlen regarding him blankly. "I mean, that's how we do things in Ironburg."

Sighing, Bohlen reached into his coat pocket, took out an ID, thumbed it, and offered it to Nast, who frowned.

"What's that?"

"A federal security ID. You might not be aware of the regs these days . . ."

"It's no good here."

"Hey, I don't want to go over your head, but—"

"I said it's no good here."

Putting the card back in his pocket, Bohlen turned to Mary Ann. "May as well knock off on those forms, sister. You won't need 'em."

Nast allowed himself a smile. "It's okay, Annie. Some people got no patience."

Bohlen went to the door. There were shouts from the hallway as he opened it. "That's him, Sheriff, the man who roughed up my boys."

Nast followed and saw Lassiter coming down the hall trailed by a vig in a snowmobile suit—Barnert, his name was. Hough was standing in his office doorway with a pipe in his mouth. Lassiter pointed at Bohlen. "This man terrorized a squad not half an hour ago . . ."

"Terrorized them, did he?" Hough said, lighting his pipe.

"Well, he caused a disturbance."

"Why didn't they bring him in?"

Bohlen walked past them. Barnert made a move as if to block him, but evidently thought better of it and stayed where he was.

"Fed security, out of our hands," Hough was saying to Lassiter.

Nast set out after Bohlen and caught up with him at the door. "You plan to raise any more hell, Bohlen, you check with us first."

Bohlen stared at him for a moment, then went out.

Catching the door, Nast followed. "I mean it, mister."

Whirling back at him, Bohlen raised a finger. "You want to interfere with security, pal, feel free. But it'll be the last thing you do for a while." He paused a moment, and winked. "Besides, I'll make sure you get the paperwork."

"You think people are going to talk to a Fed out here, Bohlen?" Nast called as Bohlen walked to his car.

"Watch my dust, cowboy." He opened the car door and grinned. "Happy trails."

Hough stepped out behind Nast, calling, "Just wait in my office" to someone inside, probably Lassiter. He joined him, still fooling with his pipe. "How'd you get rid of him?" he asked as the car roared off.

"Told him we'd cooperate," Nast said, "according to regs."

"Good," Hough said. He blew a puff of smoke into the cold air. "Idiot told me those implant people were running around here."

"We'll probably have more trouble with him," Nast said. "Maybe I should tank him."

"No, let's hold that in reserve." Hough turned back to the station. "Any luck, the vigs'll shoot him for us first."

While Hough went back inside, Nast watched the car pull away, memorizing the plate number. Then he went to his cruiser.

CHAPTER 7

BATHED IN SWEAT, Telford awoke and sat up in darkness. He'd been dreaming: Briggs was hanging in the shower stall, his features obliterated, but the eyes somehow remained and stared beseechingly. Telford started to move toward him when flames burst from the body, heatless but all-consuming. Within seconds Briggs was gone, not even ashes to mark where he'd been.

Rising from the couch, Telford zipped up his pants and threw his shirt on. He shivered. It had gotten damn cold.

In the kitchen he glanced at the clock. Three in the morning; hours yet until dawn. Feeling thirsty, he opened the fridge, took out a half-empty bottle of tonic water, and drank it down.

Poor Briggs. He'd been one of Nathan's experiments, his implant loaded with virtual software on the off chance that virtual reality would turn out to be good for something other than game parlors at the local mall. It hadn't worked. Within a year Briggs was living in his own world, a world of memories, illusions, wish-fulfillment dreams, anything to deliver him from the hell his life had become. The program was probably what had killed him, as it had that blond girl whose name Jason couldn't remember. Just before she shot herself, she said that the software—DEMILLE, it was called—was operating on its own, showing her only the things she most wanted to forget.

There had been many experiments: physics software, mathematics—just in case Riemannian geometry came in handy sometime—a medical program called GALEN for diagnosis and treatment, and Nathan's masterpiece, HUXLEY, the program that was supposed to tie everything together and reveal the universe as it actually was. It had been tried only once, and they had no idea whether it succeeded or not. Cooper had experienced *something* . . . But the raid came only a week later.

And a music program (another failure—perfect pitch but no feeling whatsoever), and one that analyzed situations according to game theory, and a holistic program . . . Telford often wondered why there hadn't been programs for sex, or whistling, or jumping a motorcycle across the Grand Canyon.

There were practical ones too. Analysis and rewrite software, subversion systems, command and control programs. But they could have used others. Nobody had come up with one on guerrilla warfare or terrorism or propaganda . . . Maybe Stoner's gang had looked into that.

He leaned against the counter and shook the bottle, swishing the remaining half-inch of soda. Forget about all that. He had a lot of them stored himself—DEMILLE, HUXLEY, an untested program that set up direct contact between implants—but he hadn't used them and never would. He had other worries, of a type no software could handle. Naomi hadn't said much that evening. She cooked dinner, and they sat down to eat with minimal conversation. Telford didn't push her, not wanting to hear any more about her leaving. That would be the worst thing that could happen now.

Afterward she had put on some CDs and sat down to listen. Classical stuff of a kind that Telford didn't much care for. He leafed through a magazine, trying to think of something neutral to say. Naomi just sat there on the couch, feet drawn beneath her, head resting on one arm while the music played. Bruckner, she'd told him.

After an hour she got up to go to bed. She brought him some blankets and asked if he needed anything else. Then she went to her room, stopping at her door to wish him good night.

He had stared at the door for some time after it closed. Things were not good at the old homestead. The kids usually perked up when he arrived—not a holiday atmosphere, maybe, but a definite rise in spirits, a sense that they were glad he was there. That was gone now.

He downed the last of the soda. The Page situation would have to be corrected as soon as possible. The lodge was Telford's turf, his refuge, the only place where he was able to wind down. If that was destroyed, he'd be left with nowhere to hide, out in the open with the cripples and the hunters. Thou hast set me a table in the presence of mine enemies . . .

He grimaced to himself. Stop it, Telford.

A roll of printout paper lay twisted next to the microwave. He picked it up as he went past. The lodge system was programmed to record every routine it ran. Telford checked this log whenever he passed through, on the belt-and-suspenders principle. At the moment he was thinking about Gene, concerned that he'd started tapping again. No sign of that, but there were a couple of items that gave him pause. One in particular from the other day, which could well have been an outside intrusion. There were few details—no software type, no source, a query beside the code. Only time and duration were definite, itself a bad sign. True, there were always oddities, particularly on a government system. But all the same . . .

He nearly reached the couch before he realized that he was not alone. He stepped back, gaping at the figure across the room. A small, slender woman in a white nightgown sat on the stairs a few steps up from the floor, hunched over slightly as if to avoid being seen.

Telford smiled at her. "Hello, Cora."

At first there was no response, but finally her hand, pale in the reflected snowlight, lifted from her lap and fluttered.

Telford sat down. "Why don't you come over here?"

Her head inclined as if she was considering it, then she got up and walked awkwardly over, sitting on the table across from him. This close, he could see her clearly: the wide-set eyes, the strong nose, the black hair tied in back. There was nothing written on that face; the eyes gazing back at him were the eyes of a child.

"You scared the hell out of me," Telford said. "I didn't hear you come down."

She smiled.

"So how have you been?"

The smile faded. She shrugged.

"Been working on your birds?"

She nodded. Cora was at least ten years older than he. Back in the early days, he'd considered her a knockout, utterly unattainable, far beyond his reach. She'd been a mathematician, a good friend of Nathan's who had worked with him on many of his projects.

She was still beautiful, but in a very different way. It was the beauty of a thing that has been badly damaged but still calls forth echoes of what once was. He had no idea what horror had been summoned by the shifting dance of chemicals in her brain to thrust her into childhood, the only safe place she knew. And he had no interest in finding out. To delve into that, he knew instinctively, would be an act as immoral as any ever committed.

She was happy now, cared for and secure, the horror that had struck her down forgotten. She had her work: the birds that she stuffed and mounted up in her room—birds she found dead on her walks in the woods.

Any bird was suitable; the plumage was unimportant, or the fact that she'd mounted the same species before. Her room resembled an avian museum, an Audubon's studio.

"Well, tell me about it," he said.

She hesitated before speaking. "There aren't many in winter," she said, her voice soft. "They've mostly gone away."

"But there was one," she went on. "A little brown one. I found him in the snow." She frowned. "Last week."

"Is it one you've done before?"

She shook her head. "I don't know what it's called. I'll have to look it up." She raised her eyes to his. "He was frozen, Jason."

"That's a sad thing, Cora."

Her frown deepened, and Telford noticed that her fingers were picking at the fabric of her robe.

He reached for her hand. "What's wrong?"

Her voice, when she answered, was higher than usual. "Are you going to leave us?"

He squeezed her hand. "No, Cora, never. Haven't I always come back to you?"

She grasped his hand in both of hers.

"Who told you I'd do that?"

She shook her head forcefully, but it didn't matter; he knew. It had to be Gene, the little bastard. He'd straighten him out tomorrow. Whatever it was that Gene had on his mind, he had no right to involve Cora.

Telford spoke soothingly, trying to ease her doubts. But she still seemed worried. "Is there anything else?" he asked.

She bit her lip. "Are you . . ." she began, then swallowed and started over. "Are you going to let Page live here?"

Bingo, he thought. He shook his head. "No, that's not going to happen."

"You can't," she said. "He can't live here with us. He can't. He's bad . . ."

He gripped her shoulders. "Cora, listen: Page is not moving in. I'll run him off as soon as I get a chance. That's why I'm here."

She nodded. When she spoke next, he could barely hear her. "Jason."

"Yes?"

"Did Page kill Ronnie?"

That's right, Telford thought. She'd been there when Page shot Ronnie Blaine, had seen Ronnie sprawled in a pool of blood and Page standing over him like death incarnate. No wonder she was so scared.

Cora went on, voice throaty, face twisted. "I've been trying to remember. He did something to Ronnie, I know he did, but I can't remember . . ."

"No," Telford said. "He didn't kill Ronnie." He began to stroke her hair. But for all practical purposes Page had killed him. Not with the pistol, perhaps, but Ronnie had already been far gone into Pelton's, and Page had kicked him over the edge. Ronnie walked into the ocean the next morning, at dawn, leaving a trail of blood from the reopened wound across the white Pacific sand.

"But he hurt him," Cora insisted.

"Listen," Telford said. "Page is not going to hurt anybody. I'll see to that. You think I can't handle Page?"

She stared back at him, eyes wide. "You should kill him."

He laughed. "Cora, come on. Don't worry about Page," he told her. "I'll do the worrying for all of us."

She took his hand and pressed it to her face.

"Okay then," he said. "Let's see a smile."

Her lips turned up, a little solemnly, but the intent was there. Telford felt absurdly pleased that he could do at least that much.

"Jason," she said quietly. He lifted his eyebrows. "Will you hold me?"

"Of course," he told her. She got up clumsily and moved to the couch. Dropping his arm around her, he pulled her close. She snuggled against him and laid her head on his chest.

He settled back on the couch. Suddenly he recalled something. Cora had one bad habit: whenever things grew tense at the station, she tended to wander off, taking some of her birds with her. The sheriff's office had brought her back twice, which hadn't done a lot for Telford's peace of mind. When asked why she left, her only answer was that she was "looking for something."

"Cora," he said. He heard her murmur against his chest. "I

want you to make me a promise. If you feel like going out to look for something, let me know first. We'll both look."

Cora shifted against him. "I promise," she said.

He rubbed her back, feeling the warm bulk of her. She'd been such a gorgeous woman; it was a pity. But it could be worse. She could be like Sarah, fighting the long, hopeless battle, watching the lights go out one by one.

He felt a twinge—he hadn't called Sarah. He'd have to do that first thing tomorrow.

Cora was breathing evenly. He glanced down at her and reached for the blanket carefully, so he wouldn't wake her. Pulling it over both of them, he lowered his head and shut his eyes. He smiled as he dozed off. At least someone was glad he was around.

The window was broken, shards of glass scattered across the inside ledge, a stark mosaic that caught the lights of Essex. The curtains flared slightly, touched by the cold wind. The apartment was freezing.

In the bedroom a woman cursed, her voice broken with sobs. She repeated a name. The name was Jason Telford.

On the living room floor lay pieces of notepaper, glowing whitely in the light cast by the city beyond the window. As the voice broke down completely, a gust of wind caught the torn pieces and whirled them around the room.

CHAPTER 8

AFTER HE MADE the last entry, Bohlen leaned back and stretched, working the kinks out before hitting display.

"Gotcha," he said. The screen showed him a wild patchwork of purple, green, and yellow overlaid with blue lines and red dots. A map of Ironwood, the lines representing streets and the multicolored squares government, commercial, and residential buildings. The dots marked the location of every registered comp in the area. There were a lot of them. He pressed for the total: 8,142.

Of course, there were always a few slobs who hadn't bothered to register, simply plugging in and relying on some cheap hedgehog program to keep from getting caught. If he ran across any, he'd turn them over to Treasury. Otherwise it didn't matter; he knew he had at least nine-tenths of what was out there.

He'd been at it the past three hours, beginning with the standard government map and adding whatever had been registered in the eight months since it had been compiled. Ordinarily that would have been Lu's job, but she was beat and he had told her to hit the sack. There were a few things he needed to take his mind off anyway.

Sliding the cursor to a random dot, he pressed for a readout, and up it came: Max's Jewelry, 22 Halsey Street, late-model PC, inventory and accounting. Pursing his lips, he moved to the wide blue stream that was Main Street. Let's see if he could hit it on the first shot . . .

He raised his fist triumphantly when he read what came up: Ironwood First State Bank, with a blinking X appended to show a recent intrusion. At least he was doing something right.

He'd called the bank after the debacle at the cophouse, getting the president on his way out. The banker, eager to show how co-operative he could be, gave him the number of the VP in charge of comps, a guy named Luck, of all things. When Bohlen asked Luck about the bank's CM program, Luck read him the brochure: "An aggressive, hard-edged, task-oriented counterintrusion program designed specifically for use in the contemporary software environment."

Bohlen thanked him and hung up. Aggressive. Hard-edged. The thing hadn't even twitched during the intrusion. A real pit-bull, that one.

Kicking the chair back, he got up and flexed the leg that had gone to sleep on him. He looked around the room. Lu had done good; it was the largest suite available, a business setup on the second floor of a motel on the west side. A big central meeting room with two bedrooms, strategically located but not in the middle of things where they would draw attention. As a nice bonus— or so Lu thought at the time—it was right down the road from the sheriff's station.

Bohlen hopped to the window. Outside, the road was empty except for one set of headlights. He grunted to himself when he saw it was a police car, and sneered when the car turned and the taillights faded toward town. Probably that prick Nast keeping an eye on him.

He stopped shaking his leg and left the window. He was starving, and there sure as hell wasn't any place open this time of night. Lu had gone out for burgers earlier, and he had wolfed down two of them, but now he felt as if he hadn't eaten for a week.

The ruins were still on the table. He pawed through the wrappers and was pleased to find a few fries slowly achieving oneness with a puddle of ketchup. He ate them without enthusiasm. Hell of a life: cold fries, and the cops hate you.

Damn shame about the sheriff. Bohlen had come on too strong, no question. Hough and Nast were obviously tight-asses, and then there was that business with the vigs. How was he to know that they took the committees seriously this late in the game? The war was long over. Out east, vigs were a joke: drinking clubs along the lines of the local bowling league.

Nast, now, had a showdown coming. Not that Bohlen could blame the man. It was a hard thing to take on a case, do all the legwork, get your hands dirty, and then have some yohab from dreamland-on-the-Potomac turn up and put it in his pocket. And Nast had a point about the way people felt about Feds. There was a lot of contempt for the government here in the west thanks to the war, and with good reason. Three million good reasons, in fact—the number of non-Indios killed by the Master Race after Medrano struck. Not that the Frontero Liberación Aztlan ever reached Montana; not even the cruise missiles loaded with sarin and tabun gas had gotten this far north. But that made no difference. People all over the west had lost relatives and friends, and had no particular desire to talk to an agent of the government that had let that happen.

Which didn't make Nast any less of an idiot. His story about the imp down in Mexico, for instance; that told Bohlen plenty. Some poor clown of an FLA tanker with a primitive threat alarm system wired to his scalp, and Nast thinks he's an imp. Right: if it's got wires attached, it's a comphugger. Kill it.

The fries made him thirsty, so he went out in the hall to get a soda from the machine, which chortled "Thank you" as he walked away. Nice backwoodsy touch, that. There hadn't been talking soda machines out east since before the war. They irritated people.

Back in the suite he collapsed on the sofa and went over what had to be done. First check out anyone with a comp offense on his record, then convicted felons—imps often had underworld contacts—and on to the wackballs, the loons, the local eccentrics. A lot of work; he'd be all morning just getting the names together, and he didn't imagine that the sheriff would be too keen on dumping him the department files. Well, he could always send a request through Washington.

Of course, there was a good chance that their boy—Bohlen was sure he was male, the crime said male—had only been passing through, using the town as piggybank and open-air morgue before continuing down the highway. But Bohlen didn't think so. No objective evidence, just that Ironwood was the kind of town he'd pick if he wanted to go to ground. Remote, quiet, a lot of newcomers, a perfect place to dig in and hide like a mouse while the cats were out hunting.

There were a few odd features, but that was always the case. The bank intrusion, for one. Pulled off with no finesse at all, as if to put up a sign saying COME GIT ME. But more than likely the imp was suffering from PS and incapable of any kind of reasoning.

He took a sip of the soda. Pelton's Syndrome. Named for Dr. Aynsley Pelton, neurologist at Walter Reed. A progressive and chronic brain dysfunction triggered by massive data influx as found in human/computer interfaces, causing subtle but far-reaching changes in cerebral hormones and neurotransmitters. First symptom, an increase in speed of neural firing, giving the subject a feeling of immense confidence, heightened awareness, and personal well-being. Followed by progressive memory loss, flattening of affect, hallucination, and psychosis. Terminal psychoses were variable and ran the gamut of psychiatric classification.

That summarized what was known about PS. Pelton had dropped his research, saying that there weren't enough subjects and that he was seeing them only in the final stages; if he could examine someone at an earlier point, he might learn more. Nobody else was studying it.

What it came down to was simply that the human brain

couldn't deal with the amount of data coming through an interface, even when the flow was stepped down by interposed circuitry. The mind eroded under it like limestone under a sandblaster.

It was Bohlen's considered opinion that implanting ranked right up there with the stupidest things ever done. Plugging a piece of untested, unproven, unrefined technology right into your brain—you couldn't ask for a better deal. He'd often wished he could sit down with Nathan Kahn and discover what the hell he'd been thinking when he first dreamed up the idea. No chance of that; Kahn was supposed to be dead, and if he wasn't, he'd be stone shrieking crazy by now.

Bohlen knew what the motive had been; everybody did. The technological singularity, the paradigm leap, machine-man synthesis, the next step in evolution. Put a chip in your head and spit in the eye of God Almighty. The Golden Age, the Adulthood of the Race, everybody eating baked beans in paradise next Tuesday. Homo Novus, Homo Praestamus, Homo Rationus . . .

Homo Dementius, more like it.

Bohlen had tried the books, and had nearly fallen asleep over them—they read like those New Age things that had been so popular during the Crazy Years. It was no use discussing the subject with the handful of imps who had been taken alive; they were usually so scrambled that they didn't know their own names. He brought it up with Tap one of the few times they spoke, trying to get him to open up, but Tap froze immediately and snapped, "You'd never understand," and that was that.

Maybe Tap had been right; maybe Bohlen couldn't understand. But he'd certainly seen the results. Not Kahn's group; they were just your standard academics, swilling white wine from paper cups and discussing Derrida. A pack of silly intellectuals who'd gotten in over their heads.

But the others: the Golden Dawn, with their grotesque amalgam of Gurdjieff, Crowley, Manson, and comps; the Cybernistas, young sports with a taste for torture; and don't forget Betty Stoner and her little coven. Stoner had been one of the weirdest human beings Bohlen had ever heard of, far surpassing Medrano, right up there with Adolf and Uncle Joe.

Hundreds dead, the country in chaos, paranoia running rampant . . . And all this at the tail end of a people's war, with the Southwest in ruins and the US in a death struggle with an enemy that it had itself created over the previous half-century. The country had been raped, and Kahn's pious crew of utopians had been there to kick her ribs in as she lay bleeding.

But Bohlen didn't hate them. No more than he did the Mexicans or Nicaraguans. They'd been trying to do good as they saw it, most of them, and they'd paid a high price for idealism. An incredible price . . .

That op in Chicago, two years ago. The previous months had shown activity, but COSSF had just gotten around to checking on it. They'd swept the city by process of elimination and honed in on three imps. The first shot himself as they came up the stairs. The second they had to take out. And the third . . .

He could still smell the stench of that tenement hallway. It had been on the south side, the wind off the lake bitter. They went in through a hall window from the fire escape, Bohlen taking point. He kicked the front door in, saw that the living room was empty, and continued at a crouch to the bedroom. As he nudged the door open, the imp inside screamed, and he burst in only to stumble over a makeshift barrier of cardboard boxes, toilet paper, and string. He rose just in time to stop the sawed-off shotgun aimed at the woman from firing.

She seemed like something out of a concentration camp, all stretched skin and eyes. It was the eyes that he remembered, staring at him while she screamed.

He never found out who she was. She died a few months later without uttering a coherent sentence.

Ever since then he'd wondered whether the pathetic little fortress she'd erected had been meant to stop some creature out of nightmare or only men. He had about decided that it had to be men.

You didn't hate people like that. Not where Bohlen came from you didn't.

He'd told Tap that story the fourth or fifth time he called—he couldn't remember which; he'd kept no records. He was well aware of what he would be in for if Cummins found out he was talking to an imp.

Tap was silent, and when he finally spoke, the choked sound of his voice told Bohlen that he had known the woman, whoever she was.

"At least you didn't shoot her," he said.

"I don't shoot anybody unless I have to, Tap."

"You've killed plenty of times, Bohlen. What's your score now, twelve?"

"Nine. And only six of them were—"

"Chipheads, Bohlen. You can say it." The bitterness was so thick, it gagged him. "And the rest?"

"The rest were plain goddamn gunmen. Accomplices, accessories, I don't know what you'd call 'em. Hired guns."

The silence on the line stretched on, and Bohlen let it. Finally Tap said, "All right, let's drop it," and they proceeded to the important thing: negotiating the surrender of the imps that Tap had under his wing.

Bohlen didn't know how Tap had tracked him down, how he'd even heard of him. That didn't matter; all that mattered was that for the first time in years a CEI was seriously discussing a surrender.

It had happened before. Just prior to the raid at Big Sur, Amory spoke to somebody, but the other party didn't show up for the meeting, and they never heard from him again. Two months later came South Braintree: a meeting, arranged through a well-known civil rights lawyer, between Amory and two implants in a house just out of town. It had been a setup. In the ambush Brice took a bullet in the head, the lawyer five rounds, and Marcus himself was wounded. Inside the house two imps were found dead—not shot by COSSF guns—with three more killed outside. The kill order came down that day, signed by a disgusted Amory from his hospital bed. It had never been rescinded.

Bohlen had mentioned the ambush to Tap, who claimed that the Cossacks opened fire first. Bohlen denied this, and as they hashed it out, it became apparent that some other outfit—either Stoner's or the GD—had delivered its message. Which was a breakthrough of sorts; Tap was finally beginning to trust him. Another call, maybe two, and they'd have come to an agreement.

Then he was shot himself, and while he lay with tubes sticking out of him, Key West happened.

He never heard from Tap again, and after a time concluded that he was dead.

The decision crystallized for him at that moment, rising to mind solid and complete. He wasn't going to dust this one. No; he'd net him, bring him in alive, sweat him and break him down. Bohlen knew that the man wasn't alone; they couldn't survive these days without a network; Tap had told him as much. If Bohlen could get only one good name out of him, one solid lead, it would be worth it.

He had no illusions: it would be tough. It was hard to capture an imp without taking unacceptable casualties. On top of that, the locals wanted him, and Bohlen felt certain that they were as quick on the trigger as they were at rapping the knuckles of outside law. Maybe it was a good thing they weren't cooperating.

But it had to be done. He'd killed nine people in three years. That was nine more than he'd killed in the war. He regretted none of them, not really. But he wasn't what Cummins said he was, either.

Besides, he owed it to Tap. Forcing himself to sit up, he looked over at the voice-only unit on the table across the room, half-wishing it would ring and he'd pick it up to hear that distorted, distant voice once again.

—Bohlen, that you?

—Yeah. What's the word?

—You ready for a transfer?

—Anytime, my friend.

—Okay, got a busload down the street. Be right over.

—Why so long?

—Took a while to talk 'em into it. See you in a few.

Smiling to himself, Bohlen rocked on the couch. He was tired, and wanted something to make it easy. But it was never easy. That voice had been stilled at Key West, and he wouldn't hear it again, not this side of Judgment Day.

It was late, and he needed rest. He never got much sleep during an operation, and he had no idea how long this one would last.

He noticed the screen still glowing. "Save that," he called out, and went to the bedroom as the comp clicked behind him.

CHAPTER 9

"THIS SANDWICH SUCKS. We gotta find a better place than that, Page."

"Quiet."

"Bet this is one of them plastic eggs, like they had on the news. You hear about that? They're putting plastic in eggs now. They twig the chickens' genes so they can eat plastic and it goes in the eggs. Saw it on the news."

"Bobby . . ." Page gripped the wheel tighter as he took the next turn. He'd made three circuits of the town so far. Some of the locals out on the street this early looked up as he passed, but most paid no attention, pushed on by the cold, brisk wind.

"Out here in the country, you wouldn't expect that, you know?" Bobby opened his sandwich to give the fried egg a close examination. "Figure they go out to the barn, everything fresh, right? I mean . . ."

"Bobby. Final warning."

With a grunt Bobby settled back in his seat and bit into the sandwich. Page shot him a glare. During the year that Page had been working him, Bobby hadn't been directly involved in anything. His place had always been on the sidelines. For the first time Page was getting a faceful of Bobby Golden.

Page had got him up at dawn, and Bobby hadn't much cared for that. It was below freezing, and that was gripe two. It was still dark out. The snow was too deep. The truck seats were cold. Now it was his goddamn breakfast.

"What are we looking for anyway?" Bobby said peevishly. He rolled down the window and tossed the wrappers. "I mean, you're looking for something, right?"

Page shook his head. He was a wonder, Bobby Golden—or Wolfe, or Stockdale, all the way back to Stan Kovic, his real name. Page wasn't quite sure whether he hung on to him because Bobby was useful or as a reminder of how silly the maggots could be. That empty face, handsome to the point of caricature, with its cleft chin, pouting lips, and high cheekbones. It was the kind of face that girls went for before they wised up.

And attached to a body that was five-foot-two if that. Smiling, Page looked away. Bobby amused him. "I'll let you know when we see it."

Popping the lid of his cup, Bobby took a sip and grimaced. "This is *cold*," he said accusingly.

The smile died. Page might find Bobby amusing, but he'd about reached his limit. The first thing Bobby had asked upon showing up was what happened to the girl. He'd spent the past few days at the college bars in Frisco—he liked hanging out with students, impressing them with his lowlife bullshit—and had heard that she was missing. Page told him nothing, just gave him a look that made him drop the subject.

They hit a patch of ice, and the truck skidded a few feet before gripping the pavement. At least Bobby had done well there. The truck he'd wired was exactly what Page ordered: a late-model Toyota manufactured for export to Siberia, able to take extreme winter conditions. It had proven its worth this morning on the route Page had chosen to avoid the 501 roadblocks: a rancher's trail blown nearly clear by hovercraft fans but still a little rough in places.

The streets were filling up as the workday began. Page turned onto Main, heading west. There had been no sign of anything downtown—not that he expected a banner saying WELCOME COSSF. It might take all day to track them down. "What time did Luke say he'd get here?"

"No particular time," Bobby said. "Just told me he'd be leaving soon."

Page fell silent. He could have told them to travel together, but he hadn't wanted Luke talking to Bobby. Best to keep separate elements separate, particularly where Luke was concerned. He was street, a hitter and no more, but he lived by that asinine jailhouse code that there were things you just didn't do. Page couldn't allow him to hear about the girl. Not just yet.

And Luke had been careless lately. If it wasn't for Page, he wouldn't be out walking. Page had deleted his records from both state and federal files. But good as Luke was—he knew his weapons, alarm systems, police and security procedures—there were plenty more where he came from.

It was crucial that Luke arrive on time. Bobby was no good at strongarm, and Page couldn't do everything himself. But no point worrying about it. Luke would show.

"I don't know," Bobby said as they left downtown. "I don't see how these people can stand it. It's so boring, nothing happening, nothing to do." He turned to Page. "You think they're Mormons?"

"Some of them," Page said.

"I'm a city kid," Bobby went on. "If I lived here, I'd—"

"Quiet," Page said.

Slowing to a crawl, he watched the figure emerging from the motel on their left. The man dropped his head, and Page swore under his breath. As he passed the motel, he turned for a better look. He was nearly certain . . .

He reached up to adjust the rearview mirror. Somebody was

approaching the man, speaking to him. The man listened. And now he turned toward the truck, a wide smirk on his face.

Releasing a deep breath, Page switched the mirror back and drove on. A few blocks down, he turned into a sidestreet and parked. Closing his eyes, he let his head fall back. Bohlen. Ross Bohlen. He cleared his mind to concentrate on the memory of the one picture he'd seen. Thinner now, and with less hair, but it was him. A big gun, one of the best they had, one of the few who'd been involved since the start.

Page smiled, thinking of the Skoda IW assault rifle under his seat. He could drive back right now, catch him on the street, and waste him where he stood. Unload the magazine into him from the ground up, watch him jerk as the rounds hit home. That would shake things up.

But it would have to wait. For now he had to sit out Cummins. After that situation was resolved, he'd have the resources to take on any of them.

"Did you find what you . . ."

Bobby's voice trailed off. Raising his head, Page turned to him. The little man's jaw flexed, but he didn't look away.

"Yeah," Page said. "Yeah, I found it."

Farther up the street, they came to an avenue that ran parallel to Main, and headed back to town. The homes here were large and expensive, built on big lots with plenty of space. Page's lip curled as he drove past them. A neighborhood like the one he'd grown up in. Every town on Earth had a section like this where the maggots could pretend they had it made because they owned something. A building, land, furniture, clothes, without a thought in their heads about what anything meant. That place coming up— he'd burned a house exactly like it a long time ago, when he was still in school, one of his first steps out of the wasteland. He eyed it as he drove by, wondering what was inside. They'd all burn soon enough. He drove five blocks before going back onto Main. Bobby spoke at the intersection. "What we gonna do?"

"Just keep chill, Bobby, I'll tell you in a minute."

He turned west and slowed as he passed the motel. The guy who'd spoken to Bohlen was standing across the street, stamping his feet against the cold. Nobody else was in sight; Bohlen had either returned or was still out. There were three cars in the lot, no telling who they belonged to.

"All right," Page said, pulling away. "This is what I want from you: when we get back to the house, you take the other car and drive to that motel. Register there under the name on the ID I gave you." He glanced at Bobby. "You still have it?"

Bobby felt at the pockets of the double-breasted jacket under his coat. "Yeah," he said.

"Good," Page said. Bobby had a tendency to lose things. "Memorize the name. Tell them you're a salesman, and pay in cash—make a joke about expense accounts. If possible, get a room in the front, near the first floor, by the stairway. Got that?"

Bobby nodded, and Page went on. "I'm going to show you a photograph. Keep an eye open for the man in the photo, and call me the minute he shows up. Immediately, you hear? All right. Now get this straight: nothing else is important. If you find out anything else, that's fine, but don't poke around and don't ask questions."

"Can I bring the picture with me?"

Page squeezed his eyes shut. "No. It's a clear shot, and you'll memorize it. He'll have people with him, and he'll be in charge. You won't mistake him."

"How long you want me to hang out there?"

"As long as it takes."

"Aw, Page, come on," Bobby said, rolling his head. "You want me to sit in a little room until this jerkoff shows up? That could be a week. No, man . . ."

"That's what I want you to do," Page said coldly. "It won't be a week. Two days, tops. Think you can handle that?"

Bobby nodded sullenly. They were at the outskirts of town, more snow now than buildings. After a moment's silence he asked, "Who are these people?"

"COSSF," Page said. "The strike force. You know about them."

Eyes widening, Bobby pushed himself up in the seat. "What? Jesus Holy Christ, Page. They're *federal*. I ain't messing with them. Those guys are killers . . ."

Page slammed the brakes and gave the wheel a sharp twist to the left. There was a layer of old ice on the pavement, and the truck fishtailed toward the curb. Steering with one hand, he didn't even flinch when they hit the mounded snow edging the street. Hands on his knees, he sat silently for a moment, then spoke without turning his head. "It's late in the day for you to want out, but if you do, now is the time. If you fuck me after this point, I will hurt you."

He swiveled his head to Bobby. "I told you what we have to gain here, and I told you the risks. For you they are minimal. The ID I gave you is perfect; I spent weeks processing it. The Cossacks do not know who you are and are not interested in you. If you act the way you normally do, you will be ignored." He paused, eyes boring into Bobby. "Now which is it?"

Bobby blinked at him, then dropped his eyes. Page could guess what he was thinking: he was wondering what "out" meant. Bobby knew that Page was nothing like the street scum he was used to; that was part of Page's allure. But it followed that Page had also done things far beyond the petty mischief of the average lowlife, things that involved blood and bone and screams in the night. How far he would go, Bobby had no idea. Page had deliberately instilled this uncertainty—through hints, remarks, the occasional purge of the worthless doper or carjacker. Which was one of the reasons Page had told him about the dancer: so that Bobby could wonder about it, as he was wondering now.

Bobby cracked his knuckles. "Okay," he said.

"Okay what?"

"Okay I'm in," he said, an edge to his voice.

Wordlessly Page gripped the wheel and drove on.

He could replace Bobby if he had to. Bobby wasn't worth all that much—he'd only acted as a wheelman on the Coast. But that would require using Gene Feist, and Feist was totally unreliable. He was weak, like all the rest. He'd let that myth about Pelton's get to him, that piece of disinformation planted by COSSF to demoralize the imps. A little confusion, and he'd collapsed, lacking the will to push into the heart of the interface, as Page had. Feist was a broken man. If Bohlen's team picked him up, it would be all over.

Page smiled to himself, thinking how rough it would have been going up against Bohlen even a year ago. But things were different now; the stakes had grown and circumstances had changed. *He'd* changed, grown stronger as time went by and his will drew more power from the masses of data he fed it. Not that he bought Kahn's idea of some mystical union between man and the universe; there was nothing to unite with. But something did exist, something ineffable, just beyond the reach of thought, and it was something that made an enhanced human more than he could be—if he was only able to grasp it.

Grasp it Page would, in time, but what mattered now was that they'd sent their best, their most superb assassin. This meant they were taking it seriously—just as he'd intended.

Now it all hinged on Cummins. He was the key; everything depended on when he showed up and what he did. He was in Hawaii now, at some conference the Japs were holding on comp security. Page's smile grew wider: Cummins was certainly the authority on that topic.

Page had tracked him every foot of the way since he'd heard about the conference a month ago. It had all grown from that one fact: that Cummins would be away from Washington for a set period, cut off from his resources there, and out from behind the incredibly complex web of CM that surrounded the city. An easy target.

At first Page had considered taking him in Honolulu, but decided against it. The islands were not his turf; he knew little about them. What he did know was not good: overpopulated, nowhere to hide, a massive military establishment with all the advanced electronics that went with it. Hawaii was isolated, easy to cut off—and it would be cut off if a government official was snatched from under the spotlight of an international conference, and a security man at that.

No, he'd decided to make Cummins come to him. It was better that way; it would throw the man off balance, keep him guessing up to the moment when Page kicked the door open and . . .

But first, of course, Cummins had to show up. Page felt a sudden emptiness, contemplating what would happen if he didn't. All that effort wasted, having to start over again, having to explain why he went off the scope a month ago . . .

The hollow feeling vanished, replaced with white-hot rage. To grovel before Harland Cummins—to have to apologize to *him!*

He recalled the first time they'd spoken, in that grubby apartment in Oakland, one of Page's half-dozen bolt-holes along the Coast. The phone rang—straight voice, Page didn't use tube, wouldn't allow one on in his presence. He answered and heard Cummins, who wasn't Cummins yet but just a voice reciting a list of places and dates. It took Page five seconds to realize that the voice was identifying some of the erasures he had done. He knew it wasn't a trick—the Cossacks never announced themselves—and he had no choice but to see where this led. As the voice had no doubt planned.

"So?" Page said when the list was finished.

"So talk to me," the voice answered.

Page understood: a sanity test. The man wanted to discover exactly how well wrapped he was. He'd have done the same himself.

So he told him about something he'd seen that morning: a black woman crying in the street while some ISB punks ransacked her apartment. He kept it straightforward, going into detail but not enough to sound obsessive, making the story as coherent and linear as possible. "I can tell you everything I've done for the last month if you got the time," he concluded.

"Not necessary," the voice replied. "You sound stable enough to me." A pause, and then: "So why all the killings?"

Page didn't tell him the real reason, which he only half-understood at the time himself, but instead made up something about how they'd seen him interfacing and had to be dusted.

"Sloppy," the voice said. "Very sloppy, but in lieu of the fact of other possibilities, it seems as though you're the man."

The voice went on to tell him what it wanted, and Page agreed. It fit perfectly with what he was already doing, and the paycheck made it irresistible—even ignoring the fact that the voice could have had COSSF on his ass with no effort at all.

So Page took the path that eventually led him to Montana. The partnership worked well—more for the benefit of the disembodied voice than for Page, it was true, but that was the nature of such arrangements. And he knew that as soon as his usefulness ended, the voice would drop a word or two in the hearing of certain waiting ears, and Page would become history—that too was the nature of such arrangements. After Ricelli, he knew that it was only a matter of months.

He had tried to track the call, but the voice vanished behind a wall of military defenses that Stoner herself would have been unable to penetrate. He took his time, working by process of elimination. It had to be someone in government, most likely security. He tapped into what personnel files he could, sometimes using the very codes that the voice gave him. After nearly a year he narrowed it down to five names: two in the FBI, one Bug, one in NSA, and Harland Cummins.

The voice was what finally gave Cummins away. It was distorted with electronic overlays, but even so it had a mushmouthed, backwoods quality that led Page to concentrate on men of Southern origin. For weeks he wavered between three of them—the NSA colonel, the Bureau assistant director, and Cummins—when he heard about the Congressional hearings and switched on the tube to the cable station showing them. He watched for five minutes before Cummins said something that erased all doubt. A phrase that the voice used so often, Page could almost hear it coming.

He replayed the tape a dozen times, jabbing the button over and over: "In lieu of the fact . . . in lieu of the fact . . . in lieu of the fact . . ."

Cummins would show up. He had no choice; Page had seen to that. The dead dancer was a flag, a signal understandable only by the two of them. Cummins had made it clear there was to be no more of "that kind of thing," as he called it. The dancer was a glove tossed in his face, telling him that asset A had gone feral. Throw in the fact that Asset B was right next door, and it was a provocation impossible to ignore.

He recalled how Cummins acted after he'd eliminated Ricelli. Cummins had known the Cossack had tracked Page down. He'd warned Page to stay low for a while, without any emphasis, though his tone had been urgent. By then Page knew about the Cossack connection, and it didn't take him long to put two and two together. It had been simple: he shorted Ricelli's car batteries and followed him until they ran out, then pulled up behind him, Good Samaritan ready to lend a hand.

The hysteria in Cummins's voice when Page finally got around to answering the phone two days later told him all he needed to know: Cummins could be twisted, same as all the rest.

He'd show up. He was a flatworm, turning when shocked, doing exactly as he was ordered. A face hiding a vacancy; an empty box exhibiting behavior. A maggot, an insect. And insects died when you stepped on them.

They were nearing the turnoff. The land rose slowly to the peaks beyond. Page looked in the direction of the lodge, wondering if Telford knew that Cummins had pinned him long ago, to hold him in reserve against the day when Page had to be discarded.

"Page?" Bobby said, his voice uncertain. "I'm gonna need some money."

"You'll get it at the house."

Just ahead was the last hill before the roadblock and the unpaved road that led up over the fields and into the woods. Page gunned the motor to take the first steep rise.

"Uhh . . ." Bobby said. "You haven't paid me for the truck yet."

Page made an irritated sound. "Bobby, don't worry about it. After this you won't have to think about money."

Bobby had no time to reply. Turning off the road, Page shifted to low and headed uphill. The truck bounced wildly, and Bobby cursed under his breath as they climbed the snow-covered slope.

CHAPTER 10

BOHLEN GOT UP in time to catch the *Rancher's Report* on the tube. It contained a lot that was new to him. Hard to believe how much you had to know to chase cows around.

He decided it would be wise to hold the shower until he got back in from the cold. After splashing some water on his face, he went downstairs and into the street, where he immediately had a run-in with a reporter.

Bohlen despised reporters, partly on principle but mostly due to an incident during the war. He'd been part of a unit mopping up after Wolsach's 3rd Armored broke through the Medranistas' eastern front. It was a scratch force of guardsmen and reservists; their mission, to round up the Latino refugees that Medrano's scum had been using as a shield and herd them into Red Cross camps.

Not an easy job, and made worse by lurking remnants of the FLA still lusting for gringos to shoot. They encountered a bunch that morning and had a sharp little firefight that lasted an hour. The radio was goofing, so there was no air, and the Medis fought like rats in a bucket. The unit approached this like a training problem, taking its time to surround the hill before moving in. It finished up with no KIAs and only two wounded.

Bohlen had been leaning against a beat-up highway fence, smoking a cigarette and reflecting on his first—and last, though he didn't know it yet—actual bit of combat, when a lifter with a painted blue eye set down a hundred yards away. A camera crew hopped out, followed by a woman dressed in Saks' notion of the latest in military couture.

He watched her pestering the other guys but without much interest, more concerned with the fact that the supply lifter was late and he hadn't slept in two days.

Finally she got around to him, a little irritated at the reactions of the unit, which had ranged from numb silence to outright hostility. Only the week before, an armored column had been ambushed in Mama West thanks to a newscast that tipped the Medis, and nobody was very pleased with the media.

She asked Bohlen a few dumb-ass questions about the engagement, which he answered with blank *uh*s. Her impatience mounted. Then she fixed him with an intensely sincere gaze and asked, "Soldier, what do you think of when you think of America?"

He looked at her, at her thousand-dollar safari suit, and at the camera crew poised behind her like a pack of cyborg gnomes. He was exhausted in a way he hadn't thought possible. He hadn't eaten since last night. Lunatics were trying to kill him.

He turned his face to the camera. "When I think of America," he said slowly, "I think of a goddamn big fuckin' bag of Dunkin Donuts."

Just then the supply wagon came buzzing over a hill, and he walked off. He didn't think any more about this, but the next day Gromer, the master sergeant, strode up to him wearing his listen-here-whiteboy look. Bohlen had no idea how, but Gromer had seen the clip. "Bohlen," he barked, "what the hell you mean telling that reporter the US a sack o' donuts? What, you psycho or something?"

This incident probably had something to do with his transfer to COSSF.

The Ironwood reporter wasn't wearing a safari suit. He was dressed in a gray overcoat and the same kind of fur hat they were wearing out east, the first Bohlen had seen here.

Bohlen winced, seeing the recorder.

"Morris, the *Register*," the guy said, eyebrows in a stern V. "You have anything to say about your reasons for being here?"

Bohlen leaned toward the recorder. "I decline to answer that question on the grounds that it interferes with my right to be secure in my own person as guaranteed by the Constitution of the United States of America."

"Come off it," Morris said as Bohlen turned on his heel and went down the street. "Are there chipheads in this town?"

"You may collect, collate, or compile data on individuals, events, and policies involving agencies of the federal government. You may discuss in a private setting the meaning, import, and implications of such data. However, neither data nor conclusions drawn therefrom may be disseminated, broadcast, or . . ."

Morris ran after him, talking like a bad editorial. "Don't you think people have a right to know of dangers facing them?"

"If an agent of the federal government or an associate thereof should be injured or slain due to the actions of a disseminator or broadcaster of such data, the latter may be prosecuted as an accessory. If any legitimate operation of any federal agency . . ."

They reached an intersection. Morris stopped at the curb and yelled, "All right, shithead. We have your name. See what happens to your career when things loosen up."

Bohlen crossed the street and walked on, wondering if the media *was* keeping a hit list. Must be a hell of a long one.

After buying some American symbols at a donut shop, he returned to find Morris standing across the street from the motel. The reporter glared at him as he spoke into his recorder.

Lu was in the shower, so Bohlen sat down to work some data. He discovered that the state cops had duplicate files for Ironwood, a backup in case of softbombing. He used the COSSF code for priority access, which they didn't appreciate. By then Lu was out of the shower, and they got to work, he in the bedroom with his comp propped on the dresser and she out in the main room. It was just like Washington except for the bed.

There was an algorithm for collating potential leads, but it wasn't that hot. The parameters were so subtle, the criteria so intuitive, that the program either missed obvious leads if the field was set too narrow or, if it was opened up, spat out worthless names by the truckload. The one time Bohlen had used it, he'd gotten a printout of everybody in the Milwaukee area named Neumann, Newman, and Numan, on the grounds that they obviously had something to do with cybernetics.

The job had to be done by hand, slow, boring, wearisome work, not that different from what he'd been doing for the last month.

Five donuts later he looked around and saw that the morning was gone. He got up and went to the window. No sign of Morris; too cold to stand around on a corner. God alone knew how the man had learned they were here—unless that damned Hough had passed him the word.

Bohlen went back to the comp to enter the last dozen suspects. All ex-Angelenos from over in Newtown, what they called "Dipville" here. A good preliminary list, he thought. Finish them up, collate them by area, map them, and start slogging. It'd be lunchtime before they were ready . . .

There was a knock at the door. Who the hell, he thought as Lu's footsteps sounded. He was getting up to grab his MP-8 just in case, when he heard a yell.

"*Louise!* Sweetheart!"

A quick flurry, then Lu spoke. "Floyd! I'll give you a punch!"

"Hey, you let your hair grow out. You don't look so tough anymore. What's the story?"

"I've got no stories for you, Delahanty."

"Ah, just as well. Probably give me a heart attack."

"Oh, you. Go bother Ross."

"I'll do that. Where's he hiding?"

The bedroom door swung open to reveal two hundred and fifty pounds of ex-cop swaddled in a shapeless black coat. Delahanty smiled and stepped into the room. "What you doing on my turf?"

"Your turf," Bohlen said, forcing himself not to smile too. "Who invited you here?"

"I was bored," Delahanty said. "Figured this'd be good therapy."

Stepping around the bed, Delahanty bent over the screen. "Coming together, is it? How many you got?"

"Hundred here, Lu about the same."

Pushing Bohlen's machine pistol aside, Delahanty sat down. "Check the area?"

"Had it done from D.C. Clean. No tripwires or softbombs."

"Yeah, they ain't stupid enough to do that anymore." Del gestured at the comp. "Who looks good?"

Bohlen paused. The list didn't seem so impressive now that Del was here. "Nobody. Petty felons, a few registry violators." He heard voices from the other room. "Who you got with you?"

"Jimmy Ling and Fred Navasky. New boys, thought they might be useful. They want to meet the immortal Bohlen, for some weird reason."

Bohlen smiled but said nothing.

"Now, I'm dying to hear about your plans for Cummins, but I can hold off on that," Delahanty said. "We've got a more pressing problem."

"What's that?"

Delahanty eyed him for a moment. "The locals."

"What about 'em?"

"For starters, I hear you asked the conductor of the town philharmonic to play 'Turkey in the Straw' for you."

"Where'd you hear that?"

"Don't worry about where. I heard." Delahanty shook his head wearily. "Now, I'm not going ask what became of your child-like charm, but what about your operational sense? How the hell do you expect to get anywhere without local law holding up their end? You join the Bugs while I wasn't looking?"

"Aw, Del . . ."

"Don't aw Del me, Ross. Remember who you're talking to. I know you. You fucked up, and you don't want to admit it. You even give them a courtesy call to let them know you were coming?"

Ross was silent.

"No, you didn't," Delahanty went on. "I always had to take care of that. *Always*. I bet you thought you'd clean up this bad cowtown singlehanded, huh?" He slapped his knees. "Fine, don't answer. I know, so it don't matter." He shook his gloves at Bohlen. "It's a damn good thing I came out here, my friend. You've been behind a desk too long, that's your problem." He got up and bobbed his head at the door. "Now get your coat."

"Where we going?"

"Lunch," Delahanty said, leaving the room.

Nodding thoughtfully, the sheriff poured himself more soda. "I hadn't heard that," he said. "I read a book about it, but . . ."

"Ain't in the books," Delahanty said around a mouthful of meatball parm. "The books are all wrong. Ross here," he gestured with his sandwich. "Is gonna write his memoirs when he retires. You wait for that one."

Chuckling, Hough nodded at Bohlen, who responded with a thin smile. On the way over, Delahanty had stopped at a sandwich joint and bought a bagful of heroes, fries, and onion rings, real greasy cop feed. He must have already spoken to Hough; the sheriff wasn't surprised when they walked in. Since then Delahanty had been hard-pedaling the Mick charm, overwhelming old Leon with jokes, chatter, and oozily sincere comments on the subject of music, including a lot of questions about Hough's violin: what make it was, how long he'd had it, what it had cost. Hough claimed that the bow alone was ten grand. Bohlen didn't believe it.

"Never was a group called the Archangels," Delahanty said, wiping his mouth with a paper napkin. "That was newspaper bullshit. They were seeing imps under the bed. What were some of the other ones they came up with, Ross?"

"The Brethren," Bohlen said, "the Fascisti, the Humanists, the Eighth Day . . ." He shrugged. "There were a lot of them."

"There were only three important ones," Delahanty said. "Kahn's group . . ."

"The papers called them the Humanists, because that's what their philosophy was," Bohlen said. "But people started thinking there were two different groups."

". . . the Stoner Gang," Delahanty went on, "and the Golden Dawn. That's it." He put his sandwich down and reached for a Coke. "The Cybernistas too, but they were nothing much."

"They sure took care of that town," Hough snorted.

"Desert Oaks," Delahanty said, tearing another bite out of his sandwich. "But that's the only thing they did."

Desert Oaks had been a small high-desert town in SoCal, with a population of a few hundred. One fine hot afternoon a handful of Cybernistas drove in, faces made up and earrings jangling. They cut the town off and took it to pieces for the sheer hell of it. Fifty dead, too many injuries to count, and half the place burned to the ground.

"Most were Phalangists and supposed to be funneling data to Medrano, but so what?" Delahanty shook his head. "The Latinos were beat by then anyway. No, Stoner and the GD were the real problem."

Finishing the sandwich, Delahanty wiped his fingers and reached for another. "Stoner was bad news. Everything you've heard about her is true, and you haven't heard half of it. She was some kind of throwback to the Age of Dictators. Believed that most of the human race ought to be wiped out."

Hough leaned forward confidentially. "Tell me one thing," he said. "Was it you guys that blew her away?"

"Nah," Delahanty said. "Not FBI either. It was the Swiss. We let them know that the most dangerous individual in history was within their borders, and they took it from there. By the time we got a team to Zurich, it was all over." ·

"The Swiss are a hard-nails bunch," Bohlen added. He picked up a lukewarm onion ring and nibbled at it.

"Which group do you think the perp is from," Hough asked. "Stoner's or, uhh . . . the Dawners, is that it?"

"Academic, at this point," Bohlen said. "They're all defunct as organizations. Could be either, or Kahn's group, for that matter. A lot of his people were unstable, for all their intellectual pretensions."

Bohlen didn't mention that it might be an outfit that had escaped detection—or worse, a new one using implant technology despite the dangers. No sense making explanations more complex than they had to be.

Clasping his hands, Hough frowned at the desktop. "So what are you thinking?"

As was his habit, Delahanty was peeling strips of melted cheese off the wax paper. "Have to ask Ross," he said, a string of parmesan poised in front of his mouth. "He's got it scoped out."

"We have no leads at all," Ross said, "which is not unusual. Just the murder and intrusion. We're following standard procedure, interviewing anyone who may have contact or knowledge. Petty crooks, wiseguys, hackers, that type. We might pick up something there—rumors, a tip—or we might force our boy to run for it. I've got a couple hundred lined up. Most of them," he decided to emphasize the point, "in the new section."

"Needless to say," Delahanty said, crumpling the wrapper he'd been scavenging, "you know more about the area than we ever will. Every department's got stuff that never goes into the files. Oftentimes the break comes from a local officer's input. Am I right, Ross?"

Bohlen shrugged, but Del glared at him. "Oh, yeah," Bohlen said. "All the time. Surprised when that doesn't happen."

Taking a sip of soda, Hough thought it over. "Well, I'll tell you," he said finally. "We are a bit overextended these days. Lot of patrolling, particularly seeing as this is winter." He looked slyly at Delahanty. "If I knew what you had in mind . . ."

"Informal liaison. We don't want to cut into your regular duties. We basically need info, to make sure we're not reinventing the wheel. And of course we don't want to knock down any of your fences either."

Bohlen thought that Del gave him a quick glance at this last phrase, but he wasn't sure.

"Well," Hough said, pulling at his mustache. "I don't see any problem with that."

"You'll want to be in on the bust, needless to say. You've got interests too."

Hough slapped the top of the desk. "All right," he said. "How do we start?"

"We'll want to talk to the investigating officer, see if he has any ideas. Beyond that, we'd need to speak to the rest of your force, fill them in, find out if they've heard anything. We could do that here or at our setup in town, makes no difference. They want to drop in off-shift, no problem. We'll give 'em all the coffee they can drink and plenty of tall tales besides."

Bohlen had to struggle to keep from smiling. As always, Del was handling it perfectly, the feudal vassal begging a favor from his lord while at the same time promising absolutely nothing in return. It was natural diplomacy, talent that Bohlen admired and envied.

The deputies would come around. They could hardly pass up an opportunity to be in on a national security bust, with all the prestige that involved. When they got there, Del would load them up with coffee and donuts and tell them a lot of lies with a hint thrown in here, a suggestion there, and before you knew it, half the department would be acting as a free part-time auxiliary.

Hough glanced at the clock. "I think Johnny Nast ought to be in by now." He reached for the intercom. "Johnny, step in here a second," he said when Nast answered. He sat back in his chair. "I may as well warn you about the Newtown force. Not that I'm trying to put down another department, you understand, but they aren't very good. Most are retreads from Los Angeles, don't know how to act in a rural setting." He shook his head. "They've been through a lot of personnel past couple years. As for the 501"—his eyes twinkled at Bohlen. "They aren't worth a darn either."

Nast walked in. "Johnny," Hough said, pointing at Delahanty. "This is Floyd Delahanty. He's running the federal operation."

Delahanty got up and shook his hand. "How you doing?"

"You already know Ross Bohlen," Hough said. Nast looked at Ross and nodded with distaste, then gazed stonily at the sheriff.

"We're going to give these people a hand. We're on the same side, after all, and they're not asking much. Right now they want to talk to you about the dancer. You've got a little time."

Nast's jaw worked slightly. "Fine by me."

"All right." The sheriff got up to walk them to the door. Bohlen followed.

"You know," Hough said, turning. "There's one thing that's always puzzled me. That program the implants use—the oblique one, I think it's called—why don't they just clean the comps out so they have nothing to work with?"

"Can't be done," Bohlen said. "Oblique programs are parasites on other software. You can't even tell if they exist without tearing apart the host program. To erase them all, you'd have to shut down every comp in the country and reload fresh software."

Nodding, Hough mulled that over. As Bohlen stepped into the hallway, the sheriff caught sight of his loafers and pointed at them. "You'll need something warmer than those this time of year, son."

Bohlen smiled at him. "I was thinking the same, Sheriff."

Turning to Delahanty, Hough said, "See that this man gets some decent footwear and keep me posted."

"Will do," Delahanty said. "And thanks."

"My pleasure," Hough said, going back into his office.

Poker-faced, Nast went down the hall without a word. As they followed, Del gave Bohlen an elbow in the ribs. "You owe me for the sandwiches," he whispered.

CHAPTER 11

SHUTTING OFF THE CHAIN SAW, Telford set it down on the stump. As he straightened, the ache in his back vanished. He grunted with relief.

It was colder than yesterday, well below freezing, but he felt hot despite the fact that he was wearing just a sweater. He glanced at the pile of cut branches next to the stump and wondered if he should take a break before he started chopping. He decided to get on with it.

He'd woken up this morning to find Cora back upstairs hiding with her birds. Naomi was in the kitchen. She smiled at him, in a far better mood than last night. She tried to force a full breakfast on him, but he refused, telling her coffee would do.

"You've forgotten what this weather does to one's appetite," she said as he went to wash up. "I'll get you something quick."

When he came out, she had a couple of egg sandwiches ready. While he ate, she went upstairs with a plate for Cora. Evidently Cora wasn't eating, as often happened when she was upset.

He was on his second cup when Naomi came back down. He asked if anything needed doing, and she mentioned the wood supply—Gene had let it slide. Pulling on a sweater, he went to the closet and dug up a pair of felt boots, then poked around for— yes! Gloves: a good pair, lined with sheepskin. He knew they were lying around somewhere.

"I think Gene is upstairs," Naomi said quietly. "I heard him sneak in earlier. You want me to send him out when he gets up?"

Telford nodded. "Yes, do that."

He gathered the logs in a loose pile and went to the shed for an ax. They burned a lot of wood at the station; there was a government directive to that effect, to cut operating costs. That also meant that they were bending the pollution regs, but Telford supposed that the chimney scrubbers took care of that.

He was balancing the first log when the door opened and Gene emerged, holding a steaming cup. He approached Telford with his eyes down, as if to make sure of his footing. Sinking the ax blade in the stump, Telford swung to face him.

Gene stopped at arm's length and held out the cup. "N-lady told me to give you this."

Telford took the cup without a word. N-lady—where the hell had he picked that up? He lifted the cup to his lips and took a sip. Hot chocolate—Naomi being motherly.

Gene was turning away. "One second," Telford said. Gene stopped, staring at the trees as if there was something fascinating going on amidst them.

Telford sat down on the stump. He'd never really gotten along with Gene. Not at the estate, not later on. Gene had treated him badly when he first arrived—with arrogance, sarcasm, pointless malignity. Even after Telford tracked him down in the ruins of Austin, alone in a wrecked house with no furniture but a mattress and a PC that could be powered up only two hours a day, the contempt remained, and was made worse by inverted gratitude.

He studied the crust forming inside the cup. "You feel like telling me what's on your mind?"

"None of your—"

"Goddamn business," Telford finished for him. "Okay. If

that's how you want it, I'm not going to push. Makes no difference. Only," he went on as Gene moved away. "Don't involve Cora."

Gene glared at him.

"I mean it. You can think whatever you want, but don't bother her with it. She's in bad shape, she can't take it, and it's just not fucking fair."

Gene only shook his head and lurched toward the path to the cabin. Telford got up, beginning to regret the tone he'd taken. It wasn't easy for Gene either.

After about ten feet Gene suddenly stopped. "That's smooth, Telford," he said loudly. "That's real smooth. You so worried about Cora with what you're planning."

"What am I planning?" Telford stepped toward him, flinging what was left of the chocolate into the snow. Gene scowled, eyes wet with fury.

"What am I planning?" Telford repeated. "What did Page tell you?" When Gene said nothing, he went on. "He told you I'm going to dump you, I know that. Did he tell you why? Think, for God's sake. What reason could I have? Why am I here if that's what I have in mind? Do you think I'd show up . . ."

Gene laughed, a grotesque snort. "They pinned you out east. You left a trail. You're gonna cut out and let the Cossacks take us, and they'll think they got you."

Shaking his head, Telford reached for Gene's arm. "Gene."

He jerked away. "Get your pimp's hand off me."

"I swear to you," Telford said patiently, trying to make each word count, "I'd never do that. Not to you, not to anybody." He gestured at the house. "Could I do such a thing to those women in there?"

"Page knows. Page is gonna stop you . . ." Gene was nearly babbling.

"Forget about Page. I'll take care of him . . ."

"Page'll kick your ass, man. He'll tear your fucking head off."

"Gene, you know what Page is. How can you listen to him?"

Gene fell silent, a twisted smirk on his face.

"Let's go inside," Telford said. "We'll talk this through. You'll see there's nothing to it . . ."

"Yeah?" Gene leaned toward Telford, and his voice was like a shriek even though he whispered. "Then why are the Cossacks in town right now?"

Telford could only stare as Gene walked off. It took him a moment to find his voice. "Where did you hear that?" He half-ran to the retreating figure, reaching for his shoulder to jerk him around. "Gene," he said, "have you been tapping again?"

Gene's lips pursed, as if he was about to spit. But then behind them there was a whine, followed by the crunch of crushed snow. His eyes widened, filled with sick fear, and he tore himself away and floundered to the path.

Looking back at the driveway, Telford saw a sheriff's cruiser coming to a halt. Guts twisting, he looked up. Nothing in sight, no sound of lifters or choppers . . .

A deputy got out and put on his hat. A big man, one Telford hadn't met. The deputy shut the car door and raised a hand in greeting. Telford took a few steps toward him before realizing that he was still holding the cup. He set it on the stump before going on.

Telford headed down Main, doubling back into the center of town for the fourth time. He drove slowly, studying buildings and parked cars, his eyes open for anything—a government plate, a face he'd once seen. He had no idea where they'd be. COSSF had no bad operational habits. Sometimes the town would loan them an office, or they'd rent a house or hotel suite. It was always different.

The deputy's visit had been nothing, little more than a courtesy call. Apparently there'd been a murder a few days ago, and they were poking around a bit more than usual. The deputy—a big

127

Amerind named Frostmoon—was friendly if reserved. He asked about Telford's retarded sister-in-law; it seemed that a year or so back he found her out wandering.

After the cop left, Telford went inside and gave Naomi a lame excuse for going to town. He didn't tell her about the Cossacks; there would be plenty of time for that.

But maybe it was just a fantasy of Gene's, a sign of his deterioration. Except Gene didn't seem that bad, not yet anyway, and he'd been dead serious; nobody could have been more serious.

It wasn't Telford who'd drawn them, that was certain. He hadn't tapped since the summer before, and that last interface was unbearable: the voices, the visual distortion. For a while he'd thought he'd gone over the edge for good.

That left three possibilities. First, that this was a standard, scheduled COSSF operation to flush out whatever they could. Which was unlikely; they didn't work that way. The Cossacks didn't move in unless they had a target. They might have changed tactics, but he doubted it. Their budget had been cut, like all the security outfits, and they couldn't afford casting nets. These days they sat around and waited for something to pop up. In fact, the director had publicly announced last fall that the imp problem was solved. Hearing that had cheered Telford immensely. A bit too soon, it now seemed.

It could be Page. That was more likely: Page shows up with the Cossacks right behind him. Hard to believe that that was a coincidence. On the other hand, the fact that Page was still around meant that he was being careful, that he wasn't making mistakes, that he didn't crack a code without knowing exactly what was waiting for him. Unless he was totally wasted—and Naomi had seen no sign of that—he couldn't be the one who had left a trail.

Also, Telford was convinced that Page was late-generation. He'd always taken it for granted that Page had been implanted well after the first wave, with better equipment, more adaptable software, and the early bugs ironed out. No way to be sure, but it was best to act as if that was true. And if Page was late-gen, there was next to no chance that he'd been tracked.

Unless he wanted to be. A nightmare scenario, but it had to be faced. All that Telford had seen and heard pointed to the fact that Page was a manipulator and a sadist, quite capable of carrying out such a scheme. But it didn't feel right. Page had a ritualistic personality; Telford was certain he'd be much more baroque and theatrical if he was seriously trying to set them up. After all, he'd once shot a man merely to underline a message from Betty Stoner.

The third possibility was that Gene had done it himself, tapping into the lodge system when Naomi wasn't around, bringing the Cossacks down on them out of sloppiness or loss of control. Realizing what he'd done and too overcome with guilt and anxiety to admit it, he'd taken it out on Telford, warning him at the same time. That theory felt the most comfortable, perhaps because it meant the situation could be salvaged.

He was back downtown. The street widened to four lanes, split by a parking area in the middle. He slowed further to look over the parked cars. His eyes fell on a figure emerging from a Chrysler Assegai, a bulky man in a black overcoat, his back to the street. He didn't seem to be a local. Telford's gaze followed him, hoping for a look at his face.

The collision alarm beeped, and he hit the brakes. Turning his head, he saw that the traffic light was now red. He gritted his teeth as the car stopped inches from the bumper of a pickup. There was a gun rack in the back window, a sticker reading 501 in the corner. Telford let out a deep breath. Lucky he hadn't hit him; he sure as hell didn't need a run-in with one of those bastards.

He looked for the Assegai driver and saw him crossing the street two car-lengths back. A flash of disappointment: it was a face he didn't know, bearded, wearing glasses. Still, COSSF had a lot of new people . . . But no, the man was now talking to someone on the sidewalk, an obvious native in a cowboy hat and shearling coat. A local after all.

Telford turned around and started back to the west end. He

was feeling last night's lack of sleep, compounded by frustration and foreboding. Too bad there wasn't some kind of switch to control those factors, a circuit that would cancel them out. But no implant ever made could process weariness, or fear, or anything else that mattered. Only the will could do that.

A half mile past the town center he spotted a coffee shop and pulled over. There were two sheriff's cars parked in front. He hesitated before deciding to go in. They might know something; he could fish a little, buy them a coffee, maybe . . .

The two deputies sat at the counter, deep in conversation, hats on the Formica top. Telford had run across the blond cop before, but couldn't recall his name. A simple one, the kind hard to keep in mind because it was so short. John Something.

Walking past them, he sat down two stools away and listened in. The blond deputy was speaking, and he seemed pretty angry.

". . . gave me a lesson on search procedure. One cocky son of a bitch, let me tell you."

"Well, why is the Bear playing with 'em, anyway?"

"Aw, you know Hough." The blond cop took a sip of coffee. "They bullshitted him. Bought him a grease sandwich from Rudy's, and then things were just great." He shook his head. "And to top it off, you know what this Fed wants? He tells me the perp's got to be brought in unharmed. No gunplay. Wants to give him to his boss for a paperweight."

The other cop looked puzzled. "But if it's a chiphead . . ."

"Exactly. Who bells the goddamn cat. I'll tell you . . ."

The gray-haired woman behind the counter approached. Telford nearly put his hand up for silence but caught himself and said, "Coffee," instead.

". . . I see him first, it's a round right in the chest and no questions. I know too much about comphuggers to take chances."

Telford nodded his thanks when the coffee arrived. The deputies got up. "I have it, Terry," the blond one said, throwing a bill on the counter. Then: "It'll serve him right if it turns out there's no hardware in the perp's head after all."

A name, Telford said to himself, burning his mouth as he gulped the coffee. Give me a name.

"It's about time you two finished up and got back looking for that killer," the woman called out.

"Don't worry, Pam," the blond cop said. "We've got federal help now."

"It's no laughing matter, Johnny."

"I'm not laughing," he said at the door.

"So where are these Feds . . ."

The voices were cut off by the closing door. Telford stifled a curse and put his half-finished cup down. Ask them for directions, that was it . . . He took out his wallet and flicked through the bills, finding only twenties. The woman was doing something under the counter. Hell with it; he couldn't wait for change. But he couldn't leave a twenty either; not for a cup of coffee. She might remember and mention it to somebody.

Outside a car door slammed. He went through his pockets, found a five and put it on the counter. "Keep the change," he called out. The woman smiled at him as he left.

The cruisers were pulling away in opposite directions as he stepped outside.

He stood on the step a few seconds. It was almost dusk, and the air had grown a lot colder. There was a line of light beneath the clouds on the western horizon, red-gold and icily brilliant, silhouetting the mountains in the distance. As Telford watched, it began to fade, the sky dulling to gray-white.

At least I know, Telford thought as he went to his car. It was hard fact now, not fantasy or hallucination. The danger was real. He opened the door and got in. They'd have to run for it. Head for the Coast, the Canadian cantons. If he could arrange for some way to save the lodge . . . But that was probably impossible. He needed more data. Where the Cossacks were, how long they'd been here, and, most of all, who was in charge.

There was only one way to do that.

He closed his eyes. It was risky on all levels, and particularly for him. And it probably wouldn't tell him much. But he didn't have a choice.

He started the car and drove off. By the time he found a phone booth that was isolated enough, it was fully dark. He shut off the motor and looked around. No one in sight.

A bitter wind struck him as he got out. For a moment he regretted not buying a hardwired car; it would have made things like this a lot easier. He entered the booth and closed the door—they still had enclosed booths out here, probably because of the cold.

Taking his gloves off, he reached into his coat pocket and took out what seemed to be a hand pager and in fact was. He pulled the back of it open, removed a chip that looked like all the other chips inside the unit, and pressed his thumb against it. He counted to three, then placed the chip on a spot just below and behind his right ear, holding it there until it stuck. An amplifier, to help him acquire the signal. He didn't need it but used it so he wouldn't have to run at full power. He wasn't sure if it really helped that much.

He paused, looking out into blackness broken only by his reflection on the side of the booth, then ran a short numerical sequence though his mind.

He flinched as the feeling struck, an instantaneous change of mental state impossible to describe. He had gone micro. The processor was tied in, charge clusters fading down the corridors of circuitry, converting to impulses that rode the bioplastic directly into his cerebellum. Telford supposed that it was this feeling that so many of the others found irresistible, but that was only a guess. It had never done anything for him.

Taking a deep breath, he picked up the receiver and dialed an open line, an unassigned number connecting nowhere. He held the receiver to the chip and instructed the implant to link him to the oblique program riding the phone company's computers.

The call-switching comps, the imp's best friend. Zip Dubois had grasped the hacker's grail, subverting the Bell Sister's system from within. The version of OBIE that had been entered into the phone comps was the most discreet, compact, and well-written ever devised. The Cossacks weren't aware that it existed; they believed the lines were clean. The comps were swept by rewrite programs a dozen times a day. What they didn't know was that OBIE was living fat and happy in the sweep programs themselves; as they eradicated one viroid, another was laid down right after it.

A flash in his right eye showed him the connection was made. A second later a series of symbols and words appeared, seeming to hover some distance out in the darkness, denoting program, location, status. Telford closed his eyes to avoid the disorientation that the effect always gave him, and thought the instructions that would start the implant quartering the area.

He stood there, ignoring the cold and the pressure behind his eyes that grew as the symbols and words changed. Make of hardware, type and generation of program, registration codes and addresses flashed on and off, turning first to yellow, then to pink, and back to the original green as the intrusion program finessed the primitive defenses of the local systems.

The pressure became pain, a dull throb matching his pulse. The readout went bright pink and then dull red. He read off the location: it appeared to be a shunt to the fiberoptic net, either inadequately shielded or illegally tapped by a registry violator. The network was riddled with flaws just like this one—the main reason nobody but the Feds used it anymore.

Whatever was riding that line was a powerful piece of work, with state-of-the-art countermeasures shielding each byte. There was no registry number and only a handful of symbols, none of which told him anything. He ordered the processor to push harder, to get him an ID and location. The readout went a deeper red.

The figures began to blur. He squeezed his eyelids tighter, as if that would make the picture clearer. A new line flashed into being: FEDERAL SCM PROGRAM ODIN V. XII, followed by a group of identifying symbols. Telford half-leaned, half-collapsed against the wall of the booth. Location, he shot at the program. The figures blurred more, ruby in the darkness, then flashed scarlet. Telford broke the interface, clawing at the chip on his neck.

He opened his eyes. He was slumped against the glass, the dial of the phone looming above him. There was a rasping, moaning sound, and he looked around in terror before he realized it was his own breathing.

He tried to put the receiver back on the hook, but his hand shook too much, so he let it drop. Pushing the door open, he staggered to his car, fumbled the keys into the lock, fell into the front seat.

They were here: the hunters, butchers, hired killers of the country in which he lived. "Oh, Christ," he keened, teeth clenched. "Oh, Christ, no . . ."

He had to get away from here. Unlikely that they'd tracked him, but not impossible. Forget the splitting headache; there are pills for that. Drive to where the pills are.

He left the booth behind in its oasis of light, taking the first few miles slowly. By the time he reached the highway, he felt better.

Half an hour later he reached the lodge, its windows glowing warm and secure. In the glare of his headlights he could see the ax jutting from the stump where he'd left it. The cup was gone.

Inside, Naomi was sitting on the couch. When she saw him, she rose, her hands fists, anger in her face. "Jase, where have you been?"

He closed the door and leaned back against it. "I went to . . ."

"He was here again," she cried, her voice shrill. "He left just now, you must have seen him."

There had been a truck on the road, traveling a bit fast. He hadn't paid attention to it.

Naomi took a step toward him. "You said you'd take care of him." Her cheeks were flushed. "You promised me . . ."

Telford looked at the rug under his feet, as if the answer were encoded in the weave. "Where's Gene?"

"In the cabin," Naomi said. "But what does that—"

"Later," Telford said, yanking the door open. He crossed the clearing and half-ran up the path, kicking his way through packed snow. The cabin hulked there, dark under the trees. He strode to it and pounded on the door.

He waited ten seconds. When no answer came, he took a step back and aimed a kick at the spot next to the lock.

The door crashed open. He walked in. The lights were off, but there was a fire burning and he could see that the place had become a sty, scattered with newspapers, magazines, old bottles and cans.

Gene lay on the bed and was reaching for something behind the mattress. He jerked up when he saw Telford, stared at him wide-eyed. Telford paused, realizing what he must look like: a shadowy figure that burst in from the night, a thing out of a bad dream.

He went to the bed. Gene flattened against the wall. Telford swept the trash off a chair and set it in front of the bed. "All right, my friend," he said, sitting down. "Let's talk."

CHAPTER 12

As HE DROVE to the house, Page glanced down at the intruder alarm glowing steadily on the passenger seat.

He'd set it before he left. It was Korean, one of the best on the market, with full-spectrum capabilities—sonic, vibration, and chemical. If anyone broke in, it would tell him when, how many, and whether they were still inside. Page had at least one in every place he used. They hadn't let him down yet.

Lying beside the alarm was the Skoda, loaded with a custom thirty-round magazine, the IR sight switched on. Nice weapon, the Skoda. Simple by today's standards, sturdy and well made, a rate of fire of over a thousand rounds a minute, the ammo aerodynamically designed to hit with an impact that caused as much damage as three ordinary rounds. It had done good work for the Czechs when the Serbian War spilled over their border. Page had not yet used it on a live target. Not yet . . .

The alarm's telltale glowed unchanged as he went past the house. He stopped and looked through the rear window. Good as the alarm was, the Cossacks could subvert it.

Picking up the Skoda, he peered through the sight and swung

it through an arc encompassing the house. No hot spots; the house was as gray as the sky itself.

He put the gun down, made a tight turn, and headed back.

Slinging the gun over his shoulder, he went to the door. As it opened, the alarm beeped in his hand; he glanced down to see that it was reading only him, and shut it off.

The phone rang as he went in, its readout displaying a number: the number of the motel. He picked up the receiver and listened.

"Page," Bobby said, sounding anxious. "Page? You there?"

Unslinging the Skoda, Page grunted.

"Where you been, man?"

"Taking care of business," Page said, setting the gun on the counter.

Bobby laughed nervously. "You gonna go out, you oughta tell me. I mean, I don't know what the hell to—"

"What's happening over there?"

"Uh, well, they're all back upstairs. Bohlen, the big guy, the Chink, all of 'em . . ."

"No sign of Cummins?"

"No, man, but listen: there's been cops around. Local guys, all wearing cowboy hats. I was thinking . . ."

Page waited for him to go on.

"Well, it's getting pretty hot here, Page. I was thinking maybe, you know, like I oughta . . ."

"Have any of them seen you?"

"No."

"Have any of them spoken to you? Have they taken any notice of you at all?"

"Well, no, but—"

"But nothing. You're there to do one thing. You're doing it. You'll keep on doing it."

"All right." The reply was so quiet that Page nearly missed it.

He shrugged out of his jacket. "You get that done, and you're out of there."

The phone was silent.

"You hear me, Bobby?"

There was a sigh, then: "I was thinking about getting something to eat. I'm kinda hungry."

"Do that. You don't have to make contact for the rest of the night, unless something happens. And Bobby, don't eat at the motel. I don't give a shit how cold it is. You go out and eat."

There was a sound of acquiescence. Page hung up. Shaking his head, he walked into the living room. The lights went on. He snapped his fingers, and the room darkened.

He paced slowly, boot heels scraping the hardwood floor. That goddamn Bobby and his endless whining . . . But no sense being irritated, things were moving right along. He'd heard from Luke this afternoon. On his way, with three good, hard boys. That had bothered Page—he'd specified four. But Luke told him that one of them was new, and special: an ex-Medranista, trained and blooded, who'd been living underground since the war. This pleased Page so much, he forgot to ask Luke exactly where he was.

It made no difference—as long as they arrived before Cummins.

Then there was the Telford situation. Not that Page worried about Telford, who was just a maggot with a plug in his head, after all. At first he thought that things had blown up when Feist called; it took a few minutes to get any sense out of the crip. After making sure that Telford wasn't around, Page went over, more to tone up Feist than anything else.

It turned out the silly bastard had only told Telford that the Cossacks were in town. No problem with that; in fact it would probably work in his favor, draw Telford's attention elsewhere.

He ought to stay away from the station from now on. But he had to talk to Telford, to make sure he wasn't preparing to jump. He and his little flock had to be around when the time came. Page smiled as he thought about it. Ironic, that he was obliged to Cummins for the final twist. Key West had been a worthwhile trip after all.

Call Telford, waylay him on one of his little errands, or pay him a visit at home? He could post a note on the lodge system, but there was no kick in that. It would have to be face to face, so he could tickle him a bit, watch him jump. Telford deserved the personal touch.

Page shivered as he considered how personal it could get. He'd thought about it, oh, had he! He owed Telford. The one man still living who'd ever laid a hand on him. It wouldn't hurt to give him a slap or two, a massage, nothing more. Telford couldn't run very far with both legs broken.

His eyes fell on the weights lying on the couch. He peeled off his sweater and shirt and let them drop. He stretched, holding the stretch for nearly a minute, feeling his muscles loosen, then picked up the weights and held them against his chest.

He interfaced and let the sensation wash over him, a sense of expansion, an oceanic feeling that anything was possible, that there was nothing beyond his reach. Closing his eyes, he stood and relished it.

There were some, he'd heard, who couldn't stand this feeling, who reacted to it badly. He didn't believe that. It was the best thing he'd ever experienced, better than sex, better than any drug. And it meant that he was a member of the elite, one of the handful who had stepped out of the cage of humanity to what lay beyond.

It was reality, glory, power. Anyone who said otherwise lied.

He instructed the implant to count for him, and started pumping. Twelve-pound weights dropped to waist level, then up to the chest, then back. Tonight he'd push himself. He hadn't lifted for days, and he had to make up for it.

He pumped slowly, letting his breathing settle into a rhythm that matched the swing of his arms. He cleared his mind, emptying it of thought and worry, opening it to whatever might come. It was a habit with him; he'd gotten some of his best ideas while working out.

What came now was that evening in Sacramento, the event that had changed his life. He called it the Revelation, though that wasn't quite the word.

It was the last week of May. He had just heard that Betty Stoner was cornered and killed.

He saw it on the news just like any other maggot. The network was shattered, most of the members dusted, and the few still alive isolated and broken. Page himself was supposed to have been in Falls Church with the Washington cell, but the stench of failure was too much for him. After two days watching the remnants moping around, he got a bad flash and took the first flight west instead. Hard copy, as it turned out: the cell was hit the next day by a COSSF team backed by a detachment of Army Rangers. Bohlen was in on that one.

In Sacramento Page lost himself among the thousands of evacuees from SoCal awaiting relocation. Sleeping in a tent in one of the camps outside the city; eating at soup kitchens; alone, fearful, not even looking at a comp, lest it somehow broadcast his presence; staring at each army lifter and truck that passed, as if this was the one carrying the men who would see to him.

Strange, thinking back on it—that there was ever a time when Scott Page was afraid.

He took to wandering the streets at night to get away from the throngs in the camp, all of whom seemed to have owned a house in Beverly Hills before LA was flattened. Wandering at night was not a particularly safe thing—the war had only been over for two months and the vigs were still out in force—but he had no choice, he needed to think. The money he'd saved from the allowance that Stoner's people were given was running out; he didn't dare do any tapping; and although he had a relocation card, he couldn't depend on that either. The card was good, legit Department of Interior stamp and all, but now that things were settling down, they were checking more thoroughly. Separating the sheep from the goats, making sure they weren't sending any lowlifes into Mom-Dad-and-the-kids country. If you were going to dump a few thousand refugees into some small town in Oregon, you wanted to be sure that an intact barrio gang wasn't mixed in with them.

It was a cool night for late May. He'd just dodged a National

Guard patrol when he passed a bar. Bev's Saloon. He'd never forget that name. A neighborhood joint, ferns and beer signs in the window, a small parking lot next door.

There was a chime in his head. Page lifted the weights one more time and squatted on the carpet, stretching his legs for push-ups, weights still in his hands for that extra few inches of effort.

A man had been in the parking lot, taking a piss. Page only glanced in his direction, but that was enough.

"What the fuck you looking at?" the drunk called out.

He was big, well over six feet. He swung around to face Page, still holding his cock. "You want a piece of this, DP? That it?"

Page considered going on, but no, the hell with that. He was tired of running.

The guy lurched toward him, zipping up his pants and muttering about the fucking DPs taking over the whole town. Page stared at him, saying nothing.

"You answer me, cocksucker." The drunk smiled at Page's silence and inched closer. "Whatsamatter, no speaky Ingles? You a Beaner, that it? You a puto? You comprende puto, eh?"

With a drunken sneer he swung at Page, who dodged it easily, the training of the last few months returning with the force of instinct. The drunk nearly lost his footing and with a snarl swung at him again.

Page took a half-step back and rammed stiffened fingers into the drunk's throat. Gagging, the man clutched his neck and staggered.

Page kicked him in the belly. The drunk fell to his knees, forehead resting on the pavement. There was no sign of anyone watching. The drunk lifted his head a few inches, legs shifting, trying to move away. With a small leap Page kicked him in the head, aiming for the temple, putting all his weight into the kick.

His foot struck with an awful crack. He shivered as he stared at the crumpled figure beneath him, ready to cower, to run. But the sky didn't open, and the night didn't brighten with the light of flame, and the ground didn't rumble . . . There was nothing. Faint music from the bar, the sighing of the breeze, the sound of traffic some distance off. Nothing else, nothing at all.

He dragged the body into the lot, dumped it behind some bushes and went through the pockets. He found an ID card for a construction company: a photo and the name Dennis Manning. And eighty bucks, which he stuffed in his jacket. Inside the bar someone laughed.

He walked away quickly, not looking back, and after a block he was running. He felt certain he'd hear a cry behind him, but it didn't come.

A half mile on he stopped and leaned against a fence. He was out of the city proper, well into the suburbs. The hills glowed with the lights of houses, big, expensive houses. He stared at them, the confusion and fear of the past weeks building to fever pitch . . .

Then it happened, instantaneously, as if a switch had been thrown inside him. His despair vanished, replaced by utter calm. That corpse back there—what was it, to give him fear? Nothing, absolutely nothing. An object that had once moved and that wouldn't move anymore. What had it been before? Dennis Manning? What did Dennis Manning mean? He repeated the syllables over and over, until they lost sense and became a gabble of empty noise. Nothing-nothing, a drunken animal, out of control and dangerous. No, lower than that: an insect, operating on a pre-established pattern. A maggot. It had been so easy putting an end to it, a brief shift of the muscles, a short leap. Nothing to it. The way it had moved back there on the pavement, quivering like a roach with its carapace broken, waiting for the final stomp of the boot. Would killing it have been so easy if killing meant something?

He straightened, clutching the fence, gripped by vision. Those lights out there, what did they hold? More maggots still: hundreds of them, thousands, millions beyond that, a hive stretching to the ends of the earth. There was no meaning there, no pattern, nothing beyond what *he* put into it.

He saw the whole thing clearly. All that he'd known—the beliefs, the rules, the morals pounded into him—disappeared, like ice in the burning sun. For the first time in his life he felt clean.

This must have been what Stoner knew, what she'd tried to tell the others. She hadn't failed. Page had grasped it—a lesson deeper than words and more basic than thought or theory. He had absorbed it, become one with it, made it part of his very being. He would never lose it now.

He would carry through with the plans he had made. And would make no mistakes. He would build slowly, day by day, taking his time, depending on no one. And it would come: the true world, the age of iron, the maggot race bent to his will.

The lights of the houses swam in the empty night. He felt like roaring out at them, a cry that would extinguish them like a wind, bringing darkness from here to the horizon. Instead he stepped back from the fence and turned away and lifted his hands. They were bloody from where he'd gripped the metal. Clenching them into fists, he walked down the road.

As he neared the camp, an armored car drove past, Guard troops sitting atop it. He went on with no attempt to hide himself. Nothing could touch him now.

The next night, he took out a businessman in a BMW. A slash of his hand, a twist of the neck, and that was it. He got two hundred dollars and a handful of credit cards. Tapping off those gave him over a grand, and with that he headed for the Coast.

The implant sounded again. Page got to his feet and without pausing began to thrust the weights over his head. As he pumped, he studied his reflection in the mirror: the layer of sweat shining in the light from the other room, the muscles bulging with each move.

It was all coming together now. What had begun that night was reaching its climax. This was the node, the focus, the single point of meaning in the midst of chaos. Strange that it should be this place, a backwoods town deadened by winter; but it would have been the same anywhere. And from here he would go to the next phase. The lights of civilization would dim, outshone by a flame unlike any ever seen. And that flame would be him.

In the mirror his eyes were pools of shadow. He gazed into them, his face steel, his arms moving skyward.

CHAPTER 13

THE SUITE was a goddamn zoo. Bohlen sat at the keyboard, ready to throw it at the next idiot who started with him. Delahanty was the prime candidate, but there were also the rookies and one leftover deputy who didn't want to leave.

Bohlen looked sideways at him. Zimmer, his name was. Working on his fifth cup of coffee, chewing the fat with Ling and Navasky. He was a black-glove cop, sporting a pair of tight leather driving gloves for sinister effect. Zimmer liked to talk, and he'd been doing that now for three hours. Bohlen wondered whether the man had a home to go to.

Turning to the screen, he finished tagging the suspects who'd either moved, been jailed, or died. There were a lot of them— apparently around here they didn't put much faith in keeping their files updated.

"Hey, what's this?"

Delahanty had finished shoveling in the two plates of spaghetti that were his dinner and was reading the copy of the *Keyhole*, which had found its way upstairs. He guffawed at the headline. "Love-starved chipheads. I like that. That's good."

Settling back, Ross cut off the insult he was about to throw and brought up current files. He glanced through them and swiveled in the chair. "Lu!" he shouted. "Goddamit, where is she?"

Navasky, Ling, and Zimmer inspected him for a moment and resumed chattering. Bohlen was about to cut loose when the bathroom door opened. Lu emerged, wearing a bathrobe and with a towel around her head. "What?"

"Where's the data on those intrusions?"

"They're not intrusions, Ross. They're filed under anomalies, the way they're supposed to be."

She slammed the door. Bohlen scowled, muttering under his breath.

"Now, now, Ross," Delahanty said, tittering.

"You go to hell, Floyd." He found the file and called it up. Lu had shown him a printout earlier, but this was the first chance he'd gotten for a closer look. Pursing his lips, he ran through the data. Lu had done a damn fine job setting up the detection program this afternoon. He probably should have thanked her. Well, plenty of time for that.

Couple of weirdies, these. Hadn't seen many like them before. Ultrahigh speed, both of them, no more than a two-mike's track on either, if that. The last, just after five, seemed to have been shielded, but it was hard to tell.

"Check this out," Delahanty said. Bohlen glanced over at him. "Woman Scientist at Goddard Station Gives Birth to Alien Baby," Delahanty read. He held up the paper. There was a picture of a little kid with scales all over him and a fake CLASSIFIED stamp across his face. "Cute, ain't he?"

Bohlen turned, gritting his teeth. Newspaper crinkled behind him. "You hear they saw Elvis up there?" Delahanty went on. "Right out on the surface. No suit or nothing."

"Good place for him," Bohlen snapped. He punched for location on both spikes. There wasn't enough data for an exact fix, but they had the vector and could estimate distance from strength of signal.

Number one appeared to come from the southern section of

town, a ritzy neighborhood called Reed Hollow. Old Victorian houses, no industry to speak of. A yuppie kingdom, it looked to be. Not likely an imp would hide out there: high visibility, stable population, everybody minding his neighbor's business. Still, you never knew. He'd give this one to Del and have him check it tomorrow.

The other was on the west side, not far from the motel, in fact. But there was nothing out there. Oh, a few houses, but you were getting into the mountains, and there wasn't a lot of flat ground. Most of the new construction was to the east, in the direction of the plains. The map onscreen showed only a handful of streets.

Then where had the signal come from? A standard program on a home comp wouldn't show these characteristics. A hacker, maybe, farting around with illegal software. Or something that popped out over a phone line.

He punched for phone locations. The screen displayed a new pattern of dots, most of them in the houses, but a few outside. One of those was flashing: a repair signal, out of order and calling for a crew. Coincidence, maybe—but the booth was in the middle of nowhere, and imps liked secluded spots.

There was a burst of noise from the rookies. Bohlen glowered. Evidently the caffeine had gotten to them. They'd spent the past hour feeding bullshit to Zimmer, stuff about imps taking ten rounds and still wielding the old ax, or getting up and walking around after they were dead, God knows what else. It had finally occurred to Zimmer that he was being kidded.

"Aw, get outta here." He waved a hand at them. "They can't be that tough. Anyway they're all nuts by now. I could take one of them."

Behind him Delahanty started whistling the theme from *Peter and the Wolf*. An old joke. Bohlen ignored it and said:

"They are that tough, sonny."

Zimmer gave him a startled look. The two rookies turned to Bohlen with the air of disciples about to hear a new revelation.

"I said they are that tough, and you can't take 'em." He

147

pointed at Ling and Navasky. "Don't let these two fool you. They've never been on a heavy op, and they don't know." He folded his arms. "Would either of you go after a chiphead alone?"

They both shook their heads, Ling muttering, "Nope."

"You hear that?" he said to Zimmer. He gestured at the rookies. "You make it clear to him. The chipheads have been at this for years," he said as he turned to the screen. "They've got military programs loaded and ready to go. Software to target movement, sounds—even heartbeats. We have evidence of IR and UV implants to boost night vision . . ." He went on, piling it thick but not so thick that it would seem ridiculous. All of what he was saying had been long disproven, but this kid didn't have to know that. ". . . some have nerve blocks so they can't feel pain. You wouldn't want to go up against 'em with that Beretta of yours."

Bohlen eyed Zimmer a moment before punching the keyboard for a printout. Delahanty could sit around thinking that he had the local law problem debugged, but Bohlen knew better. "I'm going to tell you this once, Zimmer," he said as the sheet rolled out. "You come across anything, you let us know." He tore the sheet off and got up. "Otherwise they'll be scraping you off the sidewalk with a shovel."

"Ross is right," Delahanty said, lowering the tabloid. "These aren't cattle rustlers. Don't do anything stupid."

"Well, rustlers can be pretty goddamn rough, too . . . ," Zimmer began. Bohlen didn't wait for the rest. Picking up his coat, he folded the map and slipped it in his pocket.

"Where you headed?" Delahanty called out.

"Getting some fresh air," Bohlen said at the door. So they still had rustlers out here, he thought as he went down the hall. It figured.

The road had no name, just a rural route number, and it took him a while to find it. The area was as empty as he'd suspected: a few old houses which looked as if they'd once been farms, a barn here and there to confirm the notion. Most of them still had satellite dishes on the rooftops, which you didn't see elsewhere. One dish was pointed north, in the opposite direction from the Clarke Belt. Bohlen smiled at that.

Finding the booth about a mile down, he pulled up and looked it over.

Odd place to put a phone. No buildings around, or traffic either. Maybe they held the county fair here come summer.

He got out. There was a set of car tracks twenty feet past the booth, footprints going inside.

Pushing the door open, he saw the dangling receiver and grunted. That was all; some slob who couldn't be bothered to hang up. He put it back on its cradle. Be strange if it rang now.

He inspected the booth, seeing nothing of interest, then turned to leave. His eyes went absently to the floor. This was a waste of . . .

He froze, hand on the door, staring at the object by his foot as if it would vanish if he looked away. He bent down slowly and picked it up. It stuck to his glove; adhesive plastic coating. He rose, bumping against the glass, raising the small lozenge to his face. It was a chip, green, featureless, a little larger than a dime. A signal amplifier, if he wasn't mistaken.

"Goddamn," he muttered, and put it in his pocket. He inspected the booth once more, then went quickly to his car and turned it so the headlights shone across the road.

Just a single set of footprints apart from his. He'd messed up the ones going in, but there were plenty more. The car had left clear tracks as well. He was crouched down, smiling fiercely at them, when he heard the crackle of tires and the glare of headlights swept over him.

He swung around, reaching for his pistol. The car was about thirty feet away. A searchlight on top flared and swung toward him. "Hold it right there," a voice said, distorted by amplification. "Get your hands over your head."

Bohlen grimaced but did as he was told. The cruiser sat mutely for a few seconds before the voice came again, its disgusted tone clear over the PA. "Bohlen."

Grinning, Bohlen dropped his arms and took a step toward the cruiser. The PA blared again. "Stand where you are," Nast ordered. "Now get 'em up."

Bohlen stuck his chin out. The searchlight went right into his eyes. He blinked. "Keep your head raised," Nast said.

"You goddamn . . ." Bohlen strode toward the car.

There was a warning wail and a red flash. He froze and looked down at his chest. The dot of a targeting laser glowed ruby-red. "This is your final warning."

"Aw, fuck you, Nast!"

"Approach the car slowly."

Fists clenched, Bohlen stomped to the cruiser. He assumed the laser was tracking him but paid it no attention. The driver's window stayed up, Nast studying him coldly. Finally it slid open. "What are you doing here?"

Jaw working, Bohlen decided not to give him any satisfaction. "Little overtime," he said mildly. He leaned against the hood to force Nast to poke his head out in order to talk. Pulling up his coat sleeve, he checked his watch: nearly eleven-thirty. "How about you? Past your shift, ain't it?"

That one hit: an uncomfortable look crossed Nast's face, followed by a scowl. He repeated, "What are you doing out here?"

Bohlen gestured at the booth. "Odd place for one of those," he said. He glanced at Nast, who continued staring at him wordlessly. He waited a moment, then gave in. "Tire tracks over there that somebody might want to make casts of. Footprints, too—the ones on the left. The others are mine."

"What did you find?"

"We had an anomaly from out here," Bohlen said. He wasn't going to tell Nast about the chip; the cop might demand it as material evidence. "I think one of our friends dropped by."

"One of them," Nast said. "What do you mean?"

Bohlen didn't know what he meant, not really. It was no more than a feeling, and a feeling not even strong enough to call a guess: the buffalo god grumbling in his sleep. But he was almost certain that the characteristics of this tap were different from the bank intrusion. They would need to do an analysis, but . . .

He upgraded it to a guess, then touched his side, where the scar was. It'd be nice if he could live a life not built on guesses. "There's more than one," he said. "There's . . . a few."

Nast snorted. "Well, that changes things."

"Changes what?"

"This no-shoot order of yours, Bohlen. If there was only one, okay. But a whole nest? Be serious."

Nest, Bohlen thought—as if they were hornets. "Doesn't change that at all."

"Bohlen, I'll be frank with you. The boys don't like this, and they won't stand for it. They've got wives and kids at home, and they don't need stupid orders that'll put them at risk, particularly from an outsider. So if you think you're gonna grab a few comphuggers to take back east, think again. We see 'em first, they're gone."

Bohlen leaned back. The snowscape, a dazzling white in the lights of the car, faded to perfect blackness beyond. "Nast," he said, "let me tell you a little story. Key West, last summer. You may have heard about that—big victory, six vicious imps dusted, the Republic heaves a sigh of relief, congratulations all hands. That's how it went, right?"

He swung to face the window. "Well, let me enlighten you. That was a bad op. We went out of control and blew the place straight to hell. We were still firing when the house was half burned down from gas grenades. A combined op—FBI, local cops, and our people.

"And you know what, Nast? They tried to surrender. The imps in that ville—they wanted to give up. You didn't see that in the papers, did you? I had to do a lot of poking around to find out myself. I still don't know how it happened, but it shouldn't have, and it wouldn't have if I'd been there, and it won't happen here."

He paused, expecting a response from Nast. All he got was a slight droop of the cop's eyelids.

Sighing, Bohlen pushed himself away from the car. "It's like the Latinos. Four years ago we're fighting like maniacs, bodies piled high. But when we beat 'em, did we keep on killing 'em? Of course not. It's the same thing with the imps, Nast, same goddamn thing. They aren't a threat anymore. The bad ones are gone, and the rest . . . losers. I've seen them and you haven't. They're wrecks, just hulks of human beings. And if we go on the way we have, hunting them down to the last crazed kid . . . that's not law, Nast, that's vengeance—and it's not good enough."

"Bohlen," Nast said slowly. "You ever actually in combat?"

Bohlen dropped his head. He hadn't convinced this cowboy, not at all. "Yeah." He looked up. "What about it?"

"You remember the niñobombas?"

"The what?"

Nast's eyes grew cold. "The kids, Bohlen, the kids. They'd strap ten kilos of plastique on them and send them across the wire. Eleven, twelve years old. First few times the guys would go out, and the Medis would trigger them. Nothing left. After that we mowed 'em down. One, and another, and another . . . But they never stopped, Bohlen. They kept coming."

Bohlen regarded him in silence. He was getting a chilly feeling that he'd felt only a couple times before, when he'd escorted captive imps to the psychiatric wing at Bethesda: the conviction that the man an arm's length away had strayed so far from the normal human path that a common mental bond no longer existed. He shook it off; this wasn't an imp, this was only a cop who'd seen too much warfighting. He was about to tell Nast to shove his combat memoirs when the cop began speaking again.

"Got a new meat lieutenant in, right before the city campaign, near Coronado." Nast's voice was quiet, no emotion in it, exactly as if he was giving a briefing. "Told us he didn't want any more of that. Had to be a better way. So okay, next day we're doing an area sweep and one pops up. Heads straight for the FNG as if the little bastard knew. We held fire and the niño tackled him, doped up like they were. Louie tried to shake him off and was just about to start yelling when it blew.

"We found a boot," Nast said. "Army issue suede. There was a foot inside."

Nast went silent, his face blank, his eyes squinted as if trying to make out something half-hidden in darkness. Stifling an urge to look over his shoulder, Bohlen said, "Sounds like you had a great war, man."

Nast didn't move, didn't shift his eyes, or give any other sign that he'd heard; he just sat gazing into the night as if expecting a bombrat to come take Bohlen off his hands that minute. Bohlen regarded him a few seconds, then reached over and rapped on the windshield in front of his face. "Hey!"

Without any sign of surprise, Nast swung his gaze to Bohlen. "So that's it," he said mildly. "We see 'em, they're gone. And you—just stay out of the line of fire."

"You're awful eager to kill something, aren't you?"

Nast's lips twitched slightly. "I'm not telling you again."

Slapping his knees, Bohlen stood up. "Okay, Mr. Deppity. It's been a treat jawing with you."

Nast said nothing as Bohlen walked off. But Bohlen got only ten feet before the acquisition system whooped.

He swung around to find the laser focused on his chest once again. He considered going back to the cruiser and wrecking the thing for good—two, three different ways of doing that—but instead opened his coat and took out his ID. He thumbed it and held it up to the beam. There was a low beep, and the laser went off.

Nast inclined his head. "Nice," he said.

"Works every time," Bohlen told him, and went back to his car. As he got in, the PA rumbled. "Bohlen," it said. He looked back. "You're forgetting the dancer. You haven't got all the bad ones yet."

Bohlen shut the door without a reply, not having one ready at the moment. He started up and, successfully combating the urge to sideswipe the cruiser, headed for town. As he drove by, he lowered the window and yelled, "Don't shoot any schoolkids, now."

Nast didn't even turn his head. When Bohlen looked in the mirror, he saw the cruiser just sitting there. It was still in the same spot when he drove out of sight.

Deciding it was necessary to ignore the past half hour, he felt in his pocket for the chip. There was a hacker due in from Frisco. He'd have Delahanty call him and put him on the redeye—they needed the chip analyzed as soon as possible. Beyond that, he had to call Washington and tell them to check the phone lines—whoever had been out here tonight hadn't been calling for a pizza. He wondered which night officer was on duty. He'd have to finesse it, make sure the message got to operations without crossing Jethro's desk . . .

His spirits lifted when he realized there was no reason now to sneak it through; the chip in his pocket put an end to that. He smiled, imagining the look on Harland's face when he heard.

"Got a nest of 'em, Mushmouth," he whispered to himself. He jerked the wheel sharply into the next turn. "A whole nest. Shit."

CHAPTER 14

TELFORD LOST COUNT of the number of times he let the phone ring. It was his third try at reaching Sarah, with no result. No recording, no message, nothing. He thought of tapping, but he didn't dare, not in the middle of town.

There was a rap on the glass behind him. Startled, he turned to see a middle-aged woman regarding him with firm disapproval. He opened the door of the booth and stepped out, smiling mechanically.

Back in the car, he lay his head back and closed his eyes. He should have called yesterday. Even with everything falling apart here, he should have remembered to do that. No telling what was going on there. He hoped she hadn't found the urn. He'd recalled the urn this morning, as he woke up. If there was anything that would send Sarah straight to the bottle, finding Briggs's ashes was it.

At least his head was clear. The pain last night wasn't as bad as he'd feared; nothing like the last time he'd tapped. A few twinges behind the eyes, and a preternatural awareness, much like the clarity that came with exhaustion. No voices yet; no sign of PS.

That was all he had going for him. Naomi wasn't talking; she went upstairs, and he hadn't laid eyes on her since. As for Gene, he didn't get much out of him. Page had evidently told Gene horror stories, filling him with paranoia. Gene said only two things before subsiding into dull, endless cursing: that the Cossacks were operating out of a motel at the edge of town, and that the two Micks were running things.

Telford had found the motel this morning, driving by just as Delahanty came out. He didn't stick around to see more, now knowing what the two Micks meant. Delahanty's partner had to be Ross Bohlen, the one who'd led the raid at Big Sur, who'd tracked the Stoner Group, who'd set up the massacre at Key West. The rest of them were good—they had to be—but Bohlen was in a different class. The Cossack who thought like an imp, who never missed a trick, who could fire over his shoulder blindfolded and hit the only chiphead within five hundred miles.

Most of the stories were just noise. That yarn about him identifying the Stoner punk in a Miami hotel lobby and taking him out with one shot, for instance. Things like that didn't happen. But there was a core of truth to it. Telford remembered how Bohlen had led him on, not that long ago: the quiet voice over the phone, so concerned, so understanding, so sincere—and all the time he'd been working up to Key West. Hafner, Llewellyn, and Chin died there, with three others he'd never met, torn to pieces by federal guns. Telford could easily have been there too. Leslie Chin had asked him to come. But something, perhaps the way Bohlen had vanished the week before, held him back.

He had no idea what rank Bohlen held; nobody knew anything about COSSF hierarchy. But the man must be pretty high up these days, with his record. The fact that he was out here told Telford that the Cossacks knew they had something.

Enough. He had to move, the sooner the better. This afternoon, tonight; after dark would be best. Head north for the Commonwealths, BC maybe, spend a week in Vancouver before deciding where to go next. The Yukon was a possibility. Plenty of territory up there—or across the straits to Siberia. The Kolyma Republic was accepting immigrants.

He started the car, absently rooting around the dashboard for the chip he'd misplaced. Where had he put it? His mind was blank as to those two minutes after the interface last night.

A beep announced that the car had warmed up. He stopped searching and turned to see if the road was clear. The chip was around somewhere, and he had plenty of replacements. Pulling out, he thought of what the cop had said yesterday—someone wanting to bring the imps in rather than the customary slaughter. The idea that there might be an alternative . . . But he couldn't take it seriously. If Bohlen was in charge, there was no hope.

He stopped at a supermarket for supplies. Simple food that didn't take a lot of preparation: bread, fruit, self-heating canned goods. He paid in cash. A check could be traced, and he didn't want to leave a trail of any sort, even with his account as clean as he c~ ˙ . make it.

About a mile west of town he hit a roadblock, with four cars and a truck waiting. He watched as the vigs let two of the cars pass but stopped the truck to check it more thoroughly. Guns, he thought, seeing the rifles they carried. It's all guns these days. Everybody had them now, wherever you went: homes, offices, stores. He had one himself, hidden underneath the dash, a Japanese rocket pistol made entirely of plastic. You could smuggle it anywhere.

The war had changed things. Before, how people would have screamed at a vig roadblock! But it was different now, after all the deaths, the panic, the chaos. This country had taken a beating and it still hadn't recovered.

This country. He smiled sadly to himself. He didn't think of it as his anymore.

At least there was a reason for this particular block. He hadn't paid much attention, but he'd heard about the murder a few days back. Must be unusual, in a town like . . .

A chill struck him. He stared down at the steering wheel,

unable to focus his mind. No, there couldn't be any connection. A coincidence, it had to be a coincidence. There was nothing unusual about murder. Not in a country degraded by war, not with guns as common as credit cards.

But a murder like this—the body mutilated and savaged the way the Stoner Group had been taught to do. And who appears the same day? The last of Stoner's assassins, a man who enjoyed his work . . .

A horn beeped behind him. Telford raised his eyes to see a vig gesturing him on. Putting the car in gear, he drove up and stopped. "ID," the vig said. Telford twisted to get at his wallet while the vig, a bearded man in a plaid jacket, waited impatiently. He had just gotten the wallet out when a voice called from the side of the road.

"Hey, he's okay."

A plump figure in a snowmobile suit was waving at him. "You're from the station? Whatsername's brother-in-law, ahh, Monique, right? Yeah, he's okay."

Waving him past, the vig turned away. Telford nodded at the man by the truck and drove on.

His thoughts were still racing as he neared the station. Talking to Gene again would lead nowhere, but he'd have to try again. And there were the newspapers. Naomi read a lot of them, from all over; not much else to do up here. He hoped she had saved them. Not that they'd help much either; the cops usually withheld the details.

He made the last turn and almost hit the brakes. There, parked under the trees, was a truck, a heavy-duty Toyota with big tires and oversized headlights. He had no time to wonder who it was; the driver came into view, standing over the stump, ax in hand, a pile of split logs at his feet.

Page didn't even look as Telford pulled up. The ax dropped neatly, cutting a log in half. Turning the piece that stood, Page quartered it and tossed the chunks on the pile, as casual as a man being paid by the hour. He'd stripped to his shirt, had left his coat on the truck hood. He wore gloves and heavy boots with the pants bloused into them. Moving with no apparent effort, he picked up another log. He seemed bigger than the last time Telford saw him.

No sense waiting; Page might think that he was afraid. Telford got out and walked toward him, glancing once at the house. There was no sign of anyone watching.

Page set up another log. Telford stopped about six feet away, watching as the ax rose.

"What are you doing here?"

"I'm chopping wood." Page swept the pieces away and reached for another log. "I come around, I see a pile of logs and an ax sitting here for three days, and I figure you've been busy. So I decide to lend a hand to a brother." The ax bit, chips flying into the snow. "Not a big thing, Telford, but us comphuggers got to stick together. Old Kahn always said that, didn't he?"

"Fine," Telford said. "Stack them at the side of the house when you're finished." He started for the lodge.

"You don't like that, Telford?" Page called out. "We can change the subject. How's this? Albert Owens, 501 State Street, Syracuse. Muriel Copland, 13 Twain Court, La Jolla . . ." He went on, reeling off a dozen names and addresses. Telford listened in silence. ". . . oh, yeah, that's right, he took on a new identity when he moved, didn't he? It's Hersey now, isn't it? James Hersey. And of course . . ." He held the ax at arm's length, pointing it at the house. "Naomi Buckner, et al." He smiled. "You like that topic better?"

Telford said nothing.

After a moment Page laughed and bent over for another log. "I don't know what you get out of it, Telford. Maybe you'd care to tell me. Here we have a headful of breakthrough technology, a shot at unlimited power, an opportunity that some would kill for, and you do what? You take care of the losers. You dedicate yourself to the ones who couldn't hack it. Incredible. It's not like they'll give you a Nobel." Page raised the ax. "Sainthood's just not in style.

"And where does it lead?" The ax fell. "Nowhere. Oblivion. You leave trails a chimp could follow, you and your network of burnouts. They call, and you come running . . . One fine day they'll call, and you'll run straight into a wall of bullets. It's a waste, Telford. A waste."

He rested the ax atop the stump and leaned on the handle. "Could happen here," he said, looking around him. "Anytime."

"Why don't you get to the point?"

"The point." Page put another log on the stump. "Is this. You're in trouble. Your little hideaway is blown. I did that. It was in my interest. Now you've got to run for it." The log wobbled a bit, and he shifted it until it sat firmly. "I want to help you. That's in my interest, too."

"I'll take care of myself, thanks."

"So you think." A flash, the thunk of metal biting into wood. "One phone call and this area would be sealed up tight as a drum. Not that I want that, not now anyway, much as you owe me. For now, I'm here to help you solve your problem." He slid his hands up the ax and inspected the head, brushing some chips off the blade.

A wave of sick dread rose in Telford. He looked at the ax, then at the house. He tensed, as if to break into a run, then looked again at Page, who followed his eyes to the ax. A smile appeared, slowly widening. "Christ almighty, what do you take me for—"

"You've already killed one out here," Telford said.

Page's face froze. He stared at Telford, tapping his palm with the ax. Finally he hefted it and split the waiting log.

Telford stepped closer. "Did she need help too?"

Ignoring him, Page grabbed another log and shattered it, no longer just letting the ax drop but putting his shoulders into the swing. "You want to hear how I did her?"

"Don't . . ." Telford began, but Page went on.

"All the way up, she sat and cried. Didn't understand, didn't want to. It got to me. Stopped the car. Told her"—a grunt as the ax flashed. "She could run, I'd let her go. Just sat there crying. I hit her. Knocked her clean on her ass into the snow. I waited a minute—one whole minute, I counted! Then got out. She'd shit herself . . ."

"God damn you."

"Hit her again. Lay there crying. Put on the gloves and laid into her and the blood flew and there was no more crying and I fucking loved it—"

With a cry Telford sprang. Page stepped back, fending him off with the ax. "No, not here, Telford. Not yet . . ."

Telford threw the gloves in his face, leaped for the ax, grabbed it and stepped away. He slipped and nearly went down, and then Page was on him.

There was a split second when Page was wide open, his torso defenseless. But Telford hesitated, and then it was too late.

Something hard and metallic struck his head, and the ax was yanked from his grasp. He lurched away, blinking through watery eyes, pawing the snow for a split log, a rock, anything . . .

He saw that Page was backing off, ax in hand. At the stump he set it down so that the handle jutted up. Putting his booted foot on the ax head, grasping the handle with both hands, Page roared, and the handle snapped with the sound of a gunshot. He flourished it, threw it at Telford. It struck Telford's chest and fell to the snow.

Page kicked the ax head off the stump and bared his teeth at Telford, eyes wide, as if to tear a wound across the very earth. Telford had never seen an expression like it.

The rictus relaxed, and Page lifted an arm to the house. "You want that trash to live, you'll think, my friend, you'll think."

He walked to the truck. Telford became aware that he was muttering curses to himself. He swallowed and let his breath out in a half-sob.

Page got in the truck without so much as glancing back. I could have taken him, Telford thought. I had him, I fucking had him . . .

In a window of the lodge a curtain fell back into place. The truck pulled out. He took a few steps toward the house and stopped. He hesitated only a second before running to his car.

The truck was gone by the time he got moving. Follow him. Find out where he's hiding. Throw his own tactics back at him . . . Telford pulled onto the highway without braking, counting on the lack of traffic. The truck, a half mile down the road, picked up speed. It vanished behind a curve but reappeared a moment later.

He followed for five miles, not pushing too hard, driving just fast enough to keep the truck in sight. He saw with satisfaction that Page accelerated at every curve, trying to lose him. Now he could see how it felt . . .

There was an intersection two miles ahead, well masked by trees—probably the best chance Page would have of shaking him. He slid into the next curve and hit the volts, smiling when he saw the truck reappear a few hundred yards before the crossing.

The car began to skid. Telford steered into it, staying off the brake until the tires got traction, but a glance to the side showed the snow-packed railing coming at him. He downshifted, but was still going fast enough when he hit to be flung against the passenger door.

He shook his head, pushed himself up. The hood was sprung, motor off, but the readouts showed no damage. He could still see the truck; it was heading southwest. He started up and pressed the pedal. The car jerked forward but ground to a halt. Backshifting, he tried to rock it out, but soon gave up.

He switched the car off. The truck was long gone, the surrounding pines dark with afternoon. He got out and looked back at the ice patch that had caught him. The plows around here were programmed just great.

There was a folding shovel in the back, standard equipment for this part of the world. He started shoveling.

He'd been at it five minutes when a rancher in a pickup pulled over. He lowered the window and smiled at Telford. "Stuck, are you?" Telford admitted that he was, and the rancher jovially pulled ahead and reeled out a towline. "You're lucky," he told Telford. "Was gonna use the hover today, but you can't drive them on the roads. Couldn't have pulled you out with that."

While Telford mulled over the logic of this statement, the rancher hooked the front axle and amid jokes about city folk, snow, winter driving, snow, automated plows, snow and more a-comin' they got the car out. Telford offered to pay him, but the rancher told him to pass it on. With a last long look at the intersection, Telford swung around and headed back to the lodge.

When he got there, Naomi was gone.

CHAPTER 15

BOHLEN WAS LOST. The houses were barracks, the streets all alike, the signs, where any existed, worthless.

On top of that, he was whipped and half out of his mind with caffeine—he must have drunk twelve cups of coffee so far today. He'd spent most of the night brainstorming with Delahanty, trying to figure out what the chip meant, the one Bohlen found. Obviously Joe Imp was around, but working with a relatively primitive system, and that didn't make any sense.

There had been no problem with Washington. Gussow was on duty and got through to ops without having to go up the ladder. He made no promises about tomorrow—today, rather—but Bohlen wasn't worried about that.

Wilbur had pulled in at dawn from Frisco, after taking a cab all the way from Billings. Del, already up, got him working on the chip immediately, and Bohlen was expecting word from him when the call from the rookies came.

He turned down another Newtown street, wondering if he'd crashed the car, was in hell, and would be driving around the place forever. The inmates called this Redding, after a Marine colonel who'd done something swell in Honduras during the war. To the locals it was Dipville. To Bohlen it was another goddamn development and Newtown fit just fine.

He'd asked directions from a few people, getting nothing intelligible to the mind of man. He imagined them going home to call the vigs, who would show up, drag him out, and subdue him with rifle butts before asking who he was . . .

He stopped and backed up a few feet. On the next street over sat a car that looked like the rookies' rental, right behind a local cruiser.

Pulling up to the cruiser, he got out. Ling and Navasky were pacing the sidewalk, and a town cop in a rather overelaborate uniform stood near them. On the front porch a woman sat wrapped in a Navajo blanket. She gave Bohlen a nasty look as he came up the walk.

"Hey, Ross . . . ," Ling said excitedly.

"One sec," Bohlen told him, going up the stairs and into the house. He had a good idea of what he'd find, and his first glance told him he was right.

The place was packed with hardware. Monitors, processors, modems, what have you. Heavy military spec radar cable crisscrossed the floor, and he could see two or three surge suppressors from where he stood, each overloaded with plugs. Along the walls were bookshelves crammed with old-style diskettes.

He was about to go back out when he caught sight of something on a table in the living room and went over for a closer look.

"I'll be damned," he muttered. It was a Mac, an early model, maybe thirty years old. All hooked up, with a bulky color monitor on top, and sitting beside it was a *laser printer!*

He reached for the switch but snatched his hand back. He would have felt the same way peering into a garage window and finding a Model T, or seeing a DC-3 flying overhead. He'd have loved to see if the thing still worked, but he knew what hackers were like.

There were footsteps behind him, and Ling called out, "Hey, lady, you can't—"

"This is my house, dammit!" she yelled.

She was about five-foot-five and maybe fifty years old. Her hair was gray and shoulder-length, cut in the dress-for-success fashion of the last century. Her face was round, with a pug nose and receding chin. The blanket, which Ross supposed was worn for purposes of pathos, hid everything else.

Glaring venomously, she approached Bohlen, who guiltily stepped away from the Mac.

"Are you the head fascist?"

"Well, yeah, I guess."

She took a deep breath, then went into a tirade covering the Constitution, the Red Guards, the 60s, how she'd hacked with Barlow, the Fourteenth Amendment, George McCarthy, the investigatory skill of Ling and Navasky, whom she called "Fu Manchu and his number one son," and Richard Nixon, Medrano, and Valley Forge.

". . . like Mao or the Nazis," she wound up, raising her chin.

Bohlen nodded earnestly. "You're right," he said. "You're absolutely right."

Her eyes narrowed. Behind her Ling dropped the smile he was struggling with.

"They're way out of line, ma'am, I agree. I'd chalk it up to inexperience, but that's no excuse. I'll deal with them right now."

He stepped past her and crooked a finger at Ling, who followed him outside, the woman trailing after.

The cop was yawning but perked up the moment they appeared. Gesturing at Navasky, Bohlen went halfway to the street before turning around.

"Now, do either of you two know what a hacker is?"

Ling looked over at Navasky, as if Navasky was the one in charge of this kind of question.

"Do you know what hackers do?"

Ling nodded slightly, while Navasky shrugged.

"Is it possible that this woman could be a imp?"

Navasky gave him a sick look. "Aw, come on, Ross . . ."

"Come on nothing. You think an imp would be sitting around with a houseful of old hardware in plain sight? You think the local branch of the Ancient Society of Programmers wouldn't have noticed anything?"

They were shuffling their feet now. "Uh, we asked her if she picked up any anomalies," Ling said.

"And what did she say?"

"She said no."

"So you brought me down here to ask her again?" Bohlen appealed to the sky. "Listen . . . suppose the ASP, or the Order of Original Hackers, or WEEL, or any of the other boards she's wired into gets together this weekend, and she tells them we gave her a hard time? It so happens that the hackers don't like imps or violators any more than we do, and they've probably scoped out a few things we missed . . ."

"Ross, she's just a nut," Navasky said.

"So you dragged me to this shithole burg to talk to a nut?" He glanced at the house. The woman was standing on the steps, gazing solemnly at him. "She's no nut. Some people like a houseful of cats, some like hardware. She—"

A squeal of brakes. The sheriff's cruiser pulled up with Delahanty in the passenger seat.

Bohlen turned back to the rookies. "And I'll tell you something else. From what I saw, she's got a couple mil in antique hardware and could buy and sell you two a hundred times over."

"What's happening?" Delahanty called out.

Bohlen answered, "Training session."

"They can use it," Delahanty said, nodding benignly. Bohlen threw his hands in the air. "All right, go on," he told the rookies. "You come across a kid using a kindercomp, don't shoot him until you talk to me."

Sullenly they turned away.

"Hey buddy." The cop was coming down the walk. "She's still pissed. Says she's gonna contact your superiors."

"Ah, hell," Bohlen said, visions of disaster crowding his mind.

A complaint on an unauthorized op—he couldn't have that. Sudden inspiration struck, and he walked to the porch. The woman stared down at him, a slight smirk on her face.

"Ma'am, " Bohlen said, "I intend to look into this matter myself, but like you said, you got your rights. So if you have to make a complaint, I'd go right to the top." He paused for effect. Her smirk vanished, replaced by a puzzled look. "I'd advise you to contact Mr. Edward Frisell, COSSF acting director. E-mail address is in the files."

"It's only for the record," she said mildly.

"Right," Bohlen slapped his knee. "For the record. Well, good day to you." He turned back to the street. "Some nice comps you got there," he called over his shoulder.

"They're called 'computers,' officer," she said in a frosty voice.

"Right, yeah, computers."

Hands on his hips, Del frowned as he approached. "Why'd you tell her to buzz Frissy?"

"Think it through. He'll sit on it for a week trying to figure out how to cover his ass. Otherwise, it might go straight to Mushmouth."

Zimmer was standing by the cruiser. Bohlen gave him a little wave, and the cop pushed his hat brim up in reply. "What are you doing with the cowboy?"

"He wanted to come along, and I didn't feel like driving. Been pumping him a bit. Seems that Nast is having old-lady trouble. Better give him some room."

"Six feet," Bohlen muttered.

"Have it your way," Delahanty said. "Ride back with you?"

Bohlen nodded, and Delahanty gestured at the deputy, who got into the cruiser.

"You track the other signal?" Bohlen said as he started the car.

"Yeah. Lu picked it up again this morning, pinned it right down. Turns out to be a retired army officer, one-star. He's writing a book about the Cuban campaign and has a direct line to the War

College archives. What we picked up was him requesting documents."

"That's all."

"Pretty interesting, though. Says he's got evidence that Castro had the bombs made."

"No wonder they didn't work."

"He'll send me a copy when he's finished. You made a wrong turn."

"How did you know that?" Bohlen stopped the car and K-turned. "You hear from Wilbur?"

"Yeah. He's got a prelim. The thing's from Kahn's group."

"You don't say."

"Standard military cybertage chip adapted to their use. No question about it."

"Kinda makes you think, doesn't it?"

Delahanty rolled his head. "Ross, will you cut it out?"

"Well, it couldn't be somebody who just started tapping, could it?"

"I knew you'd start with this BS, I *knew* it. Well, laddie, I don't want to hear it. There ain't no implant underground left. Period. Not a peep since Key West, five months ago. And before that? We spent all last summer just jerking around. It's over, man."

"So who was using that chip? The old biddy back there?"

"One last chiphead is not a goddam army. Face it, Ross—we burned 'em all."

"You agree with the Hillbilly."

"It's not just Cummins, Ross. It's everybody."

"It's Jethro's line, Del."

Raising his arms, Delahanty swung in the seat to face him. "Ross, you're kidding yourself. How many imps you think there were in the first place? Ten thousand? A million? You think the operation was simple? It was brain surgery, kiddo. And the training? How easy could that have been?"

"They used surgical robots. You were at Kahn's place, you saw 'em. Kahn had backing; he could afford anything. As for train-ing—how many did you ever see who really knew what they were doing?"

Delahanty held a hand up, finger and thumb an inch apart. "One piece of proof, Ross. Just one piece."

Bohlen decided to tell him. The promise he'd made to Tap to keep the calls secret was academic now. It had been ever since Key West. And Del ought to know. Bohlen would have told him a long time ago if he hadn't been shot.

He turned to see the big man grinning at him, his eyes twin-kling, the portrait of a man who had proven his case.

Bohlen felt his face redden. Okay, you fat shanty Harp, he thought. If that's how you want to play it. You can read it in my memoirs along with everybody else. He turned his eyes back to the road.

"Ross," Delahanty said amiably.

"What?"

"Slow down. You're gonna miss the exit."

CHAPTER 16

THE HOUSE WAS EMPTY, no sign of either Cora or Naomi. Telford looked in the dressers and closets, but they were all half-full and he couldn't tell if anything had been taken. Downstairs nothing was disturbed. He searched the living room for a note, but there was none.

He ran outside and up the hill to the cabin, but Gene wasn't there. He walked to the edge of the hill.

She might have gone to her aunt's in Fort Collins. They'd discussed it before, as a possible bolthole if things went bad. The old lady knew nothing about COSSF or imps; she thought her niece had carved out a respectable career in government work and believed that Naomi's cover identity was Naomi's boss, a hard woman that no one liked.

But what if Page had taken them? What if he hadn't been alone; what if that movement at the window had been one of his thugs, waiting to see what Telford would do, or waiting for an order from Page? Though it was hard to imagine Page working with anyone.

It was just the kind of thing he'd do: snatch them for some

grotesque reason of his own or no reason at all. Maybe to hold Telford to that mythical deal he'd mentioned.

A surge of nausea hit him when he pictured Page killing the woman. He punched the pine nearest him, cursing himself for not thinking the situation through before making a move. He'd been reacting, just as Page wanted him to.

He stumbled down the slope to the house. He could call the aunt, but she didn't know him and would tell him nothing. He'd have to wait. It wasn't a long drive for Naomi, a day, no more. This time tomorrow he could call and find out if she was there, or maybe she'd call him. Or maybe the Cossacks would roll in and blow his head off and end all his troubles.

In the kitchen he went through the cabinets. Naomi wasn't much for liquor, but he found a fifth of scotch. Throwing ice in a glass, he carried it into the living room along with a bottle of soda. He mixed himself a strong one, gulped it, and poured another. He sat there, awash with defeat. He should have killed Page when he had the chance, taken him out, he could have done it easily . . .

No, he couldn't. Not Jason Telford, friend of all things living, the man in training for sainthood. Not Mahatma Telford . . . But there were plenty who could—and a whole crew of them were in town right now.

It was an idea—but no. Out of the question. It made a kind of slapdash sense—send a killer to catch a killer—but fell apart the minute he thought about it. He didn't know where Page was bunkered down; out in the mountains, that was all. Besides, Page had the women. It would be just like offering them up to the Cossacks. Who wouldn't ask for IDs when they blew their way in.

What had that cop said at the diner? A no-shoot order, put out by someone nameless for reasons unknown. He laughed bitterly and swallowed more scotch. Depending on the local police grapevine, and at second hand. He was at the frayed end of the rope for sure.

But it must mean something. Why would the Cossacks issue such an order at this point? And who? Bohlen? No—not after Key

West. But what did he really know about the man? Was it possible that Bohlen hadn't been in on that operation after all? He'd been in on all the other raids Telford had heard of: Big Sur, Chicago, South Braintree. Whenever the wolf pack caught the blood scent, there was Bohlen, leading the charge.

What had happened at Key West, anyway? No survivors, no eyewitness accounts, just a few newspaper stories weeks later. Perhaps the imps had opened up first: some poor bastard deep in the grip of Pelton's, overcome with terror at being surrounded by the enemy. A hidden gun, a shot from a window. It had happened before. Why not then?

Telford thought back on the film footage that had convinced him to contact Bohlen in the first place. It had been taken at the estate just after the raid and broadcast only once before the government ordered the networks to pull it. He hadn't seen it then; he'd been on the road with Nathan's blanket-wrapped body in the back seat. It wasn't until months later that Telford even heard about it: a salesman in an airport lounge mentioned the film while offering his theory that the imp situation was a lot more than it seemed.

Using a fake government code, Telford ordered the raw footage from a network archive. When it arrived, he let it sit for weeks—the raid was still too close. But finally he decided to take a look, more to put names to faces than anything else.

The film didn't show the raid itself, just five minutes of cops and Cossacks celebrating how well things had gone; they'd taken no casualties. The bright California sun, a bit of wind through the chaparral, a lot of laughing, well-armed men. No shots of them with their feet braced on the chests of the dead. The public wouldn't have liked that.

The vidcam was focused on a knot of state troopers clapping each other on the back when a shout was heard: "Who told you to open on them, you worthless shit?" The camera turned, panning back and forth before zeroing in on a National Guard lifter parked on the grass. Next to it was a statie in camo gear and another guy wearing jeans, jump boots, and an old army shirt with a shoulder holster over it. The guy in jeans was leaning toward the cop, fury in his face. "We needed those people. Where do you get off mowing 'em down?"

The cop muttered something—Telford had never been able to make out what—and started to turn away, but the other guy launched himself at him and knocked him flat on his ass, even though the cop was twice his size.

Then chaos: a rush of uniformed figures, a cluster around the lifter, reinforcements arriving. A big guy in a safari jacket—Delahanty, he'd learned later—followed by the others, Salgado, Ricelli, O'Brien, each peeling away one cop and laying into him. Apparently there had been a lot of unventilated hostility around that day.

The brawl stopped as quickly as it had begun, with the blue-jeaned man being restrained by Delahanty and a statie. Somebody had maced him, and his face was bright red and wet with tears. "Goddamn Nazis," he yelled.

"Yeah, they're bastards, Ross. Now calm down," the big man said as they hauled Bohlen to a car, the camera following every step of the way.

Telford replayed the tape over the next few months, trying to get into Bohlen's head. What particularly fascinated him was the one moment before he'd swung at the cop. The expression on his face—outrage, yes, but something else too. Innocence? Idealism? Telford had never been able to decide.

But he'd thought about it, and when his despair became too great, when his exhaustion was past bearing and he could see nothing but a featureless wall where a future should be, he called Bohlen. The man who had killed a dozen people, who had led the big raids, who had slugged a cop who somehow failed to meet his standards of behavior.

Again Telford asked himself: Would such a man act as an agent of massacre? Would he wade in blood, butcher the helpless, squeal for joy as he uncovered the last hiding place? It was the question of a lifetime, the only one that mattered, the question before which everything else faded.

And again came the answer: No.

He took a sip of his drink. It was watery, tasteless, the ice nearly gone. He lifted a hand to the bottle but let it drop.

Ross Bohlen would be an interesting man to meet. The thought had occurred to him before; that they might get together some time, at a small place that served good booze and cheap food, an unimaginable neutral zone where they could sit and swap stories, old soldiers with their battles long behind them.

He got up and faced the comp. He didn't even know for sure that Bohlen was in town. It was time to find out.

"Somebody called for you," Lu said when Bohlen walked in.

"Who?"

"Didn't say. Said he'd call back. It sounded long distance."

He slipped off his coat and tossed it on the couch. Who the hell could that be? Not Cummins—Lu would have known. His shoes squelched as he stepped across the room. They were in a sorry state, soaked and clotted with clumps of slush. Stamping them on the carpet didn't help, so he hooked them off with his toes and kicked them under the table. They were shot—his best pair, too.

Delahanty was at the coffee machine pouring himself a cup. Bohlen grimaced and turned away. Somebody had put an active map on the wall. He admired it, wondering who. Probably Wilbur. And now Delahanty was leaving, mug in hand. "Del, don't steal those. The motel will charge us . . ."

Smirking, Delahanty shut the door. Bohlen shook his head.

"I wondered where those mugs were going," Lu said.

"He's probably got a dozen in his car."

"They ought to put chips inside to stop people from taking them. They'd save a lot of money that way."

Bohlen made a face. Not a bad idea. "Tell you what, Lu, you make smart mugs, I'll sell 'em, and we can both retire."

175

Lu's laughter rang bell-like across the room.

Stepping to the map, Bohlen inspected the Newtown area. Still a lot of red, but somehow he didn't think there was anything worth the effort. Best to start poking around to the west, in the high country. .

He noticed the amber dot which marked the rookies. One of them must have been carrying a monitor. He imagined them following a household trashbot out to the curb, nodding and tapping their foreheads. As he watched, the dot moved, and the light it left behind went green.

He turned to Lu. "Anything happening?"

Looking up from her screen, she shook her head. "Nothing . . . Oh, I talked to Kelly in Washington. They tracked something up in Jersey. They're all excited about it."

Bohlen grunted. That would be the Staten Island office. As bad as Delahanty's guys, if not worse.

He poked through the newspapers lying on the table, picked up a *Times* and dropped it when he saw it was yesterday's. The only current paper was a rag out of Billings, the *Democrat*, of all things— you'd have thought they'd change the name after those bums packed it in.

"You going out?"

"Taking a break," Bohlen said.

"Why don't you call Madeline?"

"Nah."

"Call her, Ross. She might be worried."

"Nah. The Madwoman's used to it by now."

"Ross, you're terrible. I'd hate to be married to you."

"Well, you're not, so rejoice." Trailing the paper, he went into the bedroom. "I'll call her later."

Plopping on the bed, he peeled off his wet socks and tossed them in the corner, then lay back to look over the paper.

It was mostly yokel bait. The front page featured a picture of a farmer under a Fuller dome, inspecting an indoor winter crop that was yea high. An old woman had written a book people liked. A judge in some village had gotten a parking ticket.

He settled in to read the few stories that could possibly be of interest. The Danube League had signed a friendship pact with Ukraine that the Russians were whining about even though Prague was making soothing noises. The Hawking Telescope on farside had photographed something at the edge of everything that might mean anything. A delegation of Mexican mayors had arrived in Washington to protest a decision to remove occupation troops from their towns. God, what a crazy world: four years ago it's no quarter, and now look . . .

The phone rang. Bohlen reached over, but Lu beat him to it. He lay there, hand poised above the receiver. Lu called out: "Ross, it's for you. Same guy."

He tucked the receiver under his ear. "Hello."

"Bohlen?" The voice was metallic, distorted by distance. He lay frozen for a moment. He sat up. "I'll be goddamned," he said as the paper slid to the floor.

"Don't try to track this. I'll know."

"Same rules, Tap. Same rules." There was no reply, and Bohlen went on. "You drop something lately? I think I might have found it."

A pause. "Maybe."

"So what happened to you?"

"Key West happened."

"You weren't there?"

"You know I wasn't."

"I don't know anything. I wasn't either."

There was a sound of what might have been disgust. Bohlen spoke quickly. "Now wait a sec, Tap. I can prove it."

Silence, but the line stayed open.

"I was flat on my back in a hospital. Somebody shot me. Beth Israel in Essex, August, most of September. Kidney transplant, some lung tissue, accelerated bone treatment."

The line was quiet.

"Tap?" Bohlen said.

"Wait. I'm checking."

Bull, Bohlen thought. You don't have that capability, nobody does.

He waited anyway.

"All right," the voice said finally. "What happened there?"

It was a moment before Bohlen realized he was talking about Key West. "I don't know for sure. Nobody talked much; total clampdown. You want my opinion, they just went wild. Were they your people?"

"They're all my people."

"It wouldn't have happened if I was there, Tap."

"Oh, yeah. Just like it didn't happen everyplace else . . ."

"Hey, we've been through this. You remember what we agreed on last time—we've both seen enough blood." Bohlen paused for a moment. "Now why don't you tell me what's on your mind."

"You've got a murder out where you are."

"That's right. You know the perp?"

"I do."

"One of yours?"

"No."

"I didn't think he was. So what do we do about it?"

"That's what I'm trying to work out . . . Bohlen, I'll be frank with you. I've got a problem with this guy, and you can help me."

Bohlen sat up straighter. "You want me to take him, that's fine," he said, trying to keep the eagerness out of his voice. "Just say the word, and it's done, no questions asked."

"It's not that simple," the voice said wearily.

"Nothing ever is, Tap. Why don't you paint me the picture." Bohlen heard what might have been a sigh. "All right," he said. "Let's do it this way: the guy is gone, PS has got him, he's out of control and a threat to your group." He waited a moment before going on. "He knows enough to crash you. Possibly he's planning to turn you over to us."

He thought of the idiot bank intrusion, and the way the body had been left in full view of the road. "Maybe he even set things up to bring us out here in the first place."

"Bohlen," the voice said, "how do you . . . No, forget it."

I'm losing him, Bohlen thought. I've pushed him too hard. "Tap, hang on, listen . . ." He lowered his voice and spoke as steadily as possible. "Before we go any further, I want you to know: the deal's still open. What we talked about last time."

"I'd like to believe that, Bohlen."

"It'll be just me, Tap. Nobody else."

"I have to think," the voice said slowly.

"Take all the time you want," Bohlen said. An idea occurred to him. "Look, Tap—if this guy's got you under pressure, we can take care of that first. Get him off your back and give you time to think about the other thing."

"Uh-huh. It would give you a chance to crack him, too."

Bohlen rolled his eyes toward the ceiling. "Uhh . . . yeah, you're right. I didn't think of that."

There was a faint chuckle on the line. "Okay. At least I know where to reach you. I'll be in touch, tonight or tomorrow."

"You do that, Tap."

"I will."

"I mean it. Don't run out like you did last time . . ."

"I didn't run out," the voice said coldly.

Bohlen squeezed his eyes shut. "Sorry. I didn't mean that the way it sounded."

"You never change, Bohlen."

A click, followed by the dial tone. Bohlen slapped the receiver against his palm, then got up and walked barefoot into the suite.

Lu looked questioningly at him, but he said nothing and she went back to her screen. He wondered what she was doing. Something crucial, he supposed, something which had to be done, and which was now utterly beside the point.

He padded up to the map. The amber dot moved slowly toward yet another red unknown. Tap hadn't said anything about a search, and he would have noticed. Best to keep the rookies where they were; it wouldn't do to shift them just after he'd called.

Bohlen ran his eyes across the map, wondering where Tap was hiding and how many he had with him.

By God, he could bring it off this time. He really could.

There was a ring behind him. He tensed. Not this soon, it couldn't be . . .

"Oh, hi," Lu said. Bohlen turned, letting his breath out. Lu put her hand over the receiver. "It's Eddie," she whispered.

Bohlen threw his head back and laughed. Eddie, on a voice line—he couldn't wait for clearance.

Winking at Lu, he went to the phone by the couch. "Hello," he said mildly.

"Ross," Eddie squeaked. "What are you doing out there?"

"Eddie!" Bohlen said as he fell back onto the couch. "How's tricks, old man?"

CHAPTER 17

THE STAIRS went on forever. Old, ram-
shackle, the risers worn and splintered, they rose endlessly, story
after story, each landing revealing yet another decrepit flight.

It was dark, cold, and damp—she didn't know how it could
be so damp this high up. At short intervals a harsh wind rose,
cutting through the thin dress which was the only thing she wore.
She was barefoot, and the splintery wood cut at her feet as she
climbed.

She could see only because of the dot of glaring blue-white
light that floated above her. No more than a pinpoint, it remained
at the same distance no matter how fast she moved. The light gave
off no heat, and when she looked behind her, she saw that it cast
no shadows either: the steps below simply vanished as if they had
never been.

There were no doors, no hallways leading from the landings,
no way to get off the stairs. Whenever she stopped, the light flared
blindingly until she began climbing once more.

She was too afraid to try to go back down.

Only a few times had she ever reached the top, the final landing that led into the room. She could never see what awaited her

there, just bare concrete walls and a single chair, but a sense of horror would grip her, and she knew that whatever was inside was something infinitely cold and cruel. Then she would back away, and her foot would not find the step it had just left, and the light would flare, and she would wake up screaming.

Sarah poured herself another glass of vodka and drank it down, trying to forget the dream. She had emerged from it only an hour before, not knowing how long she'd slept.

The room was cold. The broken window had a piece of cardboard taped over it, but that wasn't enough to keep out the chill. She didn't mind the cold—it was nowhere near as cold as that endless stairwell. Nothing could be.

Outside it was getting dark, the sky clear and cloudless, the lights of Essex flashing up into emptiness. On the table four bottles stood, one of them empty and another halfway there. On the floor were bottles of tonic water, only one opened. She was far past the point of tonic water.

She finished the vodka and poured more. It wasn't working as it should, wasn't keeping the dream away. Usually after she drank enough, she'd sleep a night in peace, but not now.

The dream came and went. For months she'd be able to rest with no trouble, but then it would appear again, and for a week or more she would not be able to close her eyes without seeing those stairs, that light, that final horror.

She thought she knew what was in the room: nothing. Absolute emptiness. If she ever stepped in there, ever sat down in that chair, then the light would vanish, the walls close behind her, and she would remain forever, unmoving, unable to wake, in darkness and cold.

The last few times, she had almost entered.

She hugged herself and rocked a little on the couch. The vodka was taking hold. The outlines of the nightmare began to blur.

She had never told Jason about the dream; he wouldn't understand. Oh, he had asked her enough times: what was bothering her, why the booze, how could he help, but that meant nothing.

He was too wrapped up in things, too busy with his crew of wrecks out there. That martyr complex of his—St. Jason the Good running across the country in search of a nice rack to be stretched on. Running off to care for others when he should be here with her.

She began humming, a song that her grandmother used to sing when she was little. A few of the words came back to her:

> Evening comes, I miss you more
> When the dark gloom's round the door.
> Seems just like you ought to be
> There to open it for me.

And he'd left her with no money! She gritted her teeth as she thought about it. He didn't have the guts to tell her he didn't want her to drink, didn't have the guts to tell her anything; just up and gone, with a lousy note left to mark where he'd been.

And that thing in the kitchen, the jar with the gray lumps inside . . . no, don't even think about that.

She poured another glass and put the top back on the bottle, promising herself that that would be the last.

Yesterday—or the day before—she'd tried to put the note back together to see what it said, but the pieces were all over and some of them were missing. She particularly wanted to know if he was mad about the bottle outside the window, if that was the reason he left . . .

She glanced at the phone. The buzzer was still off. Maybe she ought to switch it on again. Or call around to find out where he was. New Orleans or Montana, one of the places he usually went.

She could do that tomorrow. If she didn't call, maybe he would come back sooner.

He had to come back. She thought of what happened at the bank yesterday, when she tapped the automatic teller. The money had come out, but then a red light flashed and an alarm went off. Luckily it had been down in the village and nobody was around.

It didn't matter. They couldn't tell that an imp had done it;

they didn't know. It could have been anybody. But the machine—didn't they all take pictures now?

Tomorrow, she'd think about it tomorrow. Now she needed sleep. She reached for the bottle. No, vodka was no good. There was one thing that would work.

Turning around on the couch, she lifted the cushion beside her and pulled out a box. Opened it, put it on the table. Jason had never found it, even though he'd slept next to it for months. She took out a vial and twisted the cap off. Ordinary pot, but infused with a mild synthetic soporific. It would give her at least a few hours' rest, maybe even a whole night. Her head would be clearer after that and she'd be able to think.

She put a leaf of paper on the tabletop and bent close to tap the vial over it. But there was a knock at the door. She flinched and looked up. Probably Inez, the old woman from the next apartment, who had given Sarah an odd look that morning. She'd probably decided to come over with a casserole or something.

"Yes," Sarah called out, rising from the couch.

"Federal agents. Open up."

She stared at the door. Made a small moan. Stepped back, picking up the bottle and clutching it to her.

"You have five seconds."

She hugged the bottle close and shook her head. "Jason," she whispered.

The door burst open, and there were four men behind it, the one in front holding an EM slammer, the others with drawn guns.

Sarah instinctively raised the bottle, and one of the men fired. The bullet struck her in the head, catapulting her backward over the couch. For a moment her feet jerked spasmodically on the cushions, but then they too disappeared over the couch.

The men ran in, guns pointed. The leader, a tall black man, gestured at the bedroom. "Check in there," he said, going to the couch. He looked down for only a second. "She wasn't armed."

"I didn't know," the other man said. "I just saw her—"

"Forget it, call an ambulance."

"All clear," the agent in the bedroom called out. The black man nodded to no one in particular.

There was a shriek from the hall. A gray-haired woman in a house dress stood in the doorway staring at the splatter of blood on the wall. "Oh my God," she cried, her mouth twisted. "Oh my God."

The lead agent gestured at the agent carrying the slammer, who had already taken the woman's arm. The man who checked the bedroom came out and stopped at the couch. He nudged something with his foot. "A liquor bottle—Jesus."

A siren screamed off in the distance, and an old woman wept behind the building's thin walls.

When Telford awoke, it was completely dark and the room had grown cold. His head was aching from the call to Bohlen. He'd been dreaming, something disturbing and savage, with gunfire and blood.

He looked over at the station comp. The system was still up and the telltales glowed brightly. He thought of what Bohlen told him about the hospital. Perhaps that was what had triggered the dream. He ought to check the story, but it would have to wait; he was in no shape for that now.

He jerked upright. Someone was in the room, just past the table, barely visible in the dim light of the readouts.

He almost cried out, but caught himself. There was a familiarity about the figure: the thinness, the hint of a slouch, the bulky sweater it wore. He leaned forward. "Nathan?"

—Hiya, Jase.

"Hello."

Nathan chuckled. —No panic, no uproar. Calm as the day is long. I chose well when I chose you.

"I knew it was coming. It had to come."

—What's that, Jase? Pelton's? You don't have to worry about that. Not you. PS is just a bit of turbulence. You break through it and you're free.

"Like you did."

—I'm here, aren't I?

"You're not here, Nathan. You're dead."

—You know better than that. Death is a state-change, a virtual fluctuation, that's all. Information doesn't vanish, it assumes a new form. That's inherent in all I've ever said. You could have worked it out for yourself. Didn't I teach you anything?

Telford dropped his head. "Not enough."

There was a small sound, what might have been a sigh. —Did I tell you it would be easy? Nothing is easy, Jase. Do you think it was easy for Australopithecus? How many died on those dry African plains? That's the dialectic, Jase. Yin for Yang. No advance without grief.

The figure had grown darker.

"You've changed your tune."

—I didn't know then what I know now.

"You wanted me to save them."

—You can't save them. Nobody can. They'll fall anyway. Blood and death, that's the driving wheel. And if there's no one to drive the wheel, then we create someone. As we created the opposition here, the Cossacks, as you call them—not the cleverest acronym, by the way. They were needed to push us on, so we brought them into being.

"So all the deaths are necessary."

—The blood of martyrs, Jase. You know, it's odd, how religion mimics evolutionary theory. Small, isolated groups diverging from the common stem, then bursting forth, creating competition, death, transfiguration. You should understand that. You have a religious background, don't you?

"And those who don't change?"

—That's damnation, Jase.

"No," Telford said.

—You hold the key. That's what Pelton's is: the threshold, the edge of the singularity. The refiner's fire. Get through that, and you're home. Into the microworld, Jase. Where we belong . . .

"You're wrong, Nathan. You were wrong then, and you're wrong now . . ."

—You don't think this shabby world of matter is what we were meant for? Of course not. A poor assumption. It's simply not big enough. Its possibilities are too few . . .

"You fucked up, Nathan. The estate, the secrecy. It had to be a conspiracy, didn't it?"

—Down there, in the microworld, that's where we belong. That's where redemption lies. Total unity, total knowledge, total power . . .

"You could have come right out and offered it to them. Somebody would have listened. But we had to sit and scheme like a bunch of kids in a basement."

—All the theories—the TOEs, the GUTs—dead ends, every last one of them, never proven, because it cannot be proven, only perceived . . .

"And look how it turned out, man. Look what you left me. What am I supposed to do? Tell me!"

—And with omniscience will come omnipotence. What you imagine will come to be. Will rise out of virtuality whole and shining and clean. The ground state changed, the realm of probability raised to the highest power. No more dice thrown in the dark, Jase. You'll be in control.

Telford dropped his head. He swallowed deeply, and when he spoke, his voice was tight. "We shall be as gods, huh?"

—All it takes is one, Jase. And you—you're the one.

"You do it, Nathan."

—You're almost there, Jase. Almost home. Forget about these creatures. Briggs, Sarah, this group. Just walk away. You don't need them . . .

Blinking rapidly, Telford looked up. "Fuck you."

—Then you are one of the damned.

"There are no damned!"

A burst of laughter. —Oh but there are, boy. Those consumed in the fire, who cannot meet the test and are cast aside. Those who shall not find glory . . .

Telford rose, squinting into darkness. The figure's face had changed. It was wearing glasses now. But Nathan never needed . . .

He moved closer, saw the black robes, the white hair, the grim, fixed mouth. He knew that face, knew it well: Weber, the mad old priest.

He screamed and reached for the light. The lamp went over, the bulb breaking. The priest began speaking in Latin. Crunching the glass, Telford went to the comp and punched an emergency code. The station lights went on, all of them. He whirled, but the figure had vanished.

The words continued. Telford put his hands over his ears, but the words went on, loud as ever, until they ended in ringing silence.

He searched the house, working his way from room to room. The bedroom, upstairs, all of it brightly lit and empty. He went back down slowly and walked to the window. He could see his reflection, wide-eyed and ashen. The voice still echoed in his head. His lips began to move, translating:

> *Terror, and the pit, and the snare*
> *Are upon you, O inhabitant of the earth!*
> *He who flees at the sound of the terror*
> *Shall fall into the pit;*
> *And he who climbs out of the pit*
> *Shall be caught in the snare . . .*

He stood there a long time, staring out into the night.

CHAPTER 18

PAGE GOT UP before the sun and walked awhile through the dark house.

He had to admit he'd screwed up. Confronting Telford had been wrong; he should have either erased the man or let him be. He'd let his emotions dictate his actions, always a bad move. The temptation had been so great, to confront him, challenge him, take him out . . .

He threw his head back and inhaled deeply. He'd made an error, that was all. No more. Control, that was the key.

Gene Feist had called to tell him that Telford spent time on the phone after he returned to the lodge, talking to whom he didn't know. Could be trouble, but probably not: in the months Page had spent tracking Telford, he'd seen no one capable of aiding him in a situation like this. Telford's people were losers, all of them. He might have a hole card stashed somewhere, but Page doubted it.

Pity about the women. That pinhead had just sat there watching them leave, without finding out where they were going. Page needed somebody in that lodge to draw in the raid when the time came, and he'd counted on the women being there. He couldn't imagine Telford hanging around much longer, but he supposed

Gene would do. He thought of the look that worthless Jew bastard would be wearing when the lifters dropped and he realized that good ol' Page had let him down. Yeah, he liked that idea.

But he should have dusted Telford. Why he hadn't, he didn't know. It just didn't seem the moment for it; Telford hadn't been prepared, hadn't been frightened enough. There had to be time for him to see what was coming, to look it full in the face. Oblivion was good enough for the maggots, but Telford demanded something special.

It would have solved a lot of problems, though. Page nodded to himself. If Cummins didn't show up today, he'd give Telford to the gloves.

Dawn was beginning to show through the curtains. He turned to the mirror, seeing his dim image, bulky and featureless. He smiled at it and walked out of the room.

He made himself a solid breakfast, then showered and dressed. He got out the Skoda to strip and clean it, checking each part visually, not relying on the diagnostics. As he worked, he glanced at the phone. Luke had called last night. He'd reached the state line and was at a motel the other side of the Divide. Evidently a real trucker's paradise: he'd used a phone in the bar, and Page had hardly been able to hear him.

Luke said he'd be in today, but didn't know when. A lot of hard driving ahead, mountain roads in midwinter. Page told him to call if he couldn't make it by noon.

He put the weapon back together. He'd have to think about Luke, too. They'd worked together fine until now, but Luke had been getting erratic lately, almost as if he were a chiphead himself. He liked to party, and as the money piled up, his tastes had grown more exotic: beer turned into Grand Marnier and coke into Jap designer snort. It all took its toll.

Page hadn't enlightened him as to what this was all about. Luke knew even less than Bobby; he thought it was a smash-and-grab hit like the others. How would he take it when he learned there wasn't any cash involved? Page didn't know and didn't care—if he couldn't manage a streeter like Luke, he might as well pack it in.

He clicked the gas cartridge cover onto the gun, picked up the IR sight and opened it to test the circuits. All of them showed green except acquisition, but that was standard for this model; it would be okay when it warmed up. He clipped it onto the rifle, set the gun down, and reached for the gloves.

Turning them over, he pinched the right forefinger, smiling when he felt the material stiffen. It was called reactive polymet, although there wasn't any metal in it. All memory plastic, helical-chain stuff grown in orbit for one market only, the US military, which used it as lightweight armor for vehicles and flak vests. It was supposed to be secret. Page had learned about it while buying a vest from a down-and-out vet. The stuff fascinated him; totally malleable while worn, but harder than steel when struck. He'd thought for a long time before coming up with the glove idea, and ordered them from the manufacturer using a fake military code— three pair for a test program. They hadn't disappointed him.

He pulled them on and clenched his fists, relishing the feel of mastery they gave him. They looked like ordinary gloves—cheap leather, black, no highlights, a standard army gauntlet reaching just above the wrists. Nobody else knew about them. They were his, and his alone.

Flexing the fingers, he lifted them to his face.

A sound outside: a car pulling into the driveway. Without hurrying, Page took off the gloves and stuck them in his belt. Snatching a clip, he snapped it into the Skoda and went at a crouch to the side window.

It was Bobby, alone in the car. Page cursed as he watched him get out and walk haltingly to the house.

Had something gone wrong? Why hadn't the son of a bitch called? Had they pinned him, had Cummins arrived, had they all packed up and left? He'd better have a damn good explanation . . .

Page heard footsteps, then a hesitant voice. "Page?"

He remained silent, fighting the urge to knock Bobby on his ass as soon as he appeared.

The footsteps stopped when Bobby entered and saw him.

"What are you doing here?" Page asked.

"Uh, they were checking me out pretty close, Page. I heard a couple of 'em talking . . ."

"You're lying."

Bobby shuffled his feet. "I want out, Page. I stayed with it two days. You can't slam me for that. I'm through now. I'm leaving. But you owe me money . . ."

Page swung to face him. Dropping his eyes, Bobby stepped back. There was a bulge in his coat pocket—he was packing a gun. That bothered Page not at all; Bobby didn't have the guts to use it. "What happened?" Page said.

"I just want out, Page." Bobby's hands clutched together and twisted. "No hard feelings, huh? But I need cash. Just a grand for the truck, forget about the rest."

Page stepped toward him. "I asked you what *happened!*"

Backing to the wall, Bobby tried to speak, swallowed. "You killed that girl," he said, then clamped his mouth shut, as if to cut himself off. He dropped his head. "Don't tell me you didn't. I know you did. They're all talking about it." Bobby's arms swung out, as if to help him keep his balance. "You didn't have to do that. Pretty girl like her. It don't make no sense . . . What are you doing?"

Page had taken the gloves from his belt and was putting them on. He gazed calmly at Bobby. "You want out?"

"I am out," Bobby shouted. He slid a foot toward the kitchen. "I don't want your money. You can keep your goddamn . . ."

Picking up a chair, Page wrenched it apart with three blows and flung the pieces at Bobby.

They hit the wall—Bobby was running, not into the kitchen but to the front door. Page brought his fist down on the coffee table. "You want out!" he roared as the table collapsed. Bobby yanked on the doorknob, flinching as Page grabbed the smashed tabletop and threw it. The mirror exploded, shards of glass spraying the room.

Page walked to the door and threw his fist. Bobby fell shrieking as the door panel next to his head splintered. He pulled his legs up and covered his head with his hands.

Standing above him, Page smiled as he caught the smell of urine. "Go to the shed," he said quietly.

"No Page don't I'll go back Page don't please Page . . ."

"Go to the shed," Page repeated.

Whimpering, Bobby rolled away and went a short distance on his knees. He got up and backed toward the kitchen, lips quivering. Page turned slowly, his eyes following him.

He stepped to the center of the room and waited. Waited as the shed door creaked open. His smiled widened when Bobby cried out.

He heard footsteps, slow and dragging.

Bobby appeared in the doorway, his mouth slack, his face bloodless. He gestured at the shed. "Who . . ." He closed his eyes and shivered. "I'll go back to town now, Page."

Page stared at him in silence.

"I want to go to town now." Bobby's voice was higher.

The fragments of the mirror reflected Page: motionless, arms hanging loosely.

Bobby's face collapsed. "Page," he sobbed. "Tell me I can go back to town."

Almost imperceptibly Page nodded. Bobby stumbled back into the kitchen. The door slammed a moment later.

Page's lips twitched when he heard the car motor. He walked across the room, clenching and reclenching the gloves.

Three hours later the phone rang. It was Bobby.

CHAPTER 19

WHAT NAST HATED MOST about the DPs was the traffic. It used to be you could get across town in ten minutes, find parking wherever you pleased. Not anymore. The whole valley was turning into a little Tinseltown, the silly bastards clogging the roads from sunup till midnight.

Nast detested it. When he was a kid, you could see wilderness from the roof of city hall. Ironwood had seemed the very edge of civilization then: his family lived in a small house on the west side, right up against the mountains, and he went into the woods often. There'd been wolves in the hills then, down from Canada as people left and the land went back to the wild. He used to shiver, listening to them howl at night, imagining himself back in the frontier days, or even earlier, when only Indian tribes walked those hills.

But that was ended. And he could foresee the day when the whole area would be built up, covered with developments from the plains to the foothills—inhuman warrens of the kind that Dipville was turning into. Nast shook his head, wondering what his dad would have thought. It was a good thing, in a way, that the old boy had died when he had. It would have broken his heart to see Ironwood now. For a man like him, a hunting accident was not a bad way to go.

Nast picked through traffic, hoping he wouldn't come across a fender-bender like the one earlier. There had been some sleet before dawn, forerunner of the front due tonight. The roads were treacherous, just the kind of conditions that the DPs couldn't deal with. Three, four years they'd been here, and still hadn't learned how to drive in snow.

The accident itself had been nothing: an Audi skidded into the rear of a pickup, with no more damage than a smashed headlight and crumpled grille. But you'd have thought the car had been manufactured in orbit the way the driver carried on. Cursing, like they always did, as if being loud would accomplish anything. Sombart, a farmer Nast had known since his teens, was driving the pickup, and was just about to slug the DP when Nast pulled up.

Seeing the uniform, the Audi driver became polite and awful friendly—until Nast ticketed him for excessive speed. He'd been in the movie business, like all of them, and knew everybody. God, Nast wished the Feds would finish rebuilding that ruin on the Coast and get these people out of here.

For a second he thought the DP was going to try to bribe him. He would have loved that; he was in the mood for a good, solid bust. Things at home had gone from bad to worse. He'd been sleeping on the couch for two nights and was about ready to get the papers and file. Either that or . . . damned if he knew. After this morning, anything was possible. He'd asked where his boots were. Just that, one simple fucking question, and she'd gone off. Screaming at the top of her lungs while the kids sat there and watched. And he didn't say a word, not one word. He had to hand it to himself.

True, his boots were right by the door where he'd left them, but still . . .

Something had to break. He couldn't take it, not another week, not another day. He'd have to call a lawyer, get the papers. That might shake her enough to make her pull her socks up. If not, it wouldn't be his problem anymore.

But the kids—what about them? As he was leaving, Lydia came out of the kitchen dressed in her little school outfit, plaid skirt and white blouse. He spoke to her, called her Mite, their private nickname. She hadn't answered, just stared blankly ahead and ran up the stairs.

That really hurt. Lydia was his favorite. Oh, Laura was a sweetheart—a charmer, that one. But Lydia was the eldest, his first child, born just before he'd volunteered for Mexico. The one he'd thought of as he fought his way down that endless chain of worthless peaks. Two photos had gotten him through the war—one of Diane in a bathing suit and another of Lydia fresh from the hospital, face red and mouth open wide. He studied them, late nights at fire bases and villes where the temp nearly cracked 100 even at midnight, thinking of how it would be when he got back. How they'd go here, do this, see the other, the three of them, himself, Diane, and Lydia. And true, they'd done a lot of it, but there didn't seem to be time to do everything he had planned. There wasn't time for anything anymore.

He tried to recall when they last went somewhere together. Not last summer; Diane had taken the kids to her sister's for a couple weeks, but he hadn't been able to go along—hadn't tried, actually. And before that . . .

He couldn't remember. He really could not recall when he'd last done something with his children.

Nast reached the end of the circuit and turned back to town. A familiar truck in the other lane beeped at him—old Sombart, on his way home. Nast raised a hand and drove on.

Sombart had asked about the murder. Just curious, not pushy or nasty, but Nast was sick of hearing it. You'd think that nobody had ever been murdered in Ironwood, the way people were acting.

Not that he'd been able to do much with the case. No suspects, no leads, a brick wall. The only thing he had was the tire tracks

Bohlen had found, and he was convinced they were bullshit. The little prick hadn't even shown up for the casts.

Nast snickered to himself. At least he'd put the bastard in his place. He'd looked real tough back there, waving his little card in front of him. Never heard of a bombrat before—some veteran. Bohlen was no hard guy. He didn't know what hard was. Nobody did . . .

There was a hum overhead. Nast looked up but could see nothing. Pulling to the shoulder, he lowered the window and stuck his head out. He saw it then: a lifter, a big one, directly above him. He could almost feel the heat of the exhaust. Not military—it was painted blue, with a civilian registration number on the tail. As it flew toward town, he realized it was making a landing. He smiled, closed the window, and sped down the road. Flying below legal limits, unsafe operation, landing without a permit . . .

It seemed he was going to get his bust after all.

Yawning, Bohlen stared at the TV screen. Over the hill, he thought. And at my age, too. What a shame.

He'd spent half the night waiting for Tap to call, drinking coffee and smoking Lu's cigarettes, convinced that the moment he put his head down, the phone would ring. He finally drifted off, awakening to dawn seeping through the windows.

He was feeling it now. Groggy, flaked-out, his stomach acid from too much coffee. He'd moped around until the others left, and spent the morning by the phone, ready to lunge for it.

He forced himself to pay attention to the tube, afraid he'd fall asleep otherwise. A talk show was on, featuring one of the Kennedy brigade, which he hadn't quite caught—Bobby Jr. or Joe Jr. or Jack Jr., one of the juniors. They were talking about *The Bridge at the Vineyard,* a miniseries that had been on all week, about a peccadillo of Old Teddy's wild-man youth. Car crash, a woman killed, a cover-up, typical mid-twentieth political sleaze.

"My uncle was a foine, foine man," Junior was saying to the host in response to a long, detailed question. She turned to the camera with a bored expression. "We'll be back with Congressman Kennedy right after this message," and the screen switched to a commercial about a resort in Chilean Antarctica.

Bohlen got up and shuffled to the coffeepot. "Foine, foine," he muttered. What was left of the donuts lay next to the pot, a miserable ruin. He sighed as he peeled off a jelly donut with half the filling squeezed out.

Chewing desultorily, he went to the window. The sky was a flat deck of cloud to the horizon, the light dim and cheerless. He shivered. They were predicting snow tonight, a foot or more.

He wished he could tell somebody about the call. It was preying on him—doubts as to how he'd handled it, what he should do if Tap called back, what he should do if he didn't. He needed a smart and sympathetic ear; the question was who. Delahanty was the obvious choice, but Bohlen was afraid he'd go howling off with all kinds of ambush schemes. Besides, he'd be pissed that he hadn't been told in the first place. The rookies weren't worth the oil to fry them in. Which left Lu. She'd keep her mouth shut, was as discreet as they came. She hadn't even asked him why he was hanging around all morning.

The door opened. He turned, ready to speak, but it wasn't Lu. Instead Delahanty walked in, giving Bohlen a sly look, as if he'd figured out everything.

"Not much happening," he called out.

May as well get it over with, Bohlen thought. Fill him in, ask his opinion . . .

Then he heard a buzzing outside, a lifter, a big one at low altitude. He tried to ignore it, but the sound grew louder. He went to the window.

"You know," Delahanty was saying, "I think Redding is a waste of time. I told the guys to drop it and meet us back here . . . What the hell's that?"

Bohlen shrugged and went on searching the sky. Suddenly the aircraft came into sight: a big Boeing passenger model, flying parallel to Main.

"He's awful low," Del said, also at the window.

As if the lifter had heard him, it dipped lower and swung toward the motel. "Uh-oh," Bohlen said.

The lifter disappeared, but the noise increased until it was overhead. Bohlen saw traffic slowing on the street. The tone of the engines changed and grew even louder. Delahanty said something that ended with "bringing her in!" Caught by the lifter's exhaust, a veil of snow swept across the sidewalk. Then the roar ceased, replaced by the dying whine of turbines.

Bohlen turned to Delahanty. "Oh, boy," he said.

"Oh boy is right." Delahanty grinned, pointing at the sidewalk. Below, three men were walking to the entrance, two burly types flanking a stiff, well-dressed figure. "So that's what you were waiting for." He took a gulp from his mug, choked on the coffee. "Gawd," he said, wiping his mouth. "I never thought he'd show up himself. Ain't he supposed to be giving a speech someplace?"

There was a knock before Bohlen could answer. Delahanty opened the door. "How you doing?" he said jovially. "Come on in."

The doorway filled with a heavy figure in a black coat and a fur hat. Bohlen had seen him around: one of Jethro's goons, Morello or something. The man stepped in, examining the room as if expecting a squad of heavily armed Medranistas. The hat made him look like something out of a Chinese horse opera.

". . . never expected to see you here," Del was saying.

Cummins appeared, draped in a coat that must have set him back a grand, his hair slicked back perfectly, with gray patches at the temples. "That makes two of us, Floyd," he said, shaking Delahanty's hand. He gave Bohlen an odd look, then called to the hallway. "You may as well go back down to the vehicle, Al."

Delahanty closed the door. "Well," Cummins said, glancing at one and then the other. "The two Micks together again. It warms the heart."

Who you calling a Mick, Bohlen thought.

Slapping his gloves together, Cummins went to the table.

Morello sat on the couch with the air of a man witnessing something of absolutely no importance. "Ross," Cummins said without looking at him. "Running ahead of the pack again, as ever."

"Well, Harland," Bohlen said, "you see something needs doing, you go and do it. I mean, shit . . ."

"We've got a pretty solid trail here," Delahanty said hastily. "Some class-A evidence."

"So I was told," Cummins said. "Well, let's see it."

Bohlen frowned. By this time Cummins should have been ranting about hierarchical structures and the chain of command, like John C. Calhoun condemning the slaveholders. Something was wrong.

"Ross, you know where that chip is?" Del said, his hands full of printouts.

"Yeah, I got it." He went to his case and took out the evidence bag. So Jethro was preparing to examine the chip. Who was he kidding? His background was theory—he wouldn't know a piece of hardware if it showed up in his grits.

Delahanty was now laying some printouts in front of Cummins, who had sat down at the table. Walking over, Bohlen handed him the bag. Cummins practically grabbed it away from him. He made as if to set it aside, but then opened it and tried to shake the chip out. It stayed where it was, stuck to the plastic. He fished for it with two fingers, but it got away and bounced to the floor.

"I'll get it," Bohlen said as he stooped over. He snagged the chip, feeling it cling to his fingers, then rose slowly and presented it to Cummins, making sure their hands touched as he did. He suppressed the impulse to wipe his fingers on his pants. Cummins's skin was soaking wet. Not just clammy or damp, but locker-room sweaty. In the mountains, in February.

It seemed Harland had something on his mind. Bohlen eyed him as he turned the chip over, noted a slight tremor in his hands. What the hell did he have to be nervous about?

"Is this a standard device?" Cummins asked in a loud voice.

"It's an old one," Bohlen replied.

"Characteristic of the Kahn Group," Delahanty said. "Interface booster. Probably to make up for a design failure, but we don't know for sure. Haven't seen one for a while."

"The Kahn Group, eh?" Cummins said, putting the chip down. Delahanty started going over the hard copy. Bohlen didn't pay any attention, didn't respond when he tried to prompt him. Finally Delahanty finished, and Cummins nodded. "All right," he said. "It seems you boys have something here. Now I believe you may need some backup . . ."

"Oh, I don't know—" Delahanty began, but Bohlen cut him off.

"No, Harland may be right, Del. After all, there is something strange about all this."

"Strange?" Cummins stiffened and turned his head so that he was looking not at Bohlen but past him. "How is that, Ross?"

Bohlen sat on the table and leaned toward Cummins. "Hard to say, actually. Just a feeling you get when you've had a few ops under your belt. That halfwit intrusion, the chip, the dead woman—this isn't following any pattern I'm familiar with." He paused for a moment. "I think we have something new here."

"New?" Delahanty said. "What—"

Bohlen raised a hand. "Let's run the program, all right? This may be bigger than we think. The intrusion characteristics are completely different, implying two or more imps. You don't find two imps tapping in a single area, not these days."

Delahanty was staring at him, head cocked to one side, while Cummins sat unmoving.

"So let's consider the alternatives. It could be a new outfit that doesn't know the ropes. It could be they want to hit somebody, pay back for Key West . . ."

"Ross," Delahanty said. "Will you cut it out? How do you get from Key West to here?"

"Situational awareness," Bohlen said solemnly.

"Aw, get the . . ." Delahanty waved a hand at him, but Bohlen was watching Cummins, who had seemed to flinch just now. "I'm only speculating, Del. Suggesting possibilities."

"I'd like to see you back it up, partner."

"Suppose I do that, Floyd?"

Stiffening, Cummins looked squarely at him for the first time. For only an instant before turning away, but in that instant Bohlen saw something in his eyes he'd never seen there before: fear.

"Now, Key West," Bohlen went on, addressing Cummins, who was fiddling with the printouts. "Let's talk about that. All due respect, Harland, but that was a botch op. From what I hear . . ."

There was a loud rapping at the door, and a voice called out. "Hey, Chief, you better get down here."

Morello opened the door to reveal the other guard. Cummins rose and walked over, a bit too quickly. The guard mumbled something. Bohlen heard only snatches: "Bust him . . . local cop . . . cowboy hat . . ."

Without a word Cummins left, followed by Morello. Throwing Delahanty a puzzled glance, Bohlen followed.

From the lobby he heard a faint high-pitched voice outside, answered by gruff commands. Catching the glass door before it shut, he went out, with Delahanty right behind him.

". . . glad you showed up. I don't need this thing in my lot."

It was the motel manager, dressed in a sport coat and hunched against the cold. Bohlen couldn't see who he was talking to until he reached the corner and the lifter came into view. It was smack in the middle of the lot, blocking the entrance completely.

A man in a suede jacket braced himself awkwardly against the lifter's side, hands flat on the metal and legs spread. Nast was crouched down, frisking him.

"I'm telling you, it's government business. I was ordered to land here," the jacketed man was whining.

"Shut up," Nast said as he finished his search and pulled out a pair of cuffs. He was clapping them on the pilot's wrists when Cummins stepped up to him.

"Officer," he said. "I'm in charge here. I believe I can explain . . ."

"You ordered this aircraft to land?" Nast said, jerking the pilot upright.

"Yes, I did, but—"

"Okay, you too. Up against the side." He grabbed Cummins by the arm and half-flung him at the lifter. "Get 'em up."

Morello strode forward. "Hey, look here, pal . . ."

With a smooth motion Nast drew his pistol. "And you," he said, gesturing with the barrel. Morello goggled at him, then hopped toward the lifter.

Nast glanced at the rest of them. The other bodyguard was standing behind the planters that lined the lot, trying to appear aloof. Nast's eyes lit on him for only a moment before going on to Bohlen. "You got anything to say, Bohlen?"

"Not a thing," Bohlen said, making no attempt to wipe the smile off his face. He shivered slightly as the wind cut through his shirt. Beside him Delahanty muttered, "Holy shit."

Still holding his revolver, Nast turned to frisk Cummins. He was running his hands over Cummins's chest when he paused and pulled out a small automatic. "What's this?" he said.

"Officer," Cummins said in a strained voice. "If you'll look in the wallet in my jacket pocket, you will find an ID showing that I am a government security official. May I . . ."

Nast stepped back. "Okay," he said. "Slowly, two fingers only."

Cummins reached into his coat and handed the wallet to Nast.

There was a screech of brakes. A cruiser appeared, Zimmer poking his head out. "Hey, Johnny," he called. "What's going on?"

"What's it look like?" Nast growled, opening the wallet. He pulled out a blank ID. "Another one," he muttered.

Most of the motel staff was out on the sidewalk, along with quite a few of the guests. As Bohlen watched, a short, flashily dressed man pushed through to study Cummins, as if he were going to write a report on him.

Good, Bohlen thought. There should be an audience; events like this demanded no less. Too bad whatsisname the reporter wasn't around.

Cummins thumbed his ID so Nast could read it.

After looking it over, Nast handed it back and pointed at Morello. "Is that one of yours?"

"That's right," Cummins said.

"Okay, hardass, you can stand down."

Dropping his arms, Morello stepped back with a sneer. Another car pulled up. Bohlen didn't turn until he heard a voice say, "Hey, it's the director!"

Ling and Navasky. Better and better.

Stuffing his wallet into his coat, Cummins glared at the crowd, eyes stopping at Bohlen. "I can see you've established excellent rapport with local law enforcement, Ross." Turning to Nast, he forced a smile and said, "Now, if I can have my sidearm returned, we'll be on our way."

Nast gave him a look of surprise. "Oh? Are you licensed to operate this class of lifting body? Then you're not going anywhere, are you? Your pilot's busted."

Cummins reddened, glared at Bohlen. "Ross, do you know this man? Then say something, dammit."

"Uhh, Nast?" Bohlen began, scratching the side of his head. "How about letting it slide this one time . . . No, huh?" He looked at Cummins and shrugged.

The manager walked up to Nast. "Johnny, you can't leave this thing here."

Taking him by the arm, Nast stepped aside, and Zimmer followed to give advice. Cummins stood where he was, back straight. Morello inched over and mumbled something, but received no answer.

Feeling a nudge, Bohlen turned to Delahanty, who gestured at Cummins. "He's gonna tear you a new asshole."

Bohlen smiled. "We'll see."

The huddle broke up, and Nast went to the pilot. "This is your lucky day, pal," he said, taking the magkey from his belt and pressing it against the cuffs. "But you've got citations coming, so let's see your papers."

The crowd dispersed, prompted indoors by the cold. Cummins turned to Morello and spoke to him in a low voice. With a grimace at Bohlen, Delahanty went over to join them.

Bohlen noticed the rookies standing behind him. "What the hell happened?" Navasky said. Bohlen explained it to them, keeping his face straight.

"Does this aircraft have a transponder?" Nast called out. He was leaning in the cockpit door, tapping on a ticket unit. "What the hell's the number?"

Delahanty lumbered back. Behind him, Cummins was climbing into the lifter while Morello watched bleakly. "He's leaving," Del said.

"I wouldn't wonder."

Delahanty gave Bohlen a curious look. "He told Morello to hang around, keep an eye on things."

"Uh-huh."

The cockpit door slammed shut. "Hey," the other bodyguard cried as he ran to the closing passenger door.

"Better get around the corner," Bohlen said as the turbines began to whine.

They went inside to find Nast being thanked by the manager. Nast caught sight of Bohlen. "You know," he said, speaking loudly over the roar of the lifter. "I don't think you'd have minded at all if I took them in."

"Law's the law, Nast," Bohlen told him. Nast gave him a puzzled look and turned back to the manager.

"Hey, where you get something to eat around here?" It was Morello.

"Restaurant," Bohlen told him. "Down the hall," and watched with satisfaction as the man went off with a sneer.

Bohlen took the stairs two at time, getting to the suite just as Delahanty and the rookies opened the door. "Where's he headed?" he asked.

"Denver. Something about the office there."

"I'll bet." Bohlen rubbed his hands; it had been freezing outside.

"Ross," Delahanty said, unbuttoning his coat. "That Key West song and dance—what was that all about?"

Bohlen went to the window, to look for the lifter. It wasn't in sight. "You see him, Del? You see the way he acted? Weird. Just plain weird."

"So Cummins is acting weird. So what? Dogs chase cats, and cats eat mice. You want to hear weird? He came out to Frisco last fall, and you know what he did?"

Ordinarily Bohlen would have been interested in a good Hillbilly story, but not now. He paced, not listening, trying to think.

". . . so he wants this whole pile of reports, going back two-three years."

The way the man walked in virtually on tiptoe. The way he'd sat there, not paying attention, nervous as hell . . .

". . . and then he spends five hours going through 'em with two of his pet goons . . ."

And that look he gave Bohlen. Terror, he was sure of it. As if Cummins had expected him to . . . to do what? Slap cuffs on him and drag him by his feet down the stairs into the middle of the street while the mob cheered and kids threw iceballs? "Reports?" He turned to Del. "What was that again?"

In a monotone, Delahanty repeated himself. Bohlen stared at him. "What did he do with them?"

Delahanty shrugged. "Gave 'em back."

"All of them?"

Delahanty nodded.

Ross leaned across the table. "The Ricelli stuff, too?" His voice sounded loud even to himself.

Blinking, Del held up his hands. "Now wait a minute, Ross . . ."

Ignoring him, Bohlen swung around and sat on the table again. The rookies regarded him with interest. "Where's he going after Denver?"

Behind him Delahanty said, "Who knows? Back to Washington."

"When? How?"

"Tonight. Commercial flight, I guess. Why?"

Bohlen glanced around the room. "Where's Lu?"

"Lu's sacked out. Leave her alone. She's beat."

"Then you do it, Ling." Bohlen gestured at him. "Find out where Cummins is headed and when."

"How do I do that?" Ling asked.

"Access the FAA, that's what they're there for." My God, what were they hiring these days?

Ling got up and went to the comp. "What do I ask for?"

Oh, Jesus. "Flight information!" Bohlen yelled. "Passenger lists! Reservations!" Another minute, and he'd do it himself.

Ling sat down and started keying. Bohlen went to the bedroom and plopped down on the mattress, half-expecting Del to come in and resume his interrogation, but he supposed Del was too exasperated.

He ran it all through his mind, hardly able to grasp what it meant. If one iota of what he suspected was true, it would explain a lot: Cummins's half-assed policies, the third phase that never seemed to get off the ground, the way that all the ops began coming up empty-handed the past year, Key West, Ricelli . . .

He felt a twinge beneath his ribs. Even Loisaida.

Pulling the Colt out of its holster, he clicked the cylinder open and ran his fingers over the shells, as if to make sure they were really there. "Hey," he called out. It emerged as a croak, and he cleared his throat. "Don't let that idiot Morello know I said one word about the Hillbilly. Nothing, you hear?"

There was a mutter from the other room. "What?"

"I said, textbook paranoia, Ross," Del yelled back. "You're a sick man."

Bohlen smiled to himself, then slapped the revolver shut and slipped it back into the holster. Turning to the phone, he stared at it, as if willing it to ring.

CHAPTER 20

TELFORD SPENT the rest of the night in a stuporous half-sleep. He'd found some tranquilizers in the bathroom and took a few, hoping they'd knock him out. He had no dreams, but woke several times, lunging up in panic to look around the dark room.

It was late morning before he got up. He moved carefully, almost relishing the hazy barrier the drug had erected against the day.

His eyes fell on the spot where the ghosts had stood, and he looked away quickly, unable to force back a feeling of dread. A mantra rose up from childhood: Don't think about it, and it won't happen. It won't happen if you just don't think about it . . .

He'd feel better when he had some food. He couldn't remember the last time he'd eaten. Going to the kitchen, he splashed water on his face and opened the refrigerator.

He stepped back in horror, then realized that what he saw was no hallucination. A sound escaped from his throat. He was laughing uncontrollably.

On the center rack stood a bird: a good-sized, nondescript brown thing that leaned forward almost eagerly on its stand. Its wings were half unfurled, its beak slightly open. Stuck in the beak was a folded piece of paper.

He pulled the paper out, collapsed into a chair, unfolded the note, and read it.

Dear Jason
    Im writing this so you wont be woried about where we went. Dont worry about us we went to Naomis aunts house. I kno you are in trouble I saw Page try to hit you Naomi says its better if were not here so you dont have to worry about us. I think Naomi is mad I am not mad come to Naomis aunts house in colo when you are out of trouble
Love
Cora

He laughed again, but softly. This changed everything. He was free, nothing held him here now. Everyone under his protection was out of the line of fire and safe, no thanks to him.

He'd head to Billings and take the first flight to Denver. Talk to Naomi—he'd call her from the airport—make sure that everything was online there, and then . . .

Then he'd call Bohlen and set something up. Anything he wanted, as long as it wasn't completely insane. Sit across a table from him, get it over with. Meet him face-to-face for the first time. That was where the problem lay, he could see it now. He'd never met the man, couldn't really judge him. There was so little you could tell from a voice line.

He'd better leave now, before Page pulled in or something else happened. His head was still fuzzy; he wondered if he'd be able to drive. Better get something to eat.

Opening the fridge again, he smiled down at the bird and pulled out eggs, cheese, a gallon of milk. He scrambled the eggs and stuffed himself with them, drinking three cups of coffee in the process, then went to the bathroom to wash up.

After that, he felt as good as possible under the circumstances.

He went to the comp to enter a command that would crash the system if the hardware was touched without the password. It would also blow out the lights, waste the housekeeping systems, and wreck the plumbing, all the while warning the intruders that worse was coming if they didn't clear the place in ten seconds. The program was hardwired on a chip attached to the memory board and not susceptible to any manipulation he knew of.

There was another program that would burn the place to the ground, but that was a bit drastic at this point. He could trigger it by remote if he had to.

At the keyboard he hesitated and then selected Word. The keying took only a minute, which seemed short for something so important. When he finished, he studied the screen. All those names and addresses, never before committed to print. He hesitated, then pressed for hardcopy. Taking the sheet, he entered the deadfall command.

He picked up his coat and looked the place over. Fingerprints, handwriting, personal belongings—he ought to see to all that, but it would take too much time. If things crashed with Bohlen, he'd torch the place immediately.

He shrugged his coat on and paused, feeling a slight touch of sadness. This room, the kitchen, the stairs beyond. He was leaving it behind. Whatever happened from here on in, he'd never see it as he did now. It had been a good place, the best of places, a lifeboat that had gotten them through hard times.

His gloves were on the kitchen counter. He picked them up and went to the door. There was nothing else he needed.

Outside, he walked to the car, but then turned to the trees. Cora's note had said nothing about Gene. He hesitated, holding the car door handle, before going to the hill. He was halfway up the path when Gene stepped out from behind a tree. "Where you think you're going, Telford?"

Hands on his belt, Gene stood with hip thrust out to display the pistol better. "You're cutting out," he said. "You're leaving. I thought you'd do that."

"Why don't you come along?"

A spasm of contempt crossed Gene's face, and he rested a hand on the gun butt. "I don't think so," he said. "And I don't think you're going anywhere either. I think you'll wait until Page gets here."

"To hell with Page," Telford said mildly.

"You get your ass back inside."

"No, Gene, I won't."

"No?" Gene drew the pistol and waved it. "What about this, huh? What about this?"

"You won't use that on me."

The barrel dropped to Telford. Gene glared over it, trying to stare Telford down. But after a few seconds his eyes fell.

Telford waited until the pistol lowered as well before looking away himself. Christ, that a man should be reduced to this. He turned back to see Gene grasping the gun with both hands, as if to force it to obey him. "Hang it up, Gene," he said gently. "It's not going to work."

When Gene spoke, there was a catch in his voice. "You're cutting out. I knew it." And he walked off.

Telford opened his mouth to call him back. I should follow him, he thought. Try to talk to him, get him out of here. He doesn't have a chance if he stays.

He stood awhile, and went back down to the car. As he pulled out, he thought he saw movement among the trees. "Good luck, kid," he whispered as the lodge vanished from sight.

His head was clear as he approached Billings. He was tired, but no worse than that. A sign told him he was ten miles from the airport. Another hour at most, and he'd be gone.

He tried not to think of Gene as he drove. He felt sick about it; he'd never abandoned anybody before. But then nobody had ever turned on him, either.

There was nothing he could have done to make it come out differently. The cards had been stacked against him from the first, and he hadn't even known that a game was being played. Maybe he'd be able to pull Gene out yet, once he talked to Bohlen.

He still didn't know what Page was up to. But what other target could Page have but Bohlen? There was nothing else in Ironwood he could possibly want. Bohlen had crossed him somewhere along the line, and that vindictive maniac was out to settle up; it was the only conceivable explanation.

As for how Page planned to bring it off—Telford had the uncomfortable feeling that he was to have been bait.

He couldn't lose Bohlen now, not after what had happened last night. He didn't know how much time he had left, and if he blew it, the others—the helpless remnant of Nathan's dream—would have no one to stand between them and the abyss.

He'd call Bohlen from the terminal as soon as he got the tickets. Little to tell him—he could kick himself for not getting the number of Page's truck. But for Bohlen a description and make would probably be enough.

He chuckled deep in his throat. Jason Telford, helping a Cossack. What an irony that was! But life was full of ironies; if he had learned anything, he had learned that.

The airport exit was directly ahead. He cut across the slow lane, and a semi coming up fast braked and beeped at him. Telford raised his hand, a telegraphed shrug, and turned off the highway.

He parked the car and walked to the terminal. The dash readout, picking up the airport signal, told him he had half an hour until the next flight to Denver. There was no line at the counter; he bought a one-way, paying cash.

It seemed that wherever you went, they were working on the terminal. Half the waiting room was roped off, the construction crew wandering around as if they had no idea what they were there for. All the phones in the open section were in use. There were a lot more in the work area, but trying to use one of them would only get him a quick introduction to airport security.

He went to the bar, hoping to find a phone there, but no luck. He stopped at the entrance. In all the times he'd come through

Billings, he'd never so much as glanced inside. The décor was mock-Western: plastic guns, fake-looking deer heads, and sacks marked GOLD. He was about to leave when he caught sight of the huge TV screen at the end of the bar.

It was displaying a map of New Jersey with a star in the northeast corner a short distance above the bite of Raritan Bay. The star was marked South Orange.

He moved closer, to hear what was being said, but the map was replaced by the announcer talking about a storm in the Pacific Northwest.

Stepping to the bar, he signaled the bartender, who drifted casually over. "What can I do you for?"

Telford pointed to the screen. "Can you replay that last bit?"

The bartender blinked at him. An impressive set of muttonchops covered most of his face, and he was wearing a frontier shirt with silver buttons across the chest—probably the bar's uniform. "Well, I could do that for a customer."

"Okay, give me a beer."

"Bearhead?"

Telford stared at him.

"We've got Bearhead on tap," the bartender explained. "Only place in the area . . ."

"Yeah, Bearhead," Telford said.

The bartender drew him a glass and slid it over with a flourish. "Wouldn't make you buy myself," he said. "But the management, you know?"

Telford forced a smile. "Right."

"What part you say you wanted?" The bartender called out, going to the controls.

"New Jersey."

"Okay." The stocks were being quoted now, and there were groans from watching businessmen as the screen shimmered then coalesced once more.

". . . according to a government spokesman, the Quebecois

people demand no such changes in fishing rights . . ." He'd gone back too far. Telford took a swallow to ease the dryness in his throat.

The map reappeared behind the anchor's head. "And in New Jersey today, there is still no official word on the shooting that occurred in South Orange, a slumburb of Essex. CNN has verified, however, that the law enforcement agency involved was the Computer Subversion Strike Force, popularly known as COSSF."

The map was replaced by a locale shot. Telford stared, not believing, not allowing himself to believe. A group of brick buildings, old and stained, and beyond them a small, badly damaged house with a sign hanging askew.

The meaningless words went on: ". . . shooting victim is in critical condition at Beth Israel hospital in Essex . . . In Washington, COSSF director Harland Cummins, who last year told Congress that the implant threat had been removed, is unavailable for comment . . ."

There were sounds behind him as he lurched out. Just as he reached the phone bank, a woman hung up and walked off. He picked up the receiver, fumbled in his pocket for a chip, and pressed it behind his ear.

His fingers shook, and he had to redial twice. He gazed blankly out over the terminal. It was packed: families, businessmen, tourists. Were any looking back at him? Let them; he didn't care. There were usually ISB agents hanging around airports. That was fine. They could take him right now; it didn't matter.

He shivered as the system kicked in. What was the name of the hospital? Beth Israel, right. He ordered contact, then stood bobbing his head until the system got through. Now what—Admissions? No, Records. That wouldn't be realtime. Better get into the operations system. He gave the command; a single pink flash, and he was in.

He finally hit with PATIENT CARE. The names scrolled past. He halted at Jane Doe.

The data came up automatically: a series of lines, graphs, and numbers that he didn't understand. But that had to be her heartbeat, and that flat line . . . Then words: description of wounds, instructions for care, and a final note:

"Functionally brain dead. No heroic measures. Disconnect after forty-eight hours."

He closed his eyes, but the words remained. He felt nothing; no fear or pain or grief. Brain dead. Heroic measures. Disconnect. He spoke into the phone. "I'm here. I'm with you, babe."

But there was no reply beyond the silence of the cables carrying the signal. He wasn't there, and nothing would change if he were.

He hung up.

He rested his head against the phone, feeling the coolness of plastic on skin. He should have taken her to town. He should have left her the bottle. He should have told her he was going. He should never have left.

"Hey buddy, you okay?"

The face before him was pockmarked and mustached, the expression concerned.

"Yeah. I'm fine."

The face smiled. "Well, you don't look too hot."

Telford reached out and clutched the man's arm. It felt strange: too thin and rock-hard. He looked down at the hand protruding from the coat sleeve. Dull metal, with plastic fingers.

Damaged, he thought. All damaged.

He lifted his eyes and let out a sound that wasn't quite a laugh. "I'm fine. Really." Forcing a smile, he turned away.

"Hope things go better."

"Thanks."

He went on, walking carefully, stopping whenever anyone crossed his path. Halfway to the doors he realized that the chip was still behind his ear. Peeling it off, he let it drop and didn't look back.

He stepped out onto the concrete, into cold daylight. It was gray, the clouds so low that they touched the mountains. Just over

216

that horizon was the arena where the killers grappled, not caring who else was hurt. The innocent, the sick, the helpless—the more the better.

Let them have it out. Telford was finished. There was no point in going on. They had taken everything that was his.

He reached for the folded sheet in his coat pocket. To hell with them, with Bohlen, Page, with every last . . .

His face went slack. He saw Page wielding the ax, reeling off names and addresses. One name had been missing, just one out of them all.

On the clouded peaks death loomed, almost visible. An ax fell, and the sound of its strike filled the world.

A car horn blared as Telford ran across the lot. He didn't look around.

CHAPTER 21

FOR THE TWENTIETH TIME Page got out and slammed the truck door. The snow around the truck had already been paced flat. He went to a virgin spot under the trees and kicked through the icy crust, making it fly in soggy white lumps.

He'd been waiting for damn near four hours, and no Luke. That hitter was walking a thin line. If it all unraveled because of him, was delayed by even one day . . . Page clenched his gloved fists and squeezed. He turned to the truck. Feist jerked away from the passenger window. He'd insisted on coming when Page went to the lodge, had jabbered about being left alone.

It was getting dark; no sun to tell how much daylight was left, but the clouds were turning grayer as he watched. That might be an advantage; dark night, no moon, woods black as pitch. He liked that scenario.

But what the hell was keeping Luke? Page flexed his numb fingers—the polymet was a lousy insulator, and the cold was biting deep. Had Luke gotten lost? The directions were perfectly clear: Off the interstate, up two county roads, and there it was.

His eyes followed the path blown clear by the hovers. Right in front of you, after you made the last turn, impossible to miss.

Had they been stopped? That could be. State cops, not local vigs; the Feds kept the vigs off the interstates. But Luke had been on the run long enough to know every trick. He could talk his way out of just about anything.

But if he was picked up . . . It wasn't worth thinking about. He'd show. Just wait it out.

To think about something else, Page went over the script. First the signal from the lodge. He'd already set that up, this afternoon. One unmistakable spike, online just long enough for the Cossacks to get a clear trace. They'd head out immediately, not waiting for an exact fix; their technical people would acquire that. And no local law; neither of the Micks trusted townies to find their dicks with both hands.

And Feist would be there to welcome them. Page would send him back in Bobby's car just before it all came down. Maybe with Bobby driving.

As for Cummins, he was no field man, he was a rabbit at best. He'd sit it out, either at the motel or in his own vehicle well behind the lines, overseeing things from a distance and pretending he was on an op, just as he'd done at Key West.

That had been one of the last jobs Page carried out for him before he went stealth. One shot over the rooftop of the house on the south end of Big Pine, near where the Brigado Liberación Ortega had come ashore. Cummins gave Page only twelve hours' notice before the op went down, evidently afraid that he'd refuse if he knew that imps were involved. Page did know, and didn't give a shit. He'd have had to be a terminal-stage Peltonoid not to figure out what the cherry tops and unmarked cars meant, not to mention the big BurCyb electronics van outside the place.

It took him several minutes to scope Cummins out. Page was not surprised to find him far back, in a car a hundred yards or more behind the tanglefoot barriers. Page sighted in, strongly tempted to pop a round through the windshield an inch from his head. But instead he swung the rifle, fired once at the barrier, then lined the car up again. Cummins wasn't visible now, and some time passed before his shades-covered eyes appeared cautiously over the hood of the car.

Page let the rifle fall, laughing as the bullets poured into the house and the smoke curled skyward.

It would be the same here. Page would wait in front of the motel while they moved out. If Cummins went with them, Page would tag right along. If not, so much the better.

A leisurely ride into the mountains, a short discussion about the codes for the Swiss bank accounts Cummins was so proud of, and then . . . Page squeezed his fingers shut with almost feline delicacy. Oh, he could almost feel it. If there was a maggot on this mudball of a planet who needed the big hurt, it was Cummins. Thinking he could run Scott Page, make him come when he called, treat him as a toadie, a slave, a thing off the streets. He'd had the nerve to threaten him the last time they talked. That piece of shit . . .

Cummins's setup had been brilliant, but nothing that Page wouldn't have thought of if he'd been in the same position. Thousands of people closed their bank accounts after the comps crashed during the war. Stupid, ill-informed maggots, unwilling to trust the safeguards built into the system over the decades. As far as they were concerned, having their funds frozen for a week was the same as losing them. So they took their money home and stashed it where they were sure it would be safe.

Except that a Beltway security official with unlimited access to confidential files had gone over the data and carefully compiled a list of names and addresses. Then he arranged to have those individuals relieved of their financial worries forever.

Cummins chose only targets who met certain criteria. Old people living alone, with no close relatives, and who had withdrawn a quarter to half a mil after the bank crisis. Not a lot of people, but enough.

The hits were spaced weeks apart, the MO different so as to leave no trail. The only thing the murders had in common was a fancy hardwired safe that contained only a few bills and the body of a worthless cipher who could be crossed off the next census. Some appeared to have suffered heart attacks. Some had more interesting sendoffs, requiring that their houses be burned down to hide the results. Like the man who had set the samoyed on Page, screaming when he saw what happened to the dog just before the same thing was done to him. Or the aged maggot who shot him point-blank, hitting the vest he'd bought on the street, and who couldn't believe what Page did with that gun a moment later. Or the old woman in the wheelchair whose eyes followed him silently during the robbery, wordless even when he backhanded her. She began sobbing only after he set the place ablaze, her voice rising to a wail as the flames leapt higher.

Twenty-one hits, and over five million dollars.

The lion's share went to Cummins, at least three mil into those accounts he'd boasted about last summer. Page's share was a little over a quarter million, the same as Luke and the others.

He tried to access the data himself, but it was too well protected. He tried to talk Cummins into giving them more than one address at a time, to step up the number of hits, but Cummins refused. He demanded a bigger cut, only to be laughed at.

Cummins wouldn't be laughing much longer.

There was a whine behind him. He swung around but saw nothing—it was pretty dark under the trees now. Moving quickly, he went to the truck. "Is it them?" Feist asked. "Is it?"

Ignoring him, Page grabbed the rifle and flicked on the sight. By this time he could hear the crunch of tires above the motor noise. He stepped to the rear of the truck.

There it was: a black van with oversized tires. Page didn't recognize it, but that meant little; Luke never used the same vehicle twice.

The van slowed as it came into the open. When Page raised the rifle, the driver's window opened and a dark-skinned face looked out, followed by a waving arm. It was Blooch; Page relaxed and let the barrel drop.

The van stopped twenty yards off, and Luke got out, followed by Scully and a squat figure that must have been the Medranista. Luke said a few words to them before walking over to Page.

Luke Thibodeau had done time and looked it. The skin under his eyes was cracked and lined, giving him a reptilian appearance. There was a network of small scars on his right cheek, souvenir of a fight in an army stockade. His hair was thinning on top and going gray at the temples. He wore a sheepskin jacket and had a machine pistol slung over his right shoulder.

"Page," he said as he came up. "Been a while."

"You're late," Page said quietly.

Luke clapped his hands together. "Team of four," he said. "Scully and Blooch. I tried to get Groves, but he's in Quentin on an old probation rap. But I got the Mex." He waved at the van. "Calls himself Zapata. Says he knows demo, so if we run into any noncyb safe you can't bust . . ."

"You're late," Page repeated.

Luke's face went hard. "Page, gimme a break. We just drove through the biggest goddamn blizzard you ever saw. Ten inches of white in less than an hour. Roads shot from here to Portland. Lucky we got here at all."

"You've been drinking," Page said. He could smell it on Luke's breath.

"Yeah, that's right. We went to a bar, had a couple while they cleared the highway. Otherwise it was just sit. So BFD."

"You're going to pull a hit drunk?"

Luke regarded him in silence. That was his way, whenever he was pushed. Page glared for a moment, locking eyes with him, then looked away, damping the fury that was rising within him.

Luke smiled. "You all better now?" He twirled a finger over his temple. "All the circuits operating in sync? Okay. Now let's go through whatever it is you've got. You haven't told me jack yet."

"Call them over," Page said, pointing at the van.

Luke shook his head. "No, tell me first, and I'll fill them in later, one at a time, the way we always—"

"We're going in now."

"What?" Luke leaned forward. "Are you kidding? Do my ears play foolish and childish tricks on me? We're going in now—after driving two thousand miles through eight feet of snow. Well, my friend, I have to tell you that you are mistaken."

Page clutched the rifle. "You heard me, Luke."

Luke turned his head and snorted.

"Look at me," Page said.

"No. You look at me. You looking? Tomorrow. You got that? Tomorrow."

The rifle barrel rose, but Luke slapped it away. "Are you lifting a weapon at me, Page?"

Teeth clenched, Page cursed.

Luke backed off and called behind him. "Scully! Blooch! We got a problem."

There was a clatter from the van. But then Luke stopped and looked downhill. "What the hell's this?" he said as the pistol slid from his shoulder.

Page stood unmoving until he heard a voice call his name. He glanced behind him. There, silhouetted against the snow, was a running figure.

"Aww, it's Bobby," Luke said disgustedly. He stood with his hands on his hips, pistol dangling by the strap on his wrist.

"Page," Bobby said breathlessly, slowing to a walk. "He's gone."

"What?"

"I tried to call at the house. Then I drove over. Then I came here. The car got stuck." He took a deep breath. "He's gone. He got in a lifter and took off."

Page slumped, then with a roar he turned and swung his rifle at Luke.

Pistol up, Luke jumped back. "Cover me," he yelled. "Blooch!"

"Yo," Blooch called back, aiming a shotgun. The other two men, weapons in hand, ducked behind the van.

"Watch the one in the truck," Luke said. He backed away carefully, his eyes never leaving Page. "I wondered about this one," he said. "I really did."

He reached the tramped-down snow and slowed. Page watched him, feeling nothing beyond the desire to see Luke stumble, or turn his head, or anything else that would give the slightest opening. He gripped the rifle so tight, the plastic squealed in protest.

"You're a wackball," Luke said. "You've been making me sick for a while now. That old lady, Page . . . Enough's enough, you know?"

"You're there, Luke," Scully told him. Luke paused a moment, then rose to his full height. "You know what it is, Page?" he said. "Pelton's, man." He tapped a finger against his forehead. "It's caught up with you, for real."

Scully opened the door behind him, and Luke edged back into it. "Keep 'em covered," he said. Blooch got in on the passenger side, while Scully and the Mex clambered into the hatch. "You better see a doctor or get something from the store to take care of that, Page," Luke said, standing in the open door and grinning. "Don't come back to Oakland until you do."

The door slammed, the motor keened, and the truck lurched downhill. Page turned to follow it. As it drew abreast, his eyes met the Mexican's. The Mexican smiled and fired. Page threw himself down as the shots kicked snow up around him. He lay, face in the snow, until the shooting stopped, then looked up to see the van thirty yards downhill. The Mexican loosed a round at Bobby, who stood in rigid panic.

The truck door opened, and Feist stumbled out. Shivering, he said to Page, his voice a hysterical squeak, "I'm out of this. I'm gone, man."

Page struck him backhand and watched him go to his knees. Clutching his face, Feist moaned, and moaned again when he lowered his hands and saw blood. Page hit him a second time, a third, and stepped back. The body wriggled, feet kicking in a horizontal dance that left irregular wedge-shaped patterns in the snow.

"Snow angels," Page muttered. He wiped the glove clean, then raised his eyes to where the van was turning onto the road. "Get in the truck," he told Bobby.

He followed the van, steering with one hand, the other cradling the rifle with the barrel resting on the dash. Bobby sat silently, stiffening every time Page looked over at him.

The van's taillights disappeared over a hill. Good, Page thought, speeding up. There was a bridge just beyond, and then nothing but open road. He'd take them there.

At the top of the hill he hit the brakes. The truck slewed sideways, nearly going into the trees, and came to a stop on the shoulder. The 501 had blocked the bridge. As Page watched, the van slowed, and one of the vigs walked up to it. There was just enough light to see that he was bearded and wore a logger's shirt buttoned up against the cold. Another man in a snowmobile suit stood in the glare of the headlights, while a third waited at the bridge.

The bearded man leaned toward the van, but then backed away. There was a low cough, and he jerked upward and fell to the pavement. The snowmobiler had just enough time to reach for the rifle at his shoulder before the roar of a shotgun cut him down. Page didn't see what hit the last vig.

The door of the van opened. Luke swung out and pointed at the bridge. Scully ran over to search the body lying there, then went on to the car that blocked the road.

Luke looked back and waved his pistol. "Hey, Page," he called. "Come on down."

The car moved back, lurching as the rear wheels dropped into the gully behind it. Scully lowered the window as the car bobbed wildly, motor whining. He cursed and slapped the side panel as if that would force it back on the pavement.

"Come on, Page!" Luke was smiling, hands on his hips. "You like to watch 'em bleed, don't you? You're smooth on that, you sick mother . . ."

Lights flashed a half-mile past the bridge, red and blue reflecting madly off the snow. As the police siren began howling, Luke yelled to Scully and got back inside. The van began to turn, and had swung half around by the time Scully leapt aboard.

As fast as he could, Page backed up. There had been a wide spot in the road at the foot of the hill . . .

He got there just as the van burst over the hilltop. He pulled to the side and ducked as it roared past, in case they took a shot at him, but they were busy just then. Raising his head, he saw the patrol car flash by, the cop inside sparing him only a glance.

Page waited until the siren faded. He gave the wheel a savage turn and pointed the truck toward town.

CHAPTER 22

HAULING ON HIS COAT, Bohlen tromped down the stairs. He'd had it. All day up there with Dela-hanty smirking at him, the rookies laughing their heads off, and Lu nagging him about Maddie. The phone hadn't rung once except for that idiot who asked if they sold modified bull semen.

He was going out. There was an Albanian place two blocks away; he intended to stuff himself with pseudo-Greek food and think about the next move. If his mood didn't improve after he ate, he just might keep going—to one of the Indian nations to apply for political asylum. Or grow a long beard and hide out in a Mennonite town.

As he crossed the lobby, the manager, talking to a pretty woman at the counter, gave him a dour look as the man responsible for aircraft landing in his parking lot. Bohlen ignored the look and walked on.

Outside, it was freezing, and the air had lost its dryness: snow coming, and plenty of it. He shoved his hands in his pockets. Nearly dark; streetlights on; lots of traffic. The sound of roaring machinery came from beyond the buildings across the street, and he vaguely wondered what it could be. Some typical aspect of backwoods daily life, he supposed.

On the sidewalk he stopped. Was the Albanian place toward town or in the other direction? He shrugged and began to walk east.

Ahead of him, a patrol car pulled over. Bohlen eyed the departmental shield with loathing. Exactly what he needed—another encounter with the local law. He gritted his teeth. He was sick of cowboy cops.

So which one was it? That sullen prick Nast, or the Sioux who never opened his mouth, or jolly old Hough himself, come around to laugh at his shoes?

No, it was Zimmer. Zimmer smiling through the windshield, opening the door, getting out, reaching up for his hatbrim.

You tilt that hat at me, Bohlen thought, and I'll make you eat it.

But then there was a siren down the road. Looking back, he saw, over the headlights, the reflection of flashes on the low clouds.

Zimmer leaned inside for the radio mike. He got back in. Bohlen winced as the siren started shrieking and the cruiser moved to block the road.

Zimmer reemerged, shotgun in hand, and nodded at Bohlen as if to tell him to watch carefully to see how things were done. He waved at the cars to pull over. Up the street, the road was already clear. Bohlen stepped to the curb and saw a van coming down the centerline and a cruiser chasing it.

He unbuttoned his coat. The van was only a couple hundred yards off now and hadn't slowed at all. Zimmer reached to flick on his cherry tops. The van kept coming. Then there was a screech of brakes. Bohlen stepped back instinctively. For a moment it seemed the van would flip over, but the wheels caught, and it came to a stop thirty feet from the cruiser.

Shotgun pointed skyward, Zimmer raised the mike to his lips. "Please—" the speaker boomed.

A rifle barrel appeared in the van's side window. Bohlen yelled, his cry cut off by the blast. He grabbed for his pistol as the back of Zimmer's head exploded and his hat, his silly goddamn cowboy hat, flapped into the night sky.

The traffic increased when they reached town, blocking Page's attempt to close with the van. He snarled when another car pulled in front of him. Which made three now, and the drivers were slowing down as they became aware there was trouble up ahead.

He felt real fear for the first time in years. If Luke's boys were caught, even one of them, Page wouldn't be able to run fast or far enough. And here they were headed right into town. The situation couldn't possibly be worse. He should have settled it at the bridge. They'd been trapped there; boxed in and ready for the gun. But things had happened so fast . . .

The other lane was suddenly open. Good. He swung over and accelerated. There was the cruiser now, open space behind it. Another fifty yards and . . .

From a side street a car turned into his lane. Blinded by headlights, he pounded on the horn, its plastic cracking under his glove. Bobby whimpered. Page lifted his arm to hit him, but the car dodged aside and he sped past it. Blinking away afterimages, he saw that both the van and the cruiser had stopped. He grinned savagely and pressed on the pedal. Now we'd see . . .

He hit the brakes when the gunshot came. Bobby cried out as he was flung against the dashboard and Page wrestled the truck to a stop. "You stay right here," he said to Bobby. "You hear me? You stay . . ."

He took the rifle, got out, and jogged toward the gunfire. He'd gone only a few yards when he heard a sound behind him. Bobby was out of the truck and scrambling over a pile of snow. Whipping the gun up, Page aimed but saw only darkness. He cursed and switched the sight on. The display lit up, and he swung the rifle in a slow arc. But Bobby was gone.

Bohlen's aim was off; he saw sparks when his slugs hit the van's grille. The windshield shattered, and he threw himself on the pavement as a burst of automatic fire raged over his head.

A window broke high above him, a chair hit the sidewalk, and Delahanty opened fire.

Bohlen rolled to his right, coat tangling with his legs. He thumped against one of the planters and pushed himself to his knees. More fire from the van, drowning out what Delahanty was doing. Imps, had to be. He smiled to himself. You out there, Tap?

He chanced a look around the planter and pulled his head back as a burst tore up the other side. The van was moving, trying to return the way it had come. Pulling his legs under him, Bohlen readied himself for a sprint to the side of the motel, but there was an explosion, and his head banged against the wood of the planter.

His stomach knotted. Grenades. Jesus, what was this, the chip-head army? What else did they have?

A movement to his right. He whirled, raising the pistol, saw a car pulling in, a woman's terrified face behind the wheel, and held his fire. As the car passed him, he frogwalked into the lot after it. There was a stink of gasoline, the crackle of something burning. When he was far enough that the building shielded him, he clambered over the planters.

A quick survey showed the van nosed into the packed snow across the street. Beyond it, dark figures fled between the buildings. Bohlen took aim, but let the pistol drop. There might be bystanders in the line of fire.

Running at a crouch, he went to Zimmer's cruiser, and felt a surge of pity when he saw the man lying, face gone and arms flung wide. Farther up, the other car was wrapped in flame. It was a moment before he noticed someone behind the tree near it. He nodded when Nast waved to him.

A woman was sobbing hysterically in the lot. No more fire overhead; Delahanty must be on his way down. Distant sirens grew louder, closer, but Bohlen couldn't wait. He raised his fist and pumped it. Nast made an okay sign and pointed across the street. Bohlen nodded. Moving to the front of the cruiser, he counted five seconds and fired twice into the darkness between the buildings. He fell back, reloaded, looked out again. Nast had made it across and was squatting next to a driveway. He raised his hand, and Bohlen started running.

The smoke from the cruiser obscured Page's view, but wait, there . . . Figures moving from the van, still firing. He raised his rifle, but they were gone among the buildings.

"Hey, buddy, you better get down."

Page started. A man was crouched beside a car, peering past the fender. "I don't know what . . . ," he said, lifting his head. Then he saw Page's rifle, and his eyes widened.

Without thinking Page slammed down the butt. A satisfying thud, and the man crumpled. Someone ran across the street; a cop, he could tell by the hat.

Page stepped over the body and ran toward the buildings.

There were concrete steps ten yards down the driveway. While Bohlen covered him, Nast ran to them, then waved him on. Bohlen was halfway there when a burst raked the pavement. Throwing himself against the wall, he reached the shelter of the steps and shuffled up to Nast.

"How many?" Bohlen asked the deputy.

"Don't know. Four, maybe. These your imps, Bohlen?"

"Could be. Any more grenades?"

Nast shook his head. "Would have popped me if they had."

There was a noise from the street. Bohlen saw Delahanty and Ling running up. No sign of Navasky. Shots cut the pavement between them, and they scattered. He turned to Nast. "How'd you get away from the car?"

"Luck," Nast said grimly. "Saw it coming."

Bohlen heard gunfire on the other side of the building. He recognized the sound: an MP-8, standard government issue. Had to be Navasky. Maybe the kid could do something right after all. At the end of the drive he sensed movement. He threw a wild shot, then got up. "Let's go," he said to Nast.

When he got past the buildings, Page squatted and ran the scope across the landscape. The tiny green screen showed him nothing. He increased sensitivity and tried again. Even worse; a washed-out palette of green and yellow with no contrast at all. He lowered the rifle. That wasn't right; they should show up like torches out here. They were lying low. They couldn't have gotten away; not enough time.

He heard a shot to his left and aimed in that direction. Somebody ran from the buildings. No—two shapes. He sighted on the one in the rear and was about to pull the trigger but stopped.

It wasn't Luke. Cops or Cossacks, had to be. He smiled as the solution presented itself. All he had to do was work his way ahead of Luke and let the cops flush him out. Just like an old-time safari. Fitzgerald, or whatever his name was, would have loved it.

Another pair appeared. Page bit his lip. He didn't want too many around. Aiming at the biggest one, he fired. The man went down just as a fusillade erupted from the darkness.

Page got up and loped across the snow. There were lights up ahead. He ran toward them expectantly.

At the rear of the building was a small parking lot surrounded by brush, small trees, and snow. Bohlen's feet broke through the crust with every step he took. He didn't like that; he might as well be carrying a lighted bull's-eye. A few feet into the brush he stopped, and a second later Nast did the same. Better wait until Delahanty caught up . . .

A shot rang out behind them, and almost simultaneously a patch of brush thirty feet ahead exploded with gunfire. He threw himself on his back and fired between his feet. The MP-8 chattered to his left. Rolling onto his side, he emptied the gun into darkness. A scream, and the gunfire stopped.

Bohlen searched his pocket for a revolver clip and reloaded. "Navasky," he called out.

"Here."

"Cover us."

"Will do."

Nast crawled up to him. "You okay?"

"Yeah." He jerked his head at the brush. "Somebody knows what he's doing."

Snow crunched behind them. "Who's that?"

"It's Jimmy," Ling called out in a shaky voice. "Del's down, Ross."

Oh, Christ, no. "Stay where you are, Ling." A screech of brakes came from the street and a siren he hadn't even noticed went silent. "Better yet, grab the locals and fill 'em in."

Not waiting for a reply, he peeled himself from the snow and ran to Nast, who had gone on to the bushes. "Footprints," Nast said when he approached.

"What's up there?" Bohlen pointed at the faint lights through the trees.

"Public Works."

"That's where they're going," Bohlen said, running past.

Slowing down, Page went forward at a crouch. Ahead was a sharp rise silhouetted by lights. Peaked and sloping, it seemed almost a miniature of the mountains to the west, and Page approached it with puzzlement. He was nearly at the top before he realized what it was: snow. Piled high, tons of it, left for the warm weather to take care of. He peered cautiously over the top, but caution was unnecessary: the snow went on for at least sixty feet.

He climbed across, taking advantage of the dips and canyons formed when the stuff was packed in. On the other side was an open area, then another snowpile at the far end. Below, a dozen odd-looking vehicles were parked. Bright orange, massive, and low, and bearing large angled blades: snowplows.

A garage faced the lot. Lights glowed, but the doors were closed, and he could see no movement. This open space would make a perfect kill zone. He'd let them get halfway across before cutting them down, then out the lot's access road and back to the truck.

He eased himself over a parapet of snow, stepping carefully, digging footholds in the crust. Something moved across the lot. He looked down.

There they were, all four of them, passing the garage, with Luke in the lead. Luke was bent over and clutching his stomach. Behind him Scully had a leg drawn up and was leaning against Blooch.

Page raised his rifle, but Blooch saw him. Flinging Scully aside, he yelled, "It's Page," and started firing. Luke opened up too, his gun braced against his thigh.

Page threw himself back, but there was nowhere to hide. The snow collapsed under his feet, and he rolled to the bottom, bullets following him every foot of the way.

Bohlen let Nast take point, keeping about ten feet back and to one side. Every few seconds he looked over at the footprints they were following. Dark spots marked them. They'd hit one, at least.

He saw that Nast was going faster and sped up to keep him in sight. He hadn't forgotten what Nast said in the squad car the other night. There would be no Key West redux here. If Nast lost control, Bohlen would—well, he'd stop him one way or another.

He could hear Navasky stumbling through brush and, farther back, the voices of cops. He wished they'd shut up; he couldn't hear clearly.

A shout up ahead, and a sudden frenzy of gunfire. He started to drop and then realized it wasn't aimed at them. Bare hands in the snow, he considered what he'd just heard. Cage, rage, page? What was it? A name, maybe?

"Oh, shit," Nast hollered. "They're shooting up the garage." He raced toward the gunfire. Slapping his hands on his coat, Bohlen rose and went after him.

———

Page stopped rolling when he hit the pavement. He was shielded by the plows now. He crawled to one and went on his belly to look underneath. Feet were moving across the lot. Two of them separated from the rest and ran parallel to the snow. The Mex, most likely. Page let loose a burst from the Skoda, but it did nothing more than hurry the man along. Diving for the plow, Page banged his head on the rear plate. Bullets ricocheted on the underside as he tracked him.

They were all gone, the pavement empty, and the ammo readout of the rifle flashed red. With a snarl he flung the empty mag away and switched to the spare. He crawled back out and slumped against the rear of the plow. The snow peaks dazzled against a black sky. A minute, two, no more. He slid around the corner and crept toward the blade. Above him a door hung half-open. Hoisting himself hand-over-hand, he climbed inside.

There was barely room for him. The plow was an automated model, comp-driven, tied into the Navsat III system to follow the roads to within a half-foot of error, with a primitive recognition system for abandoned cars, downed trees, and the like. The driver's cabin was there in case of breakdown or maybe to meet union regs.

He lifted his head for a quick look. No one in sight, but they were out there, with a clear shot at him. He slammed the gun butt against the dash. He'd set it up for them, handed himself over. They couldn't have arranged this on their own. No maggot could. Street trash on one side, Cossacks on the other . . .

He'd let them slide in Oakland. That was it. Had let them all defy him, after burning the old woman. The remarks, the looks, their stupid faces smirking. Should have taken one out then. He'd done that at first—every few months he took one out. To keep the others slick and scared.

Outside, someone shouted. How much time? A minute? Less. He ran his eyes over the packed snow. They wanted blood? He'd give 'em blood. As he kicked the door wide and twisted to drop out of the cabin, his face turned to the dash.

And there it was, five inches away. The key, right in its slot atop the processor. All that was missing was a label saying TURN ME.

He reached and turned it. The comp lit up, readouts glowing red and healthy. He laid his arm against the panel, quivering as his own system came up.

It was a standard vehicular guidance program, the safeguards minimal. He ordered his implant to analyze it and eliminate the guidance parameters. He thought for a minute, then called for an override on every plow in the lot.

He heard laughter as his system signaled go-ahead. He ordered it to initiate.

As one, the plow engines roared into life.

"What the hell," Bohlen said at the sound of the engines. He hurried to Nast and reached him just as the crunch of tires began up ahead.

There was a rattle of gunfire, then a crash and the clang of metal. Nast started running, and Bohlen followed.

A moment later they were out of the brush, behind a low building. The noise was now a demonic symphony of overstressed engines and ear-numbing impacts. Seeing a huge pile of snow ahead, Bohlen ran to it and scrambled to the top. Nast meanwhile eased his way around the front corner of the building.

Wincing as another deafening crash occurred, Bohlen crouched to look over the edge. He hesitated a second, then poked his head over a mound of dirty snow.

Somebody should have been taking a video of this. In the lot in front of the garage a dozen snowplows were fighting it out. Below him, two faced off blade to blade like gladiators, growling at each other, rising on their rear wheels only to fall back and try again. Just beyond them, a plow was diligently clearing ten feet of bare pavement, sparks flying as it pushed forward and backed up to repeat the process. Another plow roared in circles, smashing the sides of the plows that tried to get past. As he watched, a sheriff's car came down an access road, then stopped and reversed damn quick when a plow snuck around the one circling and made straight for it.

Gunfire from the other side, barely audible over the din. Bohlen ducked, moved a few feet, and looked again. Nothing—and the shots hadn't been meant for him. He glanced at the garage and saw Nast slipping past the doors.

Sighing, Bohlen nodded once, with the air of a man asked to do something uncalled for, then threw a leg over and slid to the bottom.

Cackling to himself, Page steered the plow across the lot. Twice he collided with one of the others, and once he almost tipped over, but he made it, and opened the door and threw himself out just as the plow hit.

Scrambling away from the big wheels, he climbed, rifle held high. He knew where he was going. When the plows had started and the gunman fired, Page had seen puffs of snow from the muzzle blasts. He'd steered the plow toward a rift in the snow twenty feet over and was now climbing it, hidden from anyone at the top.

He went a short distance in before circling. No need to keep silent—he could bellow at the top of his lungs if he liked. He tried it, letting loose a kind of rebel yell broken with laughter.

He saw a rifle barrel poking out and took the last few steps slowly. It was the Mex. Lying with his shoulders pressed to his ears, looking wildly back and forth, flinching every time a plow hit something.

Rising to his full height, Page aimed the Skoda. But this was too easy. He took a lump of snow and tossed it at the Beaner's back. The gunman shouted and turned over. Page let him get halfway, yodeled, and gave him five rounds in the face. The man spasmed, rifle flying over his head and into the lot. Page stepped slowly forward, on the red emblazoned in the snow. Throwing his head back, he howled Luke's name, then Scully's, then Blooch's. He swung around, barrel up. "You earned it," he whispered. "You earned it."

Taking a deep breath, he stepped to the edge. His mouth dropped open when a figure slid down to the pavement on the other side. Face broadening into a smile, he opened up from the hip.

When the bursts appeared at his feet, Bohlen hit the deck instinctively, not realizing that this was a mistake until a plow nearly flattened him. He rolled away, shouting wildly, but another was headed for him, as if it had a personal grudge. When the blade nudged his shoulder, he jumped aside and clutched at it, losing his balance and falling against the cold steel. Another shot spanged off the metal, felt rather than heard, then the plow turned and hid him.

He hung on, feet dragging over the snow, considering this as good a shield as any until he looked ahead and saw that they were closing on the garage. A flash of blue—Nast wisely ducking inside—and he pushed himself away, hoping to God the plow wouldn't decide to swing toward him at that instant.

A second later he was in the open. Somehow he'd managed to hold on to the revolver, and he cut loose at the snowpile, not bothering to aim. There was no target anyway. He was still shouting, his voice hoarse.

He got a hideous feeling and looked wild-eyed over his shoulder, but the plow stalking him swerved off. Another rumbled by. He went after it, keeping low. The plow jerked to a stop and backed up. He raced past the blade, flinging himself facedown in the snow.

He raised his gun, but his hand shook too much, and the Python was empty. Grabbing a reload, he slapped it in, losing a round in the process. He rolled as a huge presence thundered past only a foot away, then rolled again in case something else decided to scoop him up.

To his right a plow was trying to climb the pile, wheels churning. He looked in the other direction, trying to spot the object he'd seen a moment before. There it was: a rifle lying half on the pavement, a late-model AK, it looked like.

He scrambled up the snowpile, cursing his lack of gloves. Behind him, a huge crash: the single combat had ended with one plow on its side. The other rammed it a couple of times, then turned and trundled off triumphantly. Lifting his pistol, Bohlen made for the area above the rifle. He was ten feet away when he saw that stealth was unnecessary. A splash of red told him that, then a body. He hunkered down next to it.

About five-five, Latin male, bearded . . . The man hadn't climbed up here in that condition. It had been done to him on the spot. But by whom? No cop would have—not even Nast. What in God's name was going on out here? Were the crazy bastards killing each other off, or what?

Bohlen was rising when a figure loomed over the snow. He whirled and saw a leather jacket, a badge, a hat. The deputy approached, mouth moving. Bohlen caught only the last word— "motherfucker." He dropped his pistol, raised his hands. It wasn't anybody he knew. The chase on, all hell breaking loose, and it had to be the one cop in the state he hadn't tangled with.

The deputy looked over the body, his face growing hard. He lifted his gun, but then looked past Bohlen. He nodded and waved.

Bohlen turned and saw Nast, taking things in. Nast's eyes met Bohlen's, his lips quirked, and he turned away. Bohlen started to call after him, but it was useless. The deputy pulled out his cuffs. Putting his hands on his head, Bohlen leaned forward. "Listen, you idiot . . ."

Page halted at the edge of an open field and went on one knee. He glanced back at the lot. He wasn't sure whether he'd dusted the plainclothes. Too chaotic to tell. Call it a probable.

Sighting the gun, he swung it across the field. There: all bunched together, not fifty yards off. He aimed at the leader, but then noticed that the one in the center was limping. Scully, he thought, shifting his aim. Right—save Luke for last.

He fired, and the green silhouette went down. The others ran in opposite directions, the one on the left moving faster. Page aimed low, and yelped with satisfaction when the figure fell and began crawling.

Luke vanished into brush. No sense wasting a shot. He wasn't going anywhere; he'd keep. Sighting on the crawling figure, Page deliberated. Then with a grunt he ran to intercept it, kicking his way through the snow, which was not deep enough to slow him down.

He stopped thirty feet ahead of the crawling man. Blooch, trailing one leg, moaning to himself, looked up and saw what was waiting. He swayed a little, and threw his head back with a sound that was half sob and half scream.

Page stood silently. Blooch threw aside the gun he was dragging. "Page," he said, his voice distorted. "Don't, man . . ."

Smiling, Page tapped his thigh with the gun barrel.

Blooch inched forward and with an effort rose to his knees, crying out in pain. He threw his arms wide. "They made me, Page . . ."

Page could not see the man's face. He lifted the rifle.

"Page!" Blooch screamed.

A squeeze of the trigger. Page watched as Blooch somersaulted backward. Heart afire, he ran toward the brush.

Bohlen started when the plow escorting him fell silent. He dropped low, jerking the gun up before he caught himself. Now he was challenging stalled snowplows. Great. Ready to fire on anything. He listened. No sound from the garage. All the plows were either demolished or shut down. How this one had gotten out of the lot he'd never know. They were talented, Montana snowplows. Smarter than the locals, anyway. It had taken him over a minute to persuade that GD cop to let him go.

GD. His mom used to say that, instead of actually swearing. That was how you knew she was pissed, when she said GD. Bohlen supposed he was pissed himself. Better pissed than scared, alone in the chill dark. Where the hell was everybody else—Navasky, Ling, the locals? Back there gaping at wrecked machinery, were they?

Not good, everybody separated and scrambling around in darkness. Nice way to get whacked by your own people.

Someone screamed. A male voice, and that word again: Page. He was sure it was Page. He turned to the sound, trying to see through the shadows.

A burst of fire—there! Weakness plucked at him as he moved toward it. Just as it had in Loisaida. That stairwell, and the punk smirking over the railing a second before the gun breathed fire. Then Del . . . Poor Floyd . . .

He eluded the thought and pushed on. Forget the fear, put it away. Retain only what Loisaida taught you. It had all come together there, the revelation of what it meant to be hunted, to have metal tearing through muscle and bone, to lose your heart's blood. Marcus's words had come home then: that this wasn't a game, a script, a morality play put on for the benefit of Ross Bohlen or anybody else. It was pure tragedy, a misfortune created by the cracks in the human soul, a judgment on them all.

He halted, backtracked a few feet. A trail, the prints long and indistinct, as if someone had been dragging himself. He bent closer and noticed blotches—no, streamers, as of steady bleeding. He followed it, and found the body in the snow. He looked around cautiously before going nearer. Couldn't tell much beyond the fact that it was a black man—a kid, really—and that he was dead.

Bohlen blew out a breath. Could Tap have done this? A sense of disgust rose at the thought. Sure he could. Or Nast—Nast wasn't right in the head. Running off with no backup—dumb or crazy, no third alternative. But there was that other name, Page . . .

Gunfire; muzzle flashes from a dark clump of brush ahead. Lurching to his feet, he ran toward it.

A rasping cough, then a muffled curse only a few feet away. Page slid his feet over the surface of the snow. The brush was all pine and made no rustle as he pushed through it.

He circled. After a minute there was more coughing, to his left and slightly behind him. He cut over about ten feet. Before him was a mass of trees, branches intertwining and blocking his way. He could sense Luke on the other side. He tensed, ready to burst through, when he heard a buzzing above: a lifter, coming closer. He waited until it was overhead, then pushed his way through.

Facing him was Luke, back against a mound of snow. He must have seen Page the same instant: he froze, one hand over his belly, the other reaching for the rifle at his side.

The sound of the lifter faded, and Luke let his arm fall. "I shoulda guessed," he said, as if to himself.

Page said nothing. It was too dark for him to make out the expression on Luke's face. The face was just a blank against a gray-white background.

"Whatever the hell you thought you were up to," Luke said, "I guess it's blown." He started laughing, but the laugh was cut off by a gagging sound. He turned and spat something into the snow. "Nothing to say?" he went on. "I suppose you think that's pretty damn scary."

The hand holding his stomach lifted, the fingers spread. "You can't do nothing to me, Page. You can't even kill me. You're a little late for that."

Page heard something, the ghost of a sound. He glanced in that direction, aware that Luke was trying to keep him here long enough for the law to grab him.

"I saw it coming, Page, saw it from the first . . ."

Page took a step forward. He would use the gloves. There was nothing more important in the world now than to hear Luke scream.

"You toting it all up, keeping score . . ."

Finish it by hand. Feel the bones breaking.

". . . you think I didn't? You think I don't know what 'maggot' means?" Luke laughed once more.

Page was practically standing over him. Then Luke's hand shot out, and a lump of snow hit Page in the face.

242

"Chiphead," Luke said, rolling to his gun. Page squeezed the trigger, but he'd slipped, was falling, and the shots went high. He lowered the barrel and came down on one knee, and the rounds slammed into Luke, flinging him back just as he fired.

The impact of the slug threw Page on his side. Incredulous, he lay there a moment before taking off a glove and reaching for his thigh. He snarled as his hand grew wet and sticky. Grabbing the rifle, he aimed at Luke and pulled the trigger. There was nothing but a click, a click that repeated as he squeezed again and again.

His leg nearly went out from under him when he drew himself up and staggered to the body. He swung the rifle at the head, making incoherent sounds as the first sharp cracks were followed by pulpy noises. Finally he turned and stumbled away, holding his thigh. He got only twenty feet before the leg buckled and he went down, face in the snow, gun flung ahead of him. He was reaching for it when a shot went over his head.

Unbelieving, he saw a dark shape coming toward him from the trees. "Not one move," a voice said. A second later a flashlight beam blinded him.

Bohlen had nearly reached the brush when he saw a light go on. A light out here meant a cop, and a cop meant Nast. He hurried toward the glow. It bobbed now, as if whoever held it was walking.

He crashed through a stand of trees, scratching his face nicely in the process. "Nast," he yelled. He heard an interrogatory sound up ahead. "It's Bohlen. Hold your fire."

"Right," Nast called out. The light began moving again.

"Wait," Bohlen said. More trees faced him; he decided to bypass them this time.

Nast came into view. He was bending over a man in the snow and had the cuffs out. Between the cuffs, the gun, and the flashlight, he had his hands full and didn't notice the arm moving beneath him.

Bohlen raised his gun, but Nast was already down in a tangle of arms and legs veiled by snow. He ran over, stood hesitant above them: both in black leather, the fallen flashlight not nearly bright enough. Nast was cursing, while the other keened like a dying machine.

Bohlen got them sorted out and clubbed the perp's shoulder. The grip loosened, and he pulled him away. Nast tried to roll off but was still caught by something. "Take him out," he said, his voice tight. "I said take him out!"

Bohlen dug the barrel behind the man's ear. "That's it," he said quietly. The man struggled another second then went limp.

"You don't know," Bohlen said to Nast when Nast got up. "Believe me." He looked down at a face that seemed all cheekbones, eyes, and teeth. "But we do, don't we, Page?"

Nast, brushing the snow off his nose, gazed blankly at the perp. He took a step and kicked him, with the deliberation of a man performing a nasty but necessary task.

His second kick missed when Bohlen yanked Page out of the way. "Nast . . ." he said, but the cop merely adjusted his stance and kicked Page again.

Bohlen fired into the sky. Nast jerked slightly and looked at him, his face bloodless.

Feeling the perp's hand reaching past him, Bohlen jammed the revolver into his throat, gave him a shake, and screamed into his face—an outburst of sheer fury, no sense to it.

Page dropped his arms.

Nast picked up his gun, flashlight, and, of course, his hat, which he inspected closely before he put on.

Bohlen looked down at the perp. "Anybody ever call you 'Tap'?" He studied the face and stepped back. "Ah, you ain't him."

A clatter near him. Nast had tossed the cuffs over. The cop was playing his flashlight across another body among the trees, somebody that wouldn't be causing any trouble ever again. Bohlen turned back to regard the man who had done this. He was sitting up, his face twisted.

As Bohlen picked up the cuffs, voices came from behind the trees. Somebody hollered, and without a word Nast went to meet them.

CHAPTER 23

STEERING CAREFULLY between the snow-pile and garage, Bohlen swung the plow toward Main. He was actually pretty good at this. Might look into it as a career when the Hillbilly canned him.

He'd commandeered the plow after Page collapsed twice while being marched back. Over Nast's protests; the cop had wanted to wait for a wagon. Bohlen overruled him. He had reasons for getting the suspect out of there quick, Nast himself being foremost among them.

Cop and suspect were now riding on the blade, which was bent badly enough to stand on. They glared at each other, Nast cold-eyed, the perp rigid and venomous. Every few seconds he'd mutter the cop's name and something that sounded like "earnest." Bohlen kept a close eye on them.

The buildings loomed. As he turned into the driveway, Navasky emerged. He studied the plow and then the width of the driveway. "Think you can make it?" he called out.

Bohlen waved him away, jumped from the cabin, and pulled Page off the blade. Page grunted but didn't look at him.

"Bohlen," Nast said as Bohlen started up the driveway. "This is my bust."

"I know that. But first things first."

The street looked like Red Square after Yeltsin was freed: vehicles, flashing lights, sheriff's men, town cops, and what appeared to be the dregs of Medrano's army but were probably just vigs. A crowd-control unit blared, and Bohlen kicked it over.

Page stumbled, his injured leg twisting underneath him. Bohlen gestured at the med lifter in the parking lot. "That way," he said.

Page's shoulders shook, but he pulled himself erect and did as he was told.

As they approached the lifter, a collection of sparc cops fell in step with Nast and started asking questions. He brushed them away without a word.

The medics were bandaging a head. "What's with him?" Bohlen asked the redheaded woman who seemed to be in charge.

"Fractured skull," she snapped. "Who are you?"

There was a sound from Page. He was staring at the bandaged man, lips pulled away from his teeth.

Bohlen said to the woman, "Fed security. I need a stretcher."

The woman pushed her hair back and began to say something nasty, but then caught sight of Page. "Arnie," she said over her shoulder.

"Bohlen . . ." Nast began.

A white-coveralled Arnie bustled up. Bohlen told him to get a stretcher and bandage the wound. "No drugs," he said as the medic stepped away.

"What do you mean?" the woman said. "That man needs—"

"This is security business, lady, and you'll do what I tell you."

"Goddamit, Bohlen." He felt Nast's hand on his shoulder.

"Half an hour," Bohlen said. "I need him half an hour." He turned in time to see Page down on the stretcher and Arnie lifting an injector from his arm. "Son of a bitch," he yelled. "Didn't I tell you . . ."

Nast had his arm. "Bohlen, don't push me . . ."

"Will you back off?" He shook Nast's hand away and bent over the medic, who looked up and said, "Let's get these, uh, manacles off, huh?"

Bohlen swallowed his next comment. Behind him the cops were advising Nast. "Hell with this, Johnny. Let's just take him," he heard one say, followed by a rumble of agreement. And the woman started yelling for an orderly.

Bohlen looked around for Navasky, saw him a few feet off, clutching the gun barrel as if to keep it from escaping. "Grab this cart," he hissed.

Navasky frowned back at him just as a huge horror-movie type dressed in white tried to push past him, making for Bohlen. Slapping the man in the chest, Navasky raised the gun.

The scene was cut short by Lu, camelhair coat flaring capelike as she grasped the other side of the stretcher. "Excuse us, please," she called as they started moving. Somebody poked Bohlen in the shoulder.

"Bohlen, you listen here . . ."

"That man needs to be treated," the woman called out.

Bohlen kept the stretcher rolling. "Later," he said. "He's fine now."

"Ross," Lu said. "You're all snow."

He was about to explain that it was wintertime when she looked down at Page, who was staring up at her with his teeth clenched and his eyes nearly popping out of his head. The injection hadn't seemed to affect him at all.

Lu wrinkled her nose. "Oh my," she said. "Aren't you a cutie?"

Nast caught up with them. "Bohlen, if this prisoner vanishes, I swear to God—"

"Half an hour," Bohlen said as they maneuvered the stretcher between the planters. "Step aside there," he told Nast, lifting the stretcher to the sidewalk.

They went across shattered glass to the entrance. Inside, the manager was waiting. "Who's going to pay for this?" he shouted. "There's at least two grand worth of damage . . ."

"The government!" Bohlen yelled back. "Your tax money! Don't worry about it!"

The manager blanched and stepped back. Bohlen became aware that the guy was staring at the pistol in his hand. "You better get back to work," he said. The manager retreated wordlessly to the counter.

"Del's in the hospital," Lu said as they went across the lobby.

"Good," Bohlen said, steering to the elevator. "Go upstairs and tell Wilbur to get online pronto. Go on—get." He maneuvered the stretcher into the elevator and pressed the button. Only when the doors closed did he relax and look down at Page. The drug was taking effect; his eyes were clouding over.

The doors opened, and he shoved the stretcher out. Lu was hurrying down the corridor toward him. "Wilbur's room," he told her. "Right away."

Lu regarded him solemnly as they went down the hall. He saw her MP-8 hanging inside her coat like a bellicose piece of jewelry. "Del's in bad shape, Ross," she said quietly.

"What?"

"He was hit in the spine. He's on the table now . . ."

"Right," Bohlen said. "Bad news. Listen, go in the suite and don't open the door for anybody but me or the rookies. Go to records for 'Page,' P-A-G-E, and anything that sounds like it. Then call around and find out where the cowboys are taking the bodies. City morgue, if they have one . . ."

He took in the cold expression on her face. "Lu," he sighed, "I'm worried about Del too, but look: it ain't over yet."

"What do you mean?" she asked, suddenly alert.

"I mean I was lied to," he said bitterly. He headed toward Wilbur's room.

"Ross, are there more out there?"

"At least one," he called back.

He poked his head in the room. Wilbur was frowning at the

stretcher and scratching his head, as if uncertain exactly how to start. "Wilbur," Bohlen said, "get moving."

Wilbur made a face and turned to his equipment, which was lit up like an amusement arcade. "Navasky," Bohlen said, "you stay in here, keep your weapon up, and watch him." He pointed at the stretcher. "I'm locking you in."

Closing the door, he leaned back.

This business had become grotesque. Four corpses out there, and he would bet that Tap wasn't among them. This Page must have done all four. And for what? To provide a diversion so that Mr. Voice-on-the-Phone could slip off unnoticed? No, that didn't make any sense. None of it did. Let's see, he had Cummins acting like a convicted felon, Tap calling up out of the grave, a childlike intrusion . . . and the dead woman, don't forget her. And now this gunfight at the OK Garage, with a killer chiphead apparently working the government end freelance. Grotesque wasn't the word for it. There was no word for it.

Pointless theorizing until he got hard data from Wilbur. He had other worries—the sheriff's department above all. He figured he had about ten minutes before they came roaring in demanding custody. He wouldn't be able to hold them. They'd be in no mood, not with one of their own dead.

Bohlen looked up and down the corridor. Empty, not even a door open . . . That gave him an idea. He'd go two or three doors down and stand there instead. Listen first to find a room that was occupied. Needless to say, they'd bust straight in, which would give Wilbur another few minutes to work with—more, if Bohlen kept his mouth shut about which was the right room . . .

Ah, too late. He could hear them on the stairs. He slumped against the door just as they appeared, six of them, Hough in the lead and Nast right beside him.

"There he is," one of them called out, pointing at Bohlen in case anyone was confused. Hough came on, face red, arms swinging at his sides. All but Hough and Nast were carrying shotguns.

Hough stopped in front of him. "Is the prisoner in there?"

"Yes he is, sheriff. He's undergoing an examination to verify that he is in fact a cybernetically enhanced individual . . ."

"I want him."

". . . what the hardware is, and what type and capability software . . ."

"I want him."

". . . comprises the system, and . . ."

"I want him, Bohlen."

The deputies had that obnoxious cop expression on their faces, jaws thrust out and eyes glaring. Except for Nast, who was looking at nothing, face pale and mouth a thin line.

"And you'll get him, Sheriff," Bohlen said evenly. "As soon as this procedure is over. From there we'll carry out the investigation to its conclusion."

Hough chewed his mustache. His eyes were calm, no anger or violence in them. Bohlen stepped forward. "Too bad about Zimmer . . ."

Arm already swinging, Hough took two hops and punched him in the jaw. Bohlen went down, blinking. Hough pointed at the door. "Kick that in." A deputy stepped across Bohlen and was about to do just that when it opened, Navasky peeping warily out. Navasky gasped when a shotgun was poked in his face. "Stand back," the cop said.

Just then there was a high-pitched squeal, a roar of static, and a shout. The deputy pushed the door open and ran inside, the rest nearly trampling Bohlen as they followed. Nast stayed out in the hall. "Hey," Wilbur said, and received a "Shut up" in reply. There was the sound of too many men in an enclosed space, a mild crash, then, "Get that stuff off him," from Hough.

Bohlen got up, rubbing his jaw. He'd thought musicians were supposed to watch out for their hands. He looked at Nast, but the cop just stood staring at the wall. The stretcher was rolled out, and he stepped to one side. Four deputies were pushing it, followed by Hough. None of them said a word as they passed.

Bohlen watched as they went to the stairway and lifted the

stretcher. "There's an elevator, you assholes," he muttered. Then, still caressing his chin, he went inside.

Navasky was standing next to Wilbur, who was scratching his head again, as if that was what he was paid for. Behind them the readouts were dead, and there was a stink of ozone. "What happened?"

"They just came charging in here," Navasky began, but Bohlen cut him off. "Not you," he said, pointing to Wilbur.

Wilbur was short, only about five-six, with olive skin and curly hair. He was dressed in a sweatshirt and baggy Turk pants about a decade out of style. Bohlen couldn't remember his last name — some long Greek thing with enough vowels to deplete the entire alphabet. "Ross, that's it, right? Well, Ross, it seems we got hit with some ripe static."

"What type?"

Wilbur laughed and swept a hand across the blank monitors. "You asking me? I'll tell you something, though, it had to be hardcore, to take out these babies."

"You're not saying his chip did this."

"No. Had to be external." Wilbur tapped behind his ear. "Triggered by the chip, though. Preprogrammed subroutine. No need to be conscious to run it." He smiled at Bohlen. "That's the assumption, anyway."

"Well, goddamit . . ."

Wilbur raised a hand. "Oh, I can verify," he said cheerfully. "I was hooked into the fifth floor. They'll have a record."

The fifth floor — the hacker's domain back in Washington.

"Well, get on the horn and do it!"

"Okay." Wilbur turned back to the wrecked equipment. "Fun," he assured Bohlen.

"Right," Bohlen said. "Navasky, come on."

"Leave that line open," Bohlen said, walking into the suite. Morello pouted but put down the receiver. Tearing his coat off,

Bohlen went into the bathroom. "Lu," he called, turning on the water, "buzz the sheriff's den and have them put a heavy guard on that imp. Tell 'em full auto with a round in the chamber—and keep him away from any and all cybernetic systems. Make it clear what they're dealing with."

He inspected his face, wincing when he touched his jaw. As for Hough, he'd get his revenge later, administratively. Gee, I don't know what happened to that request, Sheriff. Maybe you'd better send it through again . . . Filed it six months back, you say? Hmm, that's too bad.

As he splashed cold water on his face, he heard Lu talking then the phone being hung up. She stuck her head in. "He made a crack about grandma sucking eggs. Is that dirty?"

"May as well be," Bohlen snorted. He shook water from his hands and took the towel that Lu held out. Oh, Lord, the day was catching up with him. Another couple of hours, and he'd be able to sleep hanging out the window.

"What about the other stuff?" he asked, drying his hands.

"For page, we have two references, both from psychotic subjects, one of them that woman you brought in." She paused. "With the little fort? Remember?"

He nodded, toweling his face.

"For paged, though, there's a lot. It seems they use it as a kind of code for when someone's killed."

He threw the towel on the floor. "Uh-huh," he said, biting his lip. He went out, ushering Lu ahead of him. He went to the table, looking for what, he didn't know.

"The bodies are at the morgue."

"Uh-huh. Have to get Wilbur on them."

"And Del's okay. He's still critical, but . . ."

"Yeah."

She made a small sound, and he turned to see her staring at him with her lips compressed. She still didn't understand. "Lu," he told her, "it's good to hear, but we're on war footing here."

She dropped her eyes. "I know, Ross."

One of the rookies made a contemptuous noise. Paying no attention, Bohlen leafed through the sheets on the table. Printouts, data runs; amazing how much paper an op generated, and all of it worthless. There was nothing he could learn from this.

He was convinced he'd missed something crucial; that events had swept way beyond him, leaving him mumbling over the backwash, trying to divine what was coming from the track of what had passed. Not a good feeling.

Oh, he had Page, the first sane—relatively speaking—chiphead that anybody had captured in years. He could be proud of that, but he couldn't shake the idea that Page was debris, a small token thrown his way by fate or Jehovah or Tap to keep him busy and out of the way. He really should get to work on prying him loose from the backwoodsmen. It wouldn't take much, a few calls, an order from Justice . . .

The phone rang, and Lu picked it up. She said, "It's Wilbur."

God, Bohlen thought. Twenty feet down the hall, and he uses the phone.

"Uh-huh," Lu was saying. "He says it's Norad software," she called to Bohlen. "Named THORHAMMER. It's a standard systems defense program. Quark Secret, so forget we heard it . . ."

"What?" Bohlen walked over and took the phone. "What do you mean, Norad?"

"Norad," Wilbur said. "As in Aerospace Force, Strategic Defense System, Lasersats, all that good stuff. Just got the word."

"Wilbur, that's . . . that's ludicrous."

"Hey, don't kill the messenger, I'm just relaying this. Fifth floor says it checks out. Correlates with events here to the mike. They're excited. Seems this is a first."

"How did that lowlife get a military code?"

"You got me, Ross. I'll keep riding it, though. And hey, I need some paper to cover this hardware here. Otherwise I have to pay for it."

"Yeah," Bohlen said distantly. "I'll take care of it."

He stood holding the receiver. "Anybody know where Norad HQ is?"

"It's up in Idaho," Navasky said. "Razor Mountain. It's buried a mile beneath—"

"Okay, okay," Bohlen said. He was only going to call them, not dig for them.

He glanced at Morello and was satisfied to see him leafing through a paper, far above it all. In the bedroom he closed the door and switched on his comp. Taking out his ID, he pressed it to the screen and called up the classified numbers list. He found the one he wanted, ordered the comp to put through the call, and was sitting back when the screen displayed a young woman in black military coveralls.

"Bohlen, COSSF," he said, showing his ID again. "Your CO on duty? Get him for me, please."

The woman, nice-looking even with her red hair cut short, cocked an eyebrow. "I'm sorry, but General Romero is not taking calls. If you'll leave a name . . ."

"Lieutenant," Bohlen said. "This is in reference to an activation of your comp security—what you call it, a Broken Shield— about twenty minutes ago. He'll talk to me."

The woman eyed him. "One moment, please." She was replaced by the Norad emblem, an eagle in space crushing a missile. Bohlen stretched, but dropped his arms when another face appeared: a middle-aged man, obviously Latin but with that pilot look to him—square jaw, narrow eyes, thin lips. "General Romero," the man said.

"General, this is Ross Bohlen. I'm an agent for COSSF—"

"I know who you are."

Bohlen flipped a hand. "Okay. Now, you just had an intrusion. I'm on site, and I think there's a problem."

The general smiled slightly. "I'll agree with that. I'm in touch with your Washington office. Do you have anything to add?"

Bohlen pulled at his ear. He was scratching for data, that was what it came down to, but he strongly doubted he could bulldoze this guy. Not with the normal tactics at any rate, tried and true though they were.

"General," he said slowly. "The subject involved was street. No way he could have gotten at your codes."

"Oh, we've answered that question," Romero said. His face went hard. "Your agency set up access to our system some time ago. Without informing us, I might add."

Romero went on, but Bohlen was no longer listening. He sat as if stricken while the whole thing fell into place, spread out before him like a view from the highest peak there was.

". . . assume it's some operation that you're not aware of," Romero was saying.

"General, can you give me a date on that?"

Romero looked at him quizzically.

"When access was arranged."

The general frowned but hit a key and glanced to one side. "21 January of last year," he said. "Now, Mr. Bohlen, I'm sure your office will be getting in touch . . ."

"No sir," Bohlen whispered.

"What?"

Bohlen sat up straighter. "General, we've been penetrated."

Romero's eyes narrowed further. "On what level?"

"As high as it goes."

"Mister," the general said slowly, "are you telling me that my systems are open to manipulation by renegades?"

When Bohlen nodded, Romero reached for the board. "You'll excuse me—"

"No, wait!"

Romero hesitated, then dropped his hand.

"Before you go on alert status or whatever, hear me out. As I see it, you're being used for individual defense and that's it. They haven't gone any deeper. You'd know if they had, right? Okay. Now I can wrap this up from here. I can't go into detail, but it's wide open and can be terminated tonight." He licked his lips. "But I've got to have backup."

Romero studied him for several seconds. Finally he leaned closer to the screen. "What do you need?"

"What have you got?"

They made the arrangements and clicked off. Bohlen sat in front of the blank screen. It was all clear now. Oh, details were missing, but the outline was complete and hard-edged. It was as if an old map with angels and monsters on it had suddenly turned into a modern navigational chart with latitude, longitude, depth readings, and all the rest.

January 21. The stroke had dropped Marcus on the twelfth, and he'd been in the hospital for a week before it became obvious that the attack was mortal and that all that remained was the deathwatch. He died on the twenty-eighth, unspeaking, unaware, never regaining consciousness. And in that period, for just over two weeks, who was running things?

Why, the assistant director, Harland Lee Cummins by name.

Here there be dragons, in truth.

Bohlen got up and went to the door. Nothing but muted conversation and the sound of Lu's footsteps. Pursing his lips, he thought it over. A hard move, but it had to be done. He wouldn't feel safe turning his back otherwise.

Reaching for his holster, he found it empty and cursed, remembering that the Python was in his coat pocket. He went to the suitcase and lifted out his MP-8 and a mag. Loading up, he pulled the door open, keeping the gun low.

Morello was reading the *Keyhole,* a big smirk on his face. Lu was pouring herself a cup of coffee. Navasky was sprawled on the couch, while Ling sat at the table with his feet up.

As Bohlen came over, Ling twisted his head around. "Hey, Ross," he said, just as Bohlen yanked the pistol from his holster and kicked the chair legs out from under him. "What the hell," Ling cried as he fell to his knees. On the couch Navasky shot up, and Lu dropped the full cup when she turned to see Ross leveling the guns at them.

Out of the corner of his eye Bohlen saw Morello with the

paper still up and his right hand inching toward his lapel. He swung the barrel of the machine pistol. "Go ahead."

Morello hesitated, then let the paper fall and raised his hands. "I'm not drawing on you, Bohlen."

"Good thinking." Bohlen flicked the barrel an inch. "Okay. Two fingers."

The pistol appeared—a magnum, naturally—and thumped on the floor. "One by one," Bohlen told the others.

Navasky slipped his gun out. Lu's was on the table. She stepped away from it, an almost sorrowful look on her face.

"All right, against the wall, hands high, all except for you, Lu." He waited until they had obeyed, then he relaxed. "Lu," he said, giving her a smile that got no response. "Call the sheriff."

CHAPTER 24

NAST CAUGHT THE CALL for the motel but paid it no mind. He was on his way home. Hough had insisted on it, saying he'd seen enough for one day, and Nast had to agree. He was in war mode now, jittery sick tension coursing through him, making him jump at every sound, turn his head too quickly at every light. The shot of scotch that Hough had given him from the bottle in his desk didn't help any; it just made things distant, so that every last detail in his memory gleamed with photographic clarity. Especially the grenade—dear sweet Jesus, he'd almost lost it when he saw that thing arcing toward him. It'd take a lot of scotch to push that far enough away.

It even affected his thinking about Zimmer. The rage he normally felt over a dead cop simply wasn't there. Zimmer was just another grunt now, a squad member who was around one day and gone the next. Nast shivered. Christ, but he was back in Mama East for real this time: in the mountains where the Medis owned the night.

He shifted his leg. His calf ached, as if it was badly bruised. Shoulder too, where the perp had grabbed him. He was out of shape—hard to get enough exercise, this being winter and all. He needed to work out more often, that was it.

Whatever was going on at the motel wasn't his business. Not tonight. It had to be Bohlen raising hell about something, and if Nast was pushed just one more inch by him, he wouldn't be responsible. Pulling the suspect out from under him like that—big man from Washington! By God, when the Bear laid into Bohlen, it had been all Nast could do not to join in. He had to hand it to old Leon—he'd solved that problem nicely.

The perp was another matter. Bohlen said his name was Page, but they booked the man as a Doe until they found out for sure. It seemed he was a chiphead after all, hard as that was to believe. Which complicated things; the Feds would pocket him sooner or later—but not before Nast questioned him. Who he was, what he'd been doing, where he was from, the woman, the reason he'd killed four of his own like infected cattle. When Nast got answers, he'd be satisfied. They could grab the perp then, take all the credit, splash it as far and wide as they wanted. Nast didn't care.

All that would come tomorrow. For now the perp was in the county hospital, cuffed to a bed and with an armed guard watching him. Considering the mess that had been made of his leg and how much dope had been put in him, that was precaution enough.

He turned down his own street and drove to his own house, white siding, four bedrooms, one and a half bathrooms set on two acres with a private well. An older building, mid-20th, built the way they knew how to in those days. A familiar feeling hit him when he saw it. He gripped the wheel tighter. No, he thought bitterly, I don't need this. Not now.

The knot in his stomach tightened as he pulled into the driveway and switched the car off. He sat there. He recalled Diane as he saw her this morning: eyes ringed with black circles, mouth a hard line, ignoring him when he left. He stared at the house, the emotion rising within him, finally knowing it for what it was: fear. Simply that; fear of his wife, of the person closest to him, the one he'd slept beside all these years, the one who had borne his children.

Odd, that he'd never understood it before. It was as if the greater terror of the battle behind him allowed him to acknowledge this lesser terror. It has to end, he thought. It just has to. He laughed to himself without humor. Till death do us part.

His leg hurt, and he kept it stiff as he climbed the front steps. Opening the door, he swept his hat off, setting it crown up on the table just inside—she always bitched about sweat stains. There was movement in the living room, the sound of someone getting up, quiet footsteps on the carpet. Diane walked into the hall.

"John?" she said softly.

He stared at her in puzzlement. Her face was made up, her hair combed and falling past her shoulders. She was wearing a green dress he'd bought for her—when? It must have been before the war. In the dim light of the hall she looked little different from when they'd been married.

She stopped a few feet away, clutching her hands. "I heard . . ." she began, then swallowed and started over. "I heard that something happened in town. That there was a gunfight." She nodded toward the next house. "Irene told me. She said . . . a deputy was killed."

Nast nodded. "Zimmer."

Dropping her eyes, she took a step forward. He stood unmoving.

She stopped and smiled sadly. "Oh, John," she said. "I've been a handful, haven't I?"

When he said nothing, she raised her hand to touch his face. "If you're mad, I understand. I don't blame you. But it's still the two of us, John. I forgot that, I know. But that's over. I promise. It'll be better from now on. I'll do my—"

He slapped her, hard.

Staggering back, she stood with her hand on her cheek, shoulders hunched as if expecting him to strike again. He stepped toward her, and she flinched away.

A cry from the stairway: Lydia on the landing, in pajamas,

mouth wide open. Her scream turned into a wail, then high-pitched sobbing.

Nast threw his hands out. "Oh, Christ."

Diane looked up at him. "John . . ."

Shaking his head, he yanked the door open and ran to the car. He heard her call again, but her voice, the tears, it was too much. He pulled out without looking behind him.

The yelling, he could deal with that. The fighting, too. The broken dishes, the carrying on, the silences, the bad meals, all that could be endured. But this . . . this kindness was unbearable. He could not take it.

Nast turned onto the main road and drove, just drove, cursing softly and wiping the dampness from his face.

Shivering, Telford pulled the collar of his coat up and jammed his hands deep in his pockets. Before him a school bus blocked the road, cars and trucks parked behind it, armed men swarming in the headlights.

The group he was with stood twenty feet off the highway. A dozen of them, anyone who had been driving alone or was unknown to the 501. A vig slouched behind them, fondling his old AR-15 as if aching to use it. "What the hell's going on?" the man next to him said. A businessman, evidently, wearing a well-cut coat and a fashionable beret. There was a hint of panic in his voice, and his eyes stared whitely at Telford before flicking back to the road.

Telford shrugged. He had no idea, and no urge to find out. It had been just after dark when he hit the roadblock and was hustled from the car. He asked no questions and was given no explanations, just walked obediently to where he was directed.

And had been standing in the same spot ever since, silent, mind blank, not wondering what they wanted or what it was about. It meant nothing now, any of it. He was beyond all that, done with thoughts and plans. Everything he had worked for over the years, in cities he could not remember, aboard planes, in rented cars, in shabby rooms in old buildings in decayed neighborhoods, thinking constantly, thinking until it ruined his sleep, always thinking . . . had come to desolation. A trail of blood and tears and madness that led to this cold place, while the person who mattered most lay dying on the other side of the continent.

He pushed the thought away. A man should be an empty vessel, he had been told once, long ago. He would be that empty vessel, and he would wait to be filled.

Another car had been stopped. Four vigs clustered around it and dragged the driver out.

"All right," the man shouted, shaking a vig's hand away. "If you want me to stand here, fine. But keep your hands off me."

"Vigilantes," he said to Telford as the vigs moved back to the road. "I'm pleased to say we don't have the like in Wisconsin."

Another car pulled up, a 501 card in the windshield. A stocky man in an overcoat got out and waved the vigs over. They listened as he pointed first to the captives then at the bus. Three broke away and came toward them. "Okay," one called out. "We're taking a ride."

They walked slowly to the bus, Telford staying in the middle while a line formed at the door of the bus. "Anybody wants to run for it is welcome to try," one vig said, clicking the bolt of his rifle.

"Big day in Cowpat, USA," the trucker ahead of Telford muttered as he climbed aboard.

It took them five minutes to reach the outskirts of town, the vigs standing in the aisle, guns ready. Telford sat alone, not looking out the windows. Another ten minutes and the bus pulled into the driveway of the sheriff's station and came to a halt behind the building. A car drove up, and the portly man got out, pausing to fasten his armband.

From the building's sally port, a voice rang. "What the hell's this?"

"Suspects," the lead vig called back.

Telford could see an officer silhouetted in the doorway. "Suspects for what?"

"You just get the sheriff, son," the vig said, waving the captives forward.

The vigs marched them inside, where a handful of deputies shook their heads and muttered. Just as the door closed, Sheriff Hough walked in, his eyes angry.

"Lassiter, what is this?"

"These are suspects, Sheriff," the vig replied, his voice belligerent. "We've picked 'em up and brought 'em in, as per agreement."

Hough stepped toward him. "Ben, what in the devil's name is wrong with you? If you think for one minute—"

"Don't you start with me!" Lassiter shouted back. "We lost three fine men tonight, and I'm not going to take that lying down. You're nobody to talk. If you were doing your job . . ."

"Ben," Hough said, moving closer. "I've already slugged one . . . shithead tonight, and I wouldn't mind making that two. You watch your mouth."

Lassiter glared at him. "If you won't take them," he burst out finally, "I'll lock them up myself and declare a public emergency. You hear me?"

"Ahh," Hough sighed, flinging up an arm. "All right. I'll take this bunch, but I'll do with them as I see fit. And another thing"—he shook a finger at Lassiter. "This is it. The killers are either dead or in custody. No more suspects. You go back to normal patrols, and that's all. If I hear any different, I'll put you in with them."

Smiling triumphantly, Lassiter strode out. The vigs filed after him, all but one, who stood with his rifle slung over his shoulder.

Hough turned to him. "What are you waiting for, Fallows?"

The vig put on an elaborate expression of surprise. "I'm staying as an observer," he said.

Dropping his head, Hough said quietly, "If you're still standing there in ten seconds, you're busted."

The vig seemed about to answer back but evidently thought better of it. Hough watched him leave, then turned to the deputies. "Put them in holding," he said. "We'll sort them out when we get time."

He walked into the station, saying as he went: "I've had it. I'll have those fools disbanded even if it means going to the governor . . ."

The deputies locked them in and walked off, ignoring the questions thrown at them. It was a tight fit, and Telford found himself at the outside corner, facing the corridor. Across from him was another cell, with three men inside. Two were about his age—one Oriental, the other sandy-haired and stolid. The third, wrapped in a heavy coat, was lying on a cot with his face to the wall.

The two sitting up were talking. Telford paid no attention until the repetition of a name struck him. He listened more closely.

". . . still can't believe he did this. If Del was around . . ."

"Yeah, and that's another thing. You see the way he acted when Lu told him? Like he didn't give a shit. I think he's gone nuts, you ask me."

"I don't care what it is. I'm still kicking his ass when I get out of here." The sandy-haired kid dropped his head. "Fucking Bohlen."

"What'll this do to our records?" the other said pensively. "If it gets into the files . . ."

"It's not going into the files. Once I get ahold of him, he'll be lucky if he can talk, much less run a keyboard."

"I don't know, man. Bohlen's been around."

"You kidding? You see the size of him? From Del's stories you'd think he was this big guy, but uh-uh. If he's even one-sixty, I'm a chiphead myself. If I can't take him . . ."

The man on the cot rolled half over. "Will you two shut up? Both you assholes couldn't take Lu Ann, or whatever her name is. Hang it up, willya?"

As the man rolled back over, the Oriental kid went through a strange pantomime, sticking his fingers in his shirt pocket and flinging his arms wide with his mouth open. The blond one gave a nasty chuckle and whimpered, "Please, Mr. Bohlen, I won't draw on you. I'll be good, I promise."

The man on the bed threw out a muffled curse. Grinning, the

Chinese kid looked over and caught Telford's eye. He nudged his partner, and they both gave Telford the once-over before continuing their conversation in a whisper.

Telford looked away, wondering vaguely what they'd done to end up here. He turned and slumped against the bars. A few minutes later a deputy walked by, and the cell filled with shouts. Telford didn't even raise his head.

Page breathed shallowly, doing his best to give the impression of a man completely out. It was easier now than it had been in the lifter and the emergency room—all those maggots with their hands on him, cleaning the wound, bandaging him, removing his clothes. It had taken all his control to keep from striking out right then.

He was still doped up, but riding it, concentrating on the pain in his leg to keep from nodding off. He could feel the ache of the wound growing, and almost smiled with satisfaction. That was good; the more alert he was, the better. He tried to figure out whether there was anyone out in the hall. One cop sat in the room, leafing through a magazine, from the sound of it. Page, moving his head a fraction of an inch, peered at him through slitted eyes. He could make out gray hair. He gritted his teeth. He'd been hoping it was Nast.

He felt the weight of the cuff on his right wrist. The other was attached to the bed frame. That could be a problem, if the cop didn't have the keys on him, but Page could always pull the bed apart. His left arm was free—he'd moved it carefully a few minutes earlier, to make sure. There had been an IV needle in it, but they'd taken it out.

Letting the magazine fall, the cop got up and went to the window. As he shifted his head to follow him, Page felt the tug of a monitor. There must be others that he couldn't feel.

Calling up his system, he tied in, more disoriented than usual. It was the drug. He ordered his program to explore the hospital system, and could not believe what it reported a moment later:

there were no internal safeguards at all, only the standard outside-intrusion protection, and obsolete at that.

He ordered the monitor cut off from the hospital system but with the function readouts left operating. Then, thinking it over, he sent the program in to make a few changes, introducing some variations in the subroutines. He considered enabling another military program, as he'd done back at the motel. He could access six more by manipulating the code Cummins had given him. He decided against it. There were bigger targets waiting.

He finished, then stiffened, hearing footsteps in the hall. A woman, heading this way. The door squeaked as it was pushed open.

"Hi. Where should I put these?"

Page relaxed. Just a nurse.

"Damn," the cop answered. "They were supposed to take them to the station. He won't be wearing those for a while."

A feeling of excitement filled him. His clothes! If the gloves were there . . .

"You got a place for these?" the cop went on. "I'll take them in when my relief gets here."

More footsteps. The sound of something opening, and a grunt from the woman. "Right in there."

"Good enough. Just be sure to remind me."

There was a pause, and Page felt eyes on him.

"He's one of those computer people, isn't he?" the nurse said in a hushed voice.

"Oh, I don't know about that," the cop said. "Just a story, you ask me. People can't really go into machines that way. No, he's only a crook."

"Would you like some coffee?"

"You got some, sure."

She went out, with the cop right behind her. Page moved his head to see the man stretching in the hall, and went limp when he came back into the room. The nurse returned, and they chattered for a minute before she left. "You need anything else, just call."

"I'll do that." The cop sat down. "And don't you worry about this one. I've handled worse."

Page waited until the footsteps faded, then opened his eyes and moaned. He twitched his body, jerking himself to the left side of the bed while watching the cop out of the corner of his eye. The cop stood up and hesitantly approached the bed, the left side, where Page thumped against the railing. He halted, hand on gun butt, still too far away.

Flinging his head back, Page opened his eyes wider. "I . . ." he said, making his voice guttural. "I . . ."

The cop leaned closer. "Help me," Page said, and banged his head against the railing. Moving instinctively, the cop reached for him—and Page lunged, extended middle finger spearing the eye that had barely widened before it was obliterated.

Grabbing the man's throat, he hauled his spasming body across the bed. He braced his free arm across the shoulders, gripped the forehead, and heaved upward. There was a small, barely audible snap.

As he'd hoped, the keys were in the cop's belt. He got the cuffs off, then wiped his hand on the sheet and went to the closet. The jacket was on a hanger, the shirt and sweater in a basket underneath. No pants, but he hadn't expected to find them, bloody and torn as they must be.

He rummaged frantically, feeling the shirt and sweater. The gloves were gone; some maggot had taken them. Tearing the jacket off the hanger, he went through the pockets, and nearly cried out with relief when he found the gloves stuffed into a jacket sleeve. He slipped them on, letting the jacket fall.

Now he was complete. Now nothing could hold him.

He pulled the pants off the cop, inspecting them to make sure there was no blood before putting them on. His boots were nowhere in sight, so he took the shoes too. They pinched, but he wouldn't be wearing them long. Throwing the jacket on, he picked up the discarded holster belt and took the gun: a Beretta 9. He stuck it in his waistband and went to the door.

It was silent, the calm of a hospital at night between rounds. Soft voices from the nurses' station, the rasp of something dying a few rooms away.

He took a step toward the voices and stopped. No—the dead cop would be enough of a surprise for now. He headed for the exit, opened the door carefully, smiled when no alarm sounded, then went down the stairs.

Outside, it had grown colder, and flakes of snow were falling. He inched to the corner of the building. A solitary cruiser sat in the middle of the lot. He went over, tried the keys, and unlocked it with the third. A quick examination showed that the car was an outdated model; no comps and no homing beacon.

A wave of triumph flowed through him as the motor began whining. He'd beaten them again. He always did. Stoner, Ricelli, Luke, Telford—nothing could hold Scott Page, not as he was now, and never as he would become. The irresistible force incarnate. They could all lie down and bare their bellies now to what was coming.

The way was clear. He would track Cummins to Europe or wherever he ran. He would take back what belonged to him, and with that he would gather all the forgotten weapons he had traced: the tactical nukes in the old KGB bunker on Sakhalin, the binary nerve-gas shells buried in Southern Iraq, the Anthrax C cultures still frozen in the lab in Cuba. They would learn then how they had failed. He would teach them.

But first, Nast. Page would leave him as a mark, a sign of what they were all in for. A thing they couldn't forget, an act impossible to put out of mind. The gloves, the gloves would see to Nast. He'd think with the gloves. A unique sendoff for the cop who'd kicked him. Kicked Scott Page. Nast had earned it. See to Nast. Fix Nast.

Putting the car in gear, he drove out of the lot. He had a name, he needed an address.

The first phone booth gave him that. He got back in, picked up the cop's ticket pad and punched for directions. There it was, no more than a mile away.

But after two blocks he saw someone bent over the door of a truck, working on the lock. Seeing the cruiser, the man turned and walked away. Page pulled in front of him, blocking the sidewalk. The man stopped, then put his hands up and came forward. Page waited until he nearly reached the car, then opened the door.

Bobby's eyes bulged, as if he was seeing something that had no right to exist. His mouth gaped wide, but he had no time to scream before the gloved hand struck.

CHAPTER 25

CLOSING THE DOOR, Bohlen looked at Lu. She was sitting on the couch, staring at him, both hands gripping the cushion beneath her. Her jaw moved slightly.

The Amerind deputy hadn't said a word, just shrugged and put the cuffs on Morello and the rookies. Bohlen appreciated that; he didn't particularly care to go into explanations. Maybe the entire force had decided that he'd lost his mind and were humoring him. Well, that had its advantages.

"Lu," he said. "Are you clean?"

"What do you mean?"

"I mean, if you've got anything to tell me, any deep secrets, the time is now."

Lu lowered her head a little and glared at him through her eyelashes. "I don't have any secrets, Ross."

He swept his hand at the coffee table. "Go get your gun."

She stood, eyes fixed on him. "What's going on? Is this an infiltration response, or what?"

He nodded. "That's what it is." After an uncomfortable silence Bohlen went on. "Long story, but I'll give you an outline. I've been in touch with an imp for, oh, a year now . . ." He stopped when he saw her eyes dart to her gun. "Lu," he said wearily, "will you cut it out?"

"Well, what do you expect, Ross? You tear in here waving iron around, have everybody arrested and dragged out in handcuffs—what am I supposed to think?"

He gestured at the gun. "Take it if it makes you feel better. If you don't like my story, you can shoot me. How's that?"

Crossing her arms, Lu made a face at him. "Don't tempt me."

He smiled. "We were discussing a group surrender of his people. Why he picked me, I don't know. This went on for a while— he was hesitant, as you can imagine. We went through a lot of scenarios, different possibilities. Call it negotiating. Anyway, Key West rolls around, and he vanishes, poof, gone. I wondered why."

"Why didn't you tell anybody?"

"Are you kidding? Think! Key West! How can you ask a question like that? They'd have fucked it up, that's why!"

After a moment, he continued. "Now, I liked the idea. It's what Marcus would have wanted, wrapping things up real quick, and damn well an improvement on what we're doing now. I'd gotten a little tired of pegging people whose brains were fried."

Making a quiet sound, Lu nodded.

"So I felt lousy when he dropped out of sight, and was damn pleased when he called me out here. Yeah, yesterday. I didn't question it, I didn't think about how it tied in. I just thought of it as unfinished business." He walked to the window. "Then today he doesn't call back, and all hell breaks loose, and I get evidence that our lord and master is playing both sides . . ."

"What?"

Bohlen told her what he'd learned from Norad. By the time he was halfway through, she was nodding, and when he finished, she added one word: "Cummins."

"You got it." Morello's hat sat on the table like a dead muskrat. Bohlen hooked it and tossed it behind the sofa. "What does it all mean? Who the hell knows. But I'll tell you what I think: that

I was lied to, that my boy was in touch with the Hillbilly all along, that this is an operation planned way back, and that we've only scratched the surface."

"But if they're working together, then why didn't Cummins know about the calls, and if he did, why didn't he do something?" Lu shook her head in confusion. "I don't know, Ross."

"I don't either. It drives you nuts if you try to think it through. But there's a connection, and we've got to go worst case: that ten million chipheads with our names, addresses, and shoe sizes are coming to git us in five minutes . . . Oh, don't worry, in a while we'll have more protection than we need."

Lu stared at him, then nodded. "Good."

"So we're agreed. Let's start by getting me Hector Salgado's number . . . Don't look at me like that, Lu. I'm tired, and we have to get cracking here. Both numbers, home and office." He went to the coffee urn, picked up Lu's gun—a .38 Namura, nice piece but a little fancy. "Why don't you put this someplace?" Pouring himself a cup, he headed for the bedroom.

Lu called out, "I have both of them." He grunted his aproval and sat on the bed. "If it's no big secret, why are you calling . . ."

The screen flashed. Bohlen quickly hit delete; it couldn't possibly be anyone he wanted to talk to. He listened, but Lu was speaking too low for him to hear anything.

She appeared at the door. "It's Washington," she whispered. "They want to talk to you."

"Tell 'em I'm up in the woods drinking whiskey with the gold miners. And put a block on their number when you get rid of them. The sheriff's department too. They'll want to chat soon enough."

He switched on. Two numbers appeared, and he punched for Hector's office—Greater Delmarva Computer Security, Inc. To his surprise he got through immediately. Hec must be working late.

He leaned forward in puzzlement. Somebody was there, all right, and it seemed to be Hec, but he was in silhouette, dead black against a white background. The figure began speaking.

"I have just inserted a virus into your system," it said, then bobbed with sepulchral laughter as morbid music played.

Bohlen cut it off. Jeeze—long distance, and you get an ad. Wasn't there a law against that?

He hit the home number. Hector appeared, this time full face and in color. "Hey, Ross. What's up?"

Salgado was one of those Cubanos who looked as if he could give a detailed and scholarly lecture on the evolution of Latin magical realism if you ignored the way his jacket clashed with his pants. He now wore a wildly patterned ascot and a vest with a gaudy pin on the lapel. Ross was glad he couldn't see the rest of the outfit.

"Hec, I've got a problem you can help me with."

"Yeah? Where you at?"

"Montana, if you can believe it."

"I believe it. God, I'm glad I'm not doing that anymore."

"Right. You got a minute?"

"Well, I'm taking the woman out to dinner, but go ahead."

Out to dinner. The appetizers might have to wait.

"Okay, it's like this . . ."

Bohlen went through the story, using his hands, hurrying over the weak spots, emphasizing the main points with as much drama as he could muster. Salgado nodded once or twice, which was encouraging. ". . . so," Bohlen wound up. "He's due in at National in, oh, about an hour or so."

Salgado adjusted his ridiculous ascot. "Let me get this straight. You want me to kidnap a major security official of the US government?"

"Well, Hec, I wouldn't put it quite that way, but . . . yeah."

Salgado dropped his head and nodded to himself. "Ross— don't get me wrong now, I'd love to kick Harland's ass. But this? What does Del say?"

"Del? Well, he's kinda . . ."

"Yeah, kinda."

"No, Hec, wait." Bohlen moved closer to the screen. "You know, I was thinking about Ricelli."

He stopped there, knowing that was enough. Hec and Ric had been close. "Ross, are you telling me . . ."

"That's how it looks."

"You got hit too, Ross." Salgado's eyes narrowed to slits. "You think . . ."

"Yeah," Bohlen said. "I think."

There was a sound behind Salgado. He called out, "One second, hon." Bohlen closed his eyes for a moment. When he opened them, Salgado was punching the keyboard. "Okay," he said. "What time does the bastard pull in?"

Three minutes later Bohlen pushed the screen back and reached for his coffee. It was tepid, and he'd forgotten the sugar. He set it back down. Hec was going to treat this as a straight industrial intrusion pickup. Full team: two of his best, with a backup crew and a driver in an unmarked, noncyb van. The only difference was that they wouldn't be carrying IDs.

It was Bohlen's guess that Cummins planned to dump his guards and hop an overseas flight. They would pick him up at that moment and stash him in a house Salgado had in Alexandria, a place where he put software specialists on short-term contracts. Mushmouth could sit there until Bohlen got things straightened out or else discovered he'd made a foolish mistake that he'd have to apologize for.

He left the bedroom. Lu was bent over the printer, stacking sheets as they emerged. He saw that it was on the fax setting. "What's all that?"

"A list of active military software," Lu said.

"A *what*? You mean they cleared that for you?" He snatched the stack out of her hands. COSSF had been trying to get a look at those files since the war. "You're kidding!"

Lu shrugged. "They're worried."

He flipped quickly through the stack. The sheets kept coming. "How many are there?"

"Five hundred something, they said. The ones in bold are the most vital. Symbols at the end show coverage, type, language, mode. They're analyzing to see if anything's been compromised." She handed him a single sheet. "These are the ones they're most concerned about. Same code prefix as THORHAMMER."

He looked it over. "It's in English," he said.

"I asked them to do that." She retrieved the stack and added the new sheets. "I was thinking about you."

JERICHO, PONY SOLDIER, BLOOD & GUTS . . . God Almighty, where'd they dig up these names? The descriptions were clear, anyway. JERICHO erased anything within a thousand-klick area. PONY SOLDIER did the same for all systems using non-Ada machine language. ALEXANDER . . . Now this was cute; an ultraviroid to infest all foreign datanets in case the US ever got whipped. No wonder they were keeping this stuff under wraps. The next one, RUDOLF ABEL, whited out only software with a COSSF prefix . . .

"Those scum," Bohlen muttered. "I bet they—" He became aware of a low rumble outside. He raised a hand for silence, listened, then went to the window.

"What's that?" Lu asked.

"The cavalry." He parted the blinds and saw that it was snowing. Fat flakes drifted languidly past, as if in no rush at all to reach the pavement. The rumbling grew louder, till the pane shook. He peered through the curtain of snow. There—a huge black shape visible only in outline. He winced as searchlights flared from it. Through the afterimages he saw a figure running down the street. Black coat, fur hat . . . it was that reporter. Sticking his tongue between his teeth, Bohlen cackled evilly.

When the lifter moved out of sight, he headed for the door. "Be right back."

The staff and a good percentage of the guests were standing in the lobby. "Excuse me," he said, pushing through. Just outside the entrance he saw a figure in armor and a helmet, visor pulled down. "Where's your CO?" he asked. The soldier nodded and about-faced without a word. Shivering a bit, Bohlen followed.

He threw his head back when they turned the corner. The lifter loomed ten feet or more above him, wisps of steam still rising from beneath the hull. It was dead black, the Air Force roundels gray between antennas and weapon points.

Like to see Nast ticket this bird, he thought, walking to the group that stood at the open rear ramp.

They were dressed in torso armor over light fatigues, and probably with heated tights underneath. Most carried assault rifles, but there was an officer standing in the center with only a shoulder holster. Bohlen went over to him.

The man lifted his visor. "You Bohlen?"

"That's me."

"Well, Corporal, what's the word?"

Oh boy. They'd checked and found out he was still on the Army lists. He took in the oak leaves on the man's shoulders. Damned if he was going to salute. "Corporal? I thought I'd at least have made second louie by now."

The major smiled thinly. "Not quite. The name's Moore. What can we do for you?"

"You get a briefing?"

"Yes. And I'm here to tell you that if things get out of hand, I'm authorized to take over. Until then, you're in charge."

"Out of hand?"

"Another penetration, to start with." He stared unblinking at Bohlen. The Air Force was not happy, no indeed.

Bohlen kicked away the snow on the tip of his shoes. "Right. This isn't the whole unit, is it?" He gestured at the troops surrounding them.

"I have another heavy and two gunships." The major pointed across the street. "Open space a half-klick over. I'm told there's a lot of smashed-up machinery there."

"Yeah, I know," Bohlen said. "How many men?"

"Forty ground troops."

"Okay. I'll need two for this place, another two for a special mission, and the rest . . . Can you close up the town?"

"Nothing simpler."

"Even in this snow?"

The major sighed. "I'm fully integrated with Milstar, and I've got IR search systems that you don't have the rank for me to tell you about. Yes, I can cut this place off."

"Hmph." Bohlen stroked his jaw. The soldiers watched him placidly. "Okay, deploy your snakes out west, over the mountains. Standard interdiction pattern, I guess. Won't be much traffic, so any activity is suspect. Jump it and let me know. If you're fired on, DX 'em. This is a bad bunch."

"Number of hostiles?"

"Two to twenty. Act on the high figure. The east end . . ."

"I can cover it."

"Fine. Where's the CP?"

Moore nodded at the other side of the street. "Open area there. This special mission, what is it?"

"Pickup at the hospital. One of my people will accompany."

"Local law?"

"I'll let 'em know. Any problem, you call me. There's a gang of vigs, though . . ."

The major's gloved hand cut the air. "We'll see to them. As for the hostiles, how do we identify them?"

Bohlen smiled. "A busload of maniacs, Major."

Moore considered that and nodded. Selecting four men to go with Bohlen, he sent the rest up the ramp and followed.

"Thanks for showing up," Bohlen called as the ramp closed.

"My pleasure," Moore said, and poked his thumb in the air.

Bohlen looked at the visors surrounding him and shook his head. "We didn't have swell helmets like that in my day."

A soldier standing next to him flipped his visor up. "You were lucky," he said. "They suck."

CHAPTER 26

AFTER AN HOUR a deputy unlocked the cell and herded them into the back room. Telford stood staring through the bars until the cop banged his nightstick against the door. He followed, the last to join the group. The Indian deputy he'd spoken to yesterday was leaning against the door, arms across his chest. He gave Telford a mild frown when he saw him.

"All right," the cop who'd brought them out said. "One at a time. Names and addresses . . ."

The sheriff walked in. Seeing him, the Indian leaned over and spoke quietly. Hough nodded, and approached Telford.

"Excuse me," he said. "Deputy Frostmoon says he knows you. You've got family out at the station, that right?"

Telford nodded.

The sheriff tugged with embarrassment at his mustache. "Well, if you'll just step over here, sir."

Telford went with him.

"He's okay, Ralph," the sheriff told the deputy. "Get his things."

While Frostmoon went down the hall, Hough stood fidgeting. Behind them Telford could hear someone arguing about an expired driver's license. Finally Hough turned and cleared his throat. "I can understand it if you're a little angry. I sure would be. But it's kind of a strange situation. You wouldn't believe what's been happening in this town today . . ."

Telford let him run on. When the sheriff finished, he nodded again.

Hough laughed and clapped him on the arm. "I'm glad you're not taking this to heart. I'd feel really bad if you thought you weren't welcome in Ironwood . . . Ah, here we are."

The deputy handed Telford a small Manila envelope. Telford slipped it into his pocket.

"That's everything, Ralph? All right. Now, your car. It's still out there where those pinheads stopped you. I think we can give a lift to Mr. . . . can't we, Ralph?"

"The call from that trucker, Chief."

The sheriff's face lit up. "That's right. Well, it's not so bad, after all. That poor retarded girl who lives with your . . . sister, that it? She was picked up hitchhiking. The driver is bringing her here. I suppose you were out looking for her, that right?" Hough gave him a look of mock severity. "You should have called us. That's what we're here for, after all. Ralph, he can wait out front. When she pulls in, we'll get you both home, all right?"

The deputy said something about down the hall. Telford went through the door and saw a bald man running wildly toward him. He stepped aside as the man ran past.

"Chief," the man hollered, bracing himself in the doorway. "It's the hospital. Cole's dead and the prisoner's gone. That's what they told me. Cole's car, too. They called from a phone booth. Everything is out over there. Lights, power. They're trying to get a generator going, patients are dying . . ."

The deputy jumped to one side as the sheriff burst through. "Get everybody out there, *now*," he said. "Dammit, dammit, dammit . . ."

The two cops followed, the Indian pulling his jacket on. "And we'd better call Bohlen," Hough said over his shoulder.

It took a second for the name to penetrate. Bohlen? Why call Bohlen? Telford now thought of what the sheriff had said in the back room. He'd let it drift by him then, thinking it as meaningless as everything else. Frowning, he tried to bring it back. Something about a manhunt, a gunfight, men killed. And they'd caught one of them, and that one had escaped, with another cop dead and the hospital system down.

It could only mean one thing.

There was a chorus of moans and curses from the back room as the men returned to the cell. Turning away, Telford hurried to the front entrance. He passed an open door where he heard the sheriff shouting into a phone. Outside, he paused to get his bearings, then went in the direction of the mountains. It was snowing heavily. The flakes struck his face, obscuring his vision. With ungloved hands he wiped them away.

It was Page; he was certain of it. They had caught him without knowing what they had caught. He was loose again now, free and howling the hatred that was his sole and terrible song. They had not known; there was no way they could have known.

But Telford knew. He recognized him now, he could see clearly the mark on his forehead. He had always seen it.

It was a little over a mile to where the car was, twenty minutes—less, if he hurried. His steps widened, and in a moment he was running and sliding through the new-fallen snow.

Seeing lights, he slowed down. He heard voices muffled by snow. He approached at a walk, filled with foreboding when he beheld the bleak outline of the object ahead. It came into focus: some kind of warplane, black and ugly, perched in the middle of the road. Men stood arguing next to it.

". . . I don't give a shit what you are. You hand me that piece or you're dropped, pal."

A soldier in combat gear, his back to Telford, was confronting a red-faced vigilante. Beyond them were three other soldiers, visors down and guns aimed at a sullen knot of men.

The soldier held his hand out. "You gonna do what I tell you, or what?" The vig just glared. Turning his head, the soldier said, "Kneecap this fucker, Private."

Another soldier stepped forward, clicking a round into the chamber of his rifle. The vig paled, held a hand up, then reached for his holster.

"Real slow," the officer said. "Okay, drop it."

The gun fell into the snow.

"Now hit the road, all of you."

The vigs moved off to their cars. A soldier who had been standing near the lifter stepped into Telford's view. He threw his visor up, snapped a mike to his lips, and was saying, "Charlie Able," when he noticed Telford.

"Lieutenant," he said. "We've got another one here."

"He armed?" the lieutenant said, swinging toward Telford. "Well, are you?"

Telford shook his head. The soldier stuck his thumb over his shoulder. "You too, then," he said. "Go the fuck home."

As Telford passed, the radio man resumed his message. "Sent a pack of vigs to their kennels. Coordinates follow . . ."

It took Telford several minutes to find the car, covered with snow as it was. He cleared the windshield with his sleeve, got in, and started up. A truck was blocking him. He had to back up to go around it. For a moment it seemed he would be stuck, but the wheels finally stopped spinning and caught, and he pulled onto the road. As he headed west, the lifter took off behind him, the roar of its engines made softer by the snow.

To make one's plans . . .

The cruiser had snow tires, so he had no trouble with the road. The street was right up ahead. He slowed to make the turn, ignoring the strangled sobs from the back seat.

To choose one's victims . . .

Slowing more, he peered through the driving snow at the house numbers. It was a short crescent, only a few houses. There it was.

White, solid, impeccably middle-class. Nothing in the driveway, but the lights were on. He went past it and turned around, so that the car would be facing the main road when he was finished.

To wreak an implacable vengeance . . .

He sat for a moment, glorying in the feeling that surged through him. He flexed his gloves once, got out, and walked to the house.

The front door opened. A woman spoke, her voice little more than a whisper. "John?"

Then she saw him, and her mouth opened. Her lips began to quiver. "Who . . . ," she said, stepping back, trying to close the door. He kicked it open and stood, legs wide, watching the play of her features as she realized what had come to her.

A small creature made a sound from the top of the stairs. "Lydia, go hide!" the female maggot screamed as it backed away. He let it reach the foot of the stairs before he leaped.

There is nothing like it in the world.

CHAPTER 27

"THAT'S MY HOUSE," he said when he first heard it, and he'd been saying that's my house every foot of the way home.

Somebody came into the bar and told him his cruiser lights were flashing; all-points, all officers assist. He finished his drink, went out, and switched on the radio.

He didn't remember starting the car or pulling out. It was as if he'd been born here, hands on the wheel, headlights glaring through billowing snow, and saying over and over, "That's my house."

The radio didn't tell him much. A lot of bulletins, but nothing solid. They kept mentioning the hospital. Had Diane been taken there? And the kids, what about the kids? Should he forget the house, keep driving?

He shook his head to clear it. Just two or three boilermakers, but they'd done a job on him. Exhausted, an empty stomach . . . He'd wanted to knock himself out, and he'd been well on his way. He squeezed his eyes tight. He decided on the house. It was closer, and Hough was there. He'd be able to tell Nast what had happened.

A few more messages. It dawned on him that the perp had escaped. He reached for the mike. No, let it wait. If he waited, it wouldn't be as bad as he thought. He pressed the pedal down. The car fishtailed a little but stayed on the road. At the turn he almost skidded into the opposite curb. Ahead were flashers, broadened and softened by the snow. He pulled to a stop.

It was his house.

The med lifter sat in the middle of the street, yellow lights flashing. Near it were three cruisers. The front door of his house was open. He watched a man in white step out and go to the lifter.

It was just like on the hillside; the dancer, lying broken in the snow. He found himself walking toward the house. Crossing the lawn, passing his neighbors who turned and whispered among themselves, refusing to meet his gaze.

But it wasn't he who went through the door, who saw the dark red splattered on the stairwell, over the walls, in a trail across the carpet to the living room. It wasn't he, it was just an empty pair of eyes that took all this in.

The eyes fixed on the top of the stairs, where Lydia had sobbed only a short time ago. He opened his mouth to call out her name. Nothing emerged. Not a sound.

People in the living room: quiet movements, low voices, an occasional word. Hough, his face twisted and pale.

"No, oh no . . ."

He tried to move past, but Hough grabbed him and threw him back. "No, Johnny, you're not going in there."

Over Hough's shoulder he'd seen wrecked furniture, more red, and a cluster of men bent over something. "It's her," he mumbled to Hough. "It's the dancer."

Someone else gripped his arm, and he heard another voice behind him. "I'll get him out of here, Bear."

"Do that, Ralph." Hough dropped his eyes. "God knows it's the least . . ."

He felt an arm around his shoulder. "The dancer," he said as

Ralph led him outside. There was no answer, and he tried to think of something else. "He was here," he said finally.

"Yeah," Ralph said when they reached his cruiser. "Yeah. But we'll get him, Johnny. Don't you worry. We'll get him."

Ralph opened the door, but someone called to him. He waved and turned to Nast. "One second, Johnny."

Nast watched him walk off, then stared blankly at the house. A series of images rose in his mind: Diane in the doorway, the kids beside her, Diane working in the garden, the kids out back, Diane as he'd seen her just a few hours ago . . .

His breath caught. He lifted his hand to his face, the gloved fingers spread wide. He could still feel the sting where he had struck her. The shock on her face, Lydia's cry . . .

He looked at the open front door. He had done this. He had sent a signal, had called it down, bringing it here as if he had paid for it to be done.

He dropped his hand to his pistol. But no, that could wait. There was something he had to do first.

Turning from the house, he went down the street to his car.

The rapping jerked Bohlen out of a dream. In the dream he was wearing a fluorescent pink suit and running through darkness across the golf course behind his parents' house. Both Tap and Cummins were out there, tracking him down. Tap had turned out to be Jethro's brother. Bohlen kept moving, from a sand trap to a rise to the rough in back of the 18th hole, but no matter what he did, they spotted his suit and followed him. He tried to take at least the jacket off, but it wouldn't unbutton, and as the enemy came closer, he heard his dad's voice and turned to see him leaning over the fence. "Ross," Dad said, "didn't I tell you about those pink suits?"

He rubbed his eyes and inspected the room, carefully sorting things out until they began to take on significance. Screen, keyboard, motel room. No putting green, no Cummins, no pink suit.

The banging at the door came again. He got up and made his

way to the main room, to the door, and finally opened it, but there was no one there, so he closed it again.

He heard a whine from the street and reached the window in time to see a patrol car pull away. He let the slats drop back. What the hell did they want?

The phone rang. Picking it up, he said "Bohlen."

"Ross?"

"Yeah, yeah."

"That you? You sound funny."

It was Hector Salgado. What was he . . . Oh, yeah. "No, no, I'm fine. What's going on?"

A chuckle. "We got him. You had it pinned. He sent his boys home and was at the El Al counter when we picked him up."

"Well, that's good, Hec, real good."

"What's the matter? You don't sound too enthusiastic."

"No, it's outstanding, really. I'm proud of you."

"Okay. Now when are you gonna nail it down?"

"Tonight," Bohlen said firmly. "Midnight the latest."

"You *are* going to get it nailed down, aren't you?"

"Of course. We have the guy."

"Just kidding. Listen, I'm calling from a restaurant. Got to get back to the wife. Call me at home."

"Will do."

He hung up and went to the bathroom to throw some water on his face. He'd better start thinking how to present this to Washington. It would be a battle, that was for sure. Not that he was worried; he had Page, he had Cummins, now all he needed was Tap.

As he dried his face, he heard the wail of sirens outside. He smiled to himself. In an uproar, were they? Probably out chasing military lifters. Good. Keep 'em busy.

Leaving the car running, Nast walked to the sally port and let himself in. He listened for a moment: some grousing from the cells but nothing more. There didn't seem to be anybody around.

The cellblock exploded as he walked by, cries and pleas from an oddly crowded unit. He ignored them and went to the main hallway. It was empty except for a raggedly dressed woman sitting on a bench in front of the night desk. Going to Hough's office, he lifted the key from the rack, retraced his steps, turned into the locker room, and stopped at the armory door.

Unlocking it, he switched on the light and went in. He paid no attention to the grenade launchers and sniper's pieces but went to the assault rifles, picking up the first one: an AK-08, foam steel, light as plastic, a late-model nightsight attached. Underneath were the ammo bins. He pulled them open, selected a package and tore the wrapping off, and took out two thirty-round clusters of cartridgeless. He slipped one in the magazine and the other in his pocket and left.

Powell was at the front desk. He looked up in surprise. "Johnny," he said. "My God, I don't know what to say . . ."

Nast said, "Have they tracked him yet?"

"Who?"

He rapped the countertop as he spoke. "Him, him . . ." A name popped into his mind. "Page . . . the one from the hospital."

There was a gasp behind him. He half-turned, then looked back at Powell. "No, Johnny." Powell shook his head. "They will, though. Everybody's out on this one." He glanced at the gun. "Hey, that won't do any good. Why don't you put it down and—"

"Mind your business, Neil." He turned to see who had gasped. It was the ragged woman, standing and staring at him. She stepped forward and spoke. "Are you going to kill him?"

Nast looked at her.

"Are you going to kill Page?"

He nodded. "Yes."

She broke into a broad smile. "Good."

"Wait," he said. "Where is he?"

She blinked in surprise. "At the house."

Nast was about to ask what house, when it came to him who she was. The house; that had to be the ecology station west of town.

"He chased us out," the woman was saying. "He was trying to hurt Jase. I came back to help."

"He's out there now?"

She nodded brightly. "He took our house away."

Her things were piled on the bench. A nondescript package, a knapsack, an old suitcase. Atop the suitcase a stuffed bird was perched, wings spread as if it were ready to take off.

The woman leaned toward him. "Be careful," she said. "He's very dangerous."

"I will," he said, and turned and left the station.

Bohlen supposed he should be feeling like a man at the center of the action, the prime mover sardonically contemplating the whirlwind he had set in motion, all the while knowing how everything would turn out. He didn't. He felt more like somebody who'd lit the fuse to a pile of explosives underneath him and was now watching the flame crawl nearer and hoping it wouldn't hurt too much.

He thought of the possible consequences: disgrace, endless interrogation, public pillorying, a ten-year sentence digging out the locks in Panama. He turned each of these prospects over in his mind. Well, however bad it got, at least he'd have the pleasure of taking Jethro with him. A perfect solution: just sit blinking Eddie Frisell-like and say over and over, "Why, Mr. Cummins told me to."

It would almost be worth it.

At this point he probably should call Hough and see if the man had anything enlightening to say. He tried to recall if he'd told Lu to warn Hough about the military. If he hadn't, no problem; those cowboys needed to be taken down a notch anyway.

He went to Lu's comp and picked the command out on the damnfool high-speed keyboard she used. The screen beeped, displaying the departmental seal. A breathless voice said, "We're sorry, but there's no one present to answer your call. If this is an emergency, please contact—"

He cut off and made a face at the screen. But as he was getting up, it beeped again. He hit return; the screen stayed blank, but a voice spoke. "Bohlen?"

"Speaking."

"This is Moore."

Bohlen leaned forward. "Yeah?"

"Picked up something west of town. Patrol found an abandoned car out there . . ."

Bohlen rolled his eyes. An empty car in the middle of a blizzard. You don't say. Outstanding work, Major. Keep it up . . .

Moore was still speaking. ". . . and a bag job farther up the slope. Male, late twenties. Badly beaten, skull fracture, neck broken." The major went on more slowly. "I can't swear to this, but my medic may have detected an implant chip."

Bohlen's pulse began to race. "Honest to God."

"Hard copy. Now, a patrol car just passed the site, heading west. You want us to call them in or—"

"No," Bohlen said quickly. "Bring the body back here."

"Okay," Moore said. "You're the boss."

"Where'd they find it, exactly?"

"Coordinates are . . . you have a map?"

He tapped out access. "Give it to me."

"It's yours."

Bohlen looked up, turned to the map. There it was, in the foothills a few miles away. "Okay," he said. "Outstanding work, Major. Keep it up."

"Will do," Moore said. "Out."

He went over to the map. Nothing much out that way; a few homes, some ranches to the south, and right there . . . That must be the environmental station he'd heard about. He bit his lip. Tell

Moore to put everything he had out there? But it might be some kind of decoy . . .

Lu walked in, brushing snow from her hair. Behind her were two soldiers, their visors up.

"He escaped, Ross," she said, spreading her arms. "The CEI; he's gone."

He looked from her to the soldiers and back again. "Now, Lu, you didn't let those hicks bullshit you . . ."

Her face reddened. One of the soldiers took off his helmet. "No, sir," he said. "Not the way they were acting. Suspect killed one officer, then went off to do more of the same."

"He broke into a house," Lu said. "I don't know if it's a hostage situation or not. They wouldn't tell me."

"You got a bad one there, Mr. Bohlen," the soldier said.

"They're going wild over at the hospital, Ross. The sheriff was screaming . . ."

Bohlen had already put on his coat. "Where's Hough now?"

"He was going over to that house . . ."

"And we don't know where that is. Okay."

Standing at the urn, the second soldier said, "Hey Lu, you want a cup of coffee?"

Bohlen went to the door. So Lu had made some new friends. That was nice; he always liked to see that. "I'm going to the cophouse. You sit tight. I'll be back."

It took him some time to get there. At least four inches of snow had fallen, with more coming down. He nearly went off the road twice. Idiots couldn't even keep them plowed—but then again, there was a reason for that, wasn't there?

Pulling in front of the station, he ran inside. A small woman sat on the bench, playing with something that Bohlen saw was a bird. For a second he thought it was alive, then noticed how stiff it was.

He went to the desk and asked the bald deputy behind it, "Hough around?"

The man gave him a foul look. "Nope."

"You know where he is?"

Taking a sheet and pen, the deputy began writing something, his movements precise. "Can't say I do."

Bohlen looked at the shiny pate. "How about Nast?"

The deputy rose abruptly. "Mister," he said. "You don't want to come across Johnny right now . . ."

A door slammed in back, and Bohlen heard voices, one of them Hough's.

". . . so my advice to you is to leave while you have the chance," the deputy concluded.

Bohlen stepped down the hall and saw Hough, who was accompanied by a gray-haired man wearing a long sheepskin coat. Catching sight of Bohlen, Hough said something to the older man, then they both came toward him.

"Sheriff," the bald deputy said.

"I see him, Neil," Hough said.

"This is the man you told me about?" the older man said.

"That's him."

He looked Bohlen over. "I've got a few things to say to you, mister. Sheriff, we'll use your office."

"Who the hell is this?" Bohlen asked.

"The mayor," Hough told him.

Bohlen smiled. "Oh, the *mayor*."

"Sheriff," the deputy said again.

"What is it, Neil?"

"Johnny came here fifteen minutes back."

"Good," Hough said with evident relief. "I was wondering. Where is he?"

"I don't know. He went right out again. He had a rifle."

"Oh, Lord," Hough said. "Do you know where?"

"No sir. He talked to her—"

"Who?"

"Her." The deputy pointed at the woman. "Then he left."

Bohlen glanced at the woman, and took a closer look. He went over to her slowly, feet sliding on the floor as if he were sneaking up. He crouched down, took out his ID, and held it up, thumbing it as he did.

"Bohlen, what the hell are you doing?"

The woman gazed blankly at the card for a moment, then her face twisted and the bird fell to the floor. She started to moan.

Reaching out, Bohlen grasped her hand. "It's all right," he said. "It's okay."

She pulled her hand away and shrank back, arms wrapped around herself.

"It's been like this all week," Hough was telling the mayor.

Bohlen turned to them. "Where's she from?"

"Bohlen, what are you . . ."

He pointed at the woman. "Where does she live?"

"Out at the station," the deputy said.

Bohlen closed his eyes and saw a glowing dot on a map.

"What of it . . . ," Hough began, but Bohlen was already running for the door.

CHAPTER 28

TELFORD HALTED when the lodge came into sight. The windows glowed brightly. He couldn't recall—had he left the lights burning or were they set to go on automatically?

He resumed slogging through the calf-deep snow, keeping close to the trees. He'd parked the car on the road—it would never have made the climb.

It could be Gene. Of course it was. Who else knew about the alarm software . . . But then, with a chill, he saw an unknown car just past the truck. He squinted at it through billowing white. Keeping low, he went closer.

It was a patrol car. He sighed in relief, not caring what it meant beyond the fact that Page was not there. He'd been thinking about it on the drive over: there weren't many places Page could hide, with the cops and Cossacks and Army watching the roads. Several times he'd almost turned back himself, but there weren't many places Telford could hide either.

Something made him approach the cruiser. His possibilities closed when he saw the driver's door smeared with blood.

His mind cleared, more than it had for days, but it was the

clarity of fear. Scenes marched through his head, and he could not stop them: Page with the ax, Page standing over him, Page in a hallway long ago, with blood on the floor and a screaming man at his feet.

He closed his eyes, forcing the images away, remembering what he had been told as a child: that the bones of the Beast must crack at Judgment, and that this sound would echo across all creation.

The windows, blank lighted squares, revealed nothing. He took a hesitant step toward the house. He stopped. He went instead to the truck. The comp in the truck was integrated with the lodge system. He could query it and find out if anybody was inside, how many there were, and exactly where . . .

Gripping the door handle, he stopped again. It would also announce to Page that he was here, like arriving in a blazing chariot with trumpets blowing.

He let his hand fall and turned to the house, moving quickly so as not to allow his thoughts to gather.

At the steps he tried for silence, but the fresh snow squeaked under his boots. Then he was turning the knob, standing to one side. The door was unlocked. He pushed it open.

"Dammit, Bohlen, that's how we operate."

Bohlen grabbed for the handrail as the lifter made a steep bank. There were no extra seats, and he stood just outside the cockpit. Through the windshield he could see nothing but snow. They must be in the mountains by now. He hoped this thing had a good nav system.

Silhouetted by readout lights, Moore glared at him. "We set up a perimeter, we isolate the site, we move in. A followed by B followed by . . ."

Bohlen didn't want to be taken through the alphabet. "What you think this is, an exercise?"

Moore made a disgusted sound.

"No," Bohlen repeated. "We jump right on top of 'em—what you call it, *coup de main*. I go in first. They get a chance to surrender."

"See here, mister—"

"No, you see here. I know what we're up against and you don't."

Somebody up front called for Moore, who excused himself and stepped into the cockpit. Bohlen shook his head wearily. If he'd had the lifter pick him up at the station, it'd be over already. Fool move, driving back to the motel, but he'd been too excited to think. It was probably just as well, though, with the sheriff and mayor both trying to take him apart.

In the troop bay the soldiers resumed talking. Bohlen saw that the whole damn squad was eying him, visors and helmets making them look like a jury of trolls. He grimaced. He'd heard what they had to say: Cossack, hitman, headhunter. And his yelling at their CO probably hadn't done anything to lighten their opinion.

Moore emerged from the cockpit. "Now look, Bohlen . . ."

Taking a deep breath, Bohlen prepared to cut him off, but a beep sounded behind them. "Major," a voice called out. "We have activity."

The living room was empty, the house silent. The lighted comp screen was the only sign of life. Telford stepped inside.

The coffee table had been pushed against a wall, and something unidentifiable lay on the carpet. Red and white. He bent closer. Towels, at least a dozen of them, all soaked in blood. He let out a slow breath, audible in the stillness. He glanced around the room, trying to remember a time when the place had been this quiet.

His eyes fell on the comp screen. An URGENT blinked in the right-hand corner. He went over to it. The source line read Fort Collins.

He reached into his pocket for a chip but changed his mind.

He stepped to the comp and raised a hand to the keys. A blast of white noise struck him, a wave of power blazing across the spectrum. He fell before it.

Bohlen looked over to the ferret station. That had been a woman's voice. He hadn't known there were any women aboard.

"Details," Moore said.

"Source at target site, two nanos' duration, commercial hardware freak. Analyzing."

She was dressed the same as the rest of the unit: helmet visor, armor. Despite himself he craned his neck to get a look at her face. The voice sounded nice.

When she turned, he was disappointed to see that her visor was halfway down. "It's friendly ware, sir."

"Get a fix, Sandy."

"Sir."

Moore swung toward the cockpit. "Enable weapons suite, orbit at one klick."

There was burst of activity from the front, and the lifter turned sharply. "Moore," Bohlen said. "What the hell . . ."

"Back off, Bohlen. You're out of this."

"You wait one goddamn minute. You can't just blow that villa—"

"I have orders, mister," Moore snapped. "Contact gunboats," he told the copilot. "Tell them to station themselves one-eighty our course. Lock and load, open up on my—"

Bohlen grabbed his arm. "Moore, you just listen . . ."

The major shook him off and turned to a soldier perched directly behind Bohlen. "Lieutenant," he said calmly. "If this individual says another word, you clock him."

"Yes sir," the lieutenant answered, with more enthusiasm than Bohlen had heard all night.

Moore was headed forward. Taking a step after him, Bohlen called out, "Hey!"

A hand grabbed him from behind. He turned his head to see a blank visor confronting him.

"Shut up," it said.

His hand was touching something damp and cool. Before him he saw only a smooth surface, light brown in color, broken by regular lines.

Telford blinked and became aware that it was the ceiling of the room. He took a breath, expecting pain. It did not come. He was adrift, well separated from whatever was transpiring in this place. He considered trying to move, at least an arm or a leg. It seemed like too much effort.

Something was going on deep in his mind, far below the level of thought. With a sense of dread he tried to isolate it, but it vanished like a distant star too directly gazed at.

A shadow grew on the ceiling. Telford shifted involuntarily, surprised that he could move. He squeezed the damp thing, and with a shock realized that it was one of the bloody towels.

Page came into view above him, a pistol held high. His eyes were wide, the pupils huge and black. His lips twitched. "Got it," he whispered, and flung the pistol away. He was shirtless, splotches of blood drying on his chest. He stepped closer, and Telford saw that he was wearing a single glove.

He began slapping the glove with its mate. A metallic click each time they struck. He muttered something. It took a moment for Telford to realize he was saying his name.

"Or is it Jase?" Page's voice grew louder, its tone clipped. "That better? That's what they called you. Isn't it? Kahn. The rest. Jase. That's right."

He stepped away. "Doesn't matter. Names. What are they? Labels for maggots. All they got. I don't have a name. No name for what I am. No need."

Telford squeezed his eyes shut. The message, the comp—Page

had suckered him. Reeled him in, hit him with some type of static that he had no experience with. But there would be a record—the comp would have saved it. Codes and all. Including Page's own.

If he could access that, even for a second, he'd be able to hit back, strike Page down where he stood. It was Zip's work, written to beat the best the government had, and evolved to concentrated poison since then.

He started at a sharp sound. Page's voice, higher, cracking with excitement. "You know they vanish, Telford? Vanish, evaporate. Nothing to 'em. A vacuum, dead space. A little pain, a little blood, and they're gone . . ."

Tuning him out, Telford accessed. It took several seconds, and the effect was worse than usual. He stifled a groan as the readout appeared. The system was damaged: CPU impaired, memory halved, software still searching for optimal pathways. What in the name of Christ had he been hit with?

"Amazing how little it takes." Page's voice had dropped. "It's all stimuli. Mechanical, machines." He gave a cry of pure rage, wordless and foul. "It disgusts me . . . you don't know how it disgusts me!"

Still operational, but he'd need augmentation. He slipped a hand to his pocket, touched only his leg. His coat was twisted underneath him.

He froze as Page lunged into view. "You understand? You see? You don't, do you? Nobody . . ." He twisted away, swinging the glove. Something out of sight shattered. "But you will. Oh, you will. All of you. I'll burn it into you."

He reappeared, eyes half-closed, lips slack. "But you're not even here." He nodded to himself. Gripping the other glove, he shook it open. "That's okay, Jase. We'll bring you back."

If he gets that on, you will die, Telford told himself. Clutching the towels, he waited until Page looked away and then with all the strength in his possession flung the wet mass at his face.

———

"Gunships on station . . ."

"Missiles targeted . . ."

". . . what software, sir?"

"JERICHO," Moore said.

Bohlen almost missed it in all the uproar. He glanced over at the ECM console where the woman with the nice voice sat tapping the keys. "Hey," he called, earning a nudge from the soldier behind him. "JERICHO's an area program."

Moore acted as if he hadn't heard.

Bohlen raised his voice. "You want to knock out every comp in the state to crash this one?"

Moore looked over his shoulder. "Where'd you hear about that?"

Gripping the rail, Bohlen went forward. The lifter was in another tight bank; he had to hold on. "You don't know who's down there."

"I do," Moore said. "At least one bandit."

"And who else?" Bohlen tried to keep his voice down. The ship had suddenly fallen quiet, and there no sense embarrassing Moore in front of his unit. "The station staff—and the cop's kid, the one that's missing. The cop himself, for that matter."

Moore tightened his lips. "Make that a point measure, Sandy. CROMWELL will do." He smiled nastily at Bohlen. "Awful cute seeing a Cossack worried about bystanders."

"That's just it," Bohlen said. "Who wants to be like a Cossack?" He paused a moment. "You fire on that shack, Skipper, you're as bad as a Cossack."

Moore seemed about to answer when a cry came from the rear. "Activity, sir!"

He pushed Bohlen aside. "Smoke 'em," he shouted.

A crash as he rolled away. Lurching to his feet, Telford saw Page yank his gloved hand out of shattered wood. Page swung again, wildly, tearing the towels from his face. He made a sound that Telford did not recognize. He advanced, eyes burning through a mask of red, fingers flexing as if they had a life of their own.

Telford grabbed the chair beside him and threw it. The wood broke as Page struck it in midair. Telford backed away, hands high. He couldn't reach his pocket before Page would be on him.

This would be over quickly, one way or another. He was tired, disoriented, injured in a way he did not understand. But he did have one thing Page did not have.

Telford had not only been Nathan's protégé, his follower, his friend.

He had been Nathan Kahn's bodyguard.

Page was fast, yes, but Telford saw no sign of any serious training. The man's stance was poor: head thrown back, glove up and clenched, as if he was displaying it. Terror—that alone was his advantage. The fear kindled in the heart of the helpless. But it did not impress Telford. Telford was used to fear.

He needed three seconds, no more. He went for the door, as if trying to escape. Page had been waiting for that. As he leaped, Telford twisted aside and dropped. He was almost not quick enough—the glove caught him in the shoulder.

Grunting at the pain, he swiveled to Page, batting away another swing. He backed off and was halfway across the room when he slipped on one of the towels and went down. Page stood above him, both hands clenched. With a roar he lifted them.

Telford kicked Page's legs out from under him. Pushing himself backward, he got to his feet.

Their positions were now reversed, with Telford at the far end of the room. Page rose more slowly than he might have, favoring one leg. Telford saw that the cloth at his thigh was stained dark down to the knee.

The second glove lay on the carpet between them. Telford made a move as if to grab for it, and Page lunged, glove up, fingers stiff like spears. Swinging to his left, Telford kicked at a leg, connected, and Page cried out.

He stepped away as Page went down on one knee. He reached into his coat pocket. Page met his eyes and with a howl scrambled to the couch and grabbed his pistol, but Telford's hand had already emerged and rose and touched his head. Enabling the system, Telford smiled as the chip engaged and the readouts went bright.

A harsher light erased them.

Red telltales flickered as Nast tried to rock the car out. He gunned the motor, cursing as he listened to it whine. He knew he'd been driving too fast, but he never thought he'd skid off, not on this night.

The NO TRACTION light flashed. He pounded it with his fist and told the cruiser to open the trunk. Getting out, he rubbed his head where it had hit the side window. He reached into the trunk for a sheet of friction plastic, but seeing how deep the snow was, grabbed the shovel instead.

As he scooped at the packed snow, he thought of what awaited him. Trained killers, the fat Cossack had said, the one who'd been shot. Elite assassins brought to the peak of viciousness and capable of anything. The implants were what did it, making them machines, burning out all traces of fear, caution, mercy . . .

Nast didn't care. It would be just like the war, the patrols down in Mama East. An insert, a quick dust, then sky up. He was walking point again. One more time.

A vision appeared of his last day on the line, south of Tehuacán. The ground warm from the sun, the screaming pain in his leg, the others moaning around him—then gunfire, explosions, the clank of treads. He saw it again, the tank roaring at him, the head bobbing in the forward hatch.

He pushed the image away, but it was replaced by another, by what he'd seen at the house.

Choking back sobs, he closed his eyes. He had thought that that was the worst thing a man could experience, lying there waiting for a tank to roll over him. But it wasn't. It wasn't anything.

He heard a scraping and realized that he'd struck pavement.

Throwing the shovel aside, he took out the plastic, feeling it roughen as the cold hit it. He got back into the car and touched the pedal. The telltale glowed green. He pressed harder, catching himself as the car jerked backward. He shifted and drove on, the trunk hatch flapping wide.

The howling brought him back.

Instinctively he moved away from the sound, cupping his ears. The howling went on, growing hoarser but no lower in volume.

It was several minutes before Telford could raise his head. A few feet away lay Page, his eyes bulging as they stared into what he had always desired. The mouth was open wider than seemed possible, and the heels beat a syncopated tattoo on the floor.

You shall be as gods, Nathan had said an age ago and a world away. You shall eat of the tree, but you shall enter paradise and bring all who live with you.

The pistol. Telford crawled over, gripped it, and pushed himself into a sitting position. Holding it with both hands, aiming, he pulled the trigger.

You shall be as gods.

And he'd believed, and kept on believing—until now, until this moment, when he put the mark of Cain on himself with his own hands. That belief was what it had all been about: this refuge, the network, the years spent trying to save those who could not be saved. He had kept the dream alive, thinking that he, Jason Telford, was the anointed one, that he would carry them all into paradise at last.

He let the gun fall, a weight too great to be borne. Closing his eyes, he slumped.

And heard something: a whimpering, muffled and distant. As he turned toward it, his head spun. He realized that he was still in the system. He pulled the chip off. No readouts showing, but he could feel the system all the same.

Which was impossible. He raised his hands, as if to pluck

burning letters from the air. Swinging to the station comp, he froze at what he saw: a multicolored, infinitely complex pattern of fire, a fractal sculpture that seemed part of the machinery itself. He blinked, and it vanished, as if willed away.

He thought of his own implant and seemed to touch it. It was dead, its architecture destroyed, its functions frozen. But the programs still lived: not as names or symbols but as patterns, as things. They flickered before him and began to unfold.

"No!" he shouted, hands to his head.

The noise in back grew louder. Getting to his feet, he staggered to the bedroom door. It was dark, and he switched on the light.

A man lay on the floor. For a moment he thought it was Gene, the face was so badly mauled. When the man saw Telford, he lifted his hands. The fingers were bent back unnaturally. The man mumbled something Telford didn't catch, then once more, louder.

"Yes," Telford said, finally understanding, "he's dead."

The man shut his eyes and lay still. He groaned when Telford touched him, but said no more.

There was movement on the bed: a small form under the covers. Telford pulled them away. A girl, no older than six. She whimpered softly, but stopped when he put a hand on her shoulder. She opened her eyes and looked at him a moment before sitting up. She pointed to the injured man. "The boogeyman beat him up," she whispered. "And he hit my . . . he hit my . . ."

She started crying. "I want to go home."

"It's all right," he told her. "I'll get you home."

He could feel a presence out in the night, a harsh and powerful thing circling high in the darkness. The killers would be on their way—they could not have missed what had happened here. But he ignored it. His own safety was secondary. His responsibility lay with these, as it always had.

Why had Page brought them here? He had a sudden cold conception of ultimate insectile viciousness, Page storing victims to use at his pleasure. But no—he must have seen them as insurance, hostages in case he was stopped by the vigs or military. As to what would have become of them afterward . . .

Telford glanced toward the front room. What he'd done out there didn't seem so bad now.

He wrapped the girl in a blanket and carried her to the truck, holding her head against his chest so she wouldn't see the body. Strangeness met him as he stepped outside. He halted at the top of the steps, unable to grasp quite what it was. Lowering his head, he went on to the truck.

The man, short as he was, was still too heavy to carry. After giving him a shot from the station medkit, Telford walked him out. When they passed Page, the man muttered, "I didn't know." It sounded like a prayer.

Telford helped the man into the truck. The little girl was crying again. He touched her head, and she calmed down. He reached for the truck comp, but no sooner was the thought formed than the job was done: course laid for town, beacon set to go off when it reached the highway. He stared at the unit, fear clawing higher.

The motor started, and he stepped away. As the truck began moving, he leaned forward to slam the door shut. He slipped on the snow and sat, legs splayed. He shook his head.

This was it, the thing he'd feared all these years come at last. Something had given way deep in the foundations of his mind. He felt its awful absence, just as you feel a missing limb.

The taillights swept through the dark woods. He watched them vanish, then looked up into the whirling snow, the trees, the night beyond. Something loomed there, pressing against the fabric of darkness. His thoughts called it forth, and he screamed, burying his face in the snow, knowing he was seeing the same thing Page had seen.

It was some time before he dared sit up. That spasm of deep chaos, that mindless, meaningless complexity was gone. The pressure was still there, distorting and twisting the world he had known. He squinted, trying to force everything back the way it had been. But it remained a facade: fuzzy, insubstantial, buckling under the forces trying to push their way out.

It was happening as he'd always thought it would. He was alone, with no hand raised to help him. He struggled to his feet and turned to the house. But there was nothing in there for him.

He was halfway to the drive when he remembered the cabin. He swerved, started to climb, keeping his arms out for balance as the slope shifted beneath him. He lunged for a tree and clutched it, then went on to the next, eyes fixed on the shack above.

"Gene," he said, pushing the door open. "Guess what."

The cabin was empty. He swung around, and what met his eyes forced him back against the wall.

The scene before him was unrecognizable. Fragmented, folded in on itself. "Oh, Christ," he said as it shifted further, in what direction he could no longer tell. An auroral glow was rising from that impossible horizon, crawling slowly to the zenith. He bent over, hands to face, mouth open in a silent scream. A single word echoed in his head: Damnation.

After a time he looked up. There was movement below him, at the bottom of the hill, distinct from the mad surging of the world. A figure appeared from the trees. It held a rifle, and as Telford walked away, a rattle of gunfire cut through the winter stillness.

"Thirty seconds."

Bohlen took out his revolver and checked the load. Behind him the squad stood, visors muffling their voices. Something kept poking into his back. He hoped it wasn't a rifle barrel.

It had taken every ounce of persuasiveness he had in him to keep Moore from leveling the place, particularly with the weird, across-the-band signals they'd been getting since the last spike. Moore relented only after the off-roader had been intercepted and found to contain the missing girl and an unidentified, badly wounded male. He still wasn't happy about it.

Poked once more, Bohlen was about to turn on the soldier behind him and say something nasty, when a shudder nearly knocked him off his feet. The ramp fell open.

He was out before it hit the ground. Getting his bearings, he ran to the building, gained the steps, and plunged through the door with his pistol raised.

The place had been shot up but good, and with heavy ammo. Holes in the paneling, windows broken, furniture in pieces, and on the floor . . .

He grunted in surprise. Page. Troops rushed past him as he crouched over the body.

"That one of them?"

Bohlen looked up at Moore. "Yeah."

Footsteps thumped overhead. "Clear," somebody called from the stairs.

Moore touched the side of his helmet, a distant expression on his face. "We've got tracks heading into the woods."

"Let's go," Bohlen said, making for the door.

It was better under the trees. Still silent—the silence bothered him the most. Beyond the canopy of pine flared the sky, muted and distant. The near dark held strangeness, but he ignored it and went down the trail.

The scene shimmered. He shook his head to clear it. There seemed to be something in the woods ahead of him. He stopped to listen but could hear nothing.

A few feet on he whirled, certain that someone was behind him. When he continued on, a black shape hung over the trail. He was unable to make out what it was. He went forward, and it became clear and glowed with its own light.

It was Briggs, hanging from the branch of a tree. His face was intact, eyes bugged out, skin discolored. As Telford watched, flames began to lick at him.

He looked away, stumbled onward. The sense of presence

remained. He could feel them around him—all his dead, the ones he had led on, the ones he had betrayed.

Just ahead, someone was waiting. Another step, and he knew who it was: Anna Petruccio, emaciated, lying naked in the snow. Around her was a structure of cardboard boxes held together with twine. She held out her hands as he went past. "No," he told her. "I'm nobody's shepherd anymore."

Beyond her he saw the shadows of others: Ronnie, Carmen, Dave. He moaned when he thought he saw Sarah, but it wasn't her, it was the girl whose name he could never remember. "Patti," he said, recalling it at last.

"It's too late," he called to them. "You hear me . . ."

A bolt of agony struck him, and he stumbled against a tree. When he opened his eyes, they were all still there, watching. He lowered his head and went on.

Rifle up, Nast moved like a ghost. He couldn't get as far from the trail as he should, but that didn't matter. Only one set of tracks, so there was no danger of ambush. If others were out there under the trees, so be it. They'd never spot him in this darkness.

He'd seen the figure moving into the woods from an upstairs window while searching the place. Only a shape obscured by snow, but he could almost hear it laughing. He kicked out the window and dropped from the roof. You didn't use doors more than once in an unsecured area.

He avoided the tree branches whenever he could. When he couldn't, he bulled though, allowing the snow to cascade over him. The snow was the only difference between here and Mama East, that and the cold. Otherwise it was the same: tracking, cover, the certainty that your Beaner was a dead man as soon as you saw him. He was walking point.

His guts heaved as he recalled that last firefight: Hill 531, Sierra Madre Orientale. The sector was supposedly secure; it was just a mop-up, a patrol to shake out whatever bandits were left.

Someone had screamed "Gas!" and he turned to see a white

cloud pouring from the bush behind him. They weren't wearing BC gear—you couldn't in that heat—and anyway intel claimed the gas dumps had been destroyed.

They ran for it, down the trail to a flat area and straight into an ambush. Nast was hit immediately. He lay with half a dozen others while the platoon scattered. They were gaining ground when the armor appeared. Five tanks, cannons roaring and MGs lit up, breaking the line and sending the platoon back into the cloud that was only smoke after all. They fired, but the tanks kept coming, up the trail to where Nast and his buddies lay.

He began screaming when a tank drove over the first man. And screamed when the others were crushed, when the clanking grew louder, when he saw the thing bouncing in the front hatch, helmet blown off, eyes pools of red, wires and circuits dangling from the shaven skull. He dragged himself across the baking ground, nails tearing off as he clawed at dirt and rock, the treads not a foot behind him. His cries had turned to voiceless wheezes by the time the gunships appeared and turned the tanks to piles of burning metal. He was still crying when the men of his unit came to get him.

It had been a promise. He knew that now. That the beings who thought themselves better than men would not relent, that they would be back. He understood at last that it was they who had been behind the war—not Medrano, not his fanatics, no, the implanted ones, the enhanced humans, the supermen.

The war had never ended, it had continued, and he had been struck by it, a casual byblow without thought or meaning. He was walking point.

Pushing a branch away, he quickened his pace.

The trees began to thin out. Telford halted to examine what awaited him: a few feet of snow, normal and bland, fading into nothing he had knowledge of. A chaos of light and geometry, with no pattern, no framework, no referent.

He recalled what Nathan once said about changing the ground

state. But this couldn't be what he'd meant—this was no state at all. It wasn't anything.

"Is this what it was?" He looked around, but no one was there. "It's all right," he called. "I'm not mad anymore."

He waited a moment, but he was alone. Shutting his eyes, he plunged forward, uphill, down, he had no way of knowing. Through his closed eyelids light played, frantic and bizarre. And the pain grew, a whirlpool of darkness throbbing in rhythm with what lay outside.

He thought of them back there, waiting patiently for his arrival. There had always been a look in their eyes, as if they had seen something beyond language, beyond the power of the mind or heart to contain.

He dropped to his knees. He thought he understood now, and if he was right, there was no hope. He stared at the snow beneath him. Multicolored, glowing, a mad dance of probabilities. Don't tap, he'd told them. Don't tap, and you'll be all right.

Nothing would have made it all right. He called up the program codes, all of them: standard, experimental, baroque. Those rational, scientific, childlike attempts to put a hook into the infinite. He paused to say goodbye to everything that he had known, then ordered them to activate.

The blackness receded, and he was still there. He moved, and the snow beneath him was snow. He rolled onto his back. The sky still danced with fire, but it made sense now, at the same time that it did not.

What was it? Satellites, the defense network, something undiscovered or unfathomable? It made no difference. He would never have a chance to find out.

He pushed himself up. The world around him was distorted and broken but no longer grotesque. Carefully, he got to his feet, grasping what he'd only touched a moment before: that the reducing valve was now wide open. That he'd crossed the threshold to find no footing on the other side, broken the paradigm to be buried in the wreckage, gone beyond order to find only chaos and old night. That the Breakthrough was Pelton's and Pelton's was the Breakthrough.

He swung slowly around. He could sense the flux of power out there, fed to him in some way he did not understand. He felt the pulse of it, data flowing like thought, billions of operations flashing at lightspeed. There were too many sources. A number came: 8,142. And beyond them were others, in seething millions. He could manipulate that mass the same way he could shovel stars with his bare hands.

He was in a clear spot now, momentarily protected by remoteness. Had he been in the center of that maelstrom, he would have broken immediately, not even knowing what destroyed him. But a wrong thought, a wrong move, and he would bring it all down on him. His eyes searched the sky. There was no escape, no place far enough.

He threw his head back and laughed. "Here's your Prometheus, Nathan. Do you like him?"

There was time for one thing before the avalanche began. One gesture, that was all. It had to count.

A thought arose that was alien: Smash it, flatten it, extinguish all those precious fountains, become a wave-front of negation roaring across the world. Be like Medrano, like Stoner . . .

Be like Page.

A cry sounded, uncanny in this curdled space. He looked back the way he had come and saw a figure emerge from the dark. Nathan? Weber? But it was only a man.

He turned away, ordering the implant to find him the simplest path. He could do one thing . . .

He reached out and did it.

Behind Bohlen an alarm shrieked. The lifter shuddered, throwing him against the side. Moore pulled himself to the board, whose readouts were flashing red. "Somebody's riding us," the EC officer cried.

"Countermeasures," Moore said.

311

"They're down."

Moore stared at Bohlen. "What the hell . . ."

"They're gone, Dinty," the lieutenant said.

"Go to manual," Moore said quietly, his eyes not leaving Bohlen.

"Already have."

Bohlen shrugged.

He was standing at the top of a shabby flight of stairs. Before him was a door, ancient and thick. But it vanished at his touch, and he went inside.

The room was damp and cold. There were no walls, only a sodden grayness that faded off into nothing. A light shone, blue-white, glaring. It too faded when his gaze touched it.

Sarah sat in the center of the room. He went to her. His fingers met frozen skin. When he called her name, his voice was swallowed as it left his lips.

He bent closer. The skin beneath his fingers grew warm. He raised his other hand and stroked the rigid flesh until it began to yield. Beyond the grayness, a light bloomed, brightening steadily.

She shivered. He lowered his hands. There was movement, and laughter, his own.

The glow surrounded them, as warm and sweet as sunlight on a fine spring day. Her head moved and she looked up at him. It was too bright to see her expression.

A flat crack, and his right arm jerked. Sarah looked down, but he gripped her shoulders. "Come on," he said, lifting her toward the light. "We're going out."

And he was back in the clearing, head raised, half-blinded by snow. Blinking, he saw that the world was the world: concrete, solid, the way it should be.

A shape approached, rifle in hand. It growled, vicious and sub-human. Telford's arm ached, but that didn't matter. He smiled as the gun barrel jerked up.

The shot took him in the chest.

Nast stopped firing after the fifth round. He raised the gun, gripping the stock until his hand hurt.

He looked down at the outline of a man with patches of black splattered from body and head. Pictures flashed through his mind: the tank, the woman on the hill, the room at the house, the tank.

He slammed the gun butt against his thigh. He could walk away now. No, there was something more to be done. He had heard they could transfer their minds through the implants . . .

Dropping the rifle, he reached into his pocket, took out a utility knife, and opened the longest blade. He straddled the body, gingerly crouching on its chest. He bit his lip as he sliced and dug at the hard parts of the head.

"Two targets five hundred yards east in a clearing. One down," the weapons officer said. The system had come back up a moment before, as if nothing had ever been wrong with it.

Outside the canopy was a veil of driven snow. Bohlen went to the rear while Moore said something about lights. There was a jolt as the ramp fell open, and Bohlen fell with it. Then he was outside and flailing through snow. He raised an arm against the dazzle of the lifter's spotlights. There: a spot of darkness in the endless white.

Pulling out his pistol, he went down the hill as fast as he could. As he drew closer, he made out a man crouching over something. He leveled the gun and shouted for him to get up. The man gave no sign that he heard. Bohlen slowed, letting the gun drop when he saw the uniform jacket, the patch on the shoulder, the wide swaths of red sunk into the snow.

"Nast," he called out, pocketing the gun. He stopped when he saw what was being done, then pulled the deputy off the violated corpse.

He dragged Nast a few feet, pushed him down, and went back to the body. Two soldiers had reached it. "Jesus," one said.

Bohlen agreed. There was not enough left of the man's face to tell who he'd been. He looked up to see Moore standing next to him. The major said nothing.

Bohlen turned to Nast. The deputy raised his hands, both blood-soaked to the wrists. In one was a knife, in the other something small. Nast stared at his reddened claws for a moment, then began to weep. His fingers opened, and the objects fell into the snow. He seemed to fold into himself, hands rising to his face only to halt inches away.

"Get him out of here," Bohlen said. A soldier glanced uncertainly at Moore, who nodded.

Bohlen watched them move off and went to the spot where Nast had stood. In the snow he found the small thing that had fallen there: a chip, sticky with blood, and a medusoid tangle of bioplastic trailing from it. He let it drop and rubbed his hands in the snow.

He turned to Moore. "This," he said, gesturing at the body, "will have to be cleaned up."

"I'll see to it," Moore said, turning to go back up the hill. The men followed him.

Bohlen stepped to the body. Bending over, he reached for the coat and flipped it open. There was a folded sheet in the inside pocket, barely touched with red. He eased it out. Unfolded it. Held it high so that the lights of the lifter shone on it. And his hand clenched and crumpled the paper.

He let his arm fall and regarded the man at his feet.

Hello, Tap.

A snowflake struck his eye. He blinked it away. It had grown colder all of a sudden, but he knew that it would never get any colder than it was now. And once he was finished here, it would never get this cold again.

Two soldiers appeared, carrying a stretcher. Bohlen watched while they set it down and wrestled the body onto it. "Be careful," he said when a leg flopped over the side. They said nothing but were gentler as they settled the corpse, lifted the plastic of the attached bag, and zipped it shut.

He didn't turn when they took it away. He stood looking at the red stains, which were already being covered by falling snow. In minutes they would be gone, and when spring came, they would soak into the soil and be forgotten.

Let it be so. Folding the sheet of paper carefully, he put it in his pocket and turned to make his difficult way up the hill.

CHAPTER 29

THE WOMAN LAY on the bed, face obscured by the mask that put breath into her. The rest of her head was covered with bandages. Her skin, where it showed, was pale, dry, lifeless.

The comp behind her flickered. A small light began pulsing, first amber, then green. A buzzer sounded, low but insistent.

There were footsteps in the corridor, and a nurse entered the room. She looked first at the patient, then more closely at the comp. Bending over it, she ran a system check, frowned to herself, and pressed a pad.

A resident arrived. They spoke quietly, inspecting the machine once more before the doctor turned to the patient. When he finished studying her, he loosened the mask and lay it aside. The woman shuddered once and began to breathe on her own.

The doctor nodded, saying he'd seen this before, during the war. Compensation; the undamaged brain centers taking over from those that had been destroyed. He eyed the treatment limitation monitor. It showed nine hours until termination. He grimaced at it and told the nurse to shut it off.

The woman moaned. Her lips moved, a barely audible word. Eyebrows raised, the doctor looked up.

"It sounded like 'Jason,' " the nurse said.

"Relative?"

The nurse shrugged. Turning to leave, the doctor told her to keep a close watch.

CHAPTER 30

MARCUS ONCE TOLD Bohlen about something he called the tragic sense of life. Late days, it had been, when the only relief the old man could expect from his growing sickness and exhaustion was the longest sleep of all.

Laughter, he said, was really a cry of despair, a mask for emotions too painful to confront. The mature man goes beyond that, to the heart of the matter: the bleak acknowledgment that tragedy is the basis of life; that however hard the struggle, failure always waits at the end; that the battle must be its own reward. Total defiance, even as the door of the tomb slams shut.

Bohlen hadn't known what to make of that at the time; he thought he understood it now. And perhaps that was what Marcus had intended—that even if his idiot protégé couldn't grasp it then, it would stick, to make a difference long after his own personal darkness closed about him.

Bohlen couldn't tell if it made any difference. He was too damn tired, and the waiting room of the Ironwood Airport—glorious name for the local cropduster strip—was a bleak and chilly place. Washington had got him up at five, before he'd had a chance to do any more than close his eyes. Hec had just turned Cummins over, and the Hillbilly, with a few hours to think, had come up with an explanation that was a lot more coherent than the one Bohlen had. The depraved Bohlen had been in contact with a CEI all along; he'd been planning to crash COSSF, Washington, Western Civilization, and, worse, Director Harland Cummins himself; but the aforementioned director had cleverly been giving him enough rope . . .

Bohlen demanded that they put the bastard on. Cummins appeared, nowhere near as dapper as he'd been the day before, his eyes pinpoints and his jaw stubbled.

"Well, Ross," he said. "We've reached our Waterloo, you and I."

"Little Big Horn," Bohlen corrected him.

Face reddening, Cummins went on. "It seems the CEIs have all been terminated. So it's just us two."

"What?" Bohlen said. "You mean they didn't tell you? Page turned himself in. He's right over here."

Cummins went pale, but Bohlen didn't get a chance to learn what he thought about that. An uproar broke out, and a hand appeared at Mushmouth's shoulder to pull him away. He was replaced by an overweight BurCyb official, who gruffly explained that they'd gotten some new input. An acting officer at headquarters had arranged for a line to be emplaced at his home in case something came in when he was off duty. He'd recorded an alarm signal in the director's unit at the same time as the military intrusion . . . Who was it? Why, the assistant director, a Mr. Frisell.

"Eddie?" Bohlen asked.

He hadn't been able to grab any sleep after that.

The door to the runway banged open, and the charter pilot leaned in. "Hey, what's the holdup?"

Bleary-eyed, Bohlen raised his head. "I thought you had to refuel."

She made a face. An unhappy woman—Bohlen had been unable to tell her how long the flight would be or exactly where

319

they'd end up. "That was done ten minutes ago. Been waiting on you."

Waving her off, Bohlen got up and headed for the door.

Outside he paused, squinting against brightness. The sky was cloudless, the sun beaming away as if to convince the world that all that white stuff had found its way here on its own.

A figure stepped from a nearby hangar. It was the sheriff. Washington had desperately wanted Bohlen back on the next possible flight. Even though he'd locked up the comps, they'd called the motel desk a dozen times. He wouldn't be surprised if they'd asked Hough to snag him.

But the sheriff was alone, and smiling as he approached. Bohlen went to meet him.

"Heard you were heading out," the sheriff said.

"Didn't expect a sendoff."

Hough gave a short laugh. "Western hospitality, Bohlen."

They stood a moment, Hough pulling at his mustache. Bohlen decided it was best not to bring up Nast. At the hospital, thinking he was from the sheriff's office, the staff had told him that the deputy was still under sedation. Seeing Del had been bad enough.

The sheriff gestured at the hangar behind them. "You know what that is?"

Shading his eyes, Bohlen tried to make out what he was referring to. For a moment he saw nothing, then the shadows resolved into a box on a wheeled platform. A chill went through him. It was a coffin.

Whose? There were too many; he couldn't even guess. One body alone he knew couldn't be in there. It was lying at the morgue, waiting for Bohlen to tell them what to do with it.

"The dancer," Hough said. "She's going home."

A window in the lifter squeaked open. "Hey, we got a flight plan, you know?"

Bohlen and Hough turned to the aircraft. After a few steps Hough pointed. "Got yourself a pair of Westerns, I see. How you like 'em?"

Bohlen glanced down. Pointy toes and high heels—he'd picked them up on the way from the hospital. He was a country gent now. "Don't know," he said. "They aren't broken in yet."

When they reached the open door, Bohlen took the sheriff's hand, shook it firmly. Hough gazed at him a moment, his expression unreadable. "So it was chipheads after all."

Bohlen nodded.

"Hope we've seen the last."

"I think so," Bohlen said. He started to climb aboard.

"One more thing," Hough said.

Bohlen looked back.

"Those boys in the lockup. I get to keep them or what?"

Bohlen threw his head back and laughed. Morello and the rookies enjoying a jailhouse breakfast. He savored the thought a moment before answering. "You need a hand clearing the roads, they'll do. Otherwise, cut 'em loose."

"Figured it slipped your mind." The sheriff turned away. Bohlen watched him walk off, then closed the door. A moment later they were airborne.

He must have dozed. He jerked in his seat when the pilot told him where they were. Out the window he saw nothing but cloud, white and clean in the morning sun. The storm that had passed over last night, still dumping snow as it headed east.

Opening his jacket, he took out the sheet and ran a finger across the brown stains at the edge.

He had the growing conviction that he'd only grazed the edge of something that was bigger than he dreamed, like the fringe of a hurricane whose eye is miles away. His thoughts were unclear. Every time he tried to put it together, he saw only the dead. The dancer, Zimmer, Nast's wife, the man they found on the hill, first name Gene, last unknown, the nameless punks draped across a frozen landscape, Tap.

Delahanty, in the hospital, numb below the waist, bullet lodged in his spine. He couldn't take regen treatments; they'd tried it with his old man, and he'd gotten cancer. Del might never walk again. And down the hall from him, Nast, his mind broken. He would be awake by now, confronting again his private nightmare, with no resources to deal with it.

Red on white, forming a pattern repeated again and again, a pattern he might never know the meaning of.

He'd figure it out later. He had other business now. Opening the sheet, he glanced over the names. Nobody knew this list existed, and nobody would know until he was finished with it.

Lifting the receiver, he punched the number next to the first name. He knew why it was first—Cora had spoken it at the motel last night while he and Lu fed her.

As he waited for the phone to ring, a thought came to him, something once said by the most civilized man he'd ever known: *Think on this—that reasoning beings were created for one another's sake; that to be patient is a branch of justice, and that men sin without intending it.*

We made it, he told them all. Marcus, Tap, Del: we're almost home.

The phone was picked up at the first ring. A voice spoke, breathless and eager. "Hello?"

"Can I speak to Naomi Buckner?"

There was an intake of breath. Bohlen waited only a second before going on. "Ms. Buckner, my name is Ross Bohlen. I was a friend of Jason Telford . . ."

The lifter flew on for a while, then made a shallow, spiraling turn toward the clouds below.

PATRICIA ANTHONY

COLD ALLIES

INTO THE CROSSFIRE OF THE NEXT WORLD WAR . . .

. . . comes an unexpected player: a force of aliens who appear as hovering blue lights over the battlefields of Earth. Sometimes they save lives. Sometimes they destroy them.

And no one is sure which side they're on . . .

Cold Allies is the acclaimed first novel by Patricia Anthony, an author already set firmly on course to be one of the greatest science fiction names of the 21st Century.

'Scary and exciting'

Ursula K. Le Guin

'Absorbing . . . gripping and realistic . . . assured, imaginative, and distinctive'

Kirkus Reviews

'A gripping near-future thriller with a unique air of mystery'

Washington Post Book World

HODDER AND STOUGHTON PAPERBACKS

PIERRE OUELLETTE

THE DEUS MACHINE

The year is 2005 and a paralysing depression threatens to collapse the United States government.

In desperation, a secret military cabal sets DEUS – a supercomputer with the potential for true intelligence – on a fateful course: perpetually reinventing itself and, ultimately, creating a powerful new virus weapon. As DEUS begins to create bizarre and deadly new life-forms in an attempt to self-destruct, a troubled computer genius and a fatherless boy join forces to try to save the world from a terrifying biological catastrophe.

Technically awesome, dramatically taut, *The Deus Machine* totally transforms the high-tech thriller and introduces a novelist with the imagination of Michael Crichton, the breakneck pacing of Tom Clancy, and the humanity of Dean Koontz.

'*The Deus Machine* is an unremittingly inventive work of near-future fiction, showcasing the best, and hungriest, predators since *Jurassic Park*.'
Entertainment Weekly

HODDER AND STOUGHTON PAPERBACKS

A. A. ATTANASIO

RADIX

'An instant classic'

Washington Post Book World

Here is one of the most powerful novels of the future ever written. Brilliantly realized, richly detailed and convincingly imagined, it is the awe-inspiring story of a young man's odyssey of self-discovery, from dangerous adolescent to warrior, from outcast to near-godhood, in a far-future Earth dramatically changed from the one we know.

Radix is an epic of the highest order, at once an incandescently exciting novel of conflict and adventure and a supreme experience of transcendent vision.

'Here stands a high talent: a truly amazing, original, towering talent'

Los Angeles Times

'Alive with zest and daring'

Kirkus Reviews

HODDER AND STOUGHTON PAPERBACKS

A. A. ATTANASIO

SOLIS

A MASTERWORK OF THE SCIENCE FICTION IMAGINATION

A thousand years in the future, Charles Outis (who had his head cryonically frozen when he died in the 21st century) wakes to find his brain enslaved by a brutal technocracy. He manages to broadcast a distress signal that is picked up by the androne Munk – whose artificial intelligence is programmed with an empathy for *homo sapiens* culture. Munk, aided by tough troubleshooter Mei Nili, rescues 'Mister Charlie's brain' and the group sets off for the élite Martian community of Solis. Here lies the only hope of bodily reincarnation (through cloning) and sanctuary that Outis can expect.

But the trek to Solis is beset with lethal dangers from predatory humans, murderous alien monstrosities and the harsh Martian terrain itself. And at journey's end the destiny awaiting the pilgrims is wholly unexpected . . .

Solis demonstrates once more that the imagination of A. A. Attanasio knows no bounds.

'Here stands a high talent: a truly amazing, original, towering talent'

Los Angeles Times

HODDER AND STOUGHTON PAPERBACKS

ROBERT J. SAWYER

FAR-SEER

'A tour de force, vastly enjoyable, beautifully realized'
Asimov's Science Fiction Magazine

'The Face of God' is what every young saurian learns to
call the immense, glowing object that fills the night sky
on the far side of the world. Young Afsan is privileged,
called to the distant Capital City as an apprentice of
Saleed, the court astrologer. But when the time comes
for Afsan to make his coming-of-age pilgrimage to gaze
upon the Face of God, his world is changed forever.
What he sees will test his faith – and may save his people
from the hitherto unsuspected disaster threatening
them . . .

Far-Seer is the first book in Robert J. Sawyer's brilliant
science fiction trilogy, *The Quintaglio Ascension*.

'Inventive and engaging'

Newsday

HODDER AND STOUGHTON PAPERBACKS